BAD LIES

For Astrid and Sybil

BAD LIES

A STORY OF LIBEL, SLANDER, & PROFESSIONAL GOLF

TONY JACKLIN
SHELBY YASTROW

www.mascotbooks.com

Bad Lies

For more information, please contact:
Mascot Books
620 Herndon Parkway #320
Herndon, VA 20170
info@mascotbooks.com

Library of Congress Control Number: 2017960727

CPSIA Code: PBANG0218A
ISBN-13: 978-1-68401-602-0

Printed in the United States

AUTHORS' NOTE

Until I began working on this book with Shelby Yastrow — who opened his law office about the same time that I competed in my first Open Championship[*] — I had never appreciated the striking similarity between courtroom trials and professional golf tournaments.

In each, there is a clear winner. However, that victory can nearly always be traced back to factors that no one had foreseen, and that the most careful preparation could not have anticipated. So, as much as lawyers and golfers hate to admit it, a victory can have a lot to do with luck. Just as the golf ball can take strange bounces, memories of witnesses can take strange turns; and a critical document, like an elusive golf ball, may be hard to find. Both are games of inches.

There is an old saying in golf that "every shot makes someone happy." Likewise, I've learned that every syllable uttered by a witness brings relief to one set of lawyers and total despair to the other.

The lawyer will carefully prepare for his challenge by reviewing the law, double-checking the facts, developing a strategy, preparing his or her witnesses while preparing for the witnesses to be called by the other side,

---

[*] In the United Kingdom, the "Open Championship" refers to what the rest of the world calls the "British Open." Since ours was the first national golf championship, we never felt the need to identify it further.

judiciously selecting the jury, studying the habits of the judge and the expressions of the jurors, and rehearsing his or her questions and arguments. Meanwhile, the professional golfer preparing for the next tournament will study the turf, learn the yardages, memorize the roll of the greens, develop a game plan, study the habits of the opponents, and rehearse the precise shots he or she will have to strike over the ensuing four days.

But there are always the surprises — the eventualities always to be feared but seldom foreseen. Bad bounces and bad memories, like lost balls and misplaced documents, are all part of the game.

The seasoned golf professional or lawyer will each know how to recover from such unexpected adversities, but the recovery doesn't always save the day. That's why Hogan, Nicklaus, and Woods lost more often than they won, and that's why the most successful trial lawyers in the world don't win all of their cases. Second-guessing is the essential ingredient of each profession. And both the lawyer and tournament golfer would pay dearly for the occasional mulligan.

But none of this is to imply that luck trumps preparation and skill, either in the courtroom or on the golf course. As my good friend Gary Player famously remarked, after overhearing a fan describe his excellent bunker shot as lucky, "That's absolutely correct, ma'am, and the longer I practice, the luckier I get."

Working on this book has given me a keen appreciation of the trial lawyer's constant challenge in the courtroom, and I hope that others who read it will better appreciate the battles that we professional golfers have to fight every time we tee it up.

Within the pages to follow, you will see numbered references to notes at the end of the book. In these endnotes, I have attempted to provide you with some personal comments or historical perspective related to that portion of the text.

And with that, please join me on the first tee.

— Tony Jacklin

A lie
can be halfway round the world
before the truth has got its boots on

James Callaghan,
British Labour Prime Minister (Date unknown)

THURSDAY MORNING

MARCH 21, 2010

TRIAL BEGINS TODAY IN EDDIE BENNISON LAWSUIT AGAINST PUBLISHERS

CHICAGO, IL — Testimony begins today in the long-awaited defamation lawsuit filed by professional golfer Eddie Bennison against various media defendants, including Tee Time, *the best-selling golf magazine in the United States, and Globe Publications, its parent company and the owner of several of the largest media outlets in the country. The suit is in response to certain stories printed in the magazine about Bennison in 2006 that accused Bennison of cheating and using performance-enhancing drugs while winning a record number of professional tournaments on the Senior PGA Golf Tour. Bennison's suit claims that the defendants, by publishing these stories which he claims to be false, committed libel and other acts that defamed the golfer, damaged his reputation, and crippled his earning power.*

Bennison, 57, had been the phenomenal star of the Senior PGA Golf Tour, known as the Champions Tour, having turned the golf world upside down by winning 13 tournaments in 2004 and 2005, his first two seasons on the circuit, including both the US and British Senior Opens. During those two seasons, his tournament earnings were nearly $8 million — more than triple the next highest earner. Those earnings, however, were a fraction of his income from product endorsements, rumored to be in excess of $15 million annually during those two years.

No senior golfer in modern history has had a comparable two-year streak, and few in sports have captured the hearts of fans and sportswriters as Bennison has in such a short time. The golf world has seen nothing like this since 1945, when Byron Nelson won an astounding 18 tournaments in that one year — eleven in a row — later quipping that it was because most of the healthy tour players were still in the army fighting in World War II.

But all of this has come to a screeching halt. Bennison has not won an event since Tee Time's *publication of the allegedly false stories about him in 2006, and he has since lost many of his sponsors. He blames his crash on the staggering accusations contained in those stories. According to Bennison's lawyer, Charlie Mayfield, who has won several huge verdicts in the Chicago courts, the adverse publicity that emanated from these accounts not only tarnished Bennison's reputation, but also caused many sponsors to cancel his endorsement contracts and led would-be sponsors to avoid signing him to new contracts. In addition, Bennison claims, the acts of the defendants have destroyed his ability to concentrate mentally on his golf — concentration that is essential to maintaining the high level of play that characterized his first two years on the Senior Tour. Since the adverse publicity began, Bennison has not finished higher than eleventh place in any tournament, and he claims he has withdrawn from several events because of the pressure of facing hostile galleries and fellow Tour players who, he says, now shun him.*

The defendants admit their publication of the stories that strongly imply — if not directly assert — the cheating and drug use, but they insist that the stories are true. Further, they maintain that their actions are protected by the constitutional safeguards that shield the media from liability for defamation of public figures, even if the stories are false, unless there is proof that the stories were published out of malice or reckless and willful disregard for the truth.

Bennison's lawyer, Charles Mayfield, relishes the role of the underdog, having built a reputation of winning substantial verdicts against large national corporations. The defendants are represented by Hugo Shoemaker, a First Amendment lawyer from New York whose specialty is defending members of the media in libel suits, and who is widely recognized as a leading advocate of free speech. Shoemaker is being assisted by Roslyn Berman, a streetwise Chicago lawyer who has successfully defended many large companies, some assert, by launching frontal attacks against those who would dare to sue her clients.

Bennison's lawsuit does not ask for a specific amount from the defendants, but courthouse observers are speculating that if he prevails, the award could be in the hundreds of millions of dollars.

The accusations against Bennison in the original articles became one of the biggest sports stories of recent years, endlessly reprinted and reaired by newspapers throughout the world and by ABC, NBC, CBS, ESPN, The Sports Network, The Golf Channel, United . . . .

CHAPTER 1

The lunch room at Franklin Advertising in Detroit was a mess, and it was not yet ten o'clock in the morning. For the past two hours there had been a flow of people in and out of the room, some to confer over a cup of coffee about a new ad campaign, and some to take a break to look over the trade journals and morning papers that by now were scattered over the several tables.

Francine Curry was sitting off in the corner, checking for messages on her smartphone, when Liz Peters came in and plopped into the opposite chair. "Christ," she said with a sigh, "it's not even noon and I'm exhausted. I'll never get through the day. My life is a mess."

Liz absently picked up the morning *Free Press* and browsed through it while Francine was punching out replies to a few emails on her cell phone.

Although Liz Peters was always complaining about something, she was popular with her coworkers at Franklin. Her self-deprecating humor was, in a way, captivating, somehow drawing people to appreciate — or at least sympathize — with her. Her commentaries on her family and love life couldn't be better delivered by a standup comedienne, and she titillated the other women with reports of her sexual adventures. She had a face that was somewhere between plain and cute at the office, or somewhere between cute and seductive when she was at a party or on a date.

Francine slipped her phone into the pocket of her jacket. With her elbows on the table and her chin in her hands, she repeated to her friend what she had said so many times before. "So you think my life's a bowl of cherries? Dan comes home every night like you come to work every Monday. He whines about everything. His boss is an ogre, his customers are idiots, and everyone else is lazy. All he talks about are angles to make money, except when he's watching sports on TV. And the worst part is when he . . . Hey, Liz, I'm talking to you."

Liz looked up from the morning paper, where she had been browsing through the article about the Bennison trial starting that morning in Chicago. "Oh, I'm sorry, Francine," she said, shaking her head in embarrassment. "I was just looking at this picture here in the paper," she said, pointing to the sports page. "This Bennison guy looks familiar. I swear I've seen him somewhere."

CHAPTER 2

Because of the immense popularity of the plaintiff, the controversial nature of the accusations against him, and the importance of the issues, *Bennison v.* Tee Time *et al.* would be followed closely throughout the country — and throughout the rest of the sports world as well. The courtroom selected for this case was spacious and offered as much seating as possible, not only for the participants and their lawyers, but also for the members of the press and public. It was a good choice — on this first morning of the trial, the courtroom was jammed. The wide windows faced east and offered a view of many examples of Chicago's famous architecture.

At the plaintiff's table sat only two figures, Eddie Bennison and his lawyer, Charlie Mayfield. And that's how Charlie wanted it: two against the world. He always preferred the role of the underdog — being the little guys against the big guys. He knew the defense team would have a large cast. After all, he was suing two large corporations, each with layers of lawyers and a budget for high-priced outside experts, consultants, and advisors. *They even had consultants to advise them on how to pick a jury,* Charlie thought to himself. *Helpless bastards! They probably hire specialists to find the courthouse.*

Charlie Mayfield, having just reached the age of seventy, was an imposing man. He had a thick mane of white hair, was fairly tall, and had a girth that was well above average. He despised the extra twenty-five pounds he carried, most of it around the waist, and for years he had fought valiantly but unsuccessfully to do something about it. He could never resist that one extra bite, or slice, or drink, which collectively — and conspicuously — took their toll. But when Charlie was on trial, he didn't even go through the charade of watching his intake. Although he'd been trying cases for over forty years, he was as nervous and tense for the last one as he was for the first one. The downside of the nervous energy, for Charlie, was that it increased his already enormous appetite.

If Charlie's size alone was not enough to make him an imposing figure, his mannerisms were. His voice, which could be as loud as a bullhorn or as soft as a whisper, was punctuated with colorful colloquialisms and was often accompanied with waving arms, chuckles, sighs, groans, and even looks of scorn or disgust. If one had to describe Charlie Mayfield with a single adjective, it might be "explosive." Even when he whispered, one had the impression that there was volatile, combustible energy bubbling just below the surface. And, when trying a case before a jury, he made it a point to appear as the everyman — his suit could use a pressing, his shoes could use a polishing, and his necktie could use a tightening. It all perfectly fit the role he was playing: the underdog — the little guy against the big guys.

Everything was different at the defense table. The size of the defendants' legal team reflected the incredible net worth of the defendants and their affiliated companies — household names in the media world. But their show of force was not only because the defendants could afford to hire teams of the best lawyers, it was because they could not afford to play it cheap. As they saw it — and as every magazine, newspaper, and radio and television network in the country saw it — the lawsuit threatened their First Amendment rights to their well-guarded freedom of the press. For decades and decades, the media and the courts had been using the battle cry "Freedom of the press!" to protect the media's power to disparage celebrities and other public figures. Media from coast to coast were cheering for *Tee Time*, praying that Eddie Bennison would get summarily thrown out of court. The media that thrived on Eddie during his string of successes on the golf course were now seeing his case as a threat to their constitutional guarantee of a free press to write what they wished, and so now they had turned against him.

Although there were only two defendants in the case — Tee Time, Inc. and Globe Publications, Ltd. — everyone understood that they were surrogates for every newspaper, magazine, and radio and television network in the country that needed their First Amendment protections. If these two defendants won the case, they were *all* winners.

So Charlie's role, as he saw it, was to present his case as if he and Eddie Bennison were the two Davids against the Goliaths of the publishing world.

———————

The defendants' legal team was exactly what Charlie expected. There were enough of them to require a specially extended table surrounded by seats for trial counsel, their assistants, and representatives from the corporate defendants and their affiliated companies. Just behind their table, which was fully twice the size of the table where Charlie and Eddie Bennison were seated, were still more chairs for paralegals prepared to retrieve documents instantaneously from the portable file cabinets that had been wheeled in and placed all around them, or to print them using the computers and laser printers at their fingertips.

Hugo Shoemaker would act as lead counsel for the defendants. Tall and lean, Shoemaker was, by almost any measure, among the best known and most respected First Amendment lawyers in the country.

He was the senior partner at Shoemaker, Cashman & Bates, a large New York firm, and was a frequent guest on TV talk shows to discuss First Amendment issues. He was also a constitutional law professor at Yale Law School. His writings on the freedoms of speech and press were often cited by the Supreme Court as well as by other courts and law professors throughout America, and his views were considered by all to be well-reasoned and well-balanced. His scholarship could not be tainted by accusations that he was either liberal or conservative when it came to his interpretation of constitutional rights, but he usually seemed to be on the side of the press and always pushing to expand the limits of free speech. It was that quest that led him to defend those who burned American flags and draft cards. And although he was unquestionably a decent human being, Shoemaker was just as quick to defend the rights of Nazis, white supremacists, and others who spewed their hate as free speech.

As impressive as his credentials were, however, Shoemaker couldn't match Charlie Mayfield's experience with juries. Most of Shoemaker's court appearances involved appeals where he talked only to judges, not juries. He was an academic, and he tended to speak to heads, while trial lawyers like Charlie talked to hearts.

While Shoemaker was lead counsel for the defense — a status he insisted upon — sitting at his side was Roz Berman, a successful and respected trial lawyer from Chicago. She knew Charlie well and liked him, but that didn't diminish her determination to beat him into the ground. Her looks belied her fierce record and killer instinct; she was barely five feet tall, thin, and had gray hair pulled back into a tight bun. Not often does a gun for hire look like everyone's grandmother.

Roz Berman had a brilliant record of successfully defending "heavies" in the media world against popular or sympathetic plaintiffs. Her proudest moment was when a jury returned a verdict in favor of a notorious pulp magazine she represented. The magazine was being sued by the most popular male movie star in the country. The actor claimed that the magazine falsely reported that he had regularly participated in drug and sex orgies — reports that he and a legion of well-known witnesses denied. Roz Berman's searing cross-examination of the famous actor not only sealed his defeat, it also brought out enough of his character to ensure that he'd never work again in a major film. Even some of his witnesses never recovered from the beating their reputations took from her relentless research into their lives and revelations about their various pastimes. Her intense cross-examination of public icons was legendary. Other lawyers would drop into the courtroom just to watch her dissect a witness as if he or she were a cadaver. It was decided by the defense that Hugo Shoemaker would guide their ship through the First Amendment issues while Roz Berman, because of her trial experience, would handle the examination and cross-examination of the witnesses. But Roz Berman was determined that the case would be tried her way, and she would not, under any circumstances, permit Shoemaker — whom she regarded as a stuffy academic — to cramp her style.

Presiding over this imposing cast of characters was Judge Harry Krause. It was not only because his was one of the largest courtrooms in the county building that the Chief Judge of the Cook County Circuit Court assigned the case to Harry Krause. He had been given the nod because he had a well-deserved reputation for controlling a complex, highly-publicized trial, as this one was sure to be. This trait was essential where, as here, a lack of control could lead to bedlam. Having several lawyers in one courtroom, all hamming it up for the members of the press who were filling most of the seats, was a recipe for chaos. Krause was a short and somewhat frail-looking man who looked older than his seventy-five years, but he had a well-known and highly respected reputation as a stern and forceful judge who ran a tight courtroom and tolerated no sloppiness or poor decorum from the lawyers coming before him. Nonetheless, he had a wonderful sense of humor that he revealed only sparingly in the courtroom, but the ribald stories he told in his chambers, often while puffing on a cigar, were legendary.

In the course of pretrial motions, the defense urged that television cameras be allowed in the courtroom. Judge Krause had expected this, considering that all of the defendants justified their existence by the notion that the public had an unbridled right to know everything, not that evening or the next morning, but instantly. Following the guidelines of the Illinois Supreme Court, Judge Krause denied the request, but did so with a dose of his own thoughts. "I'm sorry," he announced, "but I'm obliged to keep the cameras out of my courtroom. If the lawyers before me knew that they were going to be on the ten o'clock news, they would be clamoring for the attention of the camera's eye. Every question would prompt six objections; every witness would confront six inquisitors, each with one eye on the witness and the other on the little red light; and each day counsel would wrestle for the seats showing their best sides. We're conducting a trial, not a stage show."

As is normal, the selection of the jury was preceded by Judge Krause explaining the gist of the case to the entire pool of available jurors who were summoned for the case. In his explanation, he touched upon the basic laws of libel and slander in everyday language that they would understand. "Under the law," he told them, "a person may not say or write untrue things about another person which damage the reputation of that other person. If that happens, the person whose reputation has been damaged is entitled to sue the person who said or wrote the untrue things, and to recover money to compensate him for the damage to his reputation. I should add," he said, "that if the defamatory words were oral, that is, spoken, they are considered to be *slander*. But if those words were written, it's called libel. I'll have more to say on that when we impanel the final jury."

When the process was completed after a full day, both sides were satisfied that the jury would be fair and impartial.

Charlie was pleased that four of the jurors played golf with some regularity; Roz Berman and Hugo Shoemaker were equally pleased that none of those four considered themselves to be avid golfers or were close followers of Eddie Bennison's accomplishments on the Champions Tour.

While twelve jurors would eventually return a verdict in the case, two additional jurors — alternates — were empaneled. The alternate jurors would hear the case with the others, and each would be available to substitute for one of the original twelve if any were taken ill or otherwise became unavailable to stay on the jury. If all of the original twelve jurors were still serving when the jury began final deliberations, the alternates would be excused.

CHAPTER 3

Now that the final jury was selected from the pool, Judge Krause said to the twelve jurors and two alternates, "Earlier I explained the nature of this case to the entire jury pool, of which each of you was a part. Was that explanation clear to you? Was there anything I said at that time that you don't understand or that you'd like me to clarify? Please speak up or raise your hand if that's the case."

Hearing nothing and seeing no raised hands, the judge said, "Fine. Now I'd like to tell you a little more about the legal issues that you will be considering. As I explained earlier, a defamation case can be either for libel or for slander. If defamatory statements are uttered verbally or orally, they are considered to be slander; and if the defamatory statements are in writing, they are considered to be libel. Since the plaintiff in this case, Edward Bennison, claims that he was defamed by written stories in a magazine, this is a libel case. Is that clear to all of you?"

Seeing nodding heads from the jury box, the judge continued. "Of course, if the person who is being sued for slander or libel can show that what he said or wrote was true, then he has done nothing wrong and will win the lawsuit. In other words, if you should decide that the *Tee Time* stories about Mr. Bennison were true, you would find in favor of the magazine and against Mr. Bennison.

"But," Judge Krause added in a slightly louder tone to ensure the attention of the jury, "there is one important exception to the law as I have explained it to you. This exception is based on the First Amendment to the United States Constitution. That is the amendment which guarantees the freedom of speech and freedom of the press. If the person whose reputation is injured is a public figure — that is, someone in the public eye — he cannot recover money for the damage to his reputation unless the lies about him were written with malice or a wanton or reckless disregard for the truth.

"Let me explain it another way. A newspaper or magazine may safely print false things about a public figure as long it wasn't done with malice, deliberately, or with a total or reckless disregard for the truth. That's why political newscasters may safely say things about the President of the United States, or a presidential candidate, that they may not say about you or me. So, in effect, public figures are fair game — unless the things said or written about them are malicious, deliberately false, or said or written without any regard for their truthfulness or falsity.

"All of the lawyers and parties in this case have stipulated — that is, they have agreed — that the plaintiff, Edward Bennison, is a public figure because of his widely reported successes as a professional golfer. Therefore, at the conclusion of this case, you may not return a verdict in Mr. Bennison's favor unless you unanimously agree on three things: one, that the defendants printed false statements about Mr. Bennison; two, that those statements were deliberately false, or printed maliciously or without any concern for the truth; and three, that those false statements damaged Mr. Bennison's reputation. Before you go back to decide the case at the close of the evidence, I will give you more detailed instructions on those three points. But for now, if any of you have any questions, please raise your hand."

The judge looked from juror to juror to confirm that none had a question. "As I said, when all the evidence has been presented, but before you deliberate your verdict, I will give you further instructions, and I will specifically talk to you about the meaning of 'malice' and 'reckless disregard for the truth.' But for now, you may assume that 'malice' will be proven if you believe from the evidence that the defendants published false statements about Mr. Bennison that they knew to be false. Likewise, if you believe that the false statements — assuming you find that there were false statements — were printed recklessly, or without taking the time to verify if they were true or false, that would be a reckless disregard for the truth and you would return a verdict in Mr. Bennison's favor. If, on the other hand, the defendants published false statements without knowing they were false, they would not be liable, unless you find that their negligence was gross — that is to say, that the defendants did not bother to ascertain whether the statements were false, and that they could have checked but didn't."

The judge then smiled and added, "I sure hope that I'm not confusing you with this little lecture about the law, but we all want to be sure that you understand what a libel case is all about."

CHAPTER 4

Now that the jury was selected and these issues were fully explained to them, the lawyers made their opening statements to the jury. Charlie Mayfield outlined how he intended to prove to them that the defendants published lies about Eddie Bennison, that those lies were published deliberately, maliciously, and without regard for the truth, and how these lies destroyed not only his client's reputation but also his earning power.

Next, Roz Berman told the jury that nothing written by her clients about Bennison was false — the published stories that he cheated and used performance-enhancing drugs to win golf tournaments were absolutely true, she declared, and she would prove that to be the case. And in any event, she explained, nothing written about Bennison was written out of malice or out of a reckless disregard for the truth. Whatever was written about him, she said, was nothing more than the fair reporting of facts.

Although the lawyers had asked the prospective jurors questions during the jury selection process to test their impartiality, the opening statement was the first opportunity for them to talk directly to the jurors about the case, looking each of them in the eye, smiling, and doing everything possible to show sincerity and credibility. Evidence is essential for winning a case, but so is likability, and both attorneys knew it.

Now the actual trial was about to begin. All the preliminary sparring was over. The lawyers were now armed with all the weapons they would get. These weapons were now prepped, loaded, and aimed.

CHAPTER 5

harlie Mayfield called his first witness.

Judge Krause instructed the witness to raise his right hand, and then asked, "Do you swear to tell the truth, the whole truth, and nothing but the truth, so help you God?"

"Yes, sir, I sure will."

"Please be seated."

Then Charlie Mayfield, with his thick mane of white hair and wearing his standard wrinkled, off-the-rack blue suit, raised his hefty frame from the counsel's table. He smiled toward the jury as he lumbered to the podium, but once there he focused on the witness. "Please state your full name for the record."

"My name is Eddie — I mean, Edward — Edward Joseph Bennison. But everyone calls me Eddie."

Eddie Bennison was now fifty-seven years of age, but no one could have guessed it from looking at him. His lean body showed none of the softness that accompanies middle age, and his face showed no evidence of the sun exposure common to golfers, farmers, or other outdoor laborers. He was above average height — just over six feet tall — and his jet-black hair had a tinge of gray, visible only at close range. By any account he was a handsome man, and his good looks were accentuated by his perfect teeth, broad smile, and twinkling blue eyes. If Eddie looked like the stereotypical matinée idol, it was because that's exactly what he was. His picture regularly appeared on magazine covers, ads, and commercials. He was seen on national television being interviewed by Larry King and Jay Leno, and at the White House being congratulated by the president after winning still another tournament or donating a winning purse to this or that charity. In short, Eddie Bennison looked like the national hero he was — until the fates conspired against him and his perfect world began to crumble, at first in almost imperceptible vibrations, and later in crushing avalanches.

After a few preliminary questions, Charlie Mayfield continued. "Now, Eddie, by way of background, I'm going to ask some questions to help the jury learn about your introduction to golf."

"You mean going back to when I was only twelve or thirteen years old?"

"Yes, we'll start when you were twelve or thirteen."

Charlie asked his opening question, and Eddie Bennison began telling his story . . .

Everybody's always asking me how I got into this game. That's not easy to answer, but I can tell you how I *didn't* get into this game. I didn't get into golf like most of the guys on the professional Tour got into it; their folks were members of elegant country clubs with organized junior programs for their kids. Lord, most of the tour players have had custom-made clubs since they were ten years old. They had multiple pros to teach them specific shots, and nearly every one of them had trainers working on their bodies and psychologists working on their heads to deal with pressure, adversity, course management, goals — that sort of thing.

I guess you could say that I, too, was on the golf course when I was a kid, but I wasn't there as a player — and I sure wasn't there as the son of a member. The place was called Midland — a small club a few miles outside of my home town, Kewanee, Illinois. It was a private club, but certainly not a fancy one. Only nine holes and surrounded by cornfields on three sides. Remember, this was in Kewanee, and there weren't enough fancy society types in Kewanee to make a foursome, let alone fill up a club.

Now, I'm not proud of what I'm about to say, but I want to be perfectly honest with the court and with the jury.

I was in seventh or eighth grade at the time, and one afternoon some of my school friends asked me to join them for a bike ride out to Midland. Their intention was to hunt for golf balls to sell to the golfers at the municipal course in town, Baker Park. They generally looked for balls in the cornfields to the left of the 6th and 8th holes. The cornfields are easy places to find balls because, once you're in there between the rows of corn, you can see the ground very clearly for a long way. So if a ball was hit in there, it's easy to spot when you're in the field, but it's hard to see in there from the golf course. Because of this, the golfer who hit a ball in there tends to abandon it and just hit another ball and take the penalty for hitting it out of bounds.

Well, on this particular day, we were finding some balls in the field to the left of the 6th hole. From where we were standing we could look across the fence and see balls that were hit off the 6th tee and lying in the fairway. But the golfers who hit those balls couldn't see them because they came to rest near the bottom of the hill on the fairway to a place the golfers couldn't see from the tee.

Since I was the newest and smallest kid in our group, the others convinced me to dart out into the fairway and grab a few of those balls. They told me that if they lifted me over the fence, I'd have time to grab the balls and get back into the cornfield without being seen by the golfers. They said they did this all the time.

Being young and daring, I did as they asked, but I got caught red-handed! On one of my dashes out into the fairway, a maintenance cart came storming toward me, the driver yelling at me to stop right there. He jumped out of the cart and told me he'd been watching me. Man, was I scared.

I didn't know it then, but it turned out that this was the best thing that ever happened to me. The maintenance man was not really a maintenance man at all. His name was Walt Clerke. Walt was actually a member of Midland but had a deal where he'd pitch in and help around the club, and in return he didn't have to pay dues. Some days he'd be sweeping out the pro shop, and on other days he'd be mowing fairways, repairing equipment, or training the few caddies who came out to Midland. Walt was a prince. Instead of calling the cops or, worse, my parents, he told me that my punishment was to rake bunkers — sand traps — for the rest of the day.

Well, to make a long story short, Walt took a liking to me, and I thought he was the greatest. After my first day of raking, he arranged to find little jobs for me around the club. I'd clean out the maintenance shed, clear tables in the men's grill, sweep floors, gather dirty towels from the locker room, that kind of thing. I suppose Walt violated some child labor laws, but who cared? I was happy, my folks — who for years didn't know the circumstances of my first meeting with Walt — were happy, and I think the club members were happy to have this little go-fer running around and helping out. I got paid out of petty cash — I still remember, it was fifty cents an hour. As soon as I was old enough, I became a legitimate employee. I did everything — even cleaned the swimming pool and locker rooms. My folks were delighted. Not only was I earning a little money and developing good work habits, but they didn't have to worry about where I was, who I was with, or what I was doing. Funny thing, though; not once did either of them ever step foot on the club grounds. If they drove me to work or picked me up, they never went past the front gate; no one would have minded, but they would have felt out of place. When I think back, I see Midland as a very plain and unpretentious club, especially after seeing places like Westchester, Oakmont, and Merion; but to my folks, it was a world where they didn't fit.

Except for retrieving practice balls on the range, I never did anything for individual members — except when it came to Walt Clerke. Officially, I worked for the club; unofficially, I worked for Walt. I did anything he asked. He'd play with his same foursome nearly every Saturday and Sunday, and since those were my days off in the summer, I'd caddie for him. I never once caddied for anyone else. Only Walt. Well, to say I "caddied" is an exaggeration, at least at first. I didn't know the first thing about club selection, yardage, or reading greens. Those things weren't necessary. We were kind of like a grandfather and grandson. My job was to lug his bag — it was almost as large as I was. I was a little runt in those days.

At that time, I thought Walt was the greatest golfer in the world. He must have been in his sixties, but he looked older, mainly because of his sunbaked skin and thin gray hair.

Anyway, after a few months of caddying for Walt, he began to say things during the rounds about some of the shots — that was how he began to teach me the game. He might say something like, "This is a good time to hit it low and let it run up," or "With this tight pin, I better go for the fat part of the green." Sometimes he'd invite my comments, like whether I thought he could reach the green or get it up over a tree.

Then one day — it was a Monday and the club was closed for play — I was in the shed sweeping grass clipping off the floor, and I heard Walt's voice just outside the door. "Eddie, put the broom down and come on out here." When I came outside, Walt was sitting on a golf cart, patting the seat next to him. I jumped on and we headed straight for the 6th fairway, and it wasn't until he stopped and we got out that I saw an unfamiliar golf bag and clubs on the back of the cart, along with a basket of balls. "Take these," he said, pointing to the clubs, "and come with me." I followed him over to a shady area under a big cottonwood tree. "Okay, let's see if you've learned anything about this crazy game."

Walt had conned the Spaulding club salesman out of a demo set, and then he cut them down to fit me and put on ladies' grips. It was not only to be my first golf lesson, it was the first time I hit a golf ball — ever!

I'll never forget that next hour. Walt showed me the grip and stance, then sat down against that big old cottonwood and watched me try to hit balls. The only thing I remember him saying while he sat there was, "Slower, Eddie, slower." I asked him a lot of questions, like, "Why does it keep going to the right?" or "How do I make it go higher?" But he'd only say, "Never mind that, Eddie. Slower."

Later, when we got back to the equipment shed, Walt went over to the sink to wash his hands. Speaking over his shoulder, he explained, "It's a crazy game, Eddie. Everything defies logic. Hit down on the ball and it goes high, swing to the left and it goes right, swing slow and it goes far." He chuckled and added, "That's why smart people can't play it. They try to understand it, but it can't be understood. You've watched me on weekends — I beat those guys every time. Well, one's a doctor, one's a lawyer, and the other's the richest guy in the county, and they're lucky to break 85. Me? I don't even have a high school diploma, but I have to give 'em all strokes. And you know why that is, Eddie? It's because I don't think about all the things those guys worry about, like, 'Is my club open at the top?' or 'Am I bringing it back too far to the inside?' I'm just thinking about being smooth — get all the jerkiness out of it.

"And that's the secret of this darn game, Eddie," he told me. "Just forget everything else and think about smooth, slow, and loose. That's what it's all about. The pros call it *tempo*, but that's just shorthand for smooth, slow, and loose. Once that becomes automatic — second nature — then you can start thinking about the mechanics."

Walt had this wonderful way of explaining things. For example, I asked him what he meant by "loose." I told him that I thought I had to hold the club tight to hit the ball far. Without saying a word, he tossed me a golf ball and told me to throw it as far as I could. Just as I was about to make the throw, with my arm reaching way back behind me, he yelled, "Stop right there! Now tell me, Eddie, are you holding the ball tightly, or is it just sitting there loosely in your fingers?"

I felt my fingers loosely holding the ball, and then I looked to confirm it. "It's loose, Walt."

"Of course it's loose. You couldn't throw the ball across the room if you were squeezing it. It's the same with a golf club, Eddie; you can't swing it fast if you're squeezing it or holding it tightly."

We walked to the parking area behind the shed — him to his old pickup truck and me to my bike — and he said something else I'll always remember: "Watch the good players — not to imitate their swings, but to see how they play certain shots. Doc Winters always does better in the wind 'cause he keeps it low. Watch to see how he does it. And old Herman Kelly — he hardly hits the ball out of his shadow, but he has great finesse around the greens and gets it up and down better than any of us. Watch him, Eddie. Watch how he hits the little runner along the ground, and watch how he hits the soft little pitch shot that hits and stops. But more important than *how* he hits them, Eddie, is *when* he hits them. It's called course management. Hitting the ball perfectly is no good if you have the wrong club in your hand, or if you misread the wind or the bounce. And hitting it where you aim is no good if you're aiming at the wrong place."

———

"Your Honor," Charlie Mayfield said as he turned toward the bench, "this may be a good time to break for lunch. It's just about noon, and we're about to start a whole new line of testimony."

"Any objection from the defense?" asked Judge Krause.

In the entire history of American jurisprudence, no lawyer has ever objected to a lunch break in a jury trial; the risk of alienating a hungry juror is too great. "No, Your Honor," Hugo Shoemaker replied on behalf of the defendants.

"Alright, then. Please plan to be back and ready to proceed by two this afternoon." The judge then turned toward the jury and said, "Ladies and gentlemen, we're breaking now for lunch. The bailiff's staff has made lunch arrangements for you. In the meantime, you are not to discuss the case among yourselves or with others."

———

Charlie's office was only a few minutes' walk from the courthouse, and he preferred to have lunch brought in during trials so he could confer with his client and witnesses or tend to other office business. On the way there, Eddie asked Charlie the question asked by every witness at every trial: "How'd I do?"

Charlie replied that he was generally pleased with the morning's testimony. "But it's starting to drag. We have to move this along a little faster, Eddie. You've been on the stand for over an hour and you're still thirteen years old. Interesting background, and it's important that the jurors know about it, but we have to tell them how you became a leading pro on the Senior Tour. And we can't do that without saying something about the thirty-seven years that intervened. So let's spend some time over lunch going over this afternoon's testimony."

CHAPTER 6

That damned picture! It was nagging at Liz Peters all morning. *I know that guy.* Just before lunch, she returned to the lunch room to take another look at the paper, but nothing rang a bell — not even the name. *Eddie Bennison. I never knew an Eddie Bennison. Ed? Edward? Edwin? No, nothing.* The story was something about a golfer, but she didn't know any golfers — certainly not any famous golfers. She tore out the page, folded it, and slipped it into her jacket pocket. Something to think about later.

THURSDAY AFTERNOON

CHAPTER 7

After the lunch break, all of the players — the lawyers, assistants, parties, judge, jurors, court personnel, and spectators — were back in their assigned places in the courtroom. "I hope you enjoyed your lunch," Judge Krause said to the jurors, "and that you remembered my direction that you not speak about the case. We will now proceed. Mr. Mayfield."

Charlie motioned for Eddie Bennison to return to the witness stand, and when he did so, Eddie was reminded by the judge that he was still under oath.

"Eddie," Charlie began, "we've talked about your first introduction to golf as a young boy. Moving ahead, did you play golf on your high school or college teams?"

"No, sir. I tried out for the high school team when I was a sophomore but just wasn't good enough. It wasn't only that I was still small and new at the game, but I got so nervous that I could barely hit the ball. Everything I thought I had learned, and everything that Walt told me about tempo, disappeared. I just kept swinging too hard, straining to hit the ball a mile. The try-outs were embarrassing, and I never tried it again. I did work for Walt at Midland the following summer, but didn't play at all again until I was in my thirties."

This last answer brought raised eyebrows and questioning looks among the spectators. They were asking themselves how one of the greatest golfers in the world had not been good enough for his high school golf team and how he achieved his fame in a game that he didn't play regularly until he was in his thirties.

"Okay," Charlie was saying, "I'll ask you some questions about that . . . "

─────

After I got out of high school in 1970, I joined the Marines and was soon shipped out to Vietnam. By the time I came back home in late 1973, I knew I ought to go to college. My folks couldn't afford to send me, but I was able to manage it between the GI Bill and part-time work. In the fall of 1974, I enrolled at a community college and later transferred to the University of Illinois in Champaign. One of my best friends at Illinois was Mickey Laster, also a Vietnam vet. We hung out together a lot, and managed to be roommates our senior year. Sometimes I would spend weekends or holidays with his family in Chicago. His dad was the manager of a corrugated box plant for National Container Corporation, a large company with plants across the country. Mr. Laster — his first name was Norm — was in charge of the Chicago plant, but the company headquarters were in Tulsa, Oklahoma. Norm Laster took a liking to me and treated me almost like a son.

On graduation weekend, in the spring of 1978, Mickey's folks drove down to Champaign. My mom came too, with my brother and sister, but Dad was just starting a new job and couldn't take the time off. After the graduation ceremony, Mr. and Mrs. Laster asked us to join them at dinner. While at dinner, Norm Laster looked over at me and asked, "Eddie, now that you've graduated from college, what are your plans?"

"I'm looking for a job," I replied, "but no luck so far. I have a lot of copies of my résumé out there, but no calls for interviews." I added that I was already twenty-five and it was time I found a job to support myself.

Mr. Laster leaned back in his chair and, imitating the voice of the Godfather from the movies said, "Well, young man, I have a proposition that you can't afford to turn down." He went on to explain that he'd love for Mickey to come to work at National Container, but that the company had a strict rule against nepotism. He joked that that was probably a good thing, since Mickey would bankrupt the place in six months. "However," he went on to say, "since *friends* of sons are not excluded, I went to the head of Human Resources and told him all about you. He called me last week and said that if I liked you, they'd like you, and he authorized me to offer you a position in our training program. Of course," he added, "once there, you'll be on your own. Do well and you can move up the ladder. Do poorly and you'll be back in the employment lines."

My mom's excitement was dampened when she heard that the training program was at the company headquarters in Tulsa, Oklahoma. Mr. Laster explained that that couldn't be avoided, but that the training program was only for two years. It would take that long to rotate through the various departments — Sales, Production, Purchasing, Marketing, and so forth. "After that," he explained, "Eddie might be transferred to one of our other plants" — maybe even to Chicago, which was only a couple of hours' drive from Kewanee. I told Mom that Tulsa was a lot closer to Kewanee than Vietnam, and that I'd write, call, and come home for Mother's Day. She bit her lip, nodded, and it was a done deal.

By the time I completed the training program at National Container, the company and I agreed that Sales would be the best place for me. The customers seemed to enjoy working with me, and I was able to write more new business than they expected from a trainee. I also liked that selling got me out of the office.

The Vice President of Sales told me, after my training ended, that there were openings in Sales in two of our branch offices — Minneapolis and Tulsa. If I chose Tulsa, I wouldn't technically be part of the home office, but the Tulsa plant was on the same property as the national headquarters. I asked the Vice President — his name was Mike Morrissey — what he would do if he were in my shoes, and he said he'd pick Tulsa. "If you're not real good at your job," he explained, "you want to keep a low profile, and it helps to be far away from the top brass. But if you're good at what you do — and you are — then you want to be right there where they can see you do your stuff. Take Tulsa, Eddie." And that's what I did.

I was glad that Mike influenced me to stay there. I liked Tulsa and was making new friends every day. Moreover, I had been dating this young lady I met at a mixer at the apartment complex where we both lived, and I was hoping that something serious might develop. Her name was Carol. In fact, something did develop, and we eventually got married — but not for several years — and now we have two children, Betsy and Wally. Wally was named for Walt Clerke.

"And is this your wife, Carol Bennison?" Charlie Mayfield asked as he walked back toward the gallery and held his hand close to an attractive woman. She was wearing a smart blue-gray suit over a white blouse and showed only a minimum of jewelry. Her short hair was just starting the journey from blonde to silver. She smiled broadly to acknowledge Charlie's gesture.

"Yes, sir, it is."

Walking back to the counsel table, ostensibly to consult some notes, Charlie stole a glance at Hugo Shoemaker. *Okay, Hugo, now we're ready for some golf.*

"Eddie, you told us earlier that you didn't play golf again until you were in your thirties. According to my arithmetic, you were about twenty-seven when you finished the training program. Tell us how golf came back into your life."

I think it was in 1986 — I was thirty-two or thirty-three — when the company announced that it would hold a sales and marketing conference in a few months at a new resort in southern Wisconsin. It was called the American Club but was better known simply as "Kohler," the name of the plumbing fixture company that owned it. Like at a lot of these conferences, there was time set aside for leisure. Some golf was being planned, and a couple of weeks before the conference, a few of the guys from the Tulsa division asked if I'd be part of their foursome. At first I tried to beg off, but then thought, *What the heck, why not?* It might be fun, and I thought I should re-learn the game since it could help me with my sales. So I agreed to play after warning them that I hadn't played since I was a kid.

In the few weeks before the conference, I decided I'd better do some practicing so I wouldn't embarrass myself when I got to Wisconsin. I didn't even own a set of clubs — years ago, my folks had given away the set Walt Clerke cut down for me — so my first step was to go to one of those driving ranges where you hit balls at night off a mat, and where they had racks of clubs you could use. There was one of these places in Tulsa not far from where I lived. It was called Morrie's Stop and Sock, and I went over there after work the same day I agreed to play at the conference.

The next few hours were just wonderful. Thankfully, Morrie's stayed open until fairly late in the evening. I started with a bucket of balls and took a driver off the rack — it probably wasn't worth five dollars — and found a spot off to the side. As soon as I gripped the club, all of Walt's words came surging back to me*: tempo, hold it loose, tempo, take it back slow, swing easy, it's a game of opposites, tempo, tempo, tempo.* I stretched a little, took a few practice swings, and suddenly some of the technical things that Walt later taught me flashed through my mind — take the club back low, keep my head still, keep my left arm straight. Then I teed up the first ball. I was nervous, but not nervous like when I tried out for the high school team. That was a bad nervous — a scary nervous — but this was more of an excitement nervous, like I couldn't wait. When I think back on the moment, and I do it often, I always see a smile on my face.

My first thought when I finally stood over the ball was that I was so much taller than the last time I swung a club. When I was a little runt back at Midland, my arms and legs were so short it seemed the ball was right under my nose. But now I had room. I could have a wider arc and generate club head speed without forcing it. And when I hit that first shot, I was hooked. It didn't go all that far, and it didn't go all that straight, but it *went!* By the time I got through that first bucket, I was consistently hitting the ball solidly. I knew I had fundamental errors in my swing, but I was having fun and wanted to keep doing it. After two more buckets, hitting only drivers and 5-irons, I was determined to buy a set of clubs the next day and give this thing a real try.

The next day, I passed on lunch and used the time to shop at a local sporting goods store. I didn't bother with getting custom fitted clubs; an inexpensive set with standard specs would do for the time being. I also picked up a pair of golf shoes to get better footing on the mats at Morrie's and a glove to guard against the blisters and chafing I was feeling from the night before. I made up my mind not to go onto a course until I spent another week or so at Morrie's, so I didn't bother to buy balls yet.

The clubs I bought for myself were just fine; in fact, I used them for over a year, and I hit hundreds of balls with each one that next week. The shots kept getting longer and straighter, and when I made a mistake, I was able to figure it out and correct it. I even bought a couple of instruction books. Soon I was figuring out how to hit the ball higher or lower, or make it curve to the left or right. I don't know how many buckets of balls I went through at Morrie's, but everyone who worked there was soon calling me "Eddie," and I knew their names as well.

"Hey, Eddie?" Morrie said to me one night. "Whaddya wasting your time out here for? Why don't you take that swing out to a golf course and see if it works when you have to deal with water, bunkers, and out of bounds?"

I told him I wasn't a member anywhere but that I was planning to go to one of the public daily fee courses and give it a try. "Go on over to East Side Links and ask for Jake," Morrie urged. "He's the starter over there and a good pal of mine. I'll call him so he'll expect you. Jake'll take care of you — set you up with some nice guys who won't give a damn how you play. That's the thing at East Side; they all have a good time and nobody gives a hoot about anything. Wanna hit a mulligan? Hit a mulligan. Wanna pick up a putt? Pick it up."

Well, that's just what I did. Jake — I never did learn his last name — set me up with some good guys. I played twilight golf after work, and I played 36 holes on the few Saturdays and Sundays remaining before the conference, and at nights I was back at Morrie's. Fortunately, I didn't have any business trips during that time. Until I played at East Side Links, I hadn't hit any short shots — chips, pitches, or shots out of the sand — and I hadn't even hit any putts, so I spent a lot of time on those things once I started paying at East Side. Another thing, and this was kind of funny when I think back, was that at Morrie's I had no idea how far the ball was going. They had a few yardage signs, but you could hardly follow the ball at night under the lights. Then, on the very first hole I played at East Side, after hitting a pretty good drive, I had about 135 yards to the green. But I had no idea what club to hit for 135 yards. Trying to remember how far my different irons went when I was at Midland, and adjusting for my growth, I took out an 8-iron . . . and hit the darn ball at least 30 yards over the green. For you folks who have maybe never played golf, the green is the small area where we need to hit the ball in order to putt it toward the hole.

By the time we got to the conference in Wisconsin, my game was passable for that kind of outing. The guys in my foursome scored better than I did, but that's because they knew their games and I was just starting to learn mine. Still, I hit several shots during those two rounds that drew good comments from the other guys, and that was important to me. And I was hitting it farther than most of them. I came home even more determined to get serious about the game — to make up for lost time.

CHAPTER 8

harlie Mayfield took a long drink from his water glass, pondering his next line of questions and determined to speed things up. He could see the jurors were really into Eddie's story and hanging on every word, but he could spend only so much time on background. Further, there was one subject he had to cover, one he had carefully rehearsed with Eddie and Carol, and he might just as well get it out of the way right now.

"Eddie, you told us a little while ago that you were already dating Carol and that things were getting serious. Do you recall that?"

"Yes, of course."

"How did she react to your new interest in golf?"

"She was great, she really was, and I've always loved her for how she handled it. Golf is one of those activities that takes a lot of time. A round of golf takes about four hours, and that can mean about six hours away from home when you add in driving to and from the course, loosening up on the practice range, and showering. And, as Carol had already learned, I'm the kind of guy who tends to overdo things, so I was spending more time with golf than I had expected — a *lot* more time! But she was very understanding, and without that I would never have become serious about golf. My success is as much hers as it has been mine." Here Eddie glanced over Charlie's shoulder and smiled at his wife, who was reaching for a handkerchief.

The interplay wasn't lost on the jurors, all of whom followed Eddie's eyes to his wife and saw her reaction to his testimony. Nor was it lost on Hugo Shoemaker, who imperceptibly cringed, nor on Judge Krause, who not so imperceptibly smiled.

After milking the moment for all it was worth, Charlie Mayfield resumed. "Your job at National Container must have required a great deal of time. How did the people at the company, specifically your superiors, take to your newfound preoccupation with golf?"

"Well, of course I couldn't let golf interfere with my job, but as it turned out, golf soon became a big plus at work. One thing about golfers: they all like to play with someone who plays well. That explains why, as I got better, I began to get invited by customers to their clubs and even to their meetings and conventions where time was set aside for golf. As my golf scores went down, my sales orders went up. So, to answer your question, my superiors were not complaining; in fact, they were often inviting me to *their* clubs."

"In a word, Eddie, please tell the jurors how your game progressed over the next few years."

"Sure. A few years after I got back to the game, I was starting to play in amateur tournaments around the Southwest, and even played in the National Amateur once. Except for the Tulsa Amateur, which I won twice, I hadn't won any tournaments by then, but I had a few respectable finishes."

"I assume that you had joined one of the private country clubs."

"No, sir, I didn't. I could have afforded it, I suppose, after the first few years, but there was no need. Carol never played golf and, frankly, neither of us cared much for the country club scene."

Charlie smiled inwardly. *Another point scored for Bennison family values.* "But wouldn't your game have improved even more if you played on the better, tougher private courses where most professional tournaments are played?"

Eddie smiled innocently. "As a matter of fact, I played on those courses often. Many of my friends and customers, and even some of the executives at National Container, were members at those clubs, and, like I said, they frequently invited me to play, and as my amateur record improved, many of the clubs themselves offered me an open invitation to play as a complimentary guest of the club."

Charlie was facing a dilemma. Spending too much time on Eddie's early days trying to qualify for the Tour was a diversion from the central issues in the case and, further, it ran the risk of boring the jury. But Charlie, keeping a close eye on the jury to register their reactions to Eddie's story, sensed that they were keenly interested in his climb to the top, and they seemed to be fascinated with his early struggles to get there. More importantly, Charlie was aiming for more than a victory in this trial — he wanted a *big* victory with a verdict in the multimillions of dollars. For that he needed the jury to love Eddie and to identify with him, and for that they had to know him and everything about him. They wouldn't know how much money to award him for his fall *from* the top unless they could see how hard it was to get *to* the top.

"Eddie, before the recess, you were about forty years old and playing in amateur tournaments. Did you later play on the regular professional tour before you were fifty years old and eligible to play on the Senior Tour — the Champions Tour, as it's officially called?

"No, sir."

"So, what did you do during those ten years?"

Eddie Bennison smiled at Charlie's attempt to cover ten years in one answer. "I worked very hard on my game, of course. By then I was hitting the ball far enough to be competitive at the highest levels, and I could hit the ball straighter than many of the better professionals. And my short game was pretty darn good. But there were still a few areas where I needed to work harder.

"For one thing, I had to learn how to gear down or gear up on a certain club. I knew, for example, that my standard 7-iron carried between 180 and 185 yards in the air. But if the hole was, say, 177 yards away, and the green was soft, I had to know how to take a few yards off the shot, or hit an 8-iron a few yards farther, or maybe even hit a light 6-iron. Those couple of yards are the difference between birdie and par — between winning and just playing.[1]

"And I had to learn how to 'work' the ball to the left or right, or higher or lower. If there was a tree in front of me, I had to learn how to curve around it, or hit the ball under or over it. And if I were faced with a shot that was 170 yards out, and the hole was on the right side of the green, it would be very helpful to be able to start the ball toward the center of the green, and then have it move — or cut — slightly to the right toward the hole. That way, if the ball happens to go straight, it will still be safely in the middle of the green. That gives me a greater margin of error, and is part of what we call 'course management.'

"Course management, and calculating the margin of error, are really important. What are the risks and rewards of trying to hit the ball over, under, or around the tree? Should I run the ball up the mound or pitch it over the mound? How will a ball struck off Bermuda grass behave differently than one struck off rye grass or bluegrass? When do I play for the pin, and when do I play for the wide part of the green? It's all a question of percentages that I had to learn.

"Finally, and most important, I had to learn to deal with pressure. As I reached my mid-forties, I was determined that I would take a shot at the Senior Tour when I was fifty — that Tour is not open to anyone younger than fifty. It's one thing to play amateur golf when you have a day job and you know that you don't have to play well to feed your family. It's another thing to give up your job when you have a family to support, and know that one mistake — one bad shot — and there's no paycheck. People sometimes forget that golfers aren't like football or baseball players who get paid even when they have a bad day. We don't. On top of that, we have to pay for our own transportation, hotel room, caddies, and everything else, including tips. We even have to pay entry fees to play in each tournament. Professional golfers are not pampered."[2]

Charlie moved a few steps closer to the jury box. "Tell us, Eddie, what are the expenses of playing on the Senior Tour? How much did you have to earn before you could break even?"

"Well, that's a tough question, Mr. Mayfield. Some of the guys eat at fancy restaurants, others eat at McDonald's; some stay at expensive hotels and others stay at the no-frill motels; some share rooms and others don't. Also, since most of the senior players don't have young kids who are still at home, we often bring our wives, and that adds to the expenses. And if there are kids who come along, that adds even more to the expenses. Another thing: we have our regular homes that have to be maintained even while we're out on the Tour.

"Assuming someone plays in, say, 25 tournaments, he'd need somewhere between $150,000 and $200,000 in annual earnings just to cover his travel and basic living expenses — and," he added with a smile, "that wouldn't leave much for Christmas shopping."

"So, to leave your job to play on the Tour would be a big risk."

"Absolutely! By the time I was 50, I was a Vice President of Sales at National Container. I had a good salary, plus all the other benefits like insurance and a company car. And stock options. I was worried about putting all that on the line. On the other hand, my game was coming together better than I thought was possible, and I really wanted to give it a try. If I didn't, well, I'd never know.

"The company was great. They told me to try the Tour for one year, and they'd continue my salary and benefits during that time. Part of the deal was, when I wasn't on the road, I'd be keeping my contacts with customers. Then, after the first year, we'd see how it was working out."

"What about Carol? What did she think about it?"

"She was very supportive. We both talked about it for a long, long time, and it was a joint decision. The main concern was our two children, Betsy and Wally. Since we married fairly late, they were still at home, so Carol wouldn't be able to travel with me. We figured that if I didn't do well, I'd be back home soon and forget about the Tour. My job at National Container was waiting for me. And even if I played well and won fairly good money, I still wouldn't play more than twenty or twenty-five tournaments a year, so I'd still be home for at least half the year. Heck, when I was selling boxes for National Container, I was out on the road about a third of the time, so Carol and the kids were used to my being away."

"Is that still the case, that Carol doesn't travel with you?"

"Well, not often. The kids are now in college, but still at home during the summer, and she's busy with charity work. Besides that, when I'm on tour I spend a lot of time on the course playing or practicing, and she has better things to do than sit around in a hotel room. Still, she comes out for some of the events. The kids did come out for a few of the tournaments during the summers, but it was hard to plan meals and everything else around my playing and practicing. And the traveling for a family is hard — the Tour moves all over the country, and we're never in one place more than five or six days at a time."

Charlie Mayfield walked back to the counsel table and sat down. "Tell us, Eddie, about when you actually started on the Tour."

CHAPTER 9

I always thought it was a good omen that I was born on November 3, back in 1953. That put my fiftieth birthday on the day before the beginning of Senior Tour Qualifying School on November 4 of 2003. Q School — that's what we call it — is the toughest experience any professional golfer has to face. First, there are regional qualifying events around the country, and only the top finishers are eligible to go to the finals. That year the finals were to be held in Coral Springs, Florida. I can't remember how many guys tried out that year in the regionals — probably over a thousand. And for those lucky enough to advance to the finals at Coral Springs, only the low seven scorers in the finals would make it to the Tour. That's only seven out of maybe a thousand — tough odds.

I played the regional qualifier in San Antonio, Texas, and knew that only fourteen of us would advance from there to the finals in Florida. My nerves were a wreck over the previous few weeks, but during the practice rounds, and especially when the tournament began, I became very calm and focused. I began to feel a level of confidence I didn't deserve. Until then, this was the most pressure I ever had to face, and I can't describe the relief I felt to know that I was able to deal with it. In fact, I learned for the first time that week that I play even better when the pressure is intense.

During all four days of the San Antonio qualifier, I played unbelievably well. My good shots were great, and even the poorer shots — and there weren't many — always ended up in pretty good places. It was the best golf

I ever played over four days. I placed sixth, and might've done better, but I decided to play the final round conservatively. I knew after the third day that my scores were good enough to get me to Coral Springs, and I didn't want to shoot myself out of it on the last day by taking risks. My goal was Coral Springs and then the Tour, and placing first in the regional was not important — it wouldn't be any better than fifth or even fourteenth since the low fourteen would qualify for the finals in Coral Springs. As it happened, my sixth-place finish qualified me with a cushion of seven shots.

The finals were held two weeks later in Coral Springs. Everything I had worked for over the past several years came down to the next four rounds of golf. I was feeling well, physically and mentally, but I'd never played under such pressure before, and I was worried that I might not be able to hold it together over the final rounds. It was Carol's idea that she come to Florida to be with me, and her parents were happy to come to Tulsa to stay with the kids. She was right; it was a big help. I could focus on golf and not worry about driving, parking, running to the ATM, figuring out where and what to eat, all that kind of stuff. And I had someone to talk to when I couldn't sleep or if I wanted to get my mind off golf. Most important, I had someone nearby pulling for me. About 150 of us reached the finals, and we were all fighting for just seven spots. Let's just say I didn't have a lot of friends around and having Carol there doubled my cheering section.

When I got to the course in Coral Springs for my first practice round, I was assigned a local caddie who knew the course inside out. This was a tremendous piece of luck. His name was Arturo Escalara. He knew the breaks on the greens, the bounces on the fairways, and the yardage to and over every hazard. "Eddie," he'd say, "you got 156 yards to carry the front bunker, 167 to the pin. Keep it a little right of the flag and let the slope feed you down." Or he'd say, "If you're gonna miss this green, miss it in the left; it's the only place you have a chance of getting up and down and saving par." More than once he counseled me to leave my driver in the bag. "The driver'll put you on a down slope," he'd say. "Better to hit the 3-wood to where it's level." Local knowledge like that is invaluable.

Arturo — everyone calls him Artie — was the best and only caddie I ever had on the Tour. He was about twenty-five years old at the time, and even though he was short and skinny, he had tremendous energy and strength. He carried my golf bag down the fairways and up and over the hills like it was a feather, and in no time he became everybody's buddy out there on the Tour.

As I mentioned, I played better in San Antonio Regionals than I ever had before. The bigger miracle was that I played even better in Coral Springs. My shots were straighter and more solid than ever before, and I was controlling my yardage perfectly. Even so, I don't think I'd have done nearly as well if it weren't for Artie. He told me everything I had to know about the course, and, equally important, he had this knack of saying the right thing to cheer me up or calm me down. I remember reaching a par five in two shots, and leaving myself a triple-breaking 80-foot putt. I three-putted and was steamed, but as we left the green, Artie said, "Hey, Eddie, that was okay; give Tiger a dozen balls and he couldn't get down in two from there. I'm just glad you got it down in three putts and didn't need four!"

The talk around the clubhouse was that something around five to ten under par was needed to make the low seven and qualify unconditionally for the Tour. This meant averaging something like 70, or two under par, on each of the four rounds. Eagle Trace — that was the name of the course — played tough that week, and averaging 70 was a big challenge. On the first day, I was right on the number: a 70 with two birdies and no bogies, and I was tied for fifth place. *Darn*, I thought, *here I am playing the best golf of my life and I'm still on the edge of the cliff hanging on by my fingernails. What did I get myself into?*

I caught fire the second day! Three birdies on the first five holes, and I never looked back. I ended the day with a six-under 66, and that was with the three-putt I just told you about. What made me the proudest that day was making birdie on the 18th hole after learning on the tee that I was leading the tournament. It confirmed what I saw during San Antonio and again at Coral Springs — the stronger the pressure, the better I played. Every aspiring golfer worries about how he'll deal with pressure, but we never know until we confront it. As I signed my scorecard that afternoon, I knew that I had stared the devil in the eye and didn't blink. I was leading the field after the second round!

I should mention that Carol was invisible while I was on the course. I knew she was out there somewhere, but she had this same superstition that many tour wives have: a fear that their husbands will be distracted and lose their concentration if they see their wives in the gallery. Those of us who have been out there a while laugh about it. We're out there surrounded by thousands of fans in the galleries, and often being watched by millions on TV. We're thinking about the wind, the distances, the grain of the grass, and what we want to do with the next shot. Heck, Carol could be doing cartwheels across the green and I probably wouldn't notice. Nevertheless, it's a common concern, even with wives of many of the seasoned veterans, and we appreciate it.

That night, after the second round, I wanted to relax and avoid restaurants, crowds, and traffic. Our hotel provided a small sitting room next to the bedroom, so we had a comfortable place to sit and put our feet up. I asked Carol and she agreed to having pizza ordered in, but she had a suggestion: "Let's ask Artie to join us." She knew I might want to talk to him about the next day's strategy; he would already have a chart of the pin placements for the third round. I called him and he agreed to join us.

Some years earlier, Artie's family had immigrated from Cuba to escape the Castro regime. They came to Miami full of hope and ready to work. After receiving a high school diploma, Artie enrolled in a trade school to learn about appliance repairs, but all he learned was that he hated to work indoors. He then took a job with the ground crew at a fairly modest private golf course, and soon figured out that he'd prefer to be one of the caddies; they made more money and didn't get nearly as dirty. The caddie master had him train with the other new caddies, and it wasn't long before members were requesting Artie on their bags. A year or so later, he realized that the caddie rates and tips were much higher at fancier clubs with wealthier members or at resorts catering to wealthy tourists. So he scouted around and landed a caddie job at the Eagle Trace TPC course in Coral Springs.

When I met Artie that week, he was still living at home. He hadn't married because it would mean having less money to share with his family. I'm sure he never felt deprived; on the contrary, he was proud that he was able to help his parents, brothers, sisters, and any other Escalaras who might be in need of the few dollars he could spare.

Over pizza and Cokes — none of us hardly ever drank anything stronger than Coke — Carol and I were surprised to hear how well-versed Artie was in current events. Clearly, he read the newspapers and watched the news, and his opinions were well-reasoned. Carol asked him how well he played golf, but he surprised her by saying he didn't play. "Never had the time or the money," he explained. "I don't have to hit the ball out there. I only have to know which way it'll roll or bounce, how far it should go, and where to find it. Caddies who know more than they have to know say more than they have to say." I loved it when Artie came up with those things. After another hour or so going over the next day's pin placements and agreeing on how to play some of the holes, Artie got up to leave. I asked him to sit for a few more minutes and to wait while I discussed something with Carol in the next room.

When Carol and I came back, I told him that we still had a lot more golf and that anything could happen over the two final rounds, but that in the meantime I wanted him to go home and discuss something with his family. "Carol and I agreed, Artie, that if I qualify for the Tour, I'd like to have you on my bag." His eyes got as big as saucers — I'm sure it was something he had never even dreamed about. "It would mean being away from home a good part of the year. I asked around today and found out that the standard fee for caddies is $400 a week plus 7 percent of whatever I win — maybe more if we get first place. I'll get some more details, like about travel arrangements, but in the meantime, I want you and your family to think about it. Okay?" He only nodded, but at the door he turned and gave me a hug, and then he left without saying a word.

When I met him the next morning he said, "I guess my family doesn't like me very much. They all agreed that I should get the hell out of town and go with you."

I said that would be great, provided I could keep it going and finish in the top seven. Actually, the next eight finishers would get conditional exemptions for the next year's Tour, meaning they'd get to play, but in only a limited number of tournaments. That didn't interest me. For me it would be all or nothing, and that meant finishing in the top seven.

"No sweat, Boss," Artie said, "I'll make sure you do it. I'll prove that you made a good choice last night."

That third round was a lot of fun. For one thing, I continued my good play in spite of a stiff wind. For another, Artie outdid himself. He had come to the course before dawn to pace the greens, not trusting the pin sheets they distributed before we teed off. He drew his own diagrams and was able to give me exact distances from every angle and from every edge. He had a spring in his step like a kid on his way to the circus and did everything humanly possible to keep me buoyed up. He even put his fingers to his lips to warn the other caddies — and even the other players — in our group to be silent when I was hitting. I put a 70 on the board and was now in second place, but I was in even better position than the day before, when I was in first place. That's because only one of the other leaders did well, probably because of the wind. The night before, I was leading and five strokes ahead of eighth place. Now I was second but seven strokes ahead of eighth place, and that was fine; the mission was to be in the top seven, and that meant getting as far ahead of eighth as I could get.

For the final round, after talking to Artie and Carol, I decided to change my San Antonio strategy. I was in second place, and instead of playing conservatively to protect myself, I decided to go for birdies — at least at the start — for my last round at Coral Springs. I had a good cushion and high confidence in my game. If I started to get shaky, I could always revert to safer play, but the chance to win the thing outright was too much to resist. It wasn't so much the $45,000 first-place money or the chance to pick up some endorsements — not that all that wasn't important — but this was a golden opportunity for me to win my first professional tournament. And finishing first in the finals is a much bigger deal than finishing first in the regionals — and a much better introduction into the Senior Tour. The day turned out to be a walk in the park. Every single thing went right. Putts that could've lipped out went in, shots headed for the rough took lucky bounces into the fairway. I couldn't miss, and ended up shooting 64, tying the course record and finishing in first place by five shots.

Artie and I were headed for the Senior Tour! Life was perfect!

———

Eddie Bennison's many references to his caddie, Artie, were not entirely spontaneous. This was something that he and Charlie had planned at length. For one thing, it showed that Eddie was fair and generous in acknowledging how invaluable Artie's help was to his — Eddie's — success. For another, these references would be a good prelude for Artie being called later as a witness. The more the jury already heard about the helpful and good-natured Artie, the more receptive they would be to his later testimony.

"Mr. Mayfield, it's almost five. Might this be a good place to adjourn for the day?"

"Well, Your Honor, I'd like just another minute or two."

"Go ahead."

———

Charlie walked over and leaned against the railing in front of the jury box, inviting Eddie to look toward the jury when he spoke. "Tell us, Eddie, does playing golf on the Senior Tour take much of a toll on your health?"

Eddie looked from juror to juror as he answered. "A lot of people don't think of golf as a very strenuous sport. Some don't even think of us as athletes. After all, you can play golf after a big meal, and judging from what we see on TV, it looks like a lot of the guys on the Senior Tour do that too often. And I'm now fifty-seven — an age when most athletes are well over the hill.

"But most people don't see the grind we put our bodies through to make a living out there. A single round of golf involves walking about six miles, up and down hills, and adding up the tournaments, practice rounds, and pro-ams, that's a lot of walking: maybe thirty or thirty-five miles a week. Then there's the practice. I average at least two hours of practice a day, and that means hitting hundreds of shots. It takes a toll on the back, shoulders, wrists, and elbows — even the knees. Then add in the racing to airports, grabbing meals on the run, finding a washer and dryer for our clothes, and the constant phone calls to check in with our families, making and changing plane and hotel reservations, dashing off for a haircut, and doing everything else that most people do from a comfortable office. And this is the Senior Tour; we're not spring chickens."[3]

"And how have you stood up to this lifestyle?" Charlie asked.

"Well, not so well. Since I went so many years without playing golf, my middle-aged body wasn't used to the rigors of long practice sessions. And because I didn't play my whole life, I felt that I had to practice more than the other guys to be competitive. As a result, I paid the price."

"And how was that?"

"I developed a chronic sore back, and my right wrist, elbow, and shoulder are always giving me problems."

"What do you do about it?"

"Fortunately, the fitness trailers at most of our tournament sights provide access to heating pads, ice packs, and even some massage therapy. I also talk to my regular doctor fairly often by phone, but can't see him unless I take time off the Tour."[4]

"Do you take any medication?"

Eddie smiled. "Mr. Mayfield, many of the guys have the same aches and pains that I do, and some are a lot worse. Everyone's gulping pain pills, muscle relaxants, sleeping pills — you name it. Some of the golf bags out there look like drug stores."

"And what do you take?"

"Mostly over-the-counter stuff like Advil and Tylenol. My doctor gave me a few prescriptions for something stronger, but I only took that when the pain was worse than usual. However," Eddie leaned forward as if talking to each juror individually, "I never abused these things. I took only what I needed to control the pain, and even then I was careful never to exceed the proper dosages. Honestly, I hate putting things like that in my body. In fact, I'm very careful about what I eat, I've never smoked, and my alcohol is limited to an occasional beer or glass of wine — and even that's rare."

"Just a few more questions, Eddie. Does the PGA Senior Tour — or the Champions Tour, as it's now called — have any rules or restrictions on the taking of medication?"

"They adopted rules against using certain drugs in 2008. Before that, there were no restrictions at all."

"Okay, Eddie, let's talk about the three articles that were written about you in *Tee Time* in 2006 — before the Tour banned performance-enhancing drugs. They were in the May, June, and July issues. Do you recall those articles? They were written by Max Reed."

Eddie Bennison sighed, his shoulders sagged, and his eyes turned downward. This was going to be painful for him. "Of course. I remember every word of them. Max Reed wrote that I was winning tournaments because I cheated, and because I took drugs that supposedly make me play better. He actually wrote that!"

Charlie continued. "Can you tell us how your life changed in the months following publication of those stories?"

Roz Berman knew what was coming, and she'd love to be able to stop the testimony that the jury was about to hear. She could raise an objection because the question called for an open-ended answer, but such an answer would be better than having Charlie break it down into thirty interminable questions and answers. More important, the jury seemed interested in what Bennison had to say, and they might resent her for trying to block it.

"I guess you could say it became a downward spiral. Just before those articles came out, I was the leading money winner on the Tour. And I had more wins and top ten finishes than any of the other players out there. But those accusations upset me so much that I had trouble focusing on my game — I just couldn't concentrate. All I could think of were those terrible things written about me in the articles, knowing that they were read by millions of golf fans, and repeated over and over in the sports pages and on the Golf Channel. From then on, I was a wreck every time I walked onto the golf course. I kept imagining what people were thinking about me. And they weren't only thinking! I heard the nasty comments from hecklers that came several times during every round. People would say things like, 'Hey, cheater, did you take your pills today?' Everyone heard them — my wife, my caddie, everyone! I had once been a hero out there, and now I was a villain. My golf game deteriorated to the point where I was not even competitive anymore.[5]

"And it really hurt to see how much this all affected my personal and social life. I had been popular with the other players, and we were always having dinner together. Our conversations at dinner, in the locker rooms, and on the course were always friendly, and covered everything — golf, politics, our families, the economy, world events, and even other sports. The guys out there are very well-read, and we're all up to date on what's going on in the world. But once Max Reed's articles came out, the invitations to dinner began to dwindle. Fewer guys came up to me to chat or ask me to play a practice round with them. At first I thought it was my imagination, but it became obvious that the guys were going out of their way to avoid me. And God knows what they were saying about me behind my back. I guess they figured that there must be some truth behind those terrible stories — otherwise how could Reed write them and how could *Tee Time* print them?

"And worse, my wife, Carol, told me that things began to change for her in the same way. She and the other wives would always spend a lot of time together when they were with us on the Tour — shopping, playing bridge, running errands, that kind of thing. But after the articles, her phone stopped ringing. She was being shunned by her friends, no question about it, and it was very hurtful to her.

"Even my caddie, Artie, would tell me things he was hearing from the other caddies, and they weren't nice things. Things like, 'Keep an eye on Bennison.' Once he was asked, 'Are you Bennison's caddie or his supplier?' He nearly got into a few fistfights because of these comments.

"There was a time when I felt like everyone out there loved me — the press, the fans, caddies, other guys on the Tour, and even their families. But since those articles came out, people cross the street when they see me coming. And it's taking its toll."

Charlie Mayfield looked to Judge Krause. "That's all I have for now, Your Honor."

The judge gave the standard admonition to the jurors about not discussing the case, and reminded them not to read, watch, or listen to anything about the trial. Then he rapped the gavel. "We'll reconvene at 9:30 tomorrow morning."

CHAPTER 10

Back in Roz Berman's office after court adjourned, she and Hugo Shoemaker were debating how to cross-examine Eddie Bennison. Shoemaker, ever the gentleman, wanted a non-confrontational cross-examination. "Eddie Bennison is a national hero," he argued. "The jury will resent us if we don't treat him with respect."

Predictably, Berman thought just the opposite. "If we treat him with respect, the jury will treat him with respect, and decide in his favor. We can't win this case unless the jury believes he's a cheater and druggie, and that's the way we have to treat him on cross-examination — like he's a cheating, drug-abusing bum. We have to show the jury who he really is: tear the son of a bitch apart, bring him to his knees. We want the jury to get the idea that Bennison is nothing more than a low-grade jock who can hit a golf ball, and to do that we have to treat him like that's what he is. How can we treat him better than we want the jury to treat him?

"Fortunately, we don't have to worry about how to cross-examine him yet. I'll tell the judge in the morning that we'll reserve cross-examination until we call Bennison as a witness when we put on our case — and there's a good chance that we won't even call him then."

———

Three blocks away, in Charlie Mayfield's conference room, the plaintiff's much smaller team was assembled. Charlie was at the head of the table, flanked by Eddie and Carol. His associate, Pete Stevens, and two young law clerks were seated toward the other end. Charlie had already slipped into the cabinet in his office for a couple of fingers of gin.

"Okay," he announced, after downing the gin in one gulp, "a few general observations, and then we can talk about tomorrow." As one, the two law clerks poised their pens over the legal yellow pads before them. "First, the media is covering this trial like a blanket." Looking around the table, he continued. "I already told you not to talk to the press under any circumstances. But what I didn't say is that these damned reporters are relentless. They'll stop at nothing to get a good quote, or even something they can misquote. And they don't wear signs on their chests that read 'PRESS.' Watch out for someone acting like he or she is another lawyer, or just a spectator, asking an innocent question or making an innocent comment. Something like, 'Is Bennison nervous?' If you don't deny it, tomorrow's headline will be 'BENNISON WORRIED HAS WEAK CASE.' And if you do deny it, the headline will read 'BENNISON'S LAWYER DENIES HE HAS WEAK CASE.' In either event, the jurors will read a headline that contains 'BENNISON' and 'WEAK CASE,' and their minds will make the connection. Don't even nod or shake your heads. Just ignore anyone you don't know, period."

Carol Bennison said, "I thought the judge told the jurors not to read anything about the case in the newspapers."

Charlie laughed. "Sure, and my dentist told me to floss after every meal."

"One other thing, and this applies to Eddie and Carol too. Trials have a lot of surprises. Maybe a witness says something outrageous, or the judge makes an important ruling. There is a strong tendency to react visibly, either with a big grin or an ugly grimace. Don't do that! It's kid stuff, and it's unprofessional. Moreover, the jury may miss some small piece of testimony that's harmful to us — but not if you groan or slap your head and make a scene."

Charlie looked around to make sure everyone got that last point. "Now, about tomorrow. I'm all done with Eddie, and I have a hunch that the defense will reserve asking any questions until they call him when they put on their own case. That way, they won't be limited to asking about the things I asked him on our direct examination." He chuckled and then added, "I can just imagine how they're arguing over there about how to handle Eddie. Hugo would probably pussyfoot if he had Hitler on the stand, and Roz Berman — hell, she'd go for Mother Teresa's throat.

"Earlier, I thought I'd follow Eddie with Artie, but I decided to go with A.J. instead." A.J. was A.J. Silver, Eddie Bennison's business manager and a boyhood friend. "If we want Eddie to get what he's entitled to, we have to let the jurors know how much he was earning and how much those bastards cost him. And I want them to have that information in their heads as they hear the rest of the case. A.J.'s the guy that can put it there." Charlie, looked toward one of his assistants and said, "Roy, I assume A.J. is prepped and ready to go." It wasn't a question.

"He's chomping at the bit," the handsome but obviously exhausted young lawyer said. "We went over his testimony again last night, until past midnight, and we've set aside another couple of hours tonight. He's damned near memorized his depositions; they'll never trip him up with inconsistent statements."

"Good, but be sure to let him get some sleep tonight. Then have him here by seven in the morning so I can have an hour or two to put the edge on."

CHAPTER 11

That damned picture of Eddie Bennison was still on Liz Peters' mind as she was finishing dinner. Then she had a thought that turned her stomach inside out. *Oh God! It couldn't be!* "Mom, just leave the dishes in the sink," she said as she hurriedly ran out of the kitchen. "I'll finish them right after I check something on my computer."

She ran up to her room and powered up her laptop, waiting anxiously for the screen to light up. As soon as the computer came to life, she clicked on the Internet browser and went straight to Google. As soon as the browser asked for an entry, Liz typed in "eddie bennison golf." She had barely finished typing the cue when the screen began flashing a seemingly endless cascade of sites with references to the face she had seen in the paper. Liz already knew that this Bennison guy was famous — that much was obvious from the story in the *Free Press* — but the guy she was asking Google about seemed to be an icon — a superhero megastar. Page after page after page lauded his miraculous accomplishments. She quickly stopped reading about his tournament scores and stats, and instead scanned for pictures. *Maybe there'll be another picture of this dude that'll ring a bell.*

It didn't take long. Not long at all. *Put on a sport jacket and a pair of glasses, and it's that same miserable son of a bitch.* It all come back with a flash of light. It was two or three years ago — Nancy's birthday, when the gang got together for dinner at Luigi's.

After dinner, they had decided to walk over to the Marriott, which was nearby and in the same mall. There was a cozy cocktail lounge at the Marriott, and they had a nice combo there most evenings. Liz was free-wheeling that night. Her singleness, plus a few Manhattans, a throaty laugh, and a great look all combined to put a virtual target right over her heart, and it seemed that every male in the place held a bow and arrow.

A few of the younger guys made clumsy passes, but she flicked them off as if they were lint on her dress. When her friend Alice raised her eyebrows after the last dustoff, Liz just shrugged and said, "Kids." She was just past thirty but looked younger, and she was turned off by the college types who always managed to descend into her airspace.

Once or twice she made eye contact with the man wearing glasses and a sport coat sitting alone at a table in the corner, and they exchanged smiles, but he didn't seem interested. He was reading a book — *reading a book in a bar!* She reckoned him to be a little older, but certainly within "range." Being in her cups, and getting that adventurous feeling that comes with a third Manhattan, she took a big breath, stood, straightened her dress, and sashayed over.

"That has to be one hell of a book."

He looked up with a start, and grinned broadly. "Not bad, but good enough to keep me from making a fool of myself."

"What's that supposed to mean?"

"It means that I'm a little old for this crowd, and I don't want you and your friends to think I'm some dirty old man on the hunt."

"Ha!" Her short laugh came from somewhere a little north of her pubis. "Then why are you here?"

"It's convenient. I'm staying in the hotel."

"I'm Liz," she announced.

He stood politely and offered her a seat. "Ben, Ben Edwards."

"Ben Edwards? I like that. Two first names."

FRIDAY MORNING

CHAPTER 12

s expected, the morning began with Charlie announcing that he had no further questions for Eddie Bennison. Hugo Shoemaker requested the right to reserve all questioning of Eddie until the defense put on its case, mainly because Shoemaker and Berman could not agree on whether the cross-examination should be aggressive or docile.

Judge Krause granted the request with no objection from Charlie.

Charlie then announced, "I'm calling A.J. Silver to the stand."

Eddie Bennison's business manager was tall, with dark brown hair, and he had an easy smile. He wore Ben Franklin glasses that he constantly readjusted as he moved his eyes from Charlie to the documents before him. Preliminary questions established that Silver and Eddie were both born and raised in Kewanee, lived on the same block, and were in the same class from first grade through high school. After graduating from Kewanee High, A.J. Silver went to Northwestern University to study accounting, and then to Northwestern's School of Law where he graduated with honors.

"Is 'A.J.' your given name?" Charlie asked.

"No, sir. My given name is Adam Jeffrey Silver, but I've been called 'A.J.' all my life, both socially and in business."

The lawyer smiled. "I can understand that. No one has called me 'Charles' since I was in grade school.

"And when did you and Eddie resume your friendship?" Charlie asked.

"Well, we never stopped being good friends, and we corresponded while he was in the Marines. I was still at Northwestern when Eddie returned from Vietnam and came back home to go to college. We stayed in touch and saw each other over the summers and other vacations times, and we visited each other a few times while he was downstate at Illinois and I was at Northwestern near Chicago. Even after he moved to Oklahoma we stayed in touch."

"Do you now have a professional relationship with Eddie Bennison?"

"Yes, sir, I guess you'd say I'm Eddie's business manager. It includes handling his investments, representing him in his dealings with sponsors, and overseeing his legal matters. My office even handles his travel arrangements and all scheduling. I try to maximize his earnings, protect his assets, and look out for his future, and leave him free to take care of his family, his health, and his golf."

Charlie nodded. "Does that mean that Eddie is incapable of doing those things for himself?"

"Not at all," came the quick, and rehearsed, reply. "Eddie is one of the more financially sophisticated athletes I know. However, his fast — and can I say meteoric? — success has presented more complex financial issues than any one person could possibly handle. I myself have a staff to assist me in these things. If he tried to do much of this himself, he wouldn't have time to play golf."[6]

"Do you do this for other athletes as well?"

"Yes, but Eddie was my first."

———

After Eddie won the Senior Qualifying School championship in 2003, he called to tell me that several sponsors had already contacted him. These sponsors were mostly manufacturers of golf balls, clubs, shoes, that kind of thing, and the deals they offered were fairly standard. He sent me copies to read, and I called the manufacturers' reps, but there wasn't much I could do. Remember, Eddie was hardly a household name at the time, and he had no negotiating power. It was either take it or leave it with those deals. Also, we're talking the Senior Tour, officially known as the Champions Tour, and not the regular PGA Tour where there's a lot more money to spread around.

At this time, I was a partner in a mid-size Chicago law firm. I was what they call a "transactional lawyer": I handled a variety of business issues for clients. I'm also a CPA, and my accounting background was very helpful for the things I did in my law practice.

But things started to change in a hurry as soon as Eddie started on the Tour. In his first couple of months he had two wins and three seconds, and he wasn't out of the top ten even once. His earnings were soaring, and after only five or six weeks he was getting serious calls from sponsors. When he first qualified for the Tour, he might get a call from some rep, but after those first several weeks he was getting calls from the rep's bosses, and sometimes even from the company presidents. And they were talking real money. Magazines were calling to put his face on the cover. At the same time, he was being solicited by sports agents from all over the country, every one of them promising the moon if he'd just sign on the dotted line.

I recall getting this frantic call from him. "A.J., I'm going nuts out here. I can't get off the phone. They're waiting for me in the hotels and coming up to me on the range. I need help. They want me to endorse clubs, balls, shoes, shirts, watches — all that kind of stuff. I need help."

I talked to my partners, and they agreed that I should spend as much time as necessary to help Eddie. Whatever I charged him — and that in itself was a complicated arrangement that we're still always changing — would go to the firm. We all agreed — Eddie, the firm, and I — that we'd try this for a few months and then take a look at things and figure out what to do next.

Eddie kept winning, and soon I realized I needed more help just to help him, and it wasn't the kind of help that my law firm could provide. I needed people versed in what I call "sports law" — people with experience negotiating endorsement contracts, exhibition fees, professional sports pension plans, and so on. I even needed help on the income tax laws in the various states, since local winnings are taxed by the state where the tournament is held. That meant preparing about thirty state income tax returns every year. In any event, within the year I made the decision to leave the firm and hire a few people who could help me. My plan — and Eddie consented to this — was that I would then try to recruit other athletes as well.

Eddie said nice things about me to the other guys on the Senior Tour, and pretty soon I started getting calls from some of them. Then I'd get calls from guys on the regular Tour, and before long I was picking up athletes in other sports: football, basketball, baseball, and tennis. Today we have clients in about every sport, even NASCAR drivers. In short, Eddie put me in this business, and with his success it was easy for me to succeed. But even if I had no other clients, representing Eddie has been very good for me.

I mentioned how well he did during his first two months on tour. Let me break it down. His first two wins during that time gave him about $450,000; his three seconds produced close to $400,000; and the other three events brought in another $250,000. That came to over a million dollars in just two months. But that was just a small part of it. Eddie was getting calls every day from people who sold golf clubs, balls, bags, gloves, and shoes, all offering him money to use and endorse their products. Those offers alone eventually guaranteed Eddie close to another three million dollars during his first year on tour. Add to that the offers to endorse clothes, cars, hotels, and even wrist watches, and Eddie could count on nearly five million dollars during his first year even if he didn't win another dime from golf tournaments. But he did keep winning money. In fact, he won six tournaments in 2004, and with those added winnings came even better endorsement offers for the following year.

It was incredible! Money was being offered from places he never dreamed of. Corporations were offering $75,000 to $100,000 if he'd just come and hit some balls and play golf with their executives and major customers. He was even being offered money to help design golf courses.

Eddie was the perfect person for all of this. First, he had a golf game that wouldn't stop. Most professional golfers start to lose their games a little bit at a time after reaching fifty, but Eddie's was getting stronger. He was a late starter, and he was still improving while his contemporaries were starting to fade. Second, Eddie's physical appearance is just right; he's handsome in a dignified way, he radiates health and energy, and he has a smile that's, well, contagious. Put his face on a product, or clothes on his back, and they sell. And if that's not enough, he's a heck of a nice guy. Until all this happened with the magazine articles, everyone on the Tour was his good friend and they all spoke highly of him. His character and his reputation were flawless.

CHAPTER 13

Francine Curry was on the phone when Liz Peters came into her office. With her index finger, she pointed to a chair and then held up the finger to indicate that she'd be done with the call in a minute. While finishing up the conversation, she couldn't help but notice that Liz was fidgety, wringing her hands and looking at her watch. "What's up?" Francine asked as soon as she put the phone down. "You look like you have ants in your pants. What's the problem?"

"Not a problem, but a real shocker." Liz pulled out the article from yesterday's paper and slid it across the desk. "Remember, yesterday I said that guy looked familiar?" She pointed to the small picture of Edie Bennison that accompanied the article.

Francine looked at the photo, which was upside-down to her yesterday, and then leaned back in her chair and laughed. "Where have you been, girl? This is one of the best-known guys in the country. Christ, Dan is glued to the TV whenever Eddie Bennison is playing. And you can't go a day without seeing his face in an ad or on a commercial. Even one of our clients uses him."

"Hey, take it easy. What do I know about golfers? I don't pay attention to sports, not even football or baseball. And I don't remember ever seeing him in a commercial." Liz paused, and then looked her friend in the eye and smirked. "Anyway, the asshole told me his name was Ben Edwards."

CHAPTER 14

After a short recess, Charlie rose to face A.J. Silver who was already back on the witness stand. "Before the break, Mr. Silver, you were telling us about Eddie Bennison's extraordinary start on the professional tour. Did his winning continue?"

"Yes, Mr. Mayfield, it sure did. As I mentioned, Eddie had six outright wins in 2004 and ended the year leading the Senior Tour money list — that is, the total winnings for the year. It came to nearly four million dollars, which broke the previous record by nearly a million dollars.[7]

"The player who came in second had less than half of that. Eddie did even better in 2005; he had seven wins that year. His endorsement opportunities almost got out of control. We had to turn down at least twenty or thirty for each one we accepted."

"And why is that?"

"If an athlete or other celebrity endorses too many products, or endorses the wrong ones, it dilutes the value. Coca Cola, for example, wouldn't pay Eddie as much for his endorsement if his face were plastered all over the place endorsing toothpaste, hotels, rental cars, underwear, vitamins, and orange juice. Also, endorsements take time; there are contract negotiations, photo sessions, and demands to play golf with the company executives, and Eddie had to be careful to budget his time. He couldn't just be available on a moment's notice whenever a sponsor wanted him to drop everything and show up for a photo shoot or to entertain customers."

Following their script, the lawyer asked the next question. "I take it that time is a precious commodity for a Tour golfer."

"Absolutely. A highly competitive golf game requires that all the edges be kept sharp. That requires constant practice, and practice requires time — lots of it. There also has to be time for family and relaxation. Finally, since the Tour moves from city to city each week for ten months a year, at least one day each week has to be set aside for travel." Here the witness looked directly at the jury and said, "Travel is, by far, the biggest headache of the Tour golfer. He tries to make his reservations in advance, but he doesn't know what time he plays on Sunday until after the Saturday round is done. If he plays well through Saturday, then he tees off late on Sunday and can't get on a plane until Sunday night. Otherwise he can get an afternoon flight to the next tournament or exhibition site. But he never knows until Saturday night, and that makes it tough."

"How does Eddie Bennison deal with that problem?" Charlie asked.

"Well, he eventually signed up for a fractional interest in a private jet. First, it enables him to get from tournament to tournament without the hassles of changing flights, schedule changes, and waiting in airports. Second, it makes it easier to fly home to see Carol and the kids between tournaments. Third, it makes it possible to attend exhibitions and corporate outings which are usually held on Mondays. Let's say he finishes a tournament in Ohio on Sunday afternoon, and he's been invited to a corporate sales meeting and exhibition in Pennsylvania the following day that might pay him $100,000 — a fee he often gets because of his record and reputation. With access to a private jet, he can shoot over to Pennsylvania that night, and then fly home Monday night to spend some time with his family, get some rest, and still get to the next tournament site in, say, Illinois, in time for a practice round or two and the standard pro-am event held the day before the tournament begins. An added benefit is that by getting home often, he can pick up clean clothes, get caught up on mail, get a haircut, and in general do all the things to keep some normalcy in a hectic life."

Charlie Mayfield walked over to stand in front of the jury so that the witness would be looking toward the jurors when he answered the next question. "Mr. Silver, isn't it terribly expensive to buy an interest in a private jet?"

"Well, it is, but it more than pays for itself."

"How's that?"

"It would be impossible for Eddie to get to more than a couple of those corporate events and all of those photo sessions and other meetings if he had to rely on commercial flights. The money he earns by this travel flexibility more than covers the expense of the plane." By prearrangement with Charlie, Silver left it at that. They decided it might alienate, or at least confuse, the jury by getting into the tax breaks through depreciation, the strong likelihood of being able to sell his interest down the line for a profit, and the other benefits.[8]

Mayfield now shifted so that he stood behind the podium to review some notes. "Do I understand from your testimony a while ago that Eddie's winnings during those first two years — 2004 and 2005 — came to about eight million dollars?"

"Approximately."

"And what about his earnings from endorsements and corporate outings during those two years?"

"The answer to that requires a little explanation. His outside deals during those two years were very lucrative, but a good part of that income was deferred. In other words, if a company offered him a lump sum of $500,000 to wear their shirts or endorse their brokerage business, we might counter by asking for $700,000, but have it spread out over three or four years. In fact, I made some ten- and even fifteen-year deals for him. The sponsors actually prefer spreading out their payments over a few years. But the real advantage to us is that we can keep Eddie's current taxes down and assure him of income in later years. Remember, he's already pushing sixty, and he can't continue to play at this level forever."

"Any other sources of income during those two years?"

"Yes, sir. All earnings beyond what he needed for bare living expenses were invested. Eddie's investment yield, including income and growth, during those two years alone came to nearly two million dollars."

"So, can you give us a figure that fairly represents Eddie Bennison's total income from all sources during 2004 and 2005, and I'm only asking about income attributable to his golf career. I'm not interested in any amounts he may have earned from National Container or prior investments."

"Sure. His earnings from golf during each of those two years, adding up the endorsement deals, his Tour winnings, the corporate outings, and fees for consulting on golf course designs, was between $12 million and $15 million. That includes the investment income earned on those amounts."

There were audible murmurs from the back of the courtroom, and the reporters' ballpoint pens began to race across their notebooks. Charlie Mayfield paused to let the information get properly absorbed before going on.

"How about the next year, Mr. Silver — 2006? Did that level of earnings continue?"

"No, sir."

"And why not?"

"Well, 2006 started strong. In the first five tournaments, Eddie had a win, a second place, and two or three top tens. His game was solid and his scores were consistent, even a little better than the previous two years. But that's when those terrible, vicious lies started circula — "

"Objection!" The word was out of Roz Berman's mouth before she even started to stand. "This witness has no right to — "

"Sustained," Judge Krause ruled before Berman could articulate her reason for objecting. "Mr. Silver, those people sitting over there are the jurors, and they will be the ones to decide if Mr. Bennison has been the victim of lies or distortions of the truth. We only want you to tell us what you know and not what you heard, without characterization." The judge then turned to face the jury. "Ladies and gentlemen, the witness's remarks have been stricken from the record. You are to disregard his characterization of the magazine articles in question."

Turning back to face Charlie, the judge said, "You may proceed, Mr. Mayfield."

"Mr. Silver, tell us about Eddie Bennison's golf winnings in 2006."

"The year started off well, but in April things began to fall off. Just a little at first, but then his play became very ragged. Each week he seemed to slip further and further — it was like watching a train wreck in slow motion." A.J. Silver paused to take a sip from the water glass beside the witness stand, and then continued. "The first of those articles came out in the May 2006 issue of *Tee Time*, and that issue hit the street in mid-April. And by then there were already rumors circulating about the articles, and Eddie was hearing them. That's when his game began to fall apart."

"For the record, Mr. Silver, were you traveling with Eddie during this time, and did you witness the slip in his performance with your own eyes?"

"At the beginning of 2006, I spent a week or so out at the Senior Tour where I had several clients, and I spent some time with Eddie during that time. From there I stopped by the regular PGA Tour site to visit with some other clients of mine. Then I had to get back to my office. A week or two later I got a call from Carol, Eddie's wife."

"And what was the nature of her call?"

"Well, I already knew that Eddie had a couple of bad weeks in April, and the rumors started by those articles kept getting stronger and stronger. It was the talk of the golf world — in fact, it was the biggest story in all of sports. It was on everyone's lips, and reported in the papers and all over radio and TV. Carol told me that Eddie had been hearing all these things, and it was really getting to him. These stories were not only on the sports news, but also on NBC, CBS, ABC, CNN, and all the rest. It was coming from all over — from hecklers in the galleries to stories on the Golf Channel. And the other players were treating him much cooler than they had in the past. He told me that he wasn't sleeping well, and he knew, as we all did, that everyone was talking about him behind his back. It kept getting worse and worse. He had been a popular guy surrounded by friends, and now he was often alone. He even dropped out of one or two tournaments, and withdrew from a few others before they started. Carol was very worried about him. I dropped everything and flew out to see him."

"Okay, but for now just tell us what happened to his earnings for the balance of 2006, and since."

A.J. Silver referred to some notes he had made, copies of which had already been given to the defense team. "Let's see. Eddie won $356,000 by the first week of April, 2006. During the next two weeks, after the articles came out, his winnings came to only $31,000. During the rest of the year he won a grand total of less than $70,000. During 2007, the next year, his total winnings were barely $83,000. That put him 98th in Tour winnings." A.J. looked at the defense table with ice in his eyes and added, "A far cry from being No. 1 for his first two years."

"One more question, Mr. Silver. Even though Eddie's winnings dropped through the floor during 2006 and 2007, did his other income from endorsements and exhibitions continue at the previous level?"

"Unfortunately, no. Most endorsement contracts are for only one or two years, even if we spread the revenue over several years. Also, most of these deals have a 'morals clause' — God, how I hate that term — that gives the sponsor a right to terminate the contract if the athlete does anything that tarnishes his or the sponsor's reputation. And even if the athlete doesn't do anything wrong, a bare accusation that affects his reputation might be enough for a sponsor to cancel the deal, depending on how the contract is drawn."

"And, after the *Tee Time* story, did any sponsors terminate his contracts because of the morals clause?"

"A few did, but almost all of them waited until the expiration date and then wouldn't renew. And we certainly didn't pick up any new sponsors during that time or since. A few came around to talk, but they were talking so little money that we said no; it would've destroyed Eddie's endorsement value for the future."

"Did any of his major sponsors stay with him?"

"Only Universal Brands, and the only way they would renew is if Eddie would give them an exclusive. So, by renewing with them, he had to give up signing with others.

"Anyway, by the end of 2006 Eddie's endorsements and other outside deals dropped by about 40 percent, and by the end of 2007 his outside income was about 10 percent of where it was at the end of 2004."

All of Eddie Bennison's earnings records from 2004 through 2007 were introduced into evidence without objection. With that, Charlie Mayfield noted that it was just past noon, and that it would be a good place to break for lunch. "I'm nearly done with this witness, Your Honor. I'll have only a few questions when we get back this afternoon. Then the defense can have him for cross-examination."

"Okay, we'll get started at 2:00 p.m." With that, the judge rapped his gavel and disappeared through the door behind his bench.

FRIDAY AFTERNOON

CHAPTER 15

L iz Peters and Francine Curry met for an early lunch in the Franklin Advertising cafeteria downstairs. "Liz, are you absolutely sure?" Francine asked incredulously. "You googled Eddie Bennison, and he looks like a guy you met in a bar? That's not much to go on."

"Right, but — "

Francine was shaking her head. "No, I want to get this straight. Let's start from the beginning."

"Okay. It was almost three years ago. The night I met him, a bunch of us were at a party for Nancy Gold. It was her birthday — August 17, 2007. We were at Luigi's, which is about ten or fifteen miles east of the city. It's in one of those office centers, and there are a couple of hotels out there. We went over to the Marriott after dinner for a few drinks, and they had a pretty good combo there. Anyway, I'm having a good time, and I probably had more to drink then I should. By the way, I was looking pretty hot that night. A few young guys tried to move in, but I shooed 'em away. Then I spot this cool one off at a corner table, reading a book and nursing a beer. We smile at each other once or twice. After a while, when I'm sure he's alone, I make like I'm heading for the john and swing by his table. I say something about the book. He looks up and then — get this! — he stands like I'm some kind of queen. And he offers me a seat. I sit down, give him my name, and that's when he tells me his name is Ben Edwards."

"So how does Ben Edwards become Eddie Bennison? Why do you think they're the same guy?"

"I didn't, not until last night. Some of the pictures on Google looked a lot like him — more so than the one in the *Free Press* yesterday. And some of the things in his bio checked with things he told me about himself. Like, he told me that he lived in Tulsa and sold cardboard boxes. Well, this Bennison guy lives in Tulsa, and he used to sell boxes for National Container. And then, sitting there at the computer and reading about him, it hits me. Edward Bennison, Ben Edwards. Get it? Very convenient. He reversed his friggin' names so I wouldn't know who he really was."

"Whoa, girl! What you have is a partial look-alike, and a cute twist of names. It's a long stretch from there to being able to ID a guy who probably hasn't ever been in Detroit."

"Fair enough," Liz said with a mischievous grin. "But I did my homework last night. Let's try this on for size. Number one," she began, holding up one finger, "this was in 2007 and Nancy's birthday party was on Friday, August 17. No doubt about *that*. Number two, Luigi's is out by Oakland Hills golf course. And number three — "

Francine saw what was coming.

" — that very week there was a golf tournament at Oakland Hills, and would you care to take a guess who played in it?"

CHAPTER 16

After the lunch break, A.J. Silver resumed the stand and was reminded that he was still under oath. He looked to Charlie for a question.

"Mr. Silver, how long have you known Eddie Bennison?"

"As I said this morning, ever since we were kids. Nearly fifty years."

"And you were close throughout that entire time."

"We sure were. Best friends."

"Did you hang out with the same crowd? Go to the same parties?"

"Yes, sir."

"Tell us, Mr. Silver, was Eddie much of a drinker? Or did he smoke marijuana, or take any other illegal substances?"

Silver smiled broadly and shook his head. "I hope Eddie won't mind my saying this, but he's really square, and always was. He never smoked at all, and he was always the designated driver after we were old enough to drive. As for smoking pot, or using any drugs at all, no way. He's just never been that way. Heck, Mr. Mayfield, if you showed me a picture of Eddie Bennison under the influence of alcohol or drugs, I'd know it would be a fake. He doesn't touch that stuff — not even a cigarette. Oh, maybe an occasional beer, or maybe a glass of wine, but that's it."

Charlie stood up to announce that he had no further questions of A.J. Silver.

"Mr. Shoemaker?"

Hugo Shoemaker stood and made the statement that the entire defense team had agreed upon during the lunch break. "Your Honor, with the Court's permission, the defense would like to reserve cross-examination of Mr. Silver until we put on our case."

"Is that acceptable to you, Mr. Mayfield?"

"It is."

"Then call your next witness."

CHAPTER 17

Everything up to this point was fairly routine. Now it was showtime! Charlie stood and announced, "The plaintiff calls Max Reed as an adverse witness."

Max Reed was the author of the articles that led to the filing of this lawsuit, and it was Reed who had been in the crosshairs of Charlie's rifle since the day he was retained by Eddie Bennison.

By designating Reed as an "adverse witness," Charlie was saying that he expected the witness to be hostile, so his questioning of the witness could be as if it were cross-examination. Thus, Charlie could challenge Reed's answers, badger him, and do whatever he could to make Reed look like a liar — not only as a witness, but as the shameless author of scurrilous, defamatory stories about his client, Eddie Bennison.

A short, overweight man entered the room. He looked to be in his mid-forties. He proceeded down the center aisle of the courtroom, through the gate behind the counsel tables, and to the witness stand, where he stood and took the oath. Those near him might be able to see the beads of sweat forming on his balding skull that he tried unsuccessfully to hide with an ineffective comb-over. As soon as the witness was seated, Charlie, still at the table, posed a few innocuous questions to establish for the record the witness's name, address, educational background, and current occupation.

The silver-haired lawyer then stood and posed questions more relevant to the case. "Mr. Reed, how long have you worked for Tee Time, Incorporated?"

"Seventeen years."

"As a reporter?"

"Yes, but I prefer the word 'writer' since I do more than report."

"Since you've been there for fifteen years, Mr. Reed, would it be fair to say that you are one of the senior reporters — or writers — at your magazine?"

"Yes."

"In terms of circulation, where does *Tee Time* rank in comparison with other golf magazines?"

"We're the largest. Our circulation is well over one million monthly. Nearly a million and a half."

Charlie asked the next question very slowly, as if expecting, and maybe even inviting, an objection. "And would you say that *Tee Time* enjoys a good reputation, and has a great deal of credibility among your readers?"

The question could have brought an objection, as it called for speculation, but Berman and Shoemaker decided to let it go. Roz Berman, however, saw the danger that the answer might bring.

"Yes, it is highly regarded, not only by our readers but by the entire sports world as well."

Roz Berman winced. *I told the bastard to answer "yes," "no," or "I don't know" whenever he could, and never to dress up his answers or volunteer information. But that's just what he did, and now Charlie will milk it for all it's worth.*

Actually, Charlie got a couple of extra bases out of the answer. A simple "Yes" would have sufficed, but Reed's amplification meant that the damaging statements had even more resonance, coming from a magazine that was "highly regarded by its readers and the entire sports world as well." Charlie, inwardly smiling, knew that Reed obviously had forgotten Roz Berman's admonition just to answer the questions and not volunteer additional information. It was a standard warning given by every lawyer to every witness, but was often forgotten under the pressure of the witness stand — a pressure that loosens tongues.

"I take it then, Mr. Reed, that your written words in *Tee Time* about

Mr. Bennison were taken very seriously throughout the world of sports. Is that right?"

The witness, seeing the path down which he had been led, had no retreat. "I guess you could say that."

Charlie now asked the judge if he could have the lights turned down in the courtroom. Judge Krause nodded, and the bailiff flipped a few switches. On cue, one of Charlie's associates switched on a projector that showed an enlarged page on a huge screen on the wall facing the jury. The image was about eight feet wide by eleven feet tall and, as indicted by the print at the top, was a giant copy of a page from *Tee Time*.

Giving everyone in the courtroom a chance to get their eyes acclimated, and to see what was before them, Charlie resumed the questioning.

"Mr. Reed, I assume you recognize the words on that screen as words that you wrote in the May 2006 issue of *Tee Time*."

"I do."

"So those are the words you wrote. Please read them aloud to the jury."

Max Reed read:

> *We've all read about the great athletes who have reached stardom by running faster, jumping higher, cycling faster, and hitting more home runs, only to be discovered later to have used steroids or other chemicals. As a result, they have lost their titles, records, and reputations. And deservedly so! Athletes compete with their bodies — not with their pharmacists. The youth of our country emulate their sports heroes, and we can't have these role models encouraging our kids, by example, to shoot up, snort up, or swallow up.*
>
> *Unfortunately, not all of our sports are regulated. Professional golfers, for example, have no restrictions or regulations at this time on what they can inject, ingest, or inhale. But when the first story breaks about a golf star who helped his game with chemicals — chemicals that are prohibited in professional baseball, track, or cycling — you can bet that the golfing gods will come up with the regulations that are sorely needed. Indeed, that first story is now upon us.*
>
> *Eddie Bennison, the Senior Tour phenom since he joined the Tour, has it all: good looks, big purses and endorsements, and an all-American family. He not only has a bag full of shots, he seems to have a medicine cabinet full of*

pick-me-ups and bulk-me-ups. While we can't say for sure what he's taking, he's taking a lot of it based on the comments of his fellow competitors and locker room observers. Granted, the PGA has not yet adopted rules restricting the taking of performance-enhancing chemicals, but such rules should not be necessary for a professional golfer. This is a gentlemen's game governed by an honor system. Golfers don't need referees or umpires; they call penalties on themselves, and when faced with adverse rulings they don't throw clubs or punches. And they should not sneak drugs to give them an advantage.

It's a shame that the sport of golf may now find itself in the company of baseball, cycling, and track, where higher authorities must establish rules that shouldn't be necessary to establish for players who should rely on skills — not pills!

When Max Reed finished reading, he looked over to Charlie Mayfield who was glaring at him. "Mr. Reed, that's quite a damning story, wouldn't you say?"

"I just report facts, Mr. Mayfield. It's up to others to decide whether those facts are damning."

"I see. Now, Mr. Reed, your story says that you can't say exactly what medications or pills that Eddie took. Is that right?"

"Yes, sir."

"Is that because you don't know, or because you know but don't want to say?"

"Well, I know generally what kinds of drugs he's taking."

"And you imply that those chemicals gave him an unfair advantage over his fellow competitors? Correct?"

It would be hard for Reed to deny that that was the gist of his story, but he tried to leave a little wiggle room in his answer. "Well, I'd prefer to say that it gave him an advantage and let the readers decide if it's unfair."

"But" — and here Charlie leaned forward and thrust his jaw out — "how could your readers make that judgment if you don't report the specific drugs you accuse Eddie Bennison of taking?"

Silence from the witness.

"Let me ask it another way, Mr. Reed. What if those drugs were nothing more than aspirin, Advil or Aleve, would that be wrong? Would taking those pills, and nothing more, have given Eddie Bennison an unfair advantage?"

"No, of course not."

"So, I take it, you have information that Eddie took other drugs — something more insidious?"

"I do. My information is that he has used such drugs as anabolic steroids, testosterone, and erythropoietin, which is commonly called EPO."

"Mr. Reed, is this information of yours based on your own observations, where you actually saw Mr. Bennison ingest these drugs, or is it based on what others might have told you?"

"It's based on what others told me."

Now Charlie spread his arms and asked in a louder voice, "And would you be kind enough to identify the people who told you that?"

Charlie had asked Reed the same question in pretrial depositions, and Reed answered it the same way now as he had then. "I'm sorry, Mr. Mayfield, but I refuse to disclose my sources."

Charlie, expecting that answer, nodded, but glanced toward the jury, smiling as if to imply that he, like they, recognized deception when they saw it. "That's fine, Mr. Reed. We'll come back to your sources in a few minutes." When Charlie uttered the word "sources," he did so in a sarcastic tone, and his expression was that of a man who had just bit into a bad clam.

"Those medications you mentioned. Are those what we would call 'performance-enhancing' drugs?"

"Well, I'm not a doctor, but that's my impression from everything I've read on the subject. These are the drugs most commonly associated with improperly enhancing athletic performance."

"Did you consult with any doctors or pharmacologists before writing your article?"

"No, but I've read about these drugs. Most everyone involved in the sports world knows about them."

"Mr. Reed, your article mentions the PGA. Just to be sure that everyone understands, that refers to the Professional Golfers Association, isn't that correct?"

"Yes, that's correct."

"And the PGA is the organization that has final authority over the various professional golf tours, including the Senior — or Champions — Tour. Is that right?"

"Yes, sir."

"Do you know if those medications — or "drugs," as you call them — have been banned by the PGA, or by any of the men's tours?"

"Yes, the PGA has banned most of those drugs for both the Senior and regular tours, and also for the minor tours."

"But in your article — the one you were just reading from — you wrote that the drugs were not banned."

"The article was written in 2006, but the PGA didn't begin to ban dugs until 2008."

Charlie didn't want the jury to miss the significance of his next question, so he asked it very slowly and in a louder tone. "So Eddie Bennison — assuming that he took the drugs you mentioned — was not violating any written rules of the PGA at the time you wrote those stories. There wasn't even one rule banning the use of those drugs. Isn't that right?"

"That's right, at that time there were no such rules."

To ensure that the jury did not miss the significance of his last answer, Charlie said, as if to confirm the answer, "So at the time you accused him of improperly taking drugs, there was no rule against taking such drugs. Correct?"

Reed answered meekly, "That's right."

Then Charlie turned back to the witness and asked, "Mr. Reed, let us assume that I wanted to compete on the Senior Tour. Now, I have bad feet and I have to wear orthotic inserts in my shoes. Would you say that wearing them would be 'performance-enhancing?'"

Max Reed smiled, shaking his head. "Yes, Mr. Mayfield, I'd agree that the shoe insert, in your case, would be performance-enhancing. But that would be permissible or legitimate, just as wearing a knee brace would be permissible."

"All right, then let's assume that I have arthritis, and my doctor tells me to wear a copper bracelet. Would that also be permissible?"

"I'd say so, yes."

"What if he also prescribed medications that reduced my pain and kept the swelling down? Would that be permissible?"

"If that's all they did, then yes, it would be okay. But if the purpose of the drugs was to make you stronger, or make you swing faster, then it might be a different story."

"Aha, Mr. Reed, maybe now we're getting somewhere. You say that taking something that would make me stronger and swing faster would be wrong. Is that your testimony, and isn't that what you were implying in your article?"

"Well, yes, I think that's what I'm trying to convey."

"Alright then, let's assume that I hired a personal trainer who prescribed a regimen for me to do stretching and lift weights. The purpose would be to make me stronger and enable me to swing faster. Would I be breaking your code of conduct by doing that?"

"No, certainly not.

"So it's okay to get stronger by exercise, but not by pills. Is that your testimony?"

Max Reed was being painted into a corner. "Yes, I guess that would sum it up."

"How about food? Is it okay to eat healthy food to stay strong?"

Roz Berman was on her feet. "Your Honor, I want to raise an objection to continuing this line of questioning. Pretty soon Mr. Mayfield will be asking the witness about the propriety of doing yoga or using mouthwash."

Before Judge Krause, could reply, Charlie made the point he was dying to make for the past fifteen minutes. "That's precisely my point," he said, now turning halfway toward the jury, "We all put a lot of different things in our bodies and do things with our bodies, and unless the PGA has specific rules on the subject, it's hardly in Max Reed's domain to decide what passes his own self-invented test and what doesn't. And at the time that Mr. Reed wrote those articles, the PGA hadn't seen fit to ban any medications. But now that I made that point, I'll be happy to leave the area of illegitimate performance enhancement."

"Thank you, Mr. Mayfield," Judge Krause said with a sigh. "Ms.

Berman's objection is overruled. Please proceed to another line of questioning."

"Mr. Reed, a few years ago there was an issue involving one of the PGA men's tours. It seems there was a golfer named Casey Martin who was competing on one of the minor professional golf tours. Mr. Martin had a congenital problem with his legs — he could not walk without excruciating pain, but he was a wonderful golfer as long as he was able to ride in a golf cart between shots. Do you remember that?"

"'I do, yes."

"And didn't you yourself write several stories about this?"

"Yes, I did."

"Isn't it a fact, Mr. Reed, that the PGA had a rule prohibiting a tour golfer from riding in a cart? It was right there in their written book of rules. And didn't they enforce that rule and declare that Casey Martin should not be able to ride in a cart, that it would give him an unfair advantage over other players who had to walk? Especially in very hot weather or on hilly courses? And didn't that ruling make it virtually impossible for Casey Martin to compete as a tournament golfer?"

"Yes, that's right."

"Now, Mr. Reed, didn't you write several stories condemning the PGA for enforcing that rule against Mr. Martin? Didn't you, in fact, write to defend Casey Martin's right to ride in a cart, even though it was against the rules?"

"Yes, I did."

"Well, I'm confused, Mr. Reed. In the Casey Martin case, you wrote that the PGA was too strict — you wanted the PGA to waive a rule that was right there in the books. But in Eddie Bennison's case, you want him punished for violating a rule that wasn't there.

"More succinctly, Mr. Reed, in the Casey Martin case you wanted the PGA to overlook an existing written rule prohibiting carts, but in Mr. Bennison's case, you wanted them to enforce a nonexistent rule prohibiting certain drugs. How can you square this conflict, sir? How can you want to enforce rules that aren't there, and overlook rules that are there? It makes no sense at all."

The witness spent the next thirty seconds trying to formulate an answer, but couldn't dig himself out of the hole into which Charlie had dropped him.

CHAPTER 18

hile Max Reed was still reeling on the witness stand, Charlie once again gave the signal for the lights to go down. Another giant page from *Tee Time* appeared on the wall.

"Mr. Reed, I show you parts of another article bearing your byline. This is from the June 2006 issue of *Tee Time*. Do you recognize it as yours?"

"I do."

"Please read it aloud for the jury."

"His fans claim that Eddie Bennison is a magician with his golf clubs. But, according to many golf watchers, there are few magicians who can compete with Bennison when it comes to coin tricks."

"Please continue," Charlie Mayfield prompted.

"His deft placement of a coin directly behind his ball when marking it on the green, and the ensuing replacement of his ball slightly in front of that coin when preparing to putt, leads one to speculate on the mathematics. If he snudges a mere half inch on a putt, it may be insignificant. But if he does it on every putt in a given round, it may amount, in total, to a foot or two. That could be several feet over an entire tournament, and maybe a couple of hundred feet over a season! What's it worth to a touring pro to eliminate more than a

hundred feet of putts in the course of a season? Millions, it would seem, based on Eddie Bennison's earnings."

"Thank you. Now please tell us, Mr. Reed, what the word 'snudge' means."

"Well, it's kind of a play on words — somewhere between 'sneak' and 'nudge.'"

"And it implies, does it not, something improper?"

"As I said before, Mr. Mayfield, I just write the words and let the readers make their own inferences."

"Now wait a minute, Mr. Reed! Are you telling this jury and this court that you were not writing those words to convey to your readers that Eddie Bennison is a cheater? And didn't you write those words about Eddie taking pills to convey that he is a cheating in another way?" Then louder: "Isn't that exactly what you wanted your readers to believe — that Eddie Bennison cheats and takes improper drugs, that he violates both written and moral rules, and that is how he won? And remember when you answer, you're under oath."

After a pause, during which the witness was praying for an objection from the defense, he replied. "Yes, I knew that many readers would come to that conclusion after reading those particular passages."

"Of course you did." And then, more seriously, Charlie asked, "And at the time you wrote those words, Mr. Reed, had you, with your own eyes, ever seen Eddie Bennison improperly mark and replace his golf ball?"

This was a question the defense had long anticipated, and which was the subject of more than one heated session with the witness. If Reed said he had not ever seen Bennison mismark his ball, his article would necessarily be based on hearsay and, more important, be seen as sloppy at best and reckless or irresponsible at worst. On the other hand, a yes answer would be followed up with a demand for the time and place. This presented a tough problem for the defense. They learned when they first questioned him that he had seen Bennison play only two or three rounds in person, and all the other times he saw him were on national television. If Reed saw him mismark his ball, wouldn't it also have been seen by all the other spectators, and possibly by the millions who watched the tournaments on television? If so, where are they? If not, could it be Reed's imagination? Of course, his lawyers could not tell him how to answer the question, but their explanation of the dilemma provided a virtual roadmap for how he should answer.

"No, not with my own eyes. But others who saw him mismark his ball told me that he did so. I heard it from more than one person whom I considered reliable, and that constituted sufficient corroboration to allow us to go with the story."

"And the same is true for your reporting that he took performance-enhancing drugs? That you based your story entirely on what other people told you?"

"Yes, sir. That's right."

"And I'll ask you what I asked earlier about your story on drugs. Would you care to tell us who those people are?"

"I'm sorry, I regard them as confidential sources and I refuse to identify them."

There is conflict among the courts as to whether a reporter can be compelled to reveal his sources. Illinois is one of the jurisdictions that protects the identity of the sources, so the reporter would be safe if he refused to reveal their identity. Accordingly, in his pretrial orders, Judge Krause had ruled that the lawyers could ask, but none of the defendants could be forced to divulge the names of those who gave information to the reporters. The rule was designed to protect the so-called freedom of the press and the public's "right to know." While this rule finds favor among those who prefer a broad application of the constitutional guarantee of a free press, it can be misused by a muckraking reporter who writes a reputation-damaging story and then hides behind the right not to name his sources — who may not even exist. And while the rule can seem unfair to a plaintiff like Eddie Bennison, there is the consolation that a jury, hearing a reporter refuse to identify his sources, may assume that there *are no sources*. Thus, the rule may actually work in the plaintiff's favor.

Charlie could have filed the case in another jurisdiction, where reporters were required to name their sources, but he decided against it. If Reed did in fact have sources and was compelled to disclose them, Charlie could have bigger problems.

Actually, Charlie had done his own investigation into the ball-marking and other questions about Bennison's integrity and was fairly certain that before Reed's articles it had not been an issue with anyone. He had assumed that Reed heard an off-hand comment somewhere — perhaps one instance where someone thought the ball wasn't put back precisely where it should be — and an innocent comment about the incident had been blown totally out of proportion by Reed and his bosses in order to sell more magazines.

"We'll come back to your so-called sources later," Charlie sneered, sarcasm dripping from his voice.

"Now let's shift our attention to another area. When you write an article for *Tee Time*, Mr. Reed — not necessarily the articles we're talking about here, but any article — is it customary for it to be reviewed or approved by anyone?"

"Well, we have an editorial review committee that screens everything. They go over the articles with a fine-toothed comb before releasing them for publication."

"But isn't that mainly to correct grammar and punctuation?"

"That too, but more than that. They ask questions about accuracy, substantiation, sources — that sort of thing."

"Are you saying that you submit proposed articles to a higher authority in certain cases? Not for grammar or punctuation, but to get approval for assertions or statements that might be controversial or damaging to someone's reputation?"

"On occasion."

"And did you do that with the articles about Eddie Bennison?"

"Yes, sir."

"And that was because you knew that the things you were writing about Eddie were very sensitive, and that they could be very hurtful to him. Correct?"

Reed was in a box. If he answered that the articles were not sensitive and possibly hurtful, he would appear callous. But if he answered that he knew they *were* sensitive and hurtful, and wrote them anyway, he would still be seen as callous. He took his time answering, trying to remember how he was told to handle it during the prep sessions with his own lawyers. "Yes, I knew that the articles would be, well, controversial. On the other hand, we can't not write an article just because it might offend someone, especially on a subject that has this much public interest. Let's face it, Eddie Bennison is one of the best-known athletes in the world, and when there are allegations that he did something wrong, especially like breaking the rules, he's got to expect that it would find its way into print." Regaining some confidence, the witness then volunteered: "In fact, we'd be remiss to our readers if we didn't write about it."

"Oh, I see," Charlie said in mock seriousness, "you wrote these things about Eddie as a public service. How patriotic of you."

Hugo Shoemaker was out of his chair, but the judge beat him to the punch with a rap of the gavel. "Mr. Mayfield," Krause sighed, "you know better. The gratuitous statement of counsel will be stricken from the record, and the jury is instructed to disregard it. Please continue, Mr. Mayfield, and try to be careful."

"My apologies, Your Honor." Inwardly, Charlie smiled. This was his first telegram to the jury that Max Reed, and by extension the entire media, had a sanctimonious and overly self-righteous view of their mission in life. There would be more telegrams later, and with each, Charlie would be building on the idea that free press should not be a shield for careless reporting that hurts people. And all it cost was a slight reprimand from the judge and an apology.

"Mr. Reed," Charlie continued, "since your article was, in fact, published, may I assume that your higher-ups approved of what you wrote?"

"Yes, they did."

The answer was just what Charlie wanted. Now he could portray the article as one bearing the fingerprints of the management of the magazine and that it was more than the scribblings of a single rogue reporter. Later he would lay the pavement to take the responsibility all the way up to the other defendant in the case, Globe Publications, the parent company of Tee Time, Incorporated, and the owner of the largest chain of newspapers, magazines, and radio and television stations in the country.

"Mr. Reed, with an article of this sort, isn't it also customary to have your company lawyers review it to make sure that it doesn't violate the laws of libel and defamation?"

"Yes, our lawyers read the article in advance." By now, Reed was starting to show the pressure, and Hugo Shoemaker wanted to give him a break.

"Your Honor," Shoemaker said as he stood, "I'd like to request a ten-minute recess."

Judge Krause looked to Charlie Mayfield who nodded. Then, noting the time as well as his desire for a few puffs on his cigar, the judge said, "Okay, but let's make it fifteen minutes."

CHAPTER 19

The defense team crowded together at that end of the corridor that had become "theirs." Roz Berman had her face close to Max Reed's and was talking to him much like a trainer speaks to his prize fighter in the sixty seconds between rounds. "Listen to me, Max. Your testimony is fine, but, damn it, don't be so nervous and defensive." To make her point, she raised her voice and added, "You look like Mayfield caught you wearing your mother's underwear. Try to relax. You look scared and you look uncomfortable, and to the jury those are the looks of guilt. I know this is tough, Max, and I know that Charlie can be intimidating, but you can't let it get to you. I want you to put a smile on your face when he asks you a question, like you welcome it, but don't smile after you give an answer because that will look like a smirk. Juries like smiles, but they hate smirks."

Trying to ease the pressure on an already nervous witness is like handing a condemned prisoner a blindfold and cigarette and then asking him to relax. Roz Berman knew this. On the other hand, she had seen witnesses come apart on the stand, and they begin to say anything just to get the hell out of there. So, after saying what she had to say, she gave Reed a reassuring squeeze on his arm and said, "You were great during our prep sessions, Max, and you'll be great when you get back in there. Just sit back and try to loosen up. Forcing a smile now and then will make it easier." As an afterthought she added, "And try to look at the jury once in a while when you answer — make them think you're talking to them, and that you have nothing to hide."

What she didn't tell Reed was that Charlie Mayfield, so far, was only playing footsie with him. She knew that Charlie was merely loosening Reed's shirt to expose his jugular. As she walked away, that old thought once again emerged: *If I could try a case, just once, without worrying about my own witnesses!*

———

"Mr. Mayfield," Judge Krause was saying even before he was settled in his seat behind the elevated bench, "would you like the court reporter to read back the last question and answer?"

"Won't be necessary, Your Honor. I remember where we were." Charlie turned toward the witness who was back on the stand. "Mr. Reed. A short time before the break you told us that the higher-ups at *Tee Time* reviewed your articles before they went to print. Do you remember that?"

"Yes."

"When you submitted the articles to your editors, your supervisors, and your lawyers, did any of them ask you about your sources for such serious allegations?"

Reed was prepped by his lawyers for this question, but it nonetheless made him uncomfortable. Witnesses hate to testify about their bosses for fear of inadvertently implicating them in some nefarious wrongdoing. Finally he replied: "Well, yes, we had discussions about that."

"Before your article was published?"

"Yes."

"And with whom"?

"Well, I submitted the story to Howard Wolf; he's my boss and he makes the initial decision whether to print the story. If he's okay with it, he either lets it go or, if he has any concerns, he sends it to the lawyers or the editorial review board."

"Without identifying to us the names of any of those people, tell us about your conversation with Mr. Wolf regarding these sources."

"He reminded me that I needed at least two corroborating sources for each fact; we require that when we don't identify a source by name. I told him I knew that." Reed then sat back, indicating he was done with his answer.

"And did he ask you if you had the sources and who they were?"

"He didn't have to ask me. He knew that I wouldn't write the stories if I didn't have the sources, and he knew that I wouldn't reveal the names of the sources."

"So you and Mr. Wolf didn't really talk about your sources. He merely reminded you that you needed them, but he didn't ask you if you had the sources or who they were, and you didn't tell him. Is that right?"

"That's right."

"Did you talk about these sources of yours with anyone else at the magazine?"

"Bernie Cashman. But he's not exactly with the magazine."

Charlie looked up in apparent surprise. "Bernard Cashman from New York? Mr. Shoemaker's partner in the firm of Shoemaker, Cashman & Bates?"

"Yes, that's him."

"And did you talk to him at the direction of Howard Wolf, your supervisor?"

"Yes, sir."

"So, Mr. Reed, if I were to ask you about your conversation with Mr. Cashman, would you tell me that it's confidential and covered by the attorney-client privilege?"

A quick glance toward the defense table, then: "Yes, I would."

"And suppose I didn't ask you if you disclosed the names of the sources to Cashman, but only if you told him you had sources — would you still refuse to answer?"

Reed remembered that he was instructed by Berman and Shoemaker not to relate any part of his conversation with a lawyer. To do so would risk opening the door to the entire conversation. "That's correct, I refuse to answer any question about any conversation I had with Mr. Cashman."

Charlie knew he was about to step very close to the edge of the cliff, but felt that he had to get a message to the jury — let them know what the hell was going on here. He raised his voice a notch. "Alright, Mr. Reed, let's see if we have this straight. You told the jury that you had sources, but won't name them. Then you had a conversation with Mr. Wolf, your boss, who reminded you of the requirement for corroborating sources, but he didn't ask you if you actually had sources, or who they were, and you didn't tell him who they were. Instead, he sends you off to talk about it with the lawyers, but the conversations with lawyers are confidential — locked up and put away forever. That being the case, we can't even ask you if you confirmed to Mr. Cashman that you had two sources." With his voice rising another notch, Charlie said, "For all we know, you told him you didn't have sources, and your secret would be safe because it was a privileged conversation!"

Roz Berman and Hugo Shoemaker rose in unison with their objections.

"Argumentative!" Shoemaker shouted.

"Prejudicial!" Berman declared. "Your Honor," she continued, "Mr. Mayfield is trying to convey to the jury that there were no sources, when the evidence is directly to the contrary."

Charlie couldn't let that pass. "And the only evidence that there were sources comes from Max Reed, but he turns on the mute button whenever he's asked about them. And he won't even tell us if he discussed them — or their existence — with others. Who in the world would call that evidence?"

Judge Krause sustained the objection and then summoned the lawyers and the court reporter to the bench. "Mr. Mayfield," he began, "I would remind you that your job at this time is to put questions to the witness. Later, when the testimony is complete, you'll have your chance to interpret it, and even criticize it, when you make your closing arguments to the jury. But for now, limit your conversation with Mr. Reed to questions, and please put an end to your gratuitous descriptions of the evidence. I shouldn't have to remind you of that."

Exasperated, Charlie rubbed his temples. "Judge, how can I ask questions of a witness who hides? First, he hides behind the reporter's privilege, then he hides behind the attorney-client privilege. Worse, the whole thing was a setup. His boss, this Howard Wolf, intentionally did not ask if there were sources or who they were, but instead sends him off to the lawyers where they can have a secret conversation. Now we can't even ask if the existence of the sources was discussed. You know, Judge, these guys are good, really good. They deliberately built a cocoon — a cone of silence — around themselves. It's a don't-tell-me, tell-him-because-he-can't-talk scheme. Reed and his boss, Wolf, communicate with nods, winks, and mirrors, and the only time words are used, by prearrangement, are in privileged talks with the lawyers. This isn't a trial, Judge, it's a high-stakes game of hide and seek. I appreciate the need for protecting sources, but when the defense plays these games, we can't even be sure that there are sources to protect. We have only Mr. Reed's word for it, but if a reporter's word was all that reliable, then we wouldn't need sources to begin with."

Judge Krause involuntarily nodded his head ever so slightly. He empathized with the frustration that Charlie was verbalizing. Personally, Krause believed that the reporter's privilege was often abused, and its enforcement tempted reporters to stretch the truth if not downright lie. He preferred the federal rule, where a federal judge has the discretion to order reporters to reveal his or her sources, and the reporters could be jailed for contempt of court if they refused — and remain there until they named names. However, Judge Krause had to apply the law of Illinois, and in Illinois the privilege was absolute except in rare circumstances that did not apply to this case.

"I think we've had enough for one day," he said quietly. "We'll adjourn until 9:30 Monday morning."

FRIDAY EVENING

CHAPTER 20

Francine Curry had just put the pizza on the coffee table in front of the TV. Her husband, Dan, was in his La-Z-Boy recliner, a beer in one hand and the TV remote in the other, watching the Detroit Pistons game and swearing at the images on the screen. "Shit, Fran, why have I spent my whole sorry life in Detroit? Would it violate some universal plan for me to live in LA or New York or some other damned place where they win ball games?"

As much as Dan Curry detested his hometown teams, he couldn't resist following their every game. Francine couldn't stand this compulsion of his. If she wanted to make conversation during a game, she'd better have a damned good subject.

And tonight she had one.

"Honey," she purred, handing him a slice of his favorite cheese and sausage from Piccone's, "have you been following the Eddie Bennison trial? The one in Chicago where he's suing some magazine?"

"You bet," he answered, without taking his eyes from the TV screen. "I even look at the transcript during the day on my office computer. One of the golf sites has it online."

"How's it going?"

Dan cast a sideways glance at his wife. She cared about sports like he cared about Mahjong. "He'll kill 'em. The slime bag who wrote those articles about him started testifying today. Bennison's lawyer is tearing him apart." He turned back to the TV, took a huge bite of the pizza, and added, "I hope he bankrupts those bastards. Bennison's an absolute prince of a guy, and they have no right to smear him with all this bullshit."

"What did they write about him?"

"Oh, a bunch of piddly crap. First they say he cheats. Claim he moves the ball a fraction of an inch when he marks it. Shit! The course is over 7,000 yards long, and they're jumping up and down over a few inches. And anyway, there are thousands of people standing there watching him, and millions watching on TV. Assholes!"

"I thought it had to do with drugs."

"Even more bullshit! They didn't even have a rule about drugs on the golf tour when he supposedly took them, and all they're talking about with Bennison is minor stuff for pain — stuff like aspirin or Advil. Bastards! Here's a golf magazine more interested in selling magazines than in golf. I hope he breaks 'em. After all the crap we hear about the bums in basketball and football, we need more guys in sports like Eddie Bennison. The writers ought to praise him, not attack him."

Francine was loving this. She was like a lawyer leading an unknowing witness to an inescapable trap. "So he's a good guy, huh?"

"As good as they come."

"Married?"

"Christ, Fran, what the — " He thought a moment and sighed. "Yeah, he has a wife, and she's there at the trial by his side."

"Think he cheats on her?"

Dan took a deep breath and put the Pistons game on pause, allowing them to play on without his help, and turned to his wife. "Fran, what the hell is this all about? You've never given a rat's ass about this stuff, and you wouldn't know Eddie Bennison from Elvis Presley. What's with the sudden interest in this guy — or in his sex life?"

With deliberate casualness, Francine took a sip of her wine and replied, "He screwed one of the women in my department. And then he beat her up."

Dan Curry sat straight up, stared at his wife for several seconds, and then shook his head.

"It's true, Dan. Remember the golf tournament out at Oakland Hills a couple of years ago?"

"Sure, George and I went out there during one of the rounds. I remember that Bennison played."

"He played, alright. And he was staying out at the Marriott a few miles from there."

"How in the hell — ?"

"Let me finish. There's this place, Luigi's, near the Marriott, and this gal from the office, Liz Peters, was there for a birthday party. Later, she and the others went over to the lounge at the Marriott. Bennison was sitting off in a corner by himself, and Liz waltzed over and sat down. And that was that."

"That was what? Eddie Bennison is a high-profile guy. He wouldn't take a chance of having someone recognize him in a saloon with some slut. Anyway, he probably travels with a crowd of handlers."

"Not that night," Francine said. "He could have walked into our kitchen and you wouldn't have known who in the hell he was."

"Not true. Bennison has been a star on the Senior Tour for nearly ten years, and his face was all over the sport pages. I would have recognized him from a mile away."

"Not that night, you wouldn't. He was using a fake name and was wearing fake glasses."

"Then how did your friend know who he was?"

"She didn't — not until last night." Francine briefly relayed what Liz had told her earlier in the day, beginning with how Bennison told her his name was Ben Edwards and told her he was at a sales meeting, and ending with how she made the connection through Google after she saw his picture in the paper earlier this week.

Dan Curry got up and paced around the room, stopping every few seconds to ask another question. "Is this Liz married?"

"No."

"What's she look like?"

"Great, just like someone a professional golfer would like to shack up with."

"Did he tell her he was a professional golfer? "

"No, he said he sold boxes or containers — something like that. And that's what Bennison does when he's not playing golf. Liz looked that up on Google, too. And that name — Ben Edwards. Cute, huh? A convenient alias."

Then Dan asked, "How could she remember him that well? I mean, it was a quick one-night stand a long time ago and she had no idea who he was."

"Well, things happened that made it more memorable than most one-night stands."

Finishing the pizza and ignoring the games, Dan listened carefully as his wife explained the rest of what Liz told her.

"She said that they sat and talked for quite a while. He talked a lot about his customers, and she was telling him about what she did at the ad agency. Her friends were leaving, and she was grateful that she had her own car and drove to Luigi's alone. She sensed where this was heading, and she was ready to go with it." Francine chuckled. "She wanted some action, and she told me that she did everything she could to persuade him to take her to his room.

"The guy was playing it cool, and didn't seem to be taking the bait, at least not at first. Liz figured that he was married, and that he was wrestling with what to do. Finally, she decided to go for the gold. 'Listen, Ben,' she announced, 'either I'm going to put my ass in my little Beemer and drive home, or you're going to take it up to your room. And I've had too much to drink to drive home.' Sure enough, they went up to his room."

Dan Curry was shaking his head. "There's one thing that still doesn't make sense. I can see how your friend made the connection after checking with Google, but I can't figure out what got her to go to Google in the first place, especially after all this time."

"There was a story in the paper the other day about his trial in Chicago. She saw his picture."

"Yeah, but how could a broad like Liz, who obviously has been with a ton of guys, remember him from a single picture after two or three years?"

Francine sat back and sighed. "Well, like I said, it was more memorable than a quick roll in the sack. Are you ready for more?"

"More?"

"Trust me, Liz doesn't have many inhibitions, but she told me that this Bennison guy turned out to be kind of nuts. He was like an acrobat, and he couldn't get enough. Liz loved it — she said it was like a competition to see who had more moves and more stamina. They were sweating and screaming, and damned near broke the bed and everything else in the room."

"Eddie Bennison? I can't believe this!"

"And you haven't heard the rest of it."

"There's more?

"Apparently, wild sex wasn't enough for him. The son of a bitch beat her up. It started out with a few love slaps, but he got carried away and belted her a few times — hard. She ran out of there with a black eye and a cut lip, and had some other bruises."

"Did she go to hotel security, or the police?"

"I asked that, too. She thought about it, but then decided to just chalk it up as a bad experience. She couldn't bear the thought of telling this whole story to a bunch of gawking police types. They'd figure that she was asking for it, going to the room of a strange guy. Remember, she didn't know who he was — not until this week."

Dan Curry sat quietly for several minutes while an idea began to hatch in his brain. "Do you think Liz told anyone else — I mean, besides you?"

"Probably. Judging from the things she tells us at work, she doesn't have many secrets. And now that she knows who it really is, she may want to give him a hard time because of what he did to her."

Dan Curry's brain began racing a mile a minute. Curry had a heart for larceny, but he didn't have a brain for it. Even before his wife had finished telling him about Bennison's caper with Liz, he was figuring out how to mine some gold of it. Before he could even think about a plan, though, his instincts correctly told him to get to Liz. He tried to persuade Francine to call Liz to set up a breakfast meeting for the next morning, Saturday.

"This is none of our business," Francine said, "and you have no right to get involved." She wasn't sure what he had in mind; neither did he, yet — but it didn't smell right.

"Fran, you yourself said that she might want to go after Bennison because of what he did. I only want to give her a few suggestions on how to do that. Hell, this guy has it coming — he could have killed her, and if he isn't stopped, he might kill someone later."

Francine didn't believe for a minute that her husband's motives were altruistic, but he was right about this much: abusers are repeaters, and Liz should be encouraged to destroy the bastard. If she didn't, some other poor girl might not be so lucky.

So she called Liz. By then it was still not yet nine o'clock, giving her husband plenty of time to plan what to say at the breakfast scheduled for the next morning.

SATURDAY MORNING

CHAPTER 21

Liz Peters arrived at the coffee shop to find Dan and Francine Curry already at a table. "Well, isn't this a treat?" Liz said as she joined them. "What's the occasion?"

Francine Curry glanced at her husband who nodded. Then, with some obvious discomfort, she turned to her friend. "I hope you don't mind, Liz, but last night I told Dan what you told me about this Bennison guy."

"Aw shit, Fran, why would you . . . ?"

"No, it's okay." Francine took her hand. "Let Dan explain. He wants to help you."

MONDAY MORNING

CHAPTER 22

Max Reed resumed the stand when court reconvened the following Monday morning. With the tensions of the previous Friday afternoon seemingly behind them, Charlie approached the witness with a smile on his face. "You understand, don't you, Mr. Reed, that you're still under oath?"

"I do."

"Okay, Friday we talked about your article in June 2006, describing how Eddie Bennison marks his ball on the putting green. So we'll all be clear, let's refer to that as the ball-marking issue. Is that okay with you?"

"Sure."

"And, so we're all straight on this, the May issue — that was the first one — was about the performance-enhancing drugs, right?"

"That's right."

"Good." Charlie then nodded to the bailiff who once again turned the lights down, and Charlie's assistant flipped on the projector. "Now, Mr. Reed, do you recognize the words projected on the screen as being words that you wrote the following month — that would be the third article — in the July 2006 issue of *Tee Time?*"

"Yes, I wrote that."

"And, as with the other stories from the May and June issues, did your editors, supervisors, and lawyers approve it?"

"Objection!" Roz Berman exclaimed. "Your Honor, the question assumes that the *Tee Time* lawyers approved the May story, but the witness testified only that the lawyers saw the story before it was published. What they actually said is barred by the attorney-client privilege."

Before the judge could rule, Charlie said with a broad grin, "You're absolutely correct, Ms. Berman. We only know that the lawyers saw the story before it was published, and we know that it was published after they saw it, but we don't know if the lawyers approved it. My mistake. How silly of me." Laughs were heard throughout the courtroom, including from the jury box, but no one at the defense table joined them.

"Let me rephrase the question: Mr. Reed, I'm not asking you to tell us what the lawyers said, but do you know if they saw these articles before they were published?"

"Yes, they saw them."

"And then they were published?"

"Yes." Remembering Roz Berman's instructions from the day before, Reed smiled and looked toward the jury when he answered. However, in spite of himself, his smile looked just like one of the smirks that Berman was worried about.

"Okay, please read your words up there on the screen."

Reed shifted in his seat to face the large image on the wall, and began.

"Groove" is a word often associated with Eddie Bennison. When his swing is on, it's grooved; when he's playing well, he's in the groove; and the females in his gallery have been heard to say he's groovy. But lately the "groove" word has popped up again with Bennison — this time in a less favorable context.

With a short iron to a front hole location, where too much backspin could suck the ball off the green and possibly into a hazard, Bennison's ball always seems to sit gently and stay put. Never comes back. How does he do it — every time? Well, it's all in the grooves or, more accurately, the lack thereof. Here's his secret: before making the shot, he takes one or two practice swings, and with each swing he takes a big divot. (Watch him on other shots — he doesn't take a divot with his other practice swings.) Then he wipes the mud off the face of the club with his thumb or the edge of the sole of his shoe. The result: there is compacted dirt or mud filling the grooves, and therefore less of the unwanted backspin, and therefore more birdies and fewer bogies.

I'd advise the gallery or television viewers to watch him the next time he faces such a shot, but I suspect he'll read this and be more careful in the future.

"Once again, Mr. Reed, I'll ask if you personally saw Eddie Bennison doing what you accused him of doing in that report?"

"It appeared that way from TV recordings I reviewed."

"Oh, it *appeared* that way. And I assume others told you about this. Is that correct?"

"Yes, sir. That's correct."

"And would you please give us the names of the people who told you that?"

"No, sir. I refuse to reveal the names of my sources."

Charlie looked towards the jury, shaking his head to convey again his frustration with the answer — a frustration he hoped they shared.

"To save us all time, Mr. Reed, if I asked you the same questions I did yesterday about the ball-marking article, regarding your conversations with your bosses and lawyers, would your answers be the same?"

"They would, yes."

"So, in your conversation with Howard Wolf — this time about the grooves — he didn't ask and you didn't tell whether you had sources? Is that right?"

"Yes."

"And then you saw Mr. Cashman, the lawyer, as you did with the previous articles?"

"Right."

"And you won't tell us anything about your conversation with Cashman, right?"

"Right."

Charlie appeared to review his notes for a few moments so the jurors could absorb the import of the last few questions and answers. He hoped they saw this as he did: a colossal shell game being played by *Tee Time*, its management, and its lawyers.

"Is it okay with you, Mr. Reed, if I change the subject?"

Again laughter from the spectators and a few jurors.

"That would be very nice," the witness replied with a smile of relief.

"Okay, I will. Let's talk about grooves." Charlie signaled to his assistant, Pete Stevens, who walked over to Charlie and handed him a golf club — a pitching wedge — that had been leaning against their counsel table. Charlie then lifted the club so the jurors could easily see the face of the club head. "For the benefit of the jury, Mr. Reed, doesn't the term 'grooves' refer to these indentations, or slits, running horizontally across the face of the golf club?"

"They do, yes."

"And in your article — the one you just read from — aren't you implying that dirt or mud embedded in the grooves will cause the ball to have less backspin?"

The article made that too clear for the witness to waffle. "Yes."

"Do you know that to be the case? Will dirt in the grooves actually reduce the backspin?"

"Well, one would have to assume that — "

"Don't sit there and tell us what one would have to assume! We're in a court of law, and we deal in facts, not assumptions. So I'll ask you again: Will dirt in the grooves reduce the backspin? Yes or no?"

Again Reed was in a box. Answer *no* and it makes his groove story a lie; answer *yes* and he'll have to substantiate it; answer *I don't know* and he'll be laughed out of the courtroom. He knew this came up in the prep sessions with his own lawyers, but he couldn't recall how he was to deal with it. So he waffled: "That's what I've been told."

"And would you be kind enough to tell us who told you that, or are those other sources you refuse to disclose."

"Well, let's see," Reed said, obviously stalling. "I brought it up during lunch with some of the guys at the magazine. They all play golf and know a lot about the game, and this was their consensus."

"Consensus, sure," Charlie repeated, sarcastically. "Sounds like a Gallup Poll. Do you remember who it was at that lunch whom you polled in order to ruin the life and career of Eddie Bennison?"

"Please, Mr. Mayfield," interjected Judge Krause before the defense could object.

"Sorry, Your Honor."

"No," Reed answered, "not at the moment. I can't recall who was there or who exactly said what."

Charlie looked at Reed as one might look at an insect crawling out of a salad. He then pulled out a folder and appeared to examine the contents before posing his next question. "Mr. Reed, the Rules of Golf, as published by the United States Golf Association, are quite extensive. Do you know which of those rules pertains to the groove question we're discussing?"

At last, a question for which Reed was prepared! "Yes, that would be Rule 4-2."

"Let me read that rule to the jury: 'Foreign material must not be applied to the club face for the purpose of influencing the movement of the ball.' Is that the rule to which you are referring?"

"Yes, sir."

"What is the foreign material? Is it dirt? Is dirt a foreign material?"

"Well, if it's not part of the golf club, then I would say it's foreign material."

"Therefore, is it your testimony that any time a golfer strikes a ball without first scrubbing and sanitizing his club, that he's violating the rules? Is that your testimony?"

Now the witness was shifting uncomfortably in his seat. "Well, if he deliberately left the dirt in the grooves for the purpose of affecting the shot, then I'd say he broke the rule."

"Aha!" Charlie exclaimed. "So it's a violation only if he left the dirt in the grooves on purpose, and that he did it for the purpose of affecting the movement of the ball. Is that your testimony?"

"Yes."

"And is it your further testimony that Eddie Bennison did this on purpose, and for the purpose of affecting the movement of the ball?"

Reed had no wiggle room. "Yes, that's my testimony."

"And on what do you base that extraordinary accusation?"

"Well, as I mentioned, I've reviewed television tapes of Mr. Bennison playing, and he only takes divots on his practice swings when he wouldn't want to put a lot of spin on the ball."

Charlie leaned forward and zeroed his gaze on the witness. "Tell us, Mr. Reed, as you're sitting on your couch watching Eddie Bennison on TV play a shot on a golf course hundreds or thousands of miles away, how do you know whether he wants to impart a lot, a little, or no spin on the ball? Are you able to read his mind?"

"Well, if the hole is near the front of the green, and there is water or another hazard just in front of the green, then it's obvious that he wouldn't want the ball to spin back off the green."

"But isn't it a fact that he wouldn't want the ball to spin back off the green in any event, even if there weren't a hazard there?"

"Oh, sure, but — "

"Can you think of *any* situation where the golfer would want the ball to spin off the green?"

"No, but — "

"Then let's assume the pin is near the back of the green. Would the golfer ever want the ball to land near the pin and then spin back toward the front of the green?"

"Of course not."

"Really, Mr. Reed, isn't it a fact that there may be times when the golfer would want the ball to spin backwards, other times when he'd want it to land and stay put, and still other where he may want it to land and then move forward?"

The witness could not deny this. "Yes, of course. At times he'd want a great deal of spin, and at other times he wouldn't."

"Then how in the world do you know, sitting and watching on television before Eddie Bennison hits a shot, precisely how much backspin he decides to put on the ball for any particular shot?"

After a pause, Reed answered feebly. "Well, it always seems that whenever he wants the ball to spin back, it does, and whenever he doesn't want it to spin back, it doesn't."

Charlie spread his arms out wide and smiled broadly. "What you are saying, it would seem, is that Eddie Bennison is a darn good golfer, and that he is able to control the ball better than most golfers. If that's what you're saying, Mr. Reed, then I would agree with you — as would nearly every golf fan in the country."

Reed was persistent. "But if he's able to control the ball better than others because he puts dirt in the grooves, it would be wrong."

"Then tell us exactly how he does it. You wrote that he wipes the dirt off the face of the club, but leaves it in the grooves. So, when he wants to have very little backspin, does he leave a lot of dirt in the grooves? And if he wants just a little backspin, does he leave just a little dirt in the grooves? And for a lot of backspin I suppose he digs all the dirt out of the grooves? Does he do all that careful measuring, calibrating, and cheating while the gallery and the fans at home and his fellow competitors are all watching and waiting for him to hit the ball? And even though he's one of the most popular and most observed golfers in America, you seem to be the only one who noticed all this magical sleight of hand? You and perhaps some of your unnamed sources. Is that what you want this jury to believe?"

Reed's nervousness turned to anger, and it showed in his voice. He blurted out: "You're trying to make it look like I made this whole thing up."

Bingo! Charlie thought to himself. He looked up at the judge and, with feigned innocence, asked, "Your Honor, I missed what the witness just said. May I ask the court reporter to repeat it for all of us to hear?"

Roz Berman looked at Reed with eyes that could kill as the court reporter read back Reed's last statement.

CHAPTER 23

Charlie Mayfield and Eddie Bennison were standing just outside the courtroom door during the ensuing recess. Bennison again asked, "How do you think it's going, Charlie?"

The lawyer grinned and tilted his head toward the far end of the corridor where the defense team was huddled. "Judging from that scene over there, I'd say we're doing pretty well." Eddie looked in that direction. Roz Berman looked like she was about to rip Max Reed's heart out of his chest, and the other members of the team had funereal looks on their faces. "But I don't care what the defense thinks. I'm more interested in what the jurors think, and they seem to be reacting the way I want them to. But it's early, Eddie, and we *should* be ahead — the defense hasn't started yet."

"Too bad we're in Illinois, where Reed doesn't have to name his sources."

"It's not as bad as you think. Oh, sure, I'm making a big show how that rule is hurting us, but that's for the benefit of the jury and the press. If Reed had to name his sources, you could bet he'd come up with somebody — maybe a couple of jokers from one of your galleries who'd say anything for a moment of fame. Then we'd be screwed, and we wouldn't be able to go after Reed like we are now. This is the guy I want the jury to hate, not a couple of nobodies from the gallery."

When court resumed with Max Reed back on the stand, it was clear that he was shaken. If he had any self-esteem remaining after Charlie's last onslaught, it was destroyed by the dressing down he got from Roz Berman during the short recess. In the course of just a few minutes, she pointed out where he totally forgot the things they had worked on during their prep sessions. He didn't listen carefully to the questions, he volunteered too much information with his answers, he didn't look friendly and confident, he ignored the jury, and on the last question he blew his cool and made an idiotic statement that included the words "I made this whole thing up." And Charlie, true to form, had the court reporter read those words back to the jury.

When the session resumed with Reed back on the stand, Charlie asked, "Now, Mr. Reed, we've talked about your ball-marking story and your groove story. At this point I'd like to ask you if there are any other incidents in which you believe that Eddie Bennison broke the rules of golf?"

"None that I know of."

"And before you wrote your articles about those incidents, had any other magazine, newspaper, or radio or TV station reported cheating by Eddie Bennison?"

"I don't believe so."

"So it was a Max Reed scoop, right?"

"Well, I don't know if I'd put it that way, but, yes, I was the first to report on these things."

"So, to recap your testimony, as you sit here today, Mr. Reed, the sum total of your accusations against Eddie Bennison is that he supposedly *smudges* when he marks his ball and that he sometimes leaves dirt on his club before making a shot. Oh, yes, and that he takes medicine to play better. And that you are the only one to report these derelictions. Is that correct?"

"Well, I was the *first* to report them. But they were later reported in other publications, and also in other media — television, radio, and even on blogs and various Internet sites."

"But all of those other stories were based on your stories that came out first, isn't that right?"

"Yes, I'd have to agree with that."

"So if you had never written those three articles about Eddie Bennison, then all of those other places wouldn't have written or broadcast *their* stories about him. Isn't that a fact?"

"Yes, I guess so."

"So then it all comes back to you, doesn't it, Mr. Reed? If you hadn't written those things about Eddie, no one else would have. He'd be out there winning golf tournaments, and we wouldn't be here in this courtroom. Would you agree with that?"

Max Reed again balked. After a moment he meekly replied, "Maybe, but if I didn't write those stories, someone else would have."

Charlie just shook his head, and then posed another question. "And you wrote those stories without ever, *not even once*, seeing him with your own eyes doing any of these things, but instead you based your accusations on what people told you — people whose names you refuse to disclose. Is that right?"

"Yes," the witness answered quietly.

"By the way, how many of these undisclosed sources are there, Mr. Reed?"

"Well, that's hard to say. Perhaps ten or fifteen."

"Isn't it a fact that thousands of fans are in the galleries when Eddie is competing in a tournament, and that millions are watching on television?"

"That would be correct, yes."

"And doesn't he compete in about twenty-five tournaments each year?"

"That sounds about right."

"So, wouldn't it be accurate to say that at least 30 or 40 million people see him compete — either in person or on television — over the course of a year? Maybe even 50 million people?"

"I guess so."

"And if only *1 percent* of those people saw what you heard — or what you *say* you heard — that would mean that about 50,000 people would see him cheat every year. Correct?"

Max Reed was visibly shaken. "Perhaps," he answered, barely loud enough to be heard.

"But you only heard it from ten or fifteen. Does that sound believable to you, Mr. Reed? Does it sound believable that of all the *millions* who supposedly saw watched Eddie Bennison cheat, only ten or fifteen would come forward? And why is it that other reporters would not have heard about it and written their own stories?"

There are certain moments in a trial when no answer speaks decibels louder than a verbal one — and when silence says more than "Yes" or "No." This was one such moment. The witness could think of no decent response, and the longer he thought about it, the less important his eventual response would be. So Charlie turned the flame up a notch. "Let me ask it another way, Mr. Reed. Considering that Eddie was perhaps the most popular golfer in America, if he did what you say he did in front of *millions* of people, don't you think it would have made immediate front-page news, and not remain a secret until you wrote about it weeks, months, or even years later?"

Again there was a long, excruciating silence from the witness. "Never mind," Charlie said, after letting Reed squirm for an eternity. "Since you can't think of an answer to that question, I'll ask another one."

Charlie turned and went back to his counsel table, apparently to review some notes. He bent to whisper in the ear of his associate, Pete Stevens. "Okay, Pete, it's time to disembowel the son of a bitch."

———

Charlie returned to the podium, assuming a much friendlier tone for his next line of question. "I gather from your articles, Mr. Reed, that you believe that the rules of golf should be strictly observed. Is that right?"

"Yes, I believe that," Reed replied, not sure where this was going, but relieved to see a friendlier Charlie and a change of subjects.

"And that violations should be penalized?"

"Well, sure."

"Even minor or insignificant violations, like mismarking a ball by, say, a half-inch on a 50-foot putt, or by leaving a little dirt in the grooves?"

Reed was being led into a trap, but didn't see it. He shifted in his seat and finally replied, "A rule is a rule, Mr. Mayfield, and a violation is a violation. I don't think a golfer should ignore or break a rule just because he doesn't think it's important, or because it won't make a difference."

A chill went up Roz Berman's neck. *He's spouting off again; embellishing his answers.*

"So it's a matter of integrity, right?"

"Absolutely. You either play by the rules or you don't play at all. That's true in all sports, but it's especially true in golf. It's a game of honor, with no referees or umpires to look for violations."

Berman was beside herself. *Why can't the bastard just say yes or no?* She knew Charlie Mayfield and sensed that he was driving a freight train straight at Reed, but there was nothing she could do about it.

Now Charlie rested his elbows on the podium and said in a friendly voice, "You sound like you really respect the game, Mr. Reed."

"I do," the witness answered comfortably, thinking that the answer couldn't possibly come back to bite him.

"Tell us how much golf you play."

Reed still didn't hear the whistle of the train. "Well, I play maybe once a week, sometimes twice."

"And do you play with a regular group?"

"I play at my club, and with many of the members."

"*Tee Time* is in New York, Mr. Reed. Is that where your club is?"

"Well, near there. I commute from Connecticut, and that's where my club is."

"A private country club, I assume."

"Yes," Reed answered nervously, knowing that private clubs are beyond the reach of most people who serve on juries.

"Like the kind of private club that Eddie Bennison and his family couldn't afford to belong to back in Kewanee, Illinois?"

"Objection!" Roz Berman shouted, trying to break Charlie's rhythm and derail the train. "Irrelevant and prejudicial, and Mr. Mayfield knows better."

Charlie bowed in her direction. "You're correct, Ms. Berman, and I'll withdraw the question with my apologies."

Roz Berman wasn't satisfied. She had to stop the train, and asked to approach the bench. The judge nodded. "Your Honor," she said when they were assembled, "there's no reason to clutter the record with references to Mr. Reed's golf game. This case isn't about *his* game, it's about Mr. Bennison's. This is all irrelevant and has nothing to do with the issues before the court."

Judge Krause shifted his eyes toward Charlie, waiting for a response.

"I disagree, Judge. Mr. Reed is a critical witness in this case, and therefore his credibility is necessarily an issue. Further, he's the author of widely read stories accusing Mr. Bennison of violations of the Rules of Golf. We submit that he lied in those articles, another reason why his credibility is an issue. On both scores I should have the right to challenge his credibility by inquiring into his knowledge of the game and its rules."

"I agree," Krause replied. "Ms. Berman's objection is overruled. You may proceed, Mr. Mayfield, but try to keep it short."

Back at the podium, Charlie continued in a non-confrontational tone. "Do you play in any tournaments or club events at your private country club, Mr. Reed?"

"Occasionally."

"And do you and your friends sometimes make bets? Play for money?"

"Well, yes," he smiled, "but not for much."

"How much is 'not for much'?"

"Oh, usually less than 20 or 30 dollars." He was hoping that didn't sound like much to the jurors.

"So, to repeat, you do compete in club tournaments occasionally, and you do play for money, though usually only for 20 or 30 dollars. Correct?"

"Yes," he sighed.

"By the way, Mr. Reed. that private club of yours is called Meadowbrook, isn't that right?"

"Yes," Reed answered, surprised that Charlie knew the name of his club.

"And don't they have a big event out there every year — I understand it's called a Calcutta?"

Reed shifted in his seat, sensing something in the wind. "Yes."

"Do you play in the Calcutta?"

"Usually."

"And isn't there a lot of gambling at that Calcutta? Aren't the teams auctioned off to the highest bidder and there's even pari-mutuel betting, with odds posted?"

"Yes, it's something like that."

"And aren't hundreds of thousands of dollars wagered on the event?"

Reed was visibly uncomfortable with this line of questions. "I'm not sure of the amount."

"Now you told us, Mr. Reed, that your club, Meadowbrook, is in Connecticut. Are you aware that the State of Connecticut has a law that prohibits gambling, except in certain circumstances such as licensed casinos, charitable raffles, and that sort of thing? And, by the way, unrestricted gambling at private country clubs is not one of the exceptions."

"No, I wasn't aware of that."

"Do you mean to tell us that you thought that the Calcutta gambling at your club was legal?"

"I guess I never thought about it."

"So if I understand your testimony, Mr. Reed, you believe that Eddie Bennison should obey rules pertaining to performance-enhancing drugs *that did not exist at that time*, but that you should be free to ignore criminal laws against gambling *that do exist*. Is that what you're telling us, Mr. Reed?"

Max Reed sat there fidgeting, not having any idea how to answer the question. He glanced over to Berman and Shoemaker for a lifeline, but got it from an unlikely source — Charlie Mayfield, who didn't care about the answer — he only wanted the jury to hear the question.

"We'll get back to that," Charlie said. "In the meantime, I'd like to ask a different question." Charlie backed up several steps and addressed the witness from clear back by his counsel table.

"I understand, Mr. Reed, that the rules of golf limit the number of clubs you can have in your bag. And isn't that number fourteen?"

"Yes, I think that's correct — fourteen clubs is the limit." He began to hear the train's whistle, but he didn't see it yet.

"You *think* that's correct? Is that what you said?"

"I'm sorry. Yes, that's the rule."

"Now, Mr. Reed, if I were to tell you that we had someone over at your private country club, Meadowbrook, count the clubs in your bag several times over the last few months, and that it was never less than sixteen, would I be lying?"

Hugo Shoemaker objected to the question. "Your Honor, the question here is whether the plaintiff, Mr. Bennison, violated the rules in professional tournaments, and not whether Mr. Reed violated them in friendly games at his own club."

"Your Honor," Charlie followed up, "the witness has publicly called my client a cheater. If he himself is a cheater, then it goes to his credibility — especially after lecturing us that golf is a game of honor." He then tilted his head toward the jurors and added with a clarity they couldn't miss, "The jury may well conclude that if Mr. Reed takes money from his friends, or trophies from his club, or wins the Calcutta by cheating, or violates criminal laws prohibiting gambling, he may also be willing to lie in his articles or when testifying in court." Once the jury heard that, Charlie didn't really care how the judge ruled.

"Overruled. The witness may answer."

"Never mind, Judge," Charlie announced with a friendly smile. "I'll withdraw the question."

———

Now Charlie wanted to ask a few critical questions that he knew the jurors would ask if they were allowed to interrupt the trial with questions. So he moved over to lean against the railing on the jury box and posed his questions as if he were asking for them.

"Mr. Reed, you told us that various unnamed people gave you the information you used to write your articles about Eddie Bennison. Isn't that correct?"

"Yes, that's correct."

"And you still refuse to give us the names of those people, correct?"

"Yes."

"Well, sir, did you take any steps — did you do anything — to verify the information they gave you?"

"I don't understand."

"Well, did you personally go back and review the television tapes to verify, with your own eyes, that Eddie Bennison improperly marked his ball on the putting green?"

"I tried, but it wasn't clear on the tapes. We are talking about only a half an inch or so, and none of the cameras were close enough to show that."

"So with all those fancy television cameras at all of those tournaments, not one of them was able to see what your unnamed and unidentified sources supposedly told you, is that right?"

Reed, wishing he were anywhere else in the world, replied, "That seems to be the case."

"And isn't it also true that the cameras would be unable to detect and show the amount of dirt in the grooves of a golf club being swung by a golfer who was some distance from the cameras?"

"Yes."

"That's what I thought. Now, let's get back to the drug issue, Mr. Reed. You just testified that you did not verify the information about Eddie Bennison cheating. So I'll ask if you took any steps to verify the information about him taking performance-enhancing drugs."

"I'm not sure that I . . . "

"Well, did you take any steps to find out where he acquired these drugs, or if he acquired the drugs? Or how often he took them? Did you ask his doctor, or the people he worked with for physical training?"

"No, I didn't do any of that."

"Mr. Reed, I understand that the Tour has workout facilities at the sites of all of the tournaments. Are you aware of that?"

"Yes, they're in movable trailers."

"And they're staffed with people who give massages and rubdowns, and others who help the players use the workout machines, and still others who consult with the players on nutrition and exercise. Correct?"

"Yes, that's my understanding."

"And these people — these trainers — travel with the Tour so that the golfers see the same ones with some regularity, week in and week out. Correct?"

"Yes, that would be the case."

"And there are also people in those facilities who advise the players on how to deal with their aches and pains, right?"

"I think so, yes."

"Alright, Mr. Reed, with regard to all these people who Eddie Bennison sees almost daily throughout the year about his physical condition, did you ask any of them, so far as they knew, whether Eddie took any performance-enhancing drugs? I'm not asking for their names, but can you at least tell us whether you asked any of them in order to verify the information you had?"

"I can't say that I did."

"So let's see if I have this straight, Mr. Reed. You accepted as true the information from unnamed sources that Eddie Bennison took these drugs, and took no steps to verify it, but you didn't even bother to ask the people who would really know if it were true. Is that what you're telling us?"

Roz Berman was on her feet. "Objection, Your Honor. The question is argumentative."

"Overruled. You may answer, Mr. Reed."

Reed fidgeted for a few seconds, and finally said, "I guess you could put it that way, but I had no reason to doubt my sources."

"Well, we have no way of knowing whether you had reason to doubt your sources because you refuse to tell us who they are, how many there are, or the context in which they gave you the information. But we do know who the people are who would know whether Eddie took those drugs, and you never even bothered to ask them. Isn't that right?"

This was a critical point. Under the law, not taking the trouble to verify a verifiable fact is evidence of a "disregard for the truth" — and if the jury believed that Max Reed wrote false stories with a disregard for the truth, it could clinch the case for Charlie.

Almost inaudibly, Max Reed replied, "I don't recall asking them."

Charlie walked back to his table to whisper a word or two to Pete Stevens, who listened and then shook his head.

Charlie turned and announced that he had no further questions for Max Reed.

———

Hugo Shoemaker, as shaken as Reed, did his best to rehabilitate Reed during his subsequent questioning of the witness. Through a series of leading questions, to which Charlie could have objected but didn't, Reed testified that a very small percentage of witnesses to rules violations would actually bring such news to a reporter, and that fifteen or twenty coming forward doesn't mean that thousands *didn't* witness the violations. The reporter further testified that he didn't have a reputation for writing sensational or mean-spirited stories, and that, on the contrary, he believed most professional golfers would rate him as fair. In fact, he said, he often interviewed Tour pros for his stories, and they'd never so much as speak to him if they thought he twisted or embellished the facts to hurt someone. As soon as Shoemaker thought he had stopped the bleeding, he quit. He wanted Max Reed off the stand and out of the building as soon as possible.

When Shoemaker was through with Reed, the judge looked at Charlie who slowly shook his head to indicate that he had no further questions.

"The witness may step down," Judge Krause announced, "and I think this is a good place to adjourn for the day. We'll resume at 9:30 tomorrow morning."

The success of a witness can be measured by the reception he gets as he leaves the stand. If people on his team smile and nod, it's the equivalent of the Oscar. But Max Reed saw no smiles or nods; he saw only eyes that avoided his as files were closed and briefcases were snapped shut. He trudged up the center aisle to the door at the back of the courtroom, knowing that now he had to face inquisitors more ruthless than Charlie Mayfield and judges more judgmental than His Honor Harry Krause. First it would be the reporters assembled out in the corridor, and then his superiors at *Tee Time*. Reed's fears were understandable, considering that a meeting was just convening in New York at the magazine's headquarters.

CHAPTER 24

"For crissakes," Clive Curtis was bellowing, "we're supposed to *report* the friggin' news, not *make* it!"

Clearly, this was not a good day at the New York offices of Tee Time, Incorporated, where the entire senior management team had been summoned to an emergency meeting in the company board room after the Bennison trial adjourned for the day. The meeting was called by Clive Curtis, *Tee Time*'s Editor-in-Chief, shortly after he received his daily call from one of his people in Chicago who was there to observe and report back on the trial. Curtis, a man known for not sugar-coating his words, was just getting started.

"It's not bad enough that a jury could slam us for millions, but regardless of what the jury does, we'll be the laughingstock of the media and sports worlds. This goddamned Max Reed — *our* Max Reed — is turning out to be the biggest boob since Humpty Dumpty. We probably won't have a dozen subscribers by the time this case is over. In fact — "

"As of this morning, subscriptions are still — "

"*I'm not done!*" Curtis barked at Ward Newton, Vice President of Circulation. The Editor-in-Chief then looked around the table to see if anyone else cared to interrupt him. Seeing eight people staring at the papers before them, he continued. "I want some answers, and I want them fast.

"First, how in the hell did we let those stories about Eddie Bennison slip past the people who vet these things? A story like this one is too big for the normal vetting. This guy is a national icon. Calling him a cheater or druggie — shit! It's like calling the goddamned Statue of Liberty a whore."

Angry and frustrated, Curtis shook his head from side to side. "Next, what the hell kind of lawyers do we have out there? I've been getting reports from the trial every hour, and Bennison's lawyer is murdering us. He's making us look like a bunch of slick muckrakers who deliberately lie and then hide behind legal technicalities. We sit around this table pretending that we're talking the Constitution and all that bullshit about free speech and free press, but to the public we're being sneaky and devious. Do our lawyers know what the hell they're doing? I understand we have this hotshot professor from Yale, but my guy in Chicago tells me that this professor guy is a stuffy bag of hot air.

"Next, I want to know if anyone at this table can give me one reason why I shouldn't fire Max Reed's ass the second he gets back here." He looked around the room and added, "When I'm done with that son of a bitch, he won't be able to get a job writing birthday cards for Hallmark."

Curtis again looked around at his management team. No one volunteered to speak. "Okay, Ward, let's start with you. Are we getting killed out there?"

Ward Newton was especially nervous. He was scheduled to testify at the trial in a few days, and he didn't want to suffer the same fate as Max Reed. Clearing his throat, he began to read from his notes. "As of now, subscriptions haven't been hit, and over-the-counter sales are steady. Marketing thinks we can get a big sales boost next month if we make the trial a cover story, and — "

"*What the hell is that Marketing crowd smoking?*" Curtis exploded. "I can't believe those guys. They want to write about the trial and tell the world how dumb we are just to get a one-month sales hit?" He paused to shake his head. "How 'bout this: I walk over to Marketing with a can of gasoline, pour it all over those assholes, bring in a camera crew, and then start lighting matches. If we're going to do a cover story on how fuckin' stupid we are just to sell some magazines, then let's not hold back." He shook his head again. "They want sales, I'll give 'em sales."

After a few moments of silence, Todd Slocum, the magazine's Chief

Legal Officer, took his turn at the plate. He had been at the trial during the first few days but flew back for this meeting. "We knew that Reed's stories would be lightning rods, so we took an extra precaution. Ordinarily, we have our internal editorial review committee screen all articles, and we have a libel lawyer sit on that committee. But in this case, we took the stories directly to Bernie Cashman."

"Is he that libel lawyer here in New York, the one who charges two or three grand an hour?" Curtis asked.

"That's the one. His firm is the best in the country on First Amendment law. It's his partner, Hugo Shoemaker, who's handling the trial for us."

Curtis chuckled derisively. "So we pay one lawyer to say we could publish the story, and then we pay his partner to find out if that advice was right. Is that how it works? And didn't you screen the articles yourself?"

"Yes, I did," Slocum was forced to acknowledge, "but my approval was tentative. When I realized the significance of what Reed was writing, I talked with his boss, Howard Wolf, and we decided to turn it over to Cashman, who met with Reed and took over the vetting."

"Well, let's hope Cashman's advice was better than his partner's performance in court. From what I hear, it's a toss-up as to who's the biggest dunce in the courtroom — him or Reed."

Thinking that the Editor-in-Chief was done venting, Slocum continued. "Anyway, Cashman read the stories, talked with Reed, and gave us a written opinion that the stories were defensible."

"Defensible?" Curtis asked. "Since when is the test *defensible*? I thought the test was *accurate*."

"In libel cases brought by public figures — and Bennison is a public figure — the constitutional guarantee of a free press says we can write almost anything, even if we're wrong, as long as we're not acting out of malice or a reckless dis — "

"Damn it, I know what the Constitution says! But I never figured the Constitution should be used to skirt the truth. What is it with you lawyers? Anything goes as long as you can get away with it, is that it?"

Everyone in the room — other than Clive Curtis — felt badly for Todd Slocum. He was taking the brunt for publication of Reed's articles, but they all knew that if he had rejected them as being too inflammatory, he'd be in bigger trouble. It's the never-ending dilemma of the in-house lawyer: say yes and it's your fault if things go wrong; say no and you're hurting sales.

"Anyone else have something to say?" Clive Curtis asked.

"Yeah, I do," Todd Slocum said softly. He had already felt heat from Curtis in the past few minutes and wasn't eager to stick his neck out again. "Earlier you mentioned that you wanted to fire Reed. Now, I don't want to defend the guy; he put us all in a mess, and even if we win the case, our reputation will have a blot on it. And I guess I'm partly responsible for that. I could have been more aggressive about killing the stories. But here's the thing: if we give Reed the ax, it would be like announcing that his stories were pure bullshit. We can't fire him for writing the stories while, at the same time, we're in court trying to defend those same stories."

"Are you saying that I should wait until after the jury rules?" Curtis asked.

"No, you shouldn't do a thing until all the appeals run their course. No matter who wins the trial, there will be appeals, and we don't want the higher courts to get the idea that *we* think Reed shouldn't have written those stories."

"Todd, I know that's good advice, but you might tell his boss, Howard Wolf, that if he gives Reed a bonus this year, he'll pay it out of his own pocket."

CHAPTER 25

Meanwhile, a few blocks away, three men and a woman were huddled in an office high in another New York City skyscraper. Each was a high-ranking executive at Universal Brands, a huge company that included a conglomerate of brands, at least four of which sponsored Eddie Bennison for publicly endorsing their products. They were eagerly awaiting the daily call from their observer at the Bennison trial.

The office was Jack Clausen's, Universal Brands Executive Vice President of Marketing. "I always thought the guy was too good to be true," complained Clausen. "Nobody is that perfect. Looks like Adonis, has a beautiful family, gives a great interview, doesn't play around, and can hit a golf ball through the eye of a needle in the next county. We checked this guy out twenty ways to Sunday and he comes out clean as a whistle. And now *this!*"

"Relax, Jack." This from Al Singer, President of Universal's Golf Equipment division, Medalist. "The trial has barely started, and anything can happen. If Eddie wins, his name will sell even more golf clubs, cars, watches, and clothes than it did before the scandal broke. This trial could be the best thing that ever happened to us if Bennison wins, and, according to the coverage, he's on his way to winning."

"Yeah, sure," Clausen retorted, "and if he loses we're saddled with the face of a cheating pothead all over our ads and commercials and on our products. Forget the money we pay him; who'd buy anything with his name on it? Worse, we've got over thirty million tied up in product, future commercials, and print ads featuring Bennison, and if we yank them, we have nothing in the can to go with."

Buck Starr, Universal's Vice President of Public Relations, was deeper into this mess than any of the others. Not only was he the one who, seeing the potential of Bennison before most others, fought hard to sign him, but he was also the one who had been doing the damage control since the accusations against Bennison first saw daylight. "Look, we have to keep our options open and be prepared to go both ways," he was saying. "I've got two PR campaigns ready to go, depending on the outcome of the trial. If he wins, great; we'll come out with statements that we never had any doubts of his integrity, and we'll have some pieces with him thanking us for our support throughout his ordeal. And if he loses, we'll announce that he duped us like he duped everyone else. We'll just wait and see which way to go."

Clausen looked to Gloria Shepard, Universal's General Counsel and Chief Legal Officer. "Okay, Gloria, tell me about our right to cancel Bennison's contract under the morals clause. And please do it in terms we can all understand."

Shepard flinched at the dig, resenting the insinuation that, like many lawyers, she used convoluted language to explain a simple problem.

"From a legal point of view," she began, "it isn't all that complicated. If there is strong evidence that Bennison did in fact cheat or use improper drugs, we have every right to terminate his contracts. No problem."

"So," Clausen asked, "if he loses the case we can cut him loose, right?"

"No," the lawyer replied. "The jury could believe that he didn't cheat or use drugs, but he could still lose because the magazine made an innocent mistake in its accusations. In other words, since Bennison is a public figure, he can't win unless he proves both the lie and also that it was written with malice or a total disregard for the truth. So, if he loses, we still won't know if he cheated or used the drugs.

"Stated differently," she added, "if he wins, we'll know that the jury believed that he didn't cheat or take the drugs, but if he loses, we won't know whether it's because he was a bad guy or because he failed to prove that the magazine acted with malice or a disregard for the truth."

"So if he wins we can't use the moral clause?"

"Correct."

"And if he loses we still may not be able to use it?"

"Right."

"Then how is it that Hertz and those other companies were able to cancel the O.J. Simpson endorsement contracts? He won his case when the jury decided he didn't murder his wife and that other guy."

"Easy. The morals clause gives sponsors the right to cancel if the celebrity does something terribly wrong or — and the *or* is the crucial part — if he otherwise does something that taints the brand. In the O.J. case, virtually everyone in the world except the twelve people on the jury thought Simpson was guilty and a bad guy. So it was obvious that he was injurious to the brands he was endorsing, even if he was cleared of the murder charges. The morals clause was designed for such a case.

"But our case is different. Eddie Bennison is a far cry from O.J. Simpson in the minds of the public. He is a national hero. We can't safely use the morals clause unless there is clear proof — and I mean *clear* proof — that he cheated or used improper drugs."

Jack Clausen just shook his head. Finally he said, "Alright, Gloria, I want you to prepare a memo for me and for the board of directors with clear recommendations as to what we should do depending on the various possible outcomes of the trial. And if there is anything we should be doing now, while the trial is still in progress, put that in the memo as well. Please have it on my desk by noon tomorrow."

Just then, the phone on Clausen's desk rang. He pressed the button to activate the speaker so everyone could hear.

"Hi Jack, it's Nick, out here in Chicago. Court just let out for the day."

"How'd it go?" Clausen asked.

The voice from Chicago came through the speaker for all to hear. "Bennison's doing better here than when he won the Senior US Open. I mean, his lawyer — a guy named Charlie Mayfield — is making this reporter from *Tee Time* look like a world-class putz." The caller read from his notes to summarize the day's events, concluding with the clincher: "And dig this. By the time the reporter got off the witness stand, everyone in the room — and I mean *everyone* — was convinced that *he* cheated when he played golf at his country club. This guy Mayfield is something else; he made the reporter — not Bennison — look like the cheater."

The atmosphere in the room was much calmer after the call than it had been earlier. Maybe Universal Brand's enormous investment in Eddie Bennison looked good after all.

The only lawyer in the room, Gloria Shepard, was more guarded. She had seen enough lawsuits to know that there was a long way to go before the final aria.

But not even she could foresee — and she would never know — the strange route the case would take before the fat lady would sing.

MONDAY NIGHT

CHAPTER 26

Earlier, during the meeting at the *Tee Time* offices, Todd Slocum had his cell phone turned off. Now, heading for a waiting limo to take him to LaGuardia for his flight back to Chicago for the trial, he switched the phone on to check for messages. He saw three calls had come in from Max Reed within the past hour, and also a text message from the reporter: TODD — CALL MY CELL PHONE AS SOON AS YOU SEE THIS! URGENT! He dialed Reed's number and a frantic voice answered.

"Todd! Thank God you called!"

"Hey, Max. Another rough day, huh?"

"Rough? That's not even the word for it. Sitting on a witness stand for two days and getting beaten up by a guy like Charlie Mayfield ain't for sissies."

"You said it was urgent that we talk."

"Yeah, it sure is. Are you coming back out here tonight?"

"I'm on my way to the airport right now."

"Call me when you get in — I don't care how late. I don't want to talk about it on cell phones."

"Can you give me a hint?"

"Sure. It seems like our All-American boy is a sex whacko."

"Hi, Max. I just landed. I should be at the hotel in a half-hour. Let's meet in the bar."

By the time Todd Slocum got to the Palmer House, the hotel housing the *Tee Time* people during the trial, Max Reed was sitting at a booth in the hotel's posh bar with a double Jack Daniels already in front of him — and half gone.

It was late, and Slocum didn't want to waste a lot of time. "So what's this about the guy being a sex whacko?" he asked as soon as he sat down.

"Goes like this. I finished testifying this afternoon, and when I left the courtroom, there's this guy in the hall who came up and introduced himself. Said he had to talk to me, that it was important, and asked if we could go somewhere and talk. I said sure, as long as we go someplace where I could get a drink. That Mayfield prick really worked me over, and everybody on our side was treating me like a leper. So we find a place down the street and — "

"Who was this guy?"

"Said his name was Dan Curry. Maybe it's an alias. I didn't ask for ID, but he sounds like he has information we may be able to use." Reed looked up to see if Slocum was interested.

"Go on."

"Okay, after we order drinks, he tells me he's representing a young lady in Detroit who had a one-nighter with Bennison two or three years ago. They not only had a hell of a sex orgy, but according to her, he beat the hell out of her. She left with a shiner and a split lip."

"You say he's representing her? Is he a lawyer?"

"No, I asked him that. He said it's a business arrangement, and he has a letter of authorization from her. Her name is Elizabeth Peters. He met with her Saturday morning, heard her story, got the letter and some other stuff to confirm her story, and jumped on a plane to Chicago this morning in time to catch me leaving the courtroom."

Reed then related the story as told to him by Dan Curry, emphasizing again that Elizabeth Peters had a black eye and badly cut lip. Slocum didn't seem overly interested in the fact that Bennison may have shacked up one night two or three years earlier, although it was *something*. But when Reed mentioned the woman's cuts and bruises, Slocum came alive. "Can this be verified? Do we have anything besides this woman's word?"

Max Reed laughed for the first time in two days. "That's the first thing I asked. Shit, I've been a reporter my whole life, and the first thing I look for is backup. She can produce at least six or seven friends who saw her with Bennison in a bar, and she left with him. The two of them went to a room he had at the Marriott in the name of 'Ben Edwards' — cute play on words, huh? And we can put it together by date and place. She was at the hotel — it was outside of Detroit —for a birthday party in August 2007, and Bennison was staying there at the time, playing in a tournament nearby. We can prove the Peters girl was at the bar because she came with friends who will remember her being there; the date is easy to verify because it was a friend's birthday; and it's easy to prove that Bennison was in Detroit at the golf tournament. I'm sure we can get the hotel to produce a registration or credit card charges for Eddie Bennison, or Ben Edwards, on that same night."

"How can we show that Edwards is Bennison?"

"She can swear that she recognized him from his picture in the paper the other day, and she verified it by matching what he told her with what she has found about him on Google: living in Tulsa and working for a corrugated box plant." Reed paused to see if Slocum was following him, then continued. "Once we put the bloodhounds on this, I'm sure we'll find more."

"Any proof that he assaulted her?" Todd Slocum asked. Only a lawyer would say "assaulted" instead of "beat the shit out of."

"You're gonna love this, Counselor. She got home, and when her mother saw her, she had a fit. Her face looked like it had been in a meat grinder. She told her mother that she had been in an accident, but her mother saw right through that. When she got the truth, she wanted her daughter to go to the police and insisted on taking the pictures, right then, for evidence."

"Did she go to the police?"

"No. She's smart enough to know what that would entail. She convinced her mother to drop the idea and just write the whole thing off as a bad mistake and a bad result."

"Please tell me you have the pictures."

"There are indeed pictures — thank heavens for that. Her mother took them that night, and I've seen 'em on Curry's cell phone. She was a mess. I don't have hard copies yet, but this guy, Dan Curry, said he'll give them to me. That's part of the deal."

"Okay, I'm waiting. What does this Curry guy want?"

"For sworn statements from the Peters girl and her friends, and the pictures, a cool two million. And she'll testify or do anything else we want." Reed leaned back, took a long sip of his drink, and added, "Cheap at twice the price."

TUESDAY MORNING

CHAPTER 27

harlie Mayfield presented a case to a jury like a chef presents a fine meal to his diners. As the chef would separate two heavier courses with a sorbet to clear the palate, and add the perfect wine for accent, Charlie would break up the heavy with the light, the complex with the simple. The chef's aim was to keep the diner's appetite from waning, and Charlie's was to keep the jurors' interest from waning.

"The plaintiff calls Arturo Escalara to the witness stand," he announced when court reconvened on Tuesday morning. Those not familiar with golf looked around, asking themselves who this witness could be. But the golf fans knew Artie, Eddie Bennison's caddy, as they knew about Stevie Williams, who had been Tiger Woods' caddy, or Angelo Argea, who caddied for Jack Nicklaus in his prime.

Artie, wearing a well-fitted blue suit, walked confidently to the stand, took the oath, and looked directly at the jurors with a nod and a bright smile. "How you all doin'?" he asked them.

Judge Krause, like everyone else, did a double take after Artie's cheerful greeting to the jurors. The incident, of course, was not spontaneous. It was scripted by Charlie to present a contrast to the jury: Max Reed, the shifty reporter who concealed his sources and kept information from the jury versus Artie Escalara, the open, friendly witness who was there to answer questions to help the jury.

For the first few minutes, Artie talked about his background, how he first connected with Eddie, and how Eddie offered him the job over dinner during Q-School. "If I live to be a hundred," he said, "meeting Eddie Bennison will be the best day of my life. He took me out of the *barrio*, where we had to split an apple three ways, and opened up a new life for me." He made constant eye contact with the jurors, smiled at just the right places, and was highly respectful, always addressing Charlie as "Mr. Mayfield" or "Sir."

Charlie next asked him to describe briefly his duties as a tour caddie.

"Briefly?" Artie replied in mock astonishment, but with a grin. "Mr. Mayfield, there is so much to do that it's hard to be brief."

"Try."

"Well, let's start with what I have to do on the golf course. I have to carry the bag, give the yardages, help with the club selection, select the targets, read the greens, keep the ball and clubs clean, tend the pin, rake the traps, and keep Eddie in the right frame of mind. But — "

"One moment, Artie. Tell us what you mean by keeping Eddie in the right frame of mind."

"Yes, sir. Funny things get in a player's head out there, with all the pressure, and it happens to Eddie like the rest of them. Sometimes he gets negative thoughts, like, 'I better not hit it in the trees on the left.' Or he might get overconfident when he's in the lead, and get careless. And the worst thing is when he gets angry over a bad shot or a bad break. In all those cases, it's my job to read his mind and then talk him into thinking straight. Like with the tree thing, I might say, 'Hey, I don't see any trees out there; all I see is a big, wide fairway just waitin' for your ball. Ain't nothin' else out there — just a big, fat fairway and short, green grass.'"

"What if he gets angry, or down on himself?"

"Well, Eddie's a good guy, and he never gets steamed for more than a minute or two, but that could be enough to throw him off. If that happens after he hits a bad shot, I'll remind him that he's one of the best golfers in the world, or that Jack Nicklaus on his best day couldn't have pulled off that shot. One time, it was during the British Senior Open in Scotland and we're on a short par five. He flushed his second shot perfectly, but it was a little short and ended up in a deep pot bunker in front of the green.

He turned and glared at me, like I had given him the wrong yardage. He was really hot, and I had to cool him down fast. So I said, 'Hey, dummy, did you forget we're in Scotland? I'm giving you the distance in meters, so you have to add 10 percent to get the yardage.' He looked at me like I was crazy, and then slowly he saw that I was making a joke and started to smile. Thirty seconds later we're both laughing like a couple of school kids. The gallery couldn't figure out what was going on; our ball's in a deep bunker and we're hysterical. By the time we get to his ball, we're still giggling, but I'll be darned if he doesn't get it up and down for birdie."

"Artie, does your job require you to do things when you're not on the golf course?"

"You bet! For one thing, I have to protect Eddie. I know that sounds funny, but you have to remember that he's very popular. Crowds gather around him; they want autographs, pictures, even pieces of his clothing. Sometimes I have to protect him or he could get hurt. Then there's the press people who don't give him any space at all. There are even nuts out there who want to steal his clubs. Also, Eddie doesn't like having a lot of hangers-on — you know, aides, assistants, body guards, that kind of thing, so I do stuff like running to the cleaners, finding someone to cut his hair, getting his clubs re-gripped. Heck, sometimes he's so busy, either practicing or giving interviews, that I'll call Carol to let her know that he's okay and will call later."[9]

"Thanks, Artie. Now I'd like to change the subject and talk a little about some of Eddie's playing habits. First, let's talk about the way he marks his ball on the green. Does he have a specific routine?"

"Oh, sure. All the players do."

"Please describe for the jury how Eddie does it."

"As soon as he walks onto the green, he finds and repairs the pitch mark from where his ball landed. Then he looks to see where the other players' balls are so he won't step in their line when he goes to mark his ball. Now he walks over to his ball and, facing the hole, marks his ball with a coin, then tosses it to me to clean it off. When he does this, he always marks it with the 'heads' side of the coin facing up."

"Why is that?"

"Well, if his coin is in the line of another player, he'll be asked to move it one or two club head distances to the left or right. When he does this, he'll place the coin with the 'tails' side up. That should remind him, when it's his turn to putt, to move his coin back to the original place. Otherwise it's a penalty. By the way, it's also my job to make sure he doesn't slip up and forget to move the coin back."

"Thank you. And when he puts his coin behind the ball, how close to the ball does he put it?"

"He's very careful to place the coin about a half inch behind the ball."

"And why is that?" Charlie took a quick glance at the jury; he wanted to be sure they didn't miss this exchange. "Why not place it right up against the ball?"

"Well, a lot of players do place the coin or other marker right up against the ball, but most leave a little space. The rule only says that the marker should be placed immediately behind the ball, and that the ball should later be replaced in its original spot. By leaving a little space, the player is less likely to move the ball when marking it, and that could create a mess — maybe a penalty. The grass is really short on those greens, and if the player accidentally touched the ball with the coin, it would cause the ball to roll several inches — even more if it it's on a slope. Now you're looking at a penalty. Who needs that? That's why Eddie is extra careful to leave a little space between the coin and the ball."

"So, if someone saw Eddie replace his ball a half inch in front of his coin, and that person didn't see him earlier place his coin a half inch *behind* his ball, might that person mistakenly conclude that Eddie improperly placed his ball too close to the hole?"

"Objection!" Roz Berman interjected. "It's not for this witness to assume what some other person might conclude. It calls for speculation and conjecture."

"Sustained," Judge Krause ruled. "We now have testimony as to how the plaintiff's ball is marked and replaced. It's up to the jury to decide how that may be perceived by a bystander, and that's a subject that counsel may address in their closing arguments."

"That's fine, Judge," Charlie said, knowing the jury got the message from his last question. Then, looking back to Artie, he asked, "Are you aware of the accusation, made in *Tee Time*, that Eddie somehow uses dirt to alter the amount of spin on his ball?"

Artie chuckled, according to the script, and replied, "You mean the article written by Max Reed?"

Also sticking to the script, Charlie followed up, "Yes, and may I ask what's so funny?"

"Well, when that article came out, it got a lot of laughs out on the Tour. It became a running joke. If a player's ball backed up away from the hole, he'd look at his caddie with a grin and say, 'We didn't put enough dirt in the grooves,' and if the ball rolled past the hole he'd say, 'Less dirt next time,' or 'We filled four grooves, and we should've filled only three.'" Then Artie looked at the jury and said, "That Reed guy — he must have been smokin' something when he wrote that."

The laughter throughout the courtroom ended when Charlie asked his next question.

"Artie, according to Mr. Reed, it's only when Eddie takes a practice swing with his short irons that he takes divots, and that he never takes them with his practice swings before full shots. Is Mr. Reed correct with that observation?"

"Yeah, he is. Whenever Eddie is preparing for a full shot, his practice swing is just to make sure his muscles are loose, that his shirt isn't restricting his swing, and to relieve any tension. Also, if he wants to work the ball a certain way, he may practice taking the club back a little inside or outside, or releasing it a little sooner or later, just to get the feel of what he wants to do. But those practice swings are never intended to be an exact duplicate of the actual full shot where the club head will be traveling more than a hundred miles per hour."

"What about the short shot of, say, 75 yards?"

"Well, that's different. On a full shot, the player will always swing at about the same speed. But a short shot is different. The player wants to rehearse the *exact* speed and tempo of the stroke he's about to make. With a 75-yard shot, Eddie has to get his mind set on that exact yardage; he can't make the mistake of hitting it 65 or 85 yards. So he'll take a few swings at the tempo he'll need for just that yardage, and he'll want that practice swing to be exactly the swing he wants to put on the ball for the shot, both as to tempo and for whether he wants to hit it high or low. Heck, he may do that five or six times until he feels he's got it just right and can repeat it over the ball. If he wants to hit it low, he may play the ball back and keep his wrists stiffer, and in that case, that's the practice swing he makes."

Artie paused for a moment, and then added, "You have to remember, Mr. Mayfield, that a long iron shot will travel about the same distance every time, depending on the wind. So Eddie'll hit a 4-iron only when he has to go between 225 and 240 yards. If the hole is a little farther out than that, he'll hit his 3-iron, and if he's a little closer, he'll hit his 5-iron. But he has to make a lot more adjustments for the short irons. For example, he might hit his pitching wedge anywhere from 100 yards to 150 yards, so he has to take practice swings that will duplicate the exact swing he needs for that shot. That's why his practice swings with the short irons have to be very exact, and since he always takes a divot with the short irons, he takes similar divots on his practice swings with the short irons.

"What I'm trying to say is this: with a long iron shot, the target is pretty large — usually anywhere on the putting green is okay, and within twenty feet is great. But with the short irons — we call those the scoring clubs — we try to get the ball within just a few feet of the hole. That's why we have to be more exact as we get closer."

To prove his point, Artie looked toward the jurors and said, "Next time you're watching golf on TV, take a look at what the players do before a shot. When they're about to hit a full shot with a driver or a long iron, you'll never see them take a practice swing at full speed. At the very most, they'll take a couple of slow swings just to stretch their muscles and be sure their shirt isn't restricting the swing.

"But when they're about to hit a delicate pitch shot, you'll see them take several practice swings at exactly the speed and arc that they will want to duplicate when they hit the shot."

"Okay," Charlie nodded, indicating that the testimony was clear and not open to dispute. "But after Eddie takes those practice swings for the shorter shots, doesn't he clean the grooves?"

Again, Artie smiled. "I guess it's a good question. Whenever Eddie hands me a club *after* he makes a shot, I routinely wipe it off with a damp towel, and I do this in every case regardless of the club and regardless of whether there's dirt on the club face. But he doesn't hand me the club after *practice* swings. For one thing, by then I'm standing maybe 25 or 30 feet away from him, and it would be awkward and take too much time to run back and clean off the club. For another, he's really able to get the club face clean with the sole of his shoe. Just watch the pros on the practice range; after *every single shot* they get rid of the excess mud with the sole of their shoe, *always*. They do it every time. It's a habit with them, just like a dog scratches at the grass after doing his business."

This brought more laughter throughout the courtroom. When it subsided, Charlie signaled to an assistant who turned down the lights and projected a film on the screen. The film showed a line of golfers on a practice range. "Let the record show that we are displaying a film taken before the final round of this year's US Open. It depicts sixteen professional golfers preparing for that final round, nearly all of whom are hitting iron shots. We direct your attention to what the golfers do with the club face after each shot."

Artie's canine comparison couldn't have been more accurate. Every one of the golfers, after every one of their shots, used his shoe to clean the club face of dirt. Some used the side of the sole, and some used the toe, and some even struck the club face against the heel of their shoe to shake off dirt. But, as Artie said, they all did it, and each one did it the same way every time.

Charlie then nodded to the assistant, and a moment later the screen showed another film. "This film was given to us by NBC. It was taken by their cameras during coverage of the 2005 Senior Open and shows Eddie Bennison preparing to hit a wedge shot to the 18th green. Please note that this film was made before the articles in *Tee Time*, so there was no reason for Eddie to act differently than he always does." The film showed Eddie taking two practice swings, each with a small shallow divot. After each swing, he instinctively scraped the face of the club against the sole of his shoe. It was not until after making the shot that he handed the club to Artie, who by now had returned to Eddie's side, and that was when Artie did a thorough cleaning of the club face. The two films corroborated Artie's testimony perfectly.

After the lights were again turned up, Charlie asked Artie if using the sole of the shoe does a sufficient job of cleaning the club face.

"Well, if the turf is really soft, and there's a lot of mud on the club face, then he *might* hand the club to me so I could wipe it off before he makes the shot. But if just a little dirt is left deep in the grooves, so what? It makes no difference whatsoever, regardless of what Max Reed says."

"And how would you know that?"

"Everyone who plays golf knows that."

"Objection!" This from Roz Berman. "How could this witness know what everyone — "

Before she could finish her objection, and before Judge Krause could rule, Charlie raised his hand. "Never mind, I'll use other witnesses to make that point: witnesses who play golf for a living."[10]

━━━━━━━━━━━

Over the noon recess, and back at Charlie's office for sandwiches, Charlie had a question for his client. "Eddie, when you win a tournament, what kind of bonus do you pay Artie?"

"I pay him a salary plus 7 percent of my winnings. But when I win, I give him 10 percent. Why?"

"Because, if you win this case, you should give him a bonus. He was a wonderful witness. He played off the script perfectly, and I could see that the jury ate him up."

"Swell," Eddie laughed. "Between your third and his bonus, and all the expenses, I'll have nothing left."

Charlie took another bite of his roast beef on rye and said, "You'll have your name back, Eddie, and if we win this case it'll be worth more than ever." He wiped his mouth with the napkin and added, "And anyway, Artie and I need it more than you do."

"By the way, Charlie, now that we're on that subject," Eddie said, "I want you to know that I've kept Artie on my payroll since I've been off the Tour for the trial. I figured that he wasn't earning a cent while I wasn't playing, and it wasn't fair to him to go broke because of those rotten stories. So I've been paying him about a thousand a week, even though that's less than he was earning when I was winning. Is that okay?"

"Why wouldn't it be okay?"

"Because you told me that we can't pay witnesses to testify unless they're special kinds of witnesses — like experts in some field. And Artie's a witness for us. It didn't occur to me until just now that it might be a mistake for me to have him on the payroll."

Charlie smiled. "Not to worry, Eddie, it's perfectly alright. You've been paying him as an employee — not as a witness. And it's a decent thing for you to be doing. I'm sure you want to keep him from taking another job so he'll be available when you go back on Tour, so it makes sense. But just so there are no loose ends, I'll mention it to Roz Berman. It's a way for me to show her that we're being open and not hiding anything."

CHAPTER 28

Today the defense team was having lunch at the table reserved for them at The Barrister's Grille around the corner from the courthouse. Hugo Shoemaker was complaining that Artie's testimony was obviously scripted and rehearsed, "right down to that stupid metaphor about the dog crappin' in the grass and that Max Reed must have been smoking something."

Roz Berman replied, once again making the point that Shoemaker didn't understand the first thing about trial work. "People who don't try a lot of cases don't understand the degree to which good trial lawyers prep their witnesses; they even tell them what to wear. For example, that Artie character wears an earring when he caddies for Bennison; you can see it on the film clips. But Charlie didn't let him wear it on the stand. And I'll bet that lovely suit he was wearing had a price tag on it yesterday."

To underscore her point, she reminded Shoemaker of the lame attempt he made to cross-examine Artie after Charlie was done with the witness, a cross-examination that Shoemaker insisted on handling in order to demonstrate to the jury that the caddie's testimony had been rehearsed. Unfortunately for Shoemaker, he made a classic mistake that no seasoned trial lawyer would ever make. According to the official transcript of the court reporter, it went like this:

Q: Mr. Escalara, my name is Hugo Shoemaker. Prior to taking the stand this morning, did you and Mr. Mayfield go over the testimony you would be giving?

A: Yes, sir.

Q: And did Mr. Mayfield go over all the questions he would be asking you?

A: Yes, sir.

Q: And did he tell you what answers to give to those questions?

A: No, sir, but he did give me some guidance.

Q: Guidance? Really? And what kind of guidance did he give you?

A: He said, "Artie, when you're up there on the stand, I want you to tell the truth. Even if you think the answer could hurt Eddie, you must tell the truth." And that's just what I did, Mr. Shoemaker. I told the truth like my mother's life depended on it. Even if I hadn't sworn to God to tell the truth, I knew I would disgrace myself and my family if I lied. I even went to church this morning before court and prayed to God for the strength to follow Mr. Mayfield's advice and stick to the truth even if I thought it might hurt Eddie. And God gave me the strength to do just that. I told the truth. Only the truth.

As Roz Berman had often lamented since she was retained by the defense, Hugo Shoemaker was an idiot when it came to jury trials. So he fell into Charlie Mayfield's trap. And yes, Artie's final answer to Shoemaker — *the answer that used the word "truth" seven times and "God" three times* — was precisely the answer Charlie had rehearsed with Artie, just in case one of the defense lawyers was dumb enough to ask an open-ended question about their prep sessions.

CHAPTER 29

As both legal teams were finishing their lunches, four men in golf attire were just sitting down to a buffet lunch in the men's grill at the Champions Club in Houston, the site of that week's Senior Tour event. The four were competing in the event that was to be played that week and had just come off the practice range.

"Did you guys see the paper this morning?" Denny Riggs asked. "Looks like Eddie's doing alright."

"I'd say so," Jimmy Jamison said. "They read some of the testimony on the Golf Channel last night. I always thought that Max Reed was a hack writer, but Eddie's lawyer made him sound like the biggest jackass on the planet. I think Eddie'll hit the jackpot, and *Tee Time* deserves what it gets. They had no right to print that shit about Eddie."

R.J. Wilson volunteered, "I know nothing about Eddie using drugs, but it would surprise me if it were true. The guy never smokes, and I've never seen him drink. He's very straight, and doesn't seem the type.

"And as far as cheating, I played a lot of tournament rounds with Eddie, and I've never seen him shade the rules at all. He's not even like some of the guys out here who play cute little games to distract an opponent. You know, like moving or standing too close when you're about to hit a shot. That stuff goes on all the time, but I've never seen Eddie do it."[11]

Riggs chuckled and said, "Everyone says that Seve Ballesteros was the master at distracting an opponent, but I think that Lee Trevino was the all-time champ, even though his motives were pure. It's just that he never stopped talking, and it drove the other guys nuts. One time, a competitor asked him on the first tee, 'Lee, would it be okay if we don't talk during the round today?' and Trevino said, 'You don't have to talk; you only have to listen.'"[12]

Jimmy Jamison leaned back and sighed. "People always have something to complain about. If some guy was paired with Tiger Woods on a Sunday, and he wore a red shirt, I suppose someone would say he was trying to get under Tiger's skin because Tiger always wears a red shirt on Sundays. Screw that! If I was lucky enough to be paired with Tiger on a Sunday, I'd come out there lookin' like a friggin' fire engine.

"But I've never heard anyone accuse Eddie of playing those kinds of games. As far as I'm concerned, he's a gentleman through and through. And if he did any of the things that Reed wrote, we'd all know about it long before the articles came out."

"Just the same," Dave White commented, "it hasn't been the same out here on the Tour since those damned articles came out. Eddie's been getting the cold shoulder from the other guys, and I understand that the other wives are avoiding Carol. In fact, Joey, my caddie, tells me that Eddie's caddie, Artie, hasn't been invited to the caddies' Wednesday night poker games. And Joey's pissed because Artie has a lot of money — and he's a lousy poker player."

"Right," Denny Riggs chimed in, "and I'm afraid that every time I mark my ball or wipe off my club that someone's making a video of how I do it. Goddamned reporters!

"And all that crap about drugs," Riggs added. "I have one pocket in my golf bag that could stock a Walgreens. Between my allergies, my arthritis, and my bum back, I carry around so much shit that I could probably win the Kentucky Derby." After a few seconds, he added, "And that goes for a hell of a lot of other guys out here. For cryin' out loud, we're talking about golf, not the summer Olympics where everything is based on strength and speed. Does anyone really think that a performance-enhancing drug could help us read the grain of a green or shave 3 yards off a 6-iron?"

TUESDAY EVENING

CHAPTER 30

On the Tuesday following his Monday night meeting with Max Reed, when Reed told him about Liz Peters, Todd Slocum came to the courthouse to watch Artie Escalara testify. He was impressed how Charlie Mayfield had milked the caddie's testimony to the last drop. Clearly the jury bought Artie, hook, line, and sinker.

Now Slocum had to make some decisions. Max Reed had given him an ace of spades, and Slocum was trying to figure out the best way to play it. The Liz Peters story was too good to pass up, but he feared that Hugo Shoemaker, the magazine's chief lawyer at the trial, would balk at playing that card. To Slocum, this was the stuff of the street lawyers; it was not the stuff of Yale law professors. *But if I can authenticate the story, I might be able to get Shoemaker to run with it.*

Sitting in the back of the cab after court adjourned, heading to Chicago's O'Hare Airport, Slocum took out his cell phone and dialed one of the numbers Reed had given him.

"Hello. This is Dan Curry."

"Hi Dan, my name is Todd Slocum. I'm with *Tee Time* magazine. Max Reed gave me your name. You flew to Chicago to meet with him yesterday, and I'd like to fly to Detroit tonight to meet with you — and also with your, uh, client, Elizabeth Peters . . . Okay, I'll call you within the hour to let you know when I'll be getting to Detroit, and then you can tell me where we should meet — the three of us."

━━━━━━━━━━

Dan Curry, Elizabeth Peters, and Todd Slocum were sitting in the lounge of the Hilton near the airport in Detroit, where Slocum would be spending the night.

"I want to thank you both for driving over here tonight to meet with me."

Dan Curry was smiling like the cat that ate the canary. "No problem, Mr. Slocum. Can I call you Todd?"

"Certainly. And you, too, Ms. Peters."

"Call me Liz. Everyone does."

"Okay, Liz, Dan — we all know why we're here. So, Liz, why don't you tell me what happened with you and Eddie Bennison?"

"Well — "

Dan Curry put his hand over hers and said, *"I'll* tell Todd what happened that night." Clearing his throat, he continued. "It was August 17, 2007. Liz was with some friends at a birthday party, and they ended up in the cocktail lounge at the Marriott in Pontiac. That creep, Bennison, was sitting at a nearby table — he was in town for the golf tournament being held at Oakland Hills that week. It's easy to verify that he was playing in the tournament. Anyway, he comes over to the table where Liz — "

"No, Dan," Liz Peters interrupted. *"I* went over to *his* table on the way to the john. I know it sounds crazy, but it was totally innocent. I thought it was odd that a guy his age would be sitting in a bar reading a book, especially with the loud music playing, so as I went by his table, I casually mentioned that it must be a good book. I can't remember what he said next, but we chatted for a minute and then he must have invited me to sit down, because I did. We talked some more, and I had another drink or two, and eventually he asked if I'd like to have a nightcap in his room. I said that would be fine."

"Had he already given you his name?"

"Not exactly. He told me his name was Ben Edwards — kind of a reversal of his real name."

"So how did you figure out that he was really Eddie Bennison?"

"I didn't until a few days ago. I happened to see his picture in the paper — it was a story about his trial going on in Chicago — and his name was under the picture."

"And from merely seeing his picture you remembered it was the guy you met in Detroit a couple of years earlier?"

"It's a face I'll never forget!"

"And why is that?"

"Because he beat the hell out of me. Wouldn't you remember the face of a guy who gave you a shiner and a split lip?"

"Can you tell me why he did that to you?"

"How in the hell would I know? I certainly didn't provoke him. We went to his room and were having sex," she said matter-of-factly, as if it were the most casual thing in the world, "and he got a little rough — a few slaps on my butt, that kind of thing. Then it got worse with the pinching, jabbing, and harder slaps. Right then I tried to call it quits — I tried to push him away and crawl out of the bed, but he pulled me back and belted me in the face once or twice. I actually thought the bastard was going to kill me."

Then Slocum asked, "How did you get out of there?"

"Well, first I ran into the john to look in the mirror to see what the hell I looked like. My lower lip was bleeding, and even then my eye was starting to swell. Then I came back into the room wrapped in a towel, sat down in a chair, and cried like a baby. He was still lying in the bed and didn't say a word.

"After a minute or two, I got up and dressed, then I walked over to the desk to get my purse. My mother was always worried about my safety, and she bought me some mace to carry with me in case I was ever attacked. I took out the mace, threw my coat on, and walked over to the bed and said, 'I'm leaving now.'

"Just as I opened the door to go, I turned, walked over to the bed, and, cool as a cucumber, I gave him a long shot of mace right in his eyes. He started screaming and howling, and I hightailed it out of the room, carrying my purse and coat. I was worried that he'd try to catch me, but I got a good head start; he didn't have any clothes on and was out of commission because of the mace."

Todd Slocum was taking notes. He looked up to ask, "Did you report the incident to the police, or to hotel security?"

"Hell no, I just wanted to get out of there and get home. And think about it — who would pay any attention to a girl who picked up a guy in a saloon and willingly went to his room to get laid? The police would say that I got just what I asked for."

After a minute more of taking notes, Slocum put down his ballpoint pen. "I believe every word you said, Liz, but would anyone else? Can anyone else verify any of this?"

"The girls I was with all saw me sitting with him. And then, just as we were leaving to go upstairs, I went over to tell them that I was going to his room. I'm sure they'll remember. I can give you their names and numbers."

"Anything else?"

"Well, you could check with the Marriott. I'll bet they have a room reservation for that night for Edward Bennison — or for Ben Edwards." Liz Peters paused for a moment and then added, "And if you check, you should find that a Mr. Ed Bennison — or a Mr. Edwards — put some drinks on his room tab."

"But how can we verify the injuries?"

Dan Curry, who had been silent for some time, nudged her arm. "Show him the pictures, Liz."

Todd Slocum studied the pictures that Liz Peters's mother had insisted she take, and they did indeed show the injuries she had described. After what seemed forever to Dan Curry and Liz Peters, Slocum finally leaned forward with his elbows on the table, and asked, "And why are you telling me all this? What exactly is it that you want from me?"

Though he didn't show it, Slocum was as nervous as a new bride. For one thing, his benign corporate law practice had never involved a mess as sordid as this one. But even more touchy was the fact that this was starting to smell like blackmail or extortion, and it was getting too hot to handle.

Dan Curry, looking smug, decided it was time for him to do business. "Look, Todd, we all know that your magazine is on the hook for millions of dollars if Eddie Bennison wins this case. And Vegas is giving big odds that he'll win, especially after that nutcase reporter of yours testified."

"So what does this have to do with me?"

"As if you don't know?" Dan Curry was working up a head of steam. "There's only one way you can win this case, and everybody knows it. You have to show that the famous Eddie Bennison is no angel. In fact, you have to show that he's the kind of a guy who would cheat on the golf course. And the jurors will know that a guy who can cheat on his wife would cheat on the golf course."

Curry leaned further forward, and with his nose just inches away from Slocum's, added, "And all the more so if the guy also beats the shit out of women!"

Slocum knew that Dan Curry had a point, as distasteful as it was. "Let's cut to the chase, Dan. What do you want?"

"Two million dollars, and you know that it's worth a hell of a lot more than that to that magazine of yours. Give us that, and Liz will testify as to what happened that night. If you prefer, she'll give her story to the newspapers. Or she'll do both. Up to you."

Looking to Liz Peters, Slocum asked, "Are you married, Liz?"

Curry answered for her. "No, she isn't, so she has no reason not to tell her story."

"Doing it your way wouldn't work," Slocum explained. "It would be impossible to cover up any payment — especially a large payment — to Liz or to you. Once that came out, and you can bet it will, *Tee Time* would be out of business. And if we did anything to leak that story to the press, the judge would hold us in contempt of court for improperly trying to influence the jury. And it would be even worse if we put her on the witness stand to testify and it came out later that we paid for her testimony. No thanks, jail's not for me. And I'd lose my law license to boot."

Dan Curry flashed a big grin. "But, you're here, aren't you? And don't tell me you flew out here to Detroit in the middle of the night to tell us to go to hell. You knew we had information that could save your ass, and you love our story. You've written down every word of it, and you're as excited as a dog in heat. So if our plan is no good, Mr. Slocum, tell us yours."

"I don't have a plan yet. I'd have to discuss it with our legal team. They're in charge of the case, and everything's up to them. But I can't convince them that we have anything here unless I can show them the pictures of Liz and her beaten-up face, and also a written statement from her."

Curry didn't want to turn over anything to Slocum unless he got something in return, but he understood that Slocum was probably helpless to make a deal without talking to others.

Slocum pressed on. "So here's what we have to do. Liz will have to put her story in a written statement — an affidavit, and swear under oath that it's true. She can do that before any notary public. Then we have to get documents to support it, such as copies of the hotel registration, statements from her girlfriends, and of course the pictures.

"If you can get all that to me, I'll meet with our lawyers and see what we can do for you."

"Can I talk with Liz for a minute?" Dan Curry asked.

"Sure, I'll wait out in the lobby."

A few minutes later, Curry came out to the lobby where Todd Slocum was looking at a newspaper. He handed Slocum the pictures showing a battered face, and also a couple of typed pages. "I'm going to take you at your word, Todd, that you won't do anything with these other than show them to the other lawyers. This information doesn't go any further unless Liz — and I — agree."

Slocum had begun to read the typed pages when Curry said, "You mentioned before that you wanted a notarized statement from Liz. We beat you to it. I already prepared one for her to sign, and that's what you're reading. We went to a car dealer where they had a notary." Curry grinned and said, "The guy charged us 50 cents to notarize her signature — pretty good investment, wouldn't you say?"

━━━━━━━━━━━

Later that evening, Todd Slocum phoned Hugo Shoemaker from Detroit to tell him that he was flying to Chicago on an early morning flight and would like to meet with Shoemaker and Berman as soon as possible after he arrived.

Shoemaker never asked why Slocum wanted to meet, but such meetings between the client and lawyer were routine. "Court convenes at 9:00 tomorrow morning," Shoemaker replied. "We can meet in the courtroom before then. If you're later than that, we'll meet during the first recess or over lunch."

WEDNESDAY

CHAPTER 31

With the time change, Slocum was able to book a flight back to Chicago that landed at O'Hare Airport the next morning before nine, and, without luggage, he was able to get a cab to the Cook County Courthouse in plenty of time for the mid-morning recess in the trial. He, Shoemaker, and Roz Berman were now huddled and talking softly at the far end of the corridor outside the courtroom during the recess.

"And to what do we owe the pleasure?" Hugo Shoemaker asked.

Slocum had been rehearsing for this since the night before, but he was still tense.

"I've got hard evidence, including pictures, that our fair-haired boy, Eddie Bennison, not only had an affair with a young lady in Detroit — not his wife — but also that he violently assaulted her." With that, Slocum showed Berman the horrendous pictures of Liz Peters, but surreptitiously, so that no one nearby could see them. "And here's a sworn statement from the young lady herself. I can easily get corroborating evidence, including hotel reservations and statements from people who saw them together."

Shoemaker glanced at the photos and, shaking his head, muttered, "And what are you expecting us to do with this, Todd? It has nothing to do with the case. I hope you're not suggesting — "

Roz Berman interrupted. "Wait a minute, Hugo, before you get all sanctimonious about this. We all knew that Bennison was too perfect to be true, and that there had to be a flaw — hopefully a serious flaw — somewhere. We've all been looking for that flaw since he filed this lawsuit — that was a few years ago — and we never found it, not until now. Todd just gave us the gift of a lifetime, provided we play it right."

"And just how should we play it, Roz?" Shoemaker asked, his arms folded in front of him.

"I'll have to think about it." Then, after a few seconds, she said, "Maybe I'll invite Charlie to have a drink after court this afternoon."

CHAPTER 32

"**S**omething tells me that this little tête-à-tête is not a social one," Charlie Mayfield said while stirring his martini.

Roz Berman, sipping from her vodka gimlet, smiled and playfully fluttered her eyelashes. "Oh, Charlie, you know how I've been trying to get you away from Marge for the past thirty years. I'm finally making my moves."

Charlie laughed out loud. "Come on, Roz, I'm too old and gullible for this."

"You're neither, Charlie. But you're right, this is business, and not pleasant business."

The gray-haired lawyer, so robust in a courtroom, showed no reaction other than to smile and nod, as if to say *okay, let's hear what you have to say.*

Taking the cue, Berman pursed her lips and began. "Charlie, I know you think the world of Eddie Bennison."

Mayfield nodded. "Roz, after all these years I know you well enough to know that you don't bluff. I don't know if you have a cobra in your purse or a gun in your bra, but something tells me I'm not going to like this."

"No, you won't, but I think we should talk about it before our team springs any surprises in the courtroom."

"Ah, I smell a threat."

"Your nose is good, Charlie, but please, don't use that word. What I have for you is not a threat, it's an opportunity."

"The aroma gets stronger."

Roz Berman couldn't contain her smile. "Alright, Charlie, let's get to brass tacks." With that, she leaned over to pick up her bag that was sitting on the floor beside her — it was somewhere between a large purse and a small briefcase — and retrieved a manila envelope. Then she slowly held up two pictures of Liz Peters' battered face. "Your boy, Eddie, did this two years ago in Detroit. The young lady's name is Liz Peters. The two of them shared a room at a Marriott in Detroit." Embellishing just a bit, she added, "We have the reservation confirmation. By the way, your 'white knight' client reserved the room in the name of Ben Edwards — cute play on words, right? And as you can see, their sex play got a little out of hand."

Berman then handed Charlie a couple of printed pages. "This is a copy of a sworn statement from Ms. Peters telling the whole story — under oath."

While an impassioned Charlie Mayfield could telegraph any emotion he desired in a courtroom, he could likewise become a sphinx to mask any emotion when it served his purpose. And it served his purpose this time.

After studying the photographs and the statement, he calmly looked the other lawyer in the eye and said, "Roz, this is beneath you. This is the kind of crap I expect from second-rate divorce lawyers, or from shysters who make a living from squeezing deadbeats. But you? This doesn't make sense."

Berman didn't fall for it. "It might not make sense to you, Charlie, but it will sure make sense to Eddie Bennison. If you ask him, Charlie, and it's your duty to ask him, he'll beg you to dismiss your lawsuit to avoid having the world hear Liz Peters tell her story. And that's just what you should do, Charlie, to protect your client: dismiss the suit."

"And just how would you manage to get her on the stand?" Mayfield replied. "This case involves the question of whether Eddie Bennison cheated on the golf course and whether he used certain drugs. Those are only two issues, Roz. But there is nothing in the case — nothing at all — involving Eddie Bennison's sexual activities. Therefore, any testimony of this Peters woman would be irrelevant, and I'll keep her the hell off the stand."

"You may be able to object to her testimony, Charlie, but once the jury — and the press — see her and hear her name, it won't be long before the story will be out."

"And this bimbo you found — how much are you paying her to ruin my client's life, and her life too, when I'm done with her?"

"I know nothing of any payment — or promises of payment — to her." Roz Berman was speaking the truth, because she intentionally never asked. But she knew that she'd have to find out about that if Peters took the stand because, sure as hell, that would be Charlie's first question on cross-examination.

Roz Berman was a smart lawyer, and she knew that putting Liz Peters on the stand could backfire on her. That's why she hoped that Charlie would take the bait and either dismiss the case or settle for pennies on the dollar just to keep her off the stand. Of course, she knew Charlie well enough to know that he would not take the bait, but he still had a duty to discuss this with Eddie Bennison and, Roz hoped, Bennison would panic and direct Charlie to drop the case before allowing this torrid story to be highlighted in papers and newscasts throughout the world.

Charlie took the last sip from his martini, arose, and announced, "This meeting is over, Roz. See you in the morning."

"Take these with you," Roz Berman said, handing Charlie the photographs and the two-page typed statement signed by Elizabeth Peters. "Take these with you, and show them to your client in case he needs a reminder of what he did that night."

CHAPTER 33

As Charlie Mayfield and Roz Berman were sitting down to have their cocktails, Todd Slocum nervously walked into the imposing office of his boss, Clive Curtis, Editor-in-Chief of *Tee Time*. It was just past six in the evening in New York, but almost everyone at the magazine was still working.

"Hi, Todd. What's up?"

Slocum chose the upright chair facing Curtis from the opposite side of his desk. *If he's going to shoot me, I may as well give him an easy shot.*

"We might have stumbled into a lucky break on the Bennison case."

Curtis' eyebrows shot up. "Really? Tell me about it."

"Well, we have some bombshell evidence that Bennison has been doing some bad things — some *very* bad things — and it might turn things around for us."

"What kind of bad things?"

"Well, I don't know that I should give you the details. We lose our advantage if this thing gets out before — "

Clive Curtis interrupted him in mid-sentence. "I understand your concern for confidentiality and keeping it among the lawyers, Todd, but I'm in charge here and I want to know what the hell you have up your sleeve."

"I sure understand your position, Clive, but — "

"Don't 'but' me! As soon as I heard that Reed was writing those friggin' articles, I started running around here like a nervous wreck. I knew they could explode in our faces. Our readership is full of golfers and golf fans who idolize Eddie Bennison, and I knew that throwing shit at that guy would piss all of them off. And I was even more worried that Reed's articles weren't true, and that could result in a lawsuit — like the lawsuit we have right now!

"So, scared to death that we could lose readers, and at the same time lose a lawsuit that could put us out of business, I ran straight to your office. I remember that, Todd. And I remember you telling me there was nothing to worry about. You assured me the story was thoroughly vetted by you and by Hugo Shoemaker's partner. And you also told me that it was our duty to run the story because it was newsworthy and because our readers had some kind of sacred 'right to know.'

"Every publisher in the world knows that the 'right to know' is plain bullshit used as a justification to spread more bullshit! Pulp magazines claim that the public has a 'right to know' that a movie star is really an alien from outer space, or that he screws goats. And TV networks demand the right to film executions in the interest of the public's 'right to know.'

"And I'll tell you something else, Todd," Clive Curtis said in a raised voice as he leaned toward Slocum, so close that their faces were scarcely three feet apart. "Since you're such a proponent of that 'right to know' bullshit, I've got a right to know what the hell you and your fucking lawyers have on Eddie Bennison, and I want to know about it before anyone else finds out about it! Is that clear enough for you, or do I have to paint you a picture?" Curtis paused to catch his breath and sit back in his chair. "So, Todd, if anyone has a 'right to know,' it's my 'right to know' what the hell is going on around here with you and your lawyer friends."

Todd Slocum could hardly breathe. It would be easy enough to tell Curtis about Liz Peters' story and how she could tell the world that Bennison was both an adulterer and a woman beater. In fact, Curtis would probably like to hear that. But, if he told Curtis that much, it would lead to more questions that Slocum wanted to avoid — questions like, "Are we giving her anything for her story?" or "Did you vet her story better than you vetted Reed's story?"

In desperation, Todd Slocum resorted to the age-worn excuse lawyers use when they don't want to reveal information: "Clive, I'd love to be able to tell you everything we know, but, once you know it, you'd have to testify to it if asked. So I'm really protecting you by keeping you in the dark."

Hearing that, the Editor-in-Chief quickly rose and leaned even closer to Todd Slocum, whose face was getting whiter by the second. "Protecting me? Did you say you were protecting me? You should have thought about protecting me when you approved that dog-shit article of Reed's. Now I've got a board of directors all over my ass, and the hot shots at Globe Publications — they own us, remember? — they don't even return my calls. And I get hate mail every day the papers carry news about the trial. If this case goes south, and according to the papers it's going to the deep south, I'll be the laughingstock of the entire publishing world. And for sure I'll be out of a job. So thanks, Todd, for protecting me. I owe you."

To Slocum's dismay, Clive Curtis wasn't done. "So tell me, Todd — tell me about this bombshell that's going to win the case for us. I need some good news. And don't worry about protecting me from having to testify to it — I'll say I learned it from you, my attorney, and we all know that the 'attorney-client' privilege means that I don't have to reveal what my attorney tells me in confidence. I learned that much from your goddamned trial."

The lawyer squirmed in his chair for a few seconds, and finally decided to go ahead and spill the beans — but in a way that might somewhat insulate him in the eyes of his boss.

Taking a deep breath, Slocum began. "A young lady from Detroit — her name is Elizabeth Peters — came to us with a story. She claims that she spent an evening in Eddie Bennison's room at a Marriott Hotel while he was in Detroit for a golf tournament a couple of years ago. Bennison, as you probably know, is married and has a family. According to her statement, which was signed under oath, they had wild sex, during which Bennison got more and more violent. It led to him slugging her hard in the face, giving her a black eye and a cut lip. And she gave us pictures showing the damage to her face — it was really a mess."

"You say she came to *us*. Who is 'us'?"

"Her representative approached Max Reed while he was at the trial to testify. Max passed the information to me, and I passed it along to Hugo Shoemaker and Roz Berman." Everything that Slocum told Curtis was true, but he conveniently omitted the fact that he had met with Peters and her friend, Dan Curry. He also omitted reference to the two million–dollar price tag for the Peters woman to tell her story.

Clive Curtis took a few seconds to digest the news. Then he said, "If I understand you correctly, the only person on our side who personally had contact with her or with her agent or representative, whatever the hell he is, was Max Reed. Is that right?"

Todd Slocum knew that Curtis was a news guy through and through. He was "gathering strings," a phrase used by journalists to describe how reporters put together all the facts that make a final story. As Slocum knew all too well, Clive Curtis was a top-notch editor, and before that a top-notch reporter, and he was very good at gathering strings. As such, Curtis knew all the right questions to ask to get the story. So, Slocum knew he had to face the music and play it straight.

"Well," he finally responded, "Max never met the Peters woman. He met only with a guy named Dan Curry who said he was representing her. Then Max called me to say he had this big piece of news about Bennison. He really made it sound like a big deal, and he wanted to tell me about it in person. So I flew out to Chicago to hear what he had to tell me — I was heading to Chicago anyway to be at the trial the next day. Max related the story to me, and then said that the Peters woman would not talk to us without Curry present. He said everything had to go through Curry — they insisted on that. I knew I had to check out the story — authenticate it as best I could — so the next day I called Curry from Chicago and that night I flew to Detroit to meet with him, but I told him that he had to bring her along. I thought it was important that I heard her story from her, firsthand."

"Before we go further on this, Todd, I have another question," Curtis said, "a *legal* question. Is it legal to pay a witness, or to make any other promise to her, in return for her testimony?"

"Lawyers aren't allowed to pay witnesses for their testimony, except in certain cases where the witness has been prequalified as an 'expert' witness and his or her testimony is limited to scientific or technical matters. For regular non-expert witnesses like Liz Peters, we are not allowed to pay or promise anything to them for their testimony. And, totally apart from the legal considerations, it just plain looks bad to offer testimony that has been bought and paid for."

Then came the question that Todd Slocum feared, but one he expected from Curtis, who was carefully gathering strings: "Did this Curry guy ask you for anything? Or did you offer anything? I need to know this, Todd, so let's not beat around the bush."

Slocum tried to sound casual so as not to betray his discomfort. "Well, he said the Peters woman would be willing to tell her story in court at the trial, or, if we preferred, she'd sit for an interview with any newspaper or magazine we choose. She'd do it for two million dollars."

"Two million dollars! Do you — "

Slocum held his hands in front of him as if he were trying to stop a freight train, which, in a sense, he was. "Wait, Clive. That's what he *asked* for, but I never offered — or promised — anything like that."

"Like *that*? So what did you offer or promise?"

"All I said to him was that I needed copies of her statement and the pictures showing her battered face. I made it clear that our trial lawyers were in charge of all decisions — everything — that concerned the lawsuit. I said I had to discuss this with the lawyers and with my higher-ups, and to do that I needed the statement and pictures for substantiation."

"And did he give them you — just like that?"

"Sure. They knew I couldn't do anything on my own — that I had to clear it with the lawyers and my bosses. So they knew I needed her statement and the pictures to verify her story."

Clive Curtis' mind was racing to gather more strings, but there were too many loose ends. Then, thinking out loud, he said, "Wouldn't it be wonderful if she just ran off to the press on her own, without any encouragement or cooperation from us? Then we'd get everything we want without doing a thing or getting involved."

Slocum pondered that for a moment, and then said, "Well, if they know that we won't play ball with them, and I sure don't think we should, then maybe they will run off to some outfit like *Sports Illustrated*, or one of our competitors like *Golf Digest,* and try to sell the story to them. Maybe even *National Enquirer* or one of the other tabloids. I have no idea if any of those magazines would pay for the story, or how much, but it could be worth a try for her. It would be the only way that she and this Curry guy could cash in if we don't pay them — and we shouldn't."

The Editor-in-Chief, doodling on a pad, voiced a thought. "So there's a chance that she might find someone else to buy and print her story. If so, we get all the advantages and won't have to pay a cent."

"Possibly."

"You know, Todd, this business scares the hell out of me, and part of me wants to run as far away from it as possible. On the other hand, I can see how this story about the hotel room could help our case — big time."

"Look at it this way, Clive. Curry and Peters probably lost their leverage to squeeze us when I wouldn't play ball, but now that we have the statement and pictures, we're able to squeeze Charlie Mayfield and his golden boy client, Eddie Bennison. That's what Roz Berman is working on now." Then Slocum waggled the pencil he was holding in order to make his point. "In other words, Clive, now that we have the statement and pictures, we don't need anything more from Liz Peters. As far as we're concerned, she can take a hike."

"Can you connect the dots for me?"

"Sure. Roz now has copies of the statement and the pictures. She showed them to Charlie Mayfield — he's Bennison's lawyer — and she told him that this whole thing would go away if he dismissed his case."

Seeing that his boss wasn't following him, Slocum tried to explain. "Here's how it would come down, Clive. Roz threatens to put this Peters lady on the stand to tell the world that Bennison is an adulterer, a woman beater, and a sex maniac. But if Bennison drops his case against us, we, in return, would agree to tear up the pictures and the statement and not put the woman on the stand. And if Mayfield is as smart as everyone seems to think, he'll take Roz up on it — he'll take the deal and withdraw his case. He knows that as soon as Peters gets on the stand and starts talking, Bennison's case goes up in flames. And along with it would go Bennison's reputation and Mayfield's fees — he surely took this case on a contingent fee basis, probably one-third, so if the jury gives Bennison, say, 30 million, Mayfield gets 10 million of it. But that all goes bye-bye once the jury hears Peters warble from the witness stand. So you can bet that Mayfield is seriously considering Roz's offer, and I'll bet that he takes it."

"But if he dismisses the case, he won't get a dime."

Slocum shook his head. "What we'd do is this — both sides would jointly announce that a settlement was reached, but by agreement the terms of the settlement would be kept confidential. That way, no one would know if Bennison got 25 million or nothing.

"In fact," he continued, "we'd probably have to pay *something*. Charlie Mayfield won't recommend any deal where he gets no legal fee. Therefore, we'd have to pay something so he could get a fee, even if it's not a big one, and then he'll sell the deal to Bennison." He paused, and then added, "So, big deal! That would be chicken feed compared to what we'd have to pay if we lost."

"Okay, I get it," Curtis said after giving some thought to what Slocum had been trying to explain. "We got the statement and pictures without having to pay for them, but now we're turning around and using them to blackmail Bennison and his lawyer. Have I got that right?"

"It's not blackmail, Clive, not at all. We're in the middle of a lawsuit. In lawsuits it's very common for one party to offer to withhold evidence that would be damaging to the other party, in return for the other party making some concession. And that's all we're asking here. Roz told Mayfield that she would agree not to put Liz Peters on the witness stand to tell her story, and show her pictures, on the condition that they withdraw the case. There's nothing wrong with that. In every negotiation, and in every trial, someone is using leverage to gain an advantage or get a concession, and that's all we're doing here. Happens all the time."

The main problem with Todd Slocum's analysis is that he assumed Charlie Mayfield had only two options — either dismiss the case or listen to Liz Peters bury his client.

But Charlie had a third option incubating in that creative brain of his.

CHAPTER 34

Charlie Mayfield was too good a lawyer not to take seriously any proposal that could affect his client, and, to be sure, the Liz Peters bombshell could affect Eddie Bennison in ways too horrible to comprehend. Charlie could make recommendations, but the final decision on what to do about this belonged to his client, Eddie. So, while walking back to his office after Roz Berman dropped the Liz Peters mess on his lap, and with deep sadness, he used his cell phone to dial Eddie's number.

"Hi, Charlie. I was just reading about our case on the Internet. The sport blogs can't help talking about what you did to Max Reed on the witness stand. I don't think he'll be able to get a job with *TV Guide* after all this."

"Yeah, Eddie, it's going well, so far. But something came up this afternoon. Can you come up to my office? We have to talk. I'm on my way there now. How about 6:00?"

"Sure. What's up?"

"I'll explain when you get to my office."

CHAPTER 35

"**M**ake yourself comfortable over there on the couch, Eddie," Charlie said when Eddie walked in. "I'll sit here at the desk where I can make some notes."

After fidgeting for several seconds, taking out a fresh legal pad, uncapping his pen, and telling his secretary to hold his calls, Charlie turned to Eddie and asked in a quiet voice, "Would you like to tell me about Elizabeth Peters?"

"Elizabeth Peters? Doesn't ring a bell. Can you give me a hint, Charlie? I don't recognize the name."

"You might not recognize her face, either — not anymore."

Still confused, Eddie creased his brows and looked Charlie straight in the eyes. "Sorry, Charlie, I have no idea — "

"Do you remember playing in a tournament in Detroit a couple of years ago? It was at Oakland Hills, and you stayed at a Marriott nearby."

In flash, Eddie felt a chill on the back of his neck. *Oh shit! Her!* He sat back, took a deep breath, and said, "Yeah, okay. Now I remember."

"And do you remember that she was in your hotel room?"

"Yes."

"And do you remember striking her in the face?"

Eddie nodded, sheepishly.

"And was all this in the course of having sex?"

"No, absolutely not! It was nothing like that! Not at all."

The lawyer sighed, clasped his hands behind his neck, and threw his feet up on his desk. "Okay, Eddie, give it to me, and don't leave anything out. I need to know what happened, and I need to know it all. Is that clear?"

"Yeah, sure." Eddie took a minute to assemble his thoughts, and then began. "It was a few years ago, Charlie, so I may have a couple of the details wrong, but I sure remember the night. I wish I could forget it, but I never will."

"Just tell me," Charlie demanded, pen poised.

"Okay. I was staying at the Marriott, not far from Oakland Hills. I believe it was a Friday night two or three years ago. I was still in my slump after the *Tee Time* articles but was having a good tournament — in fact, I was playing better that week than I had since those articles had come out — and I was charged up for the Saturday and Sunday rounds."

"Did you have your own room, or did you share it with any of the other golfers?"

"It was my own room. In the early days on Tour, I might share a room with one of the guys, but later on I preferred being alone. It gives me a chance to get more rest, take care of emails and phone calls, and study my charts for the next day's round."

"Charts?"

"Yeah. There's some outfit that sells booklets for each course showing yardages from various points to greens, bunkers, and other hazards. They also show the slopes on the greens. There's a separate page for each hole. Our caddies buy them for a few bucks. While we're playing practice rounds, most of us, with our caddies, add all sorts of notes to help us when we get back to that hole. For example, I might add a note to remind me of a bunker that can't be seen from the tee box. Or I might add, 'Play a fade for the drive, or 'Anything on the left runs to creek,' or 'Stay below the hole.'

"I call this book my 'charts,' and I study it every night before playing a tournament round. It helps me plan my strategy and focus on the exact shots I need to hit the next day. I'll even practice those specific shots on the range before teeing off for the next round."

"Then who is this guy Ben Edwards whose room you used that night?"

Eddie sighed. "Charlie, you're a great lawyer, but your name and face aren't splashed all over the sports pages every day, and the TV sportscasters don't know you from Elmer Fudd — no offense. But when I became the leading money winner on the Senior Tour and had my face and name on TV, newspapers, and commercials for all sorts of products, I was hounded by fans, sportswriters, and all sorts of hangers-on. At first it was flattering and a real thrill to be the center of attraction and see my face on magazine covers, but all that got old, fast. It got to the point where I'd show up at a hotel where I had a reservation, dead tired, and people would be there waiting for me. 'How about an autograph, Eddie,' or 'What did you think of the course, Eddie?' or 'Hey, Eddie, I have a tip that will help your putting.' They aren't even nice about it — literally shoving me and breathing in my face. And if I was the least bit rude, it would be all over the next day's news that I was a prick. Even the hotel clerks and car rental agencies recognize my name, and they all crowd around when I show up.

"So, Charlie, in order to have some privacy, I started using 'Ben Edwards' as an alias. I even had credit cards in that name so my car, room, and restaurant charges would match the name on the reservations. Even my luggage tags say 'Ben Edwards.' And I wear a hat and fake glasses a lot of the time. The hat is one of those fedoras like men used to wear all the time, and some still do. And the glasses have big black rims, but the glass is as clear as a window pane.

"Of course, that night at the Marriott was after the *Tee Time* stories, and I wasn't all that popular at the time, but enough people would recognize me that I was still using the 'Ben Edwards' name and wearing the fake glasses — especially because some of those who recognized me would now heckle me instead of reach out to shake my hand. So you might say that I used the alias before to protect me from the people who liked me, and I used it later to protect me from the people who hated me."

"Let's get back to Ms. Peters. What happened?"

"It was a hell of a night that I won't forget, even though I didn't recognize her name. I'm not even sure that she gave it to me."

"But you remember her in your room? And striking her?"

"Yeah, I already told you that. But let me tell you the whole story, from the beginning."

"Please."

"As I said, I was playing well and was in good position to place high in the tournament. In fact, I remember shooting a 67 that day. When Ben Hogan set the record at Oakland Hills in the 1951 National Open, that was his best round — 67.

"So I was feeling great when I got back to the hotel. I cleaned up and went down to dinner, and then, to settle down, I decided to go into the lounge and listen to some music — they had a small band playing there — before going back to my room.

"I found a table in the corner, and pulled out my charts — "

"Okay," Charlie interrupted, eager for Eddie to get to the business with Liz Peters, "so you're sitting there with your charts."

"And this young lady comes over to my table. I swear that I didn't invite her over. She was wearing this big smile and trying to look like some kind of sex kitten. She said something about the book I was reading — I keep my charts in a small leather binder that looks like a small book — but after a few awkward moments of her standing and me sitting, I asked if she'd like to sit down. She did, and I think she ordered a drink."

"Do you think she knew who you were?"

"No, not at all. I doubt if she knew a golf ball from a bowling ball. She might have told me where she worked; I don't remember, and if I told her anything about me, I probably said I was a corrugated box salesman from Tulsa, which I am, actually.

"She was obviously on the make, and even suggested coming up to my room. I *absolutely* said no, that I was married, and that I wasn't into messing around with other women. When I added that I was tired and wanted to call it a night, she said something like, 'But it's so early,' and to make her point, she grabbed my wrist to look at my watch. Then she said something that didn't seem important — until about an hour later. She looked at my watch and said, 'Wow, is that really a Rolex?' I said that it was, and that probably gave her the idea that I was loaded because she started asking me a lot of questions about what kind of car I drove, did I travel abroad, that kind of thing.

"About this time, I signaled for the waitress — maybe it was a waiter

— to bring me the tab for our drinks. In the meantime, this little bimbo is hanging on for dear life, almost begging to go to my room. When the tab came, I must have given the waitress or waiter my room number so the drinks could be charged to my room, and I probably left a cash tip; servers prefer getting tips in cash instead of on credit cards. Then I got the hell out of there. I figured that if this lady didn't know who I was, others in the hotel probably did, and it could have been a bad scene if they saw me with another woman, especially going to a room with another woman."

"But there must have been more," Charlie prodded.

"Lord yes! I got into my room, and decided to take a shower. Up until a couple of years ago, I always took my showers in the locker room at the club where we played, but more recently I prefer to wait until I get back to my hotel room. It's easier, and I don't have to carry extra clean clothes with me to the course. Anyway, I emptied my pants pockets onto the desk in the room, tossed my pants, shirt, and jacket on the chair, and went in to shower. Toweling off after the shower, I heard this knock at the door. I thought it might be housekeeping to turn down my bed. I wrapped a towel around me and, without giving it a thought, I opened the door a tad to see who was there, and in walks this woman like she owned the place. She didn't wait for an invitation or anything — just pushed the door open and came right in. She kicked off her shoes, crawled onto my bed, and said something like, 'I came up here to see if I could change your mind.' Then she looked me over and said, 'I can see you're dressed for it,' or something like that.

"I went back into the bathroom to figure things out, and after a minute or two put on one of those robes that the hotel provides, and I came out and found her standing at the desk, holding my Rolex in one hand and my wallet in the other. I went over, grabbed her wrists, and took the watch and wallet out of her hands. She actually tried to put up a fight, so I shoved her into the chair in the corner.

"Next thing I knew, she runs over to her purse, turns, and sprays something awful toward my face — I guess it was mace. It could have been a gun! Fortunately, she mostly missed my eyes, maybe because I moved away so fast, but the little I got was terrible. My eyes were on fire! She kept coming at me, spraying, and I kept ducking and covering my eyes. She wouldn't give up, so reflexively I began swinging my fists and hit her in the face. Then she started scratching, kicking, and yelling, but I don't think I hit her again — just shoved her away. It all happened so fast. I think I only hit her that one time, but I swear it was in self-defense. She could have blinded me. I tell you, Charlie, she was crazy as a loon."

Reliving the event, Eddie Bennison was visibly shaken.

"I would have called the police or hotel security, but I didn't want this to become a public thing, with my name being so well known; also, she didn't get away with any of my valuables, so I decided to end it as quietly and as soon as possible.

"'Listen,' I said, 'I want you out of here, right now! Just go. If you don't, I'm calling the authorities to have you arrested. Now *go!*'

"Without saying a word, she picked up her purse and left. And I thought that was the end of it. How dumb was that? Here she is, coming back to ruin my life."

After years of trying cases, first as a prosecutor of criminal cases, and then in the civil courts, Charlie Mayfield had good radar for detecting liars. He had seen them all: the subtle fibbers, the "shaders of truth," and the bald-faced liars who could say there's a Santa Claus and pass a lie detector test at the same time.

But this time his radar sent no signals. As bizarre as Eddie Bennison's story was, Charlie believed him.

———

After a moment of silence, Bennison asked, "So what is it that she wants, Charlie? There must be something for her to arrive on the scene in the middle of our trial."

"She didn't come to me," Charlie Mayfield replied. "She went to our friends at *Tee Time*. It was their lawyers who dropped it in my lap, but I don't know if she went directly to the lawyers or to those bastards at the magazine. So, Eddie, I can't tell you what she is asking from them. But it's money, I'm sure."

"But what do their lawyers want from us? They must want something, or they wouldn't have told you about her."

"Right on, Eddie. Here's the deal. They want us to drop our case and, if we don't, they threaten to put Liz Peters on the witness stand to tell her story — or go to the newspapers — for the whole world to hear."

This famous golfer who could, without blinking an eye, sink a curling 10-foot putt for $100,000 collapsed at the news he had just heard from his lawyer.

"Oh, my God, Charlie — "

"Just wait, Eddie. Don't go jumping off the ledge. Not yet, anyway. I've looked bigger dragons than this in the eye, and I'm still here."

"So what can we do?"

"Beats the hell out of me. But I'll come up with something. Give me some time to think about it."

Eddie Bennison groaned.

CHAPTER 36

Whil e all the lawyers for the defendants were trying to figure out how best to play the Liz Peters card, Charlie Mayfield was trying to figure out a way to ensure that it would not be played at all. As he saw it, his only option was to keep her story from seeing daylight, which meant keeping her off the witness stand and preventing her from blabbing to the press or anyone else. And he had to figure out a way to do that without giving up the case. Sure, he could put Eddie on the stand to refute her testimony, but then it would be a "he-said-she-said" battle, and it's the kind of battle where people might well believe the woman or fall prey to the adage that says, "Where there's smoke there must be fire." And, regardless of who was believed by the most people, once the story was out there, it would always be a blemish on the character and reputation of Eddie Bennison. Charlie Mayfield was a solid enough lawyer to know that winning the case was important, but protecting the reputation of his client was even more sacred. He had to keep that story from coming out, regardless of whether it was true or false.

To do that, he had to keep the name of Elizabeth Peters from even being mentioned in the courtroom, lest the reporters find her and start asking questions. He had to get her out of the case.

And the idea that had been hatching in Charlie's mind was beginning to take form.

THURSDAY

CHAPTER 37

Todd Slocum was back in his office at *Tee Time*, his head still reeling after his meeting the night before with Clive Curtis — and he was dreading the possible fallout from playing the Liz Peters card. At first he thought he was safe in turning the problem over to Roz Berman, but then he realized that he wasn't safe at all. Regardless of whether she leaked the story to the press or put Peters on the witness stand to tell her story, it would inevitably come out that his fingerprints were all over the place — phone calls with Dan Curry, a late night flight to Detroit for a secret meeting with Curry and Liz Peters, delivery of the statement and photos to Roz Berman, hearing and relaying the demand for two million dollars, and all the rest.

His depressed mood was interrupted by the buzz of the intercom on his desk. "Yes, Dorothy?"

"There's a Dan Curry on line four."

Shit! Feeling a chill on the back of his neck, but nevertheless trying his best to sound casual, Slocum picked up the phone. "Morning, Dan. You caught me just as I was going into a meeting."

"I'll be quick. I was calling to ask about the money."

"Look, Dan. I never agreed to pay you a dime. Hell, I could lose my law license for doing something like that. All I said was that I'd tell our lawyers about Liz, and if they want to make a deal with you, it's up to them. I told you I needed her statement and the pictures of her face to convince them that her story was real, and you gave them to me. And I gave them to the lawyers. From here on, it's their call."

"So what are we — uh, what is Liz supposed to do while you guys are playing with yourselves?"

"She sat on her story for nearly three years, so she should be able to sit for another few days. And what's her alternative? If she wants to go out and talk to the press right now, she's free to do so. Be my guest. There are plenty of pulp magazines that would be happy to pay her for the story. She'll be famous — and rich!"

"Very funny. But it ain't gonna happen. Your magazine is gonna be the beneficiary of her story, so you'll have to pay for it."

The fears, frustration, and angst that had been accumulating over the past days finally got the best of Todd Slocum's self-control.

"Hey, who in the hell do you think you are? Don't you go telling me what I have to do! If you were as goddamned smart as you thought you were, you wouldn't have come to *Tee Time* to peddle your sleazy fucking story. You'd have gone to Bennison or his lawyers. Or you could have gone to *The National Enquirer* and maybe they'd buy it. But no, Mr. Big Shot, you gave me her statement and the pictures, and I promised you nothing. Your mistake."

Hearing no response from Dan Curry, Slocum decided to shoot another arrow. "Let me draw a picture for you, Dan. You've been thinking that we'd pay you a pile of dough so Liz would tell the world what happened back in that hotel room. Here's what you missed: Bennison would probably pay you more — a hell of a lot more — for her *not* to tell her story. So you had two roads leading to a payoff, but you took the wrong one, and now you screwed this thing up so much that both roads are now closed — to you." *And why not shoot one more arrow?* "But since you were kind enough to give me the statement and pictures, one of those roads is open to me."

"So how are you planning to use the pictures and statement?" Curry asked.

"Well, maybe we'll do what you should have done. Maybe we'll go to Bennison and his lawyers and see what they'll give us for them. And

Bennison will never give you a dime for them because he knows that I have copies. Too bad, Dan, you blew it!" Then he slammed down the phone.

CHAPTER 38

Just as Slocum cut off the conversation, he got a call from his boss, Clive Curtis, who had a question. "Is there any way that Mayfield could keep that Peters woman off the stand? If there is, then he could tell Roz to go to hell. Why would he give up the case just to keep her off the stand if he can keep her off the stand without giving up the case?"

Slocum paused for a few seconds before responding. "I don't see how. All he could do is object after hearing what she has to say, and ask the judge to strike her testimony for some legal reason, but by that time the jury will have heard enough of her story to change whatever good feelings they had for Bennison. Moreover, half the courtroom is filled with people from the press, and once they heard even a few sentences about an incident at the Marriott, or even the name of another woman, they'll be sending out the bloodhounds and running off to file their stories."

"Okay, got it." Curtis switched off.

I hope I'm right about that, Slocum thought to himself. But being a corporate lawyer, he never learned many of the trial tactics and maneuvers that weren't taught in law school.

But Charlie Mayfield knew them all — and he was about to unleash a beauty.

FRIDAY

CHAPTER 39

Charlie couldn't get Liz Peters off his mind. He kept coming back to the same conclusion: *I have to keep that woman off the stand! Even if I can destroy her story on cross-examination, by then it will be too late. Once she tells her story, Eddie Bennison is a ruined man — the jurors will hear it and the press will be running wild.*

Once again he pulled out her signed statement and examined it for some clue that she was making up her story from thin air. There was one point that kept nagging at him. Peters clearly said that she and Eddie went up to his room together, while Eddie maintained that he went up alone and that she, without being invited, came up later.

After chewing this over for a minute or two, Charlie landed on an idea. With a smile on his face and a twinkle in his eye, he reached for his phone to buzz his secretary.

"Lillian, do you think you could track down Hank Potter and get him on the phone?"

"Hank Potter?" his secretary asked. "The private investigator you used on the Bennett case? The one you called Dick Tracy?"

"Yeah, that's him. Let me know when you find him."

In a surprisingly short time, Lillian called to say that Hank Potter was on the line.

"Hank! You old so-and-so. How's life treating you?"

"I'm fine, Charlie. What's going on?"

"Not much," Charlie replied, "but maybe you could help me with something."

"Just name it."

"Hank, don't I remember that you used to head up security at the Hilton over on Michigan Avenue?"

"Good memory, but that was before I started my own investigation firm. Left there a couple of years ago."

"That's fine. Here's my question. Is it customary for hotels to have security cameras to monitor people in the elevators or walking through the corridors?"

"Sure, especially the larger chains like Hilton and Hyatt. We call them CCTVs — closed circuit television."

"And do they keep the tapes for long — like maybe two or three years?"

"Depends," Potter added. "I urged Hilton to keep the tapes for at least two years — that's the statute of limitations in Illinois for injury claims, so people had two years after an injury to file suit. If someone claimed, say, that they fell and got hurt because a floor was wet or a rug came loose, and we had a video of the scene, I wanted it to be available for evidence. And believe me, Charlie, it came in handy more than a few times. I doubt if the small places, like the 'no-tell motels,' bother with security cameras, but I know that the large outfits do. And with today's technology, it's easy to keep the tapes for several years — and that's a good policy."

Charlie was starting to feel pretty good. "What about the Marriott? Do you think they'd have the cameras and keep the tapes?"

"I'd be surprised if they didn't. But it's easy for me to find out."

"And how would you do that?"

"Well, those of us in hotel security — or who *were* in hotel security — are kind of a fraternity. We didn't have a formal association, but we got together from time to time to share ideas. And since we all worked for hotels, we had nice places to meet and stay. I knew a couple of the guys who were with Marriott. I'm sure I still have their contact information on my computer. Would you like me to call them?"

"That would be great, Hank. I'm particularly interested in the Auburn Hills Marriott in Pontiac, Michigan."

"Got it," Potter said after writing the names of all those places. "Shouldn't be a problem. Give me your number and I'll call you as soon as I know something."

An hour later, Hank Potter called. "Charlie, I was able to reach my contact at Marriott headquarters, and he knows that particular hotel in Pontiac. He called there and was able to talk with both the manager and the security guy. They do have CCTV for the elevators and corridors."

"That's wonderful, Hank! Good work. Can I talk to them?"

"Sure. I gave them your name and told them to expect a call from you. Grab a pen and I'll give you their names and numbers."

"I owe you, Hank."

"You can buy me a drink at that fancy club of yours."

Charlie spun around in his chair to retrieve a file in the credenza behind him, and from it he pulled out two pictures of the battered face of Elizabeth Peters. Then he dialed one of the numbers Hank Potter had given him.

"Hello. Joe Andrews here." Andrews was the Director of Security at the Marriott in Pontiac, Michigan. Charlie preferred to go straight to him instead of going through the hotel manager.

"Mr. Andrews, this is Charlie Mayfield. I believe my friend Hank Potter mentioned that I'd be calling."

"He sure did. How can I be of help, Mr. Mayfield?"

"Hank tells me that your hotel has security tapes covering the elevators and corridors. Is that right?"

"That's right."

Great! "May I ask how long you keep them?"

"Sure. Our lawyers insist that we keep the tapes for at least three years before erasing or reusing them. That's the statute of limitations in Michigan of personal injury claims — three years. Is that okay?"

"Better than okay, Joe. It's fabulous!" *So far, so good,* Charlie thought, *the incident at the hotel was just under three years before.*

"I have a couple of pictures here that my secretary can fax to you, or else scan and email them to you. They are of a young lady who was in your hotel on the evening of August 17, 2007. That was a Friday night. In the pictures, her face is a mess, but I think you'd still be able to recognize it if you saw it on one of your tapes."

"Now wait a minute, Charlie. Are you claiming that this lady was injured at our hotel? If so, I'll be damned if I'll help you and then have you sue the hotel for her damages."

Charlie laughed. "Good point, Joe. But not to worry — when I send you the pictures, I'll include a statement from me assuring you that we are making no claims against the Marriott — none whatsoever. It'll be in the form of a release, and I'll make it legally binding on me. You can run it by your legal people if you'd like."

"And I don't suppose you're representing this woman's husband, and that he's trying to nail her with another guy? We respect our guests' privacy, and we don't want to get sucked into a nasty divorce case."

"No, Joe, I assure you, it's nothing like that. On the contrary, I'm hoping to show that there was no hanky-panky going on at your hotel. I'm hoping that your tapes show her going up the elevator and walking down the corridor, and that she was alone."

To help Joe Andrews in his search, Charlie explained: "The lady in question was in the hotel cocktail lounge after she went to dinner elsewhere, and she happened to meet a man there who signed the tab for their drinks. If you can check with your accounting department, you should find a tab for that night signed by a guy named either Bennison or Edwards. That tab should show the time it was signed, and I'm looking for the woman to be on the elevator or in the corridor during the next quarter hour or so. I want to know if she's alone at that time. Think you can do that for me?"

"Shouldn't be a problem," Andrews replied. "I've made some notes here, and I'll call accounting to check the time of the bar tab. That will tell me the time frame for the tapes we'll want to review. Shouldn't take me long — probably less than an hour. But I'll still need the pictures to make an I.D."

"You'll have them in a few minutes. All I need is your fax number and email address. And as I said, her face in the pictures is pretty messed up — she ought to look a lot better on your tapes."

As soon as Charlie got Andrews's email address and fax number, he hung up and drafted the statement that he had promised. In a few minutes that statement and the bruised face of Liz Peters was floating through cyberspace from Chicago to Pontiac, Michigan.

Charlie got the awaited call from Joe Andrews at about four in the afternoon.

"We're in luck, Charlie. We got that little honey. And you were sure right; in our pictures she looked a hell of a lot better than she did in yours, but it was her, alright. She was even wearing the same dress as in the photo you sent, where she had the shiner and cut lip. But her face looked okay in the ones we have on the tape. You're sure, Charlie, that this has nothing to do with a claim against the hotel?"

"I'm sure, Joe, and I put that in the statement I sent you. I promise that you have nothing to worry about."

"By the way," Andrews said, "the tapes show that she went into room 342, if that's important for you to know. And the registration for that room was in the name of Ben Edwards, the same guy who signed the tab in the cocktail lounge, like you said. Also," Andrews went on to say, "he signed the tab at 8:54 p.m., and our tapes show her going up the elevator at 9:06, so it all connects.

"The number of the room she entered isn't visible on the tape, but we know our hotel. 342 is the room right across from the fire extinguisher, and we can see it hanging there on the tape, and we can see that it's the next to last room on that end of the corridor — the rooms only go up to 344 so it has to be 342. And another thing, Charlie, if it's important — before she knocked on the door, she took out a mirror, put on lipstick, and teased her hair. Looked like she was getting ready for action."

Holding his breath, Charlie said, "Tell me she was alone when she went up to the room."

"She was alone, alright — in the elevator and in the corridor."

"Are you able to send some of the pictures to me? Especially where she's putting on the lipstick."

There was a sight pause while Andrews made a note of the request. Then he said, "If you need the entire tapes, I can send copies to you, but in the meantime, I'll make some images of the separate frames showing the things we're talking about, like the one with the lipstick and where she's alone in the elevator and corridor, and email them to you now as separate photos. I have your address — it's on the release you sent to me."

"Perfect! And will those pictures show the date and time they were taken?"

"You bet. That information is on every frame, and it's very clear."

"Oh, and one other thing!" Charlie half shouted before hanging up.

"Yeah?"

Charlie remembered Eddie telling him that Peters knocked on the door, and that as soon as he started to open, she wasted no time charging into the room. "Can you tell from the tapes if she was invited into the room? Or did she kind of barge in once the door was opened?"

"Well, the camera was at the end of the corridor, and from that angle we couldn't see who opened the door, but then something happened that seemed really odd to us. I was looking at the tape with a couple of my guys, and it looked to us from that angle like she kind of forced her way in by pushing or shoving the door with her shoulder. It all happened quickly, but one of my guys said something like, 'Wow, she really wanted to get in there — she must have been in a rush to pee.'"

"That's very helpful, Joe. Would it be possible to include a section of that tape — the part where she put on her makeup and shoved her way into the room?"

"No problem, I'll send you all the relevant tapes by courier this afternoon, but you may need to do a little hunting to find a device to play it on. I'll let you know the model of the device we use — might cost you a few bucks, but I'm sure you can find it anywhere. But just to cover all the bases, I'll send along still shots of the images on the tape. That way, you can see them before you get the tapes and a playback device."

Charlie Mayfield sat back in his chair and audibly exhaled. It was the best he had felt since cross-examining Max Reed.

He picked up the phone to call Eddie Bennison. "Eddie, can you come over to my office tomorrow morning? I hate to take you away from Carol on a Saturday, but it's important. Come any time before noon. I'll have some sandwiches brought in for lunch."

"Shall I bring Carol along?"

"I don't think that would be a good idea. We need to talk about

Elizabeth Peters and how we're going to deal with her. I don't think you'll want Carol hearing about that."

"Oh, crap!"

"Relax, Eddie. I have a few ideas that might save the day, and they seem to be coming together. In fact, I'm waiting for some good news in the next hour or two. That's why I want you to come over tomorrow morning."

SATURDAY

CHAPTER 40

Eddie Bennison arrived at Charlie Mayfield's office at 11:45, and Lillian Durant, Charlie's secretary, led him to the conference room where Charlie was waiting.

Entering the room, Eddie said anxiously, "You said on the phone that you were hoping to get some good news?"

"Right," the lawyer said, "but first let me ask you a couple of questions."

"Shoot."

"I recall you saying that when you left the cocktail lounge that night, you left alone and went upstairs by yourself, and that she came up a little later. Is that right?"

"Yep."

"So, her friends who were sitting at the nearby table . . . if any of them said that the two of you left together, they'd be lying, right?"

"Gee, Charlie, it was a long time ago. I can't swear for sure that we didn't walk out of the lounge together, and I can't remember if she went over to talk to her friends before leaving the lounge. But what I do know, for sure, is that I went upstairs alone. I thought I had seen the last of her. I also know, for sure, that she came to my room after I got there — and that I had no idea whatsoever that she was coming up there. So, whether she walked out with me and then stopped in the john or somewhere, or walked over to talk to her friends, she did not go upstairs with me. She came alone — and uninvited — a little later. I had already been up there for about ten minutes — long enough to take a shower — and then all of the sudden she's knocking on my door, and when I cracked it open to see who was there, she shoved the door open and waltzed right in."

"Okay, we're clear on that. Now, here's a copy of a statement that she signed. Read it closely. She says in there that the two of you went upstairs and to your room together. You say you both went upstairs separately. If you — "

"I know that I went up alone, and she followed me. But is that important?"

"It's damned important. *It's everything!* Would you rather have the jury — and the world — think that you brought her to your room, or that she came up uninvited?"

"But it's her word against mine, and there's no way to prove that she's lying."

Charlie flashed a big smile. "Yes there is, Eddie, and I've got the proof right here." The lawyer reached over to a folder and removed several photos. "Here is our friend, Elizabeth Peters, in an elevator, walking down a corridor, then putting on lipstick and messing with her hair, and then shoving her way into a hotel room — your hotel room. And in each picture, she's alone."

Seeing the photos, Eddie Bennison's eyebrows shot up. "How'd you get these?"

"I have my ways. And I should get a courier delivery later today with the actual tapes from which these photos were made. And," Charlie added with a big grin, "the kicker is right there on the time stamps. The first one was taken at 9:06 p.m. — exactly twelve minutes after you signed the bar tab. Everything syncs.

"Now, Eddie, study the rest of her statement and see if there are other places where she's wrong. I know she's wrong about most of it, but look for other errors — even little ones, where we can prove her wrong with other evidence. If the judge or jury sees that she lies about something, it's easier for them to believe that she is lying about other things as well."

Eddie read over the statement and looked like he saw a ghost. Since Charlie first mentioned Liz Peters to him, he thought the danger was the story that he had a woman in his room. But now he saw the real danger — a story that he was a wild sex maniac who violently slapped and slugged women for thrills.

"Oh, my God, Charlie, this is terrible — and it's all bullshit. There was no sex at all. Sure, I struck her, but only in self-defense — she was spraying stuff in my face after I caught her trying to rob me, and it burned. This could ruin me — and my marriage. Is there any way we can keep this out of the case?"

Charlie Mayfield smiled. "Well, Eddie. I have an idea. If it works, we'll get Elizabeth Peters out of the picture, and the press will never know she existed."

"If you can pull that off, Charlie, I'll buy you the biggest and driest martini they can make at that fancy Metropolitan Club of yours."

MONDAY AFTERNOON

CHAPTER 41

A trial is like the proverbial iceberg where the dangers lurk below the surface — not far below, but just enough not to be seen. The visible parts give no indication of the fatal perils beneath. Thus, the jurors in *Bennison v. Tee Time, et al.*, had been focusing only on what they had been seeing and hearing — the subtleties of the rules of golf, how Eddie Bennison marked his ball and cleaned his clubs, and whether he took improper drugs.

None of the jurors had any inkling whatsoever that other issues were at play — sensational issues such as adultery and physical abuse that had consumed the lawyers and the litigants for the past several days — issues that could send the good ship *Bennison* to the bottom of the sea. Charlie, as captain of his ship, had to steer clear of the fatal dangers presented by the Liz Peters iceberg.

Judge Krause had other business scheduled for Monday morning, so the Monday session of the trial convened at 2:00 p.m. Knowing the judge to be a stickler for punctuality, the lawyers made it a point to be there, and ready to go, on time.

At 1:50, with all the other lawyers in the courtroom, Charlie walked up to the small table where Leon Poleski, the judge's bailiff, was sitting, gavel in hand. "Hi, Leon."

"Hi, Charlie. Need anything?"

"I sure do, Leon. Can you tell the judge that I have a request? I'd like to have a conference in his chambers with all of the lawyers in our case. I have a motion to make, and I don't want to make it in open court. It's important, Leon."

The bailiff knew Charlie. If Charlie wanted to make a motion in chambers and not in open court, he must have a good reason. And if he said it was important, it was important.

"Wait here a minute." Leon disappeared through the door behind the bench. In less than a minute he was back.

"Round up the lawyers, Charlie, and bring 'em back to our chambers. He'll hear you. He wants to know if we should have the court reporter in there."

"Thanks, Leon, and yes, have the reporter there — we may need this on the record."

"Fine. I'll keep the jury in the jury room until you're done."

Charlie gave the bailiff a knowing wink. "You know how we lawyers work, Leon. We might be in there all afternoon."

"They won't mind, Charlie. They're getting along fine with one another, and we have plenty of snacks and soft drinks back there. And what the hell," the bailiff added, "the county's paying them seventeen bucks a day — best money most of 'em ever made."

━━━━━━

Five minutes later, both legal teams were in Judge Harry Krause's chambers. Charlie sat in a chair to one side, next to his young associate, Pete Stevens. On the other side of the judge's desk, a sofa and two chairs held Hugo Shoemaker, Roz Berman, and three other lawyers who were assisting them.

"What do we have, Charlie?" the judge asked, using first names since they were in chambers and not yet on the record.

"I have a motion *in limine*, Your Honor, and with your permission I'd like the record of this hearing sealed."

The judge looked at Charlie inquisitively.

"You'll understand my request, Judge, after you hear my motion. I think we should have a transcript, but I'm asking that we keep it sealed."

"Okay, I'll rule on that after I hear what this is all about. Any objection?" he asked, looking over to Roz Berman and Hugo Shoemaker.

As one, they both said, "No objection, Your Honor." But Berman, recalling her conversation with Charlie over cocktails, began to sense what was coming. And she didn't like it.

"Okay, Charlie, let's hear it." With that, Judge Krause nodded at his court reporter sitting at a table next to his desk. "Ready, Sally?"

Sally Ringer nodded and made sure that her stenotype machine was loaded with paper and placed exactly where she wanted it. Then she looked up. "I already have all your names and the case name and number," she said. "Do we need to administer the oath to anyone, Mr. Mayfield?"

"Won't be necessary, Sally — at least not yet. I may have one or two witnesses who will have to be sworn, but I'd like to defer that for now. Until then, only the lawyers will be talking, and none of us wants to be under oath." Even Judge Krause chuckled at that.

Then Charlie turned to the judge who, in spite of having his court reporter recording every word, was holding a pen above a pad of paper in preparation of taking notes.

"Your Honor, a few days ago Roslyn Berman, one of the attorneys for the defense in this case, asked to meet with me in order to give me some information. Before I reveal what the information was, I'd like to remind you of my request to have the transcript sealed."

The judge knew that Charlie would not be asking to seal the transcript unless the information he was about to disclose was highly sensitive. He thought for a moment, and then said, "Let's do it this way. We'll go off the record for the time being." He looked over to his court reporter who nodded and removed her nimble fingers from the stenotype machine. "While we're off the record, Charlie, you can briefly tell us what this is all about. Then I'll consider your request to seal the transcript once we go back on the record. If I agree with you, I'll enter an order that the transcript will be sealed. If I don't, then you'll have to decide whether to proceed with an unsealed transcript."

"Fine with me, Judge," Charlie replied. "And if you don't seal the transcript, I may have to stop and withdraw my motion *in limine*. As much as Ms. Berman would like to see this all over the evening news, I can't take the cha — "

"I object to Mr. Mayfield's rude insinuation," Roz Berman interjected as she stood to glare at Charlie Mayfield.

"Object all you want," Charlie half-shouted as he rose to his feet. "You were the one who came to me, dragging this bag of slop, and you were the one who threatened — yes, I said *threatened* — to make it public unless I withdrew our lawsuit. Now you tell Judge Krause, Roz, was I lying when I said that?"

Roz Berman, uncharacteristically, was at a loss for words.

Judge Harry Krause intervened. "This is getting us nowhere. I want you both to sit down, and, Charlie, I want you to go ahead and tell me what this is all about."

Charlie sat down and began. "As we all know, a motion *in limine* is designed to prevent the introduction — even the mention — of certain evidence, either oral or documentary, before it is actually presented or offered. Ordinarily, a lawyer can object to improper evidence that has already been offered, and, if the judge agrees that it is indeed improper, the objection will be sustained. And where there's a jury who saw or heard that evidence, they will be instructed by the judge to disregard it.

"Whether they actually can disregard it is a question that only a mind reader could answer. But one thing is certain — where the improper evidence is highly inflammatory or prejudicial, it cannot be erased from the minds of the jurors, regardless of how clearly the judge instructs them to disregard it. If, for example, a juror heard a witness say that the plaintiff or defendant was a serial killer, could she magically put it out of her mind, merely because a judge told her to disregard it? Of course not. And it's for those cases that the motion *in limine* is designed — to prevent even the offer of improper evidence before it can be seen or heard by the jury and, therefore, before it can improperly inflame or prejudice the jury."

"All right, Charlie, as long as we're off the record, why don't you tell me what this evidence is that you don't want the jury to know about? You've aroused my interest in just what it is that Roz is threatening to — excuse me, Roz — that Roz is suggesting she might introduce."

"Very well." Charlie took a folder from his briefcase and produced the two pictures of Elizabeth Peters that Roz Berman had given him. "Your Honor, these purport to be photographs of a young lady named Elizabeth Peters who lives in Detroit, Michigan." Charlie handed the photos to the Judge who winced when he looked at them. "And here is a statement signed by the same woman. It's actually an affidavit and was signed by her under oath before a notary." He handed the statement to the judge.

"In her statement, Your Honor, she alleges that she met the plaintiff in this case, Edward Bennison, in a cocktail lounge at a Marriott Hotel in Pontiac, Michigan, on Friday night, August 17, 2007, while he was in town playing in a golf tournament nearby.

"According to her statement, she left a table she was sharing with friends and approached Mr. Bennison of her own volition. He did not invite her to his table. She struck up a conversation with him. She claims that shortly thereafter they both went, together, to his room at the hotel and engaged in sex. She further claims that Mr. Bennison, without provocation, struck her about the face at least twice, causing the damage you can see in the photos.

"Ms. Berman told me that she intended to put Ms. Peters on the stand to tell that sordid story and to introduce the photos into evidence."

Judge Krause spent a few minutes reading the statement and taking another look at the photos. Then he looked around the room and said, "Charlie, I can see why you don't want all this to come into evidence, but I'd like to hear your legal grounds for barring it."

"Fair enough, Judge. We have three grounds for barring it. Possibly four. First, and most obvious, all of this so-called evidence is totally immaterial and irrelevant to any issue in this case. The *Tee Time* articles, which are the subject of this lawsuit, accuse Mr. Bennison of using drugs and cheating on the golf course. Even if he did have a sexual and physical encounter with this Peters lady, *which we emphatically deny*, it would have no bearing — none whatsoever — as to whether he did the things mentioned in the article. So, while it may be interesting to people who relish this kind of stuff, it has absolutely no relevance to any legal issue in this case. And, most important, it would deflect the attention of the jury away from the central issues they are here to consider.

"Second, the lurid details mentioned by Ms. Peters, and the photos, are so highly inflammatory that introducing them into evidence would prejudice the jury totally out of proportion to any benefits that such evidence could possibly produce, and it is our position that it would produce no benefit whatsoever toward resolving the real issues before us. In short, the introduction of this — this stuff — would work to destroy the fairness of this trial. And it would destroy the life of a man for no legitimate purpose. That is not the job of lawyers or the purpose of trials.

"Our courts have long held that evidence can be *too* inflammatory — *too* prejudicial — if its potential value is insignificant when compared to the damage it does. And that is precisely what we have here, Your Honor. This nonsense has nothing to do with the issues we're here to litigate. It's nothing more than a mud-throwing ploy.

"My third reason, Your Honor, is that this evidence — if we can call it that — is false. This entire story is a fabrication, and we will ask that Elizabeth Peters and anyone working with her be sanctioned by the court for the wrongful attempt to influence the outcome of this trial with false allegations. Furthermore — "

Judge Krause held up a hand. "Pardon the interruption, but I have a question. You contend that Ms. Peters' story is false. Is it false because you and your client *say* it's false? Or do you have some other proof to *show* it's false?"

"I have proof, Your Honor. and the proof is incontrovertible. In fact," he grinned, "you might call it eyewitness proof. Would you like me to go into that now, or shall I first tell you what my fourth point is to keep this story away from the jury?"

"Up to you. You should present your argument in the manner you feel will best serve your purpose."

"Thank you. I'll cover my fourth point first." Charlie paused to consider the best way to bring up a subject that, he knew, would cause Hugo Shoemaker and Roz Berman to wet their pants.

CHAPTER 42

"**M**y fourth point, Your Honor, is this: common sense dictates that this entire Peters story is not only false, which I promise to prove in a few minutes, but that it is also the product of some very nasty foul play." As soon as he saw Roz Berman and Hugo Shoemaker turn to look at one another, Mayfield held up a hand to silence the objections he knew would be coming as soon he uttered the words "foul play." "Please," he said, "let me finish."

Charlie looked at Judge Krause with a conspiratorial smile. "Your Honor, we've known each other a long time. I've tried cases for over forty years, and you've tried and heard cases for at least that long. We both know from our personal experiences that sensational witnesses telling scandalous stories don't just appear out of thin air for the altruistic purpose of bringing justice to the courtroom. They come for a reason.

"So, Your Honor, we must inquire as to how this witness, Elizabeth Peters, happened to come to us. What is her motive for wanting to tell a story that would surely humiliate her from coast to coast? What does she expect to get out of this?" Here Charlie glanced at Roz Berman and added, "The unavoidable question is whether any promises have been made to compensate her for selling out her reputation. Once she tells her story, she'll be forever linked with other women whose questionable behavior has graced our TV screens and newspapers — women like Monica Lewinsky and Linda Lovelace. I refuse to believe that she's doing that for nothing.

We must find out if she's *telling* her story or if she's *selling* it. It goes to her credibility. And more importantly, it would be highly improper, legally and ethically, to compensate a witness to testify — especially where the testimony is scandalous.

"We need to explore that! And, Your Honor, I respectfully suggest that if you, and not I, were defending Eddie Bennison, you would likewise want to question just how and why Elizabeth Peters appeared on our doorstep. Has she received — or will she receive — something in return for committing moral suicide on the witness stand, for the entire world to see and read about? It's not hyperbole to liken her to a suicide bomber — she is willing to blow herself up just for the pleasure of blowing up Eddie Bennison. But is she doing it for pleasure, or is she doing it for money? Is it not reasonable to ask that question? On the contrary, it would be unreasonable — in fact, a dereliction of duty — not to ask it!

"Therefore, Your Honor, in order to test the legitimacy of this witness, and the story that she brings with her, I would like to begin by asking that Roz Berman be sworn so I can ask her some questions under oath. We have a right to know how she found this witness, or if the witness found her, or if some third party produced the witness. Further, we have a right to know what motive, if any, the witness could possibly have to bring this shame onto herself. Is she getting something to make all this worthwhile to her, or has she appeared only to punish Eddie Bennison?"

Judge Krause made a quarter-turn in his chair to face Roz Berman. Still speaking off the record, he asked, "Do you have anything to say, Roz?"

"Well, Your Honor, Mr. Mayfield didn't give us any notice that he was going to make this motion today, so I am not fully prepared to respond to it. I would request that we adjourn the hearing on his motion until another time. However, I do want the record to reflect my resentment to his innuendo that I or our clients made any illicit payments to Elizabeth Peters."

"Mr. Mayfield?"

"Well, Judge, I can understand Mr. Berman's resentment to what she calls my innuendo. So, no more innuendo. Let's just clear the air and stop beating around the bush." Charlie turned his head to look Roz Berman straight in the eye. "Alright, Roz, can you tell us, unequivocally, that no one connected with your side of the case — that means you, any of the lawyers, anyone at *Tee Time*, or any of the other defendants — that none of you made any payments or promises of payments to induce Elizabeth Peters to tell this story? Can you tell us that, Roz, without any qualification whatsoever?"

"Well," Berman replied, "I can certainly give that assurance for myself. However, I would need a little time before I could make that assurance for all the others on our side of the case. I'd have to ask them."

"You should have asked them *before* you brought this garbage to us," Charlie growled. "Actually, Your Honor, there is a little more to my motion that I didn't get a chance to present. I'm worried that the defense will somehow leak the Peters story to the press, even if Ms. Peters doesn't testify, and that would make my motion moot because the damage will have been done. All they'd have to do is leak the name 'Elizabeth Peters,' Bennison's name, the Marriott, and a date. That's all it would take. Not only would the world see it, but it could not escape the attention of the jurors if it were all over the papers and on TV. Even if they didn't see it, their husbands, wives, and neighbors would, and how could they not mention it to the jurors?

"So I'll make this suggestion: I'd agree to a short — very short — adjournment of this hearing to give Roz some time to ask questions, but before I agree to that I must ask for three conditions. One, that the defense assures us that no part of this story will be leaked to the press or to anyone else; two, that I am permitted to examine Roz when we reconvene; and three, that we should reconvene no later than tomorrow afternoon. That should give her plenty of time to collect her thoughts, ask her questions, and respond to my motion.

"Oh, and by the way, I'll also have some questions on the record for Mr. Shoemaker, since he's lead counsel for the defense and should know what's going on with this odious Peters business."

Hugo Shoemaker, unaccustomed to the emotional give and take that Berman and Mayfield went through every day, had been uncomfortable since he first heard of Liz Peters, and this session in the judge's chambers was particularly stressful. *What the hell am I, a Yale professor of Constitutional law, doing in a battle over a hotel room sex brawl?* But now that he heard that Mayfield wanted to question him — under oath — he took on the look of a man in the final stages of carsickness.

Judge Krause broke the silence. "As for anything being 'leaked' to the press, I would regard such an event as contemptuous and punishable. I already admonished counsel and the parties not to discuss or otherwise communicate with the media and, even if I hadn't, doing so would fly in the face of the very purpose of having a trial where all evidence heard by the jury must first be screened and approved by the court. So make no mistake, there will be no leaking of this story to anyone, including the press. That's an order."

The judge looked around to be sure that his point was not missed. Then, in a softer tone, he said, "In order to accommodate Ms. Berman's request, we will resume this hearing tomorrow afternoon at four o'clock, after we recess the trial for the day."

Charlie Mayfield had something to say. "First, Your Honor, if you please, a few minutes ago you asked if I had proof that the Peters story was false, and I said that I did and that I would get to that. May I address that now?"

"Yes, of course."

Charlie had that look in his eye — the look of a boy about to set off a stink bomb in church.

CHAPTER 43

"Your Honor," Charlie began, "anyone in the business of trying cases knows that facts are stubborn. They sometimes hide in dark corners, but they're always there for the finding — if we look long enough and hard enough. And once we find them, they won't go away. No matter how much we may want them to disappear, they won't — they just sit there and nag at us. Like I said, they're stubborn."

Seeing that he had everyone's attention, Charlie proceeded. "I believe everyone here has a copy of the Elizabeth Peters statement, or has at least seen it." He looked around at the others for confirmation, and saw nodding heads. "Okay, it's very clear that Ms. Peters claims that she and Mr. Bennison met at the Marriott cocktail lounge, and then they went upstairs together, and then to his room — together. Correct?" Again, nodding heads.

"Obviously, the fact that they went upstairs together is key to her story. Surely she wouldn't want us to think she went up to his room alone, and of her own accord, and barged in without being invited, would she? Does anyone dispute that? No? Okay then."

Charlie leaned over to extract a folder from his briefcase, and from it he removed some photos. Handing five or six of the photos to Judge Krause, Charlie said, "Judge, these are pictures of the defendants' star witness, Elizabeth Peters. These individual photos were each separate frames of one or more tapes that I will explain to you. You will note that each photo is marked with the date and time of day when it was taken. That date is

August 17, 2007, and, as you can see, the time marked on every one of the photos is between 9:06 p.m. and 9:12 p.m. on that date — and those times correspond exactly with the date and times mentioned in the statement of Ms. Peters as to when she claims she left the Marriott lounge with Mr. Bennison. I'll prove that beyond a shadow of a doubt in a minute or two." Charlie looked around to see if anyone in the room wanted to challenge the match up of the date and times. No one did.

"And the photos of the woman that I just handed you are clearly of the same woman in the photos produced by Ms. Peters, even though her face is damaged in the ones she produced. You will notice that she is wearing the same dress in each of those sets of photos." Charlie spread his arms and said, "So this should eliminate any doubts that the woman in these photos is Elizabeth Peters."

Roz Berman showed no reaction, but she was stunned. *How in the hell did Charlie get these pictures?*

"Now, Judge, as you will clearly see in two of these pictures, Ms. Peters is standing in an elevator alone, and it's obvious that she is alone because the entire interior of the elevator is visible. No one is in there except for Elizabeth Peters. No Eddie Bennison. No anyone!

"And in the other three photos, we can see her in the corridor — alone. We can also see numbers on some of the room doors, showing her to be on the third floor, the same floor on which Mr. Bennison had his room. He was registered in room number 342, a fact we can easily prove with a statement from the Marriott management. And in a minute you will see evidence of her shoving her way — uninvited — into that room.

"And for further corroboration, Your Honor, the time and date stamps on the photos correspond perfectly with the dates and times in Ms. Peters' statement, and we are prepared to show that they also correspond perfectly with Mr. Bennison's signing of the bar tab a few minutes earlier. To be sure, we have documentary proof that he signed the bar tab at precisely 8:54 p.m. Ms. Peters claims that they both left the lounge right after that, together. But the photos before you show that she was on the elevator, alone, at precisely 9:06 p.m. And the time and date stamps prove that these are obviously not pictures we had taken of Ms. Peters in some other elevator, or in some other corridors on some other date."

Judge Krause cleared his throat and half-raised a hand to indicate that he had something to say. "Gentlemen, Roz, considering the seriousness of all this, I've decided that I want to go back on the record for the remainder of this session." He looked to his court reporter who nodded and pulled her chair closer to her stenotype machining. "However, subject to a further order, I want only one copy of transcript of this session to be prepared, and that copy will remain in my possession. If any of the other lawyers should need a copy, I will make mine available for them to review in my chambers — I don't want copies floating around. If they need a copy of their own, my court reporter will make it available to them, but subject to conditions I will then impose to guarantee the confidentiality of that transcript. I don't want one word of today's proceedings to leave this room unless and until I say otherwise. That especially applies to leaks to the press, as well as to anyone else. And later I'll rule on Charlie's motion that the transcript be permanently sealed. Is everyone clear on that?"

Seeing general assent, the judge looked to Charlie. And now that they were back on the record, a bit more formality re-entered the room. "Please continue, Mr. Mayfield."

CHAPTER 44

Before returning to the photos, Charlie paused to clarify a point which, if not explained, could become a problem down the road. "I want to point out that the hotel's records will show that Mr. Bennison's room, 342, was actually registered in the name of 'Ben Edwards.' That's also the name he used to sign the bar tab. And that's the name he gave to Ms. Peters, according to her statement. The explanation for that is both easy and innocent.

"Owing to his high public profile, especially to golf and sports fans, Mr. Bennison is frequently denied the right of privacy that the rest of us take for granted. His face and name are recognized by people everywhere, and too many of them become overly intrusive. People shove scraps of paper at him, screaming for an autograph; cameras are literally pushed to within inches of his face; and there are the endless shouting of unanswerable questions and the offering of unwanted advice.

"And worse, this night at the Marriott was not long after publication of the *Tee Time* articles, and Mr. Bennison was hoping to avoid recognition by hecklers as well as others.

"When not on the course, Mr. Bennison wears various hats and sunglasses to lessen his recognizability, and he often wears fake eyeglasses. As a matter of fact, in Ms. Peters' statement she herself says that when she approached his table on her own, Bennison was wearing a hat and also eyeglasses, which, we are prepared to prove, contained clear glass that provided no sight correction.

"When he makes a reservation at a restaurant, hotel, or car rental agency, he knows better than to use his given name, lest the crowds will be waiting for him, demanding conversation, autographs, golf tips, and uncomfortably close contact.

"In light of all this, is it any wonder why Eddie Bennison would reserve the room at the Marriott in the convenient alias of 'Ben Edwards'? And wouldn't that be all the more expected, since that particular hotel is a short distance from the golf course where he is playing a highly publicized golf tournament, and since tens of thousands of golf fans are within a stone's throw from there?

"So protective is he of his privacy that he even has credit cards and baggage tags in the name of 'Ben Edwards.'

"And, finally, the 'Ben Edwards' alias is not something he cooked up just to conceal a rendezvous with Elizabeth Peters. He registered his room in that name long before knowing Ms. Peters would approach him in the hotel lounge. We can further prove that he used that name continuously for several years for hotel reservations, restaurant reservations, and car rentals, all for his own privacy."

Charlie Mayfield was satisfied that he had now explained away the curious fact that Eddie used another name for the hotel room. Without that explanation, the use of an alias to reserve a hotel room would raise unwanted suspicions.

He then went on to talk more about the photos. "Your Honor, someone a lot smarter than I once said that a picture is worth a thousand words. When we're done with the photos I have here today, we will all appreciate the wisdom of that adage."

Charlie then raised his voice a notch to emphasize the point he was about to make. "Your Honor, since we're now on the record, I'd like to repeat a point I made earlier so there will be no gaps in the transcript. Please note that in each of these pictures of the corridor, Ms. Peters is alone, just as we saw her in the elevator. Alone! Mr. Bennison, who according to her signed statement was with her, is nowhere to be seen. Indeed, no one is with her, and no one is dragging her to Mr. Bennison's room. Contrary to her statement — her sworn statement — she is all alone and on her own.

"By the way, as you all may have figured out by now, these pictures and the tapes I have to show you were all supplied by the Marriott, and I have people there who can authenticate them — in case," he added, glancing at Roz Berman, "anyone here questions their authenticity." He couldn't resist adding, "And this evidence, as opposed to the fairy tale told by Elizabeth Peters, is trustworthy."

Judge Krause looked at the photos and passed them to the defense lawyers. After giving everyone a chance to see them, Charlie continued.

"Here are two more pictures of our Elizabeth Peters — now she's standing in front of a door. We can't see the number on the door from this angle, but the people from the Marriott will confirm that it's the door to Mr. Bennison's room, 342. They can tell because it's the next to last room on that side of the corridor, and therefore identifiable because the rooms go up only to 344. It's also across the hall from a fire extinguisher which, they assure me, hangs directly across from room 342.

"You will note that, standing at the door, Ms. Peters has a small mirror in her hand. In one of the two pictures I just handed you, Judge, she is applying lipstick. In the other she is primping her hair." Charlie couldn't resist tossing in an editorial comment: "Looks like she wants to impress whomever is on the other side of that door."

He continued. "I have the entire section of the tape that includes these frames, and," motioning to the satchel sitting beside him, "I will soon show her doing all that primping and preening and then barging into that room without invitation."

Roz Berman was doing her best to look unimpressed. Hugo Shoemaker was rubbing his forehead and staring at the floor.

Charlie Mayfield then removed two small boxes from a separate leather satchel he had brought with him. "What I have here, Your Honor, are video tapes. The pictures you have came from these tapes, but the tapes include more than what you have already seen."

He paused long enough to ensure that he had everyone's attention. Roz Berman was staring at him with eyes that could kill. *Yeah, she's paying attention, alright.* Meanwhile, Hugo Shoemaker wore the expression of a man walking into an IRS audit.

Then Charlie proceeded. "I'm not very good with this technical stuff, but if you'll give me a few seconds, I can show the tapes." Touching the shoulder of the young man sitting next to him, Charlie added, "Pete here is from my office, and he has a — what do you call it, Pete? — a projector? He can set it up to show the tapes either now or when we reconvene tomorrow. In either event, Judge, if you'll indulge me just a little longer, I can show one small part of one of the tapes now. Pete can project it on the wall over there. Okay, good. Now, as you all can see, this part of the tape shows Elizabeth Peters entering Mr. Bennison's room, and clearly not by invitation. After putting on her lipstick and tidying up her hair, she knocks on his door and then literally shoulders her way into his room once Mr. Bennison opened the door slightly to see who was knocking. Would you like for us to show you that again, Judge?"

"We can defer that for a moment. First," Judge Krause asked, looking to Berman and Shoemaker, "would either of you like to take another look at that tape?"

After glancing to Shoemaker, Roz Berman responded, "That won't be necessary, Your Honor, not right now."

"Good enough," Charlie answered as he put the boxes back into his satchel.

"Your Honor?"

Heads tuned. These were the first words Hugo Shoemaker had spoken since they came into the judge's chambers.

"Go ahead, Mr. Shoemaker."

Hugo Shoemaker cleared his throat and spoke in a very slow — and very serious — voice. "Your Honor, as you know, my court appearances have been mostly limited to the appellate courts and the Supreme Court where we don't produce evidence or witnesses. We focus primarily on the law, and we apply the law to the facts that are already in the record from the trial in the court below. We can't change the record — we accept it as it comes to us. Sometimes the record reveals conflicting facts, which we try to resolve, but we can't introduce new facts."

"We understand that. Please go ahead."

"I make that point because, now that we're back on the record, I want the record to show that I never even heard of Elizabeth Peters until her name was mentioned a week or two ago by Mr. Todd Slocum. I had nothing to do with . . . "

Roz Berman was steaming, knowing that Shoemaker was about to pin the tail directly on her ass. Judge Krause asked, "And who is this Todd Slocum?"

Berman replied quickly, "He is the General Counsel — the Chief Legal Officer — for our client, Tee Time, Incorporated. But I want you to know, Your Honor, that all I did — "

Krause cut her off. "We'll hear from you later, Ms. Berman. But first, Mr. Shoemaker has the floor, and I'd like to hear the rest of what he has to say."

"Of course," she replied through tight lips.

The judge looked back to Shoemaker.

"I only wanted to say that I never met Elizabeth Peters, I never talked with her, and I know nothing about her other than what Mr. Slocum brought to us — her statement and the photographs of her bruised face. As far as I know, neither I nor Ms. Berman had anything to do with finding her or preparing her statement. Isn't that right, Roz?"

"Yes, it is, absolutely! We knew nothing about this until a couple of days ago, when Mr. Slocum told us about it, and I told Mr. Mayfield about it the same day."

Hearing that, Charlie thought to himself, *Nice going, Roz. You make it sound like you told me about the Peters lady as a courtesy. But it wasn't a courtesy — it was extortion!*

"Perhaps we ought to hear from this Mr. Slocum," Judge Krause said. He turned toward Charlie Mayfield. "What do you think, Charlie?"

"Well, there's no question that I'd like to hear from Slocum, Judge, but I'd like to make another point here."

"Go ahead."

"First," Charlie said, after assuring himself that the court reporter was recording his every word, "I want to make it perfectly clear that I am not accusing anyone in this room of bribing a witness or suborning perjury.

By no means am I doing that. But I am raising the possibility that *someone* did. Even if the Peters woman approached the defense or someone at the magazine, I cannot believe that she would humiliate herself like this without getting — or demanding — something in return. It defies logic and basic common sense."

Charlie weighed his next words very carefully. He looked at Roz and said, "Roz, you and I have known each other for a long time. I've always respected you, your legal skills, and your professional ethics. I know you didn't do anything wrong here."

"Thank you," she said.

Then Charlie added, "*But I wonder if you didn't fail to do something that you should have done.*"

Berman sat upright and said, "I don't understand."

"Well, Roz, let me fill in the blanks. If this Peters lady had come to me, or if this Slocum guy had come to me with her story, all sorts of alarms would have sounded in my head." Peeking sheepishly over to the court reporter, he said more quietly than usual, "Excuse me for putting it this way, but we trial lawyers call it our 'shit detector.' We've learned — often the hard way — that when someone brings us evidence that sounds too good to be true, it usually *is*. Surprise witnesses who come out of nowhere with bombshell stories set off those alarms. I know that I have to test and challenge that evidence because, if I don't, my opponents sure will, and if the evidence doesn't stand up, I'll be sitting there with egg all over my face — and my client will suffer."

"And your point?" Roz Berman asked.

"My point," Charlie replied, "should be obvious. Did you challenge the Peters story as I did? Why was it I, and not you, who found the hotel tapes and pictures that showed she lied when she said that she went to the room with Bennison and not on her own? Why was it I, and not you, who asked if she was being paid for her story? Did you ask this Todd Slocum if he or his dirt-peddling magazine was paying her off?" Charlie paused, and then tossed in the clincher. "You knew of this outrageous story long before I did, Roz, but you never bothered to check it out. You just accepted it as true — or didn't want to find out otherwise."

Charlie then poured water from the carafe on the judge's desk into the glass sitting in front of him, at the same time holding up his left hand to signal that he wasn't done yet. Then he went on to say, in very measured words, "But perhaps, Roz, you did ask about payments, or other favors, for the Peters woman, as I would have expected of you. And if you did, we should know what answers you got."

He looked to the judge and spread his arms. "That's all I want to know, Judge."

To get back to his motion *in limine*, which is what brought them all there, Charlie added, "For all the reasons I mentioned earlier, this scandalous story should never be heard by the jury. And that's especially so if the story was bought and paid for."

Judge Krause put his hands behind his neck and swung around to look out the window. In a few seconds he turned back. "Okay, here's what we're going to do. And Sally," he said as he looked to his court reporter, "be sure to get this on the record." He paused just long enough to choose the right words. "Ms. Berman, if you or Mr. Shoemaker can answer Mr. Mayfield's questions about payments or other consideration going to Ms. Peters, and answer them on the record and with definite certainty, we'll hear you out. And to give you time to think it over, we'll reconvene tomorrow at four o'clock. And I don't want either of you coming back here to tell us 'I don't know' or 'I haven't checked.' You have a whole day to find out and check. And if, at that time, you can't tell us for sure if any benefits are or are not passing to Ms. Peters, in the past or in the future, then I want you to have this Todd Slocum in my chambers tomorrow at four. He'll tell us, and if he can't, we'll find someone who will. No evidence will be introduced in my courtroom that isn't on the up and up. And that's my order."

CHAPTER 45

While the lawyers were arguing Charlie Mayfield's motion *in limine,* Eddie and Carol Bennison were in their room at the Hyatt Hotel on Michigan Avenue, several blocks north of the courthouse. Clients are sometimes invited to join their lawyers for meetings in chambers, but Charlie didn't want Eddie anywhere near there for today's chambers session. "We're going to be talking about that Liz Peters crap," he told his client, "and it'll be better if you're not there. I can handle it. There'll be plenty of opportunity for you to tell your side of the story if we ever get that far, but if things go right in chambers, we'll never get that far.

"If we're lucky," Charlie went on to say, "and if I can convince the judge that I'm right about a few things, all the Peters stuff will be out of the case for good, and she'll be history as far as we're concerned."

Now, back at their hotel, Carol Bennison asked her husband, "Do you have any idea what they're talking about back there in chambers?"

Hoping his voice wouldn't betray him, Eddie tried to answer casually. "No idea, honey. Probably just a bunch of legal mumbo-jumbo." He added, with further guilt, "I'm sure it would all be very boring to us."

CHAPTER 46

Hugo Shoemaker, Roz Berman, and their three assistants shared an
elevator after leaving Judge Krause's chambers. If that elevator
were equipped with the same cameras used by the Marriott, it
would have revealed five silent people, each deep in thought, trying
to assess what transpired during the past hour or so. And none looked to
be in a good mood.

As they exited the Cook County Courthouse onto Washington Street
and headed for LaSalle Street to Berman's office a couple of blocks away,
Berman signaled to Shoemaker that they should fall back so they could
talk in private.

As soon as he did so, she hissed, "Hugo, that was a shitty thing you
did back there!"

"What?"

"You know what! You implied, strongly, that I was involved in some
skullduggery with this Peters thing. And the first words out of your mouth
were to wash your hands of the whole business, and to announce that you're
a silk-stocking appellate lawyer who doesn't get down in the dirt with the
trial lawyers who you obviously regard as disgusting hacks. We're a team,
Hugo, and you're getting paid handsomely to help win a case, and not to
shift blame for everything that could go wrong on — "

"Now you listen to me!" Shoemaker interrupted. "When Slocum
brought us that wretched story — "

"Oh, yes," Berman interrupted, "that reminds me. Good job on bringing Slocum into this and setting him up as the fall guy. Did you forget that he's the guy who hired you? And that he's the guy who has to approve your bills before you get paid? Todd Slocum is our client. He hired us to win a case, not to throw him under the bus."

"As I was trying to say, it was I who questioned the whole story when he brought it to us. But you bought it hook, line, and sinker the minute you heard it. I'll never forget how excited you were. You were bouncing around like a high school cheerleader. And to make matters worse, you ran with it straight to Mayfield in an attempt to blackmail Eddie Bennison — an attempt that is about to backfire in our faces.

"Yes, Roz, you're right. We are a team. So when you drag us through the pig sty, I get shit all over me, just like you do!"

Berman had no response to Shoemaker's outburst — an outburst that was uncharacteristic for the normally quiet law professor.

After a moment, Shoemaker broke the silence with a question that Roz Berman didn't want to hear. "So tell me, Roz, did anyone make a deal with Elizabeth Peters?"

"I certainly don't know of any such deal."

"But did you ask Slocum? Did you ask him if the Peters woman asked for anything? Or if he promised her anything? Like Mayfield said back there, aren't those obvious questions for a seasoned trial lawyer to ask? Paying a witness is highly unethical and could lead to disciplinary proceedings — maybe even disbarment. And if you put this woman on the stand, and her testimony turns out to be false, you — and maybe I — could be guilty of suborning perjury, which, I need not remind you, is a criminal offense."

Now defensive, Roz Berman replied, "I don't know a thing about any payments, and that's all I care to say about it for now."

"Fine," Hugo Shoemaker said, feeling for the first time that he finally had an advantage over the feisty woman who had been irritating him ever since he got into this case. "But I need to know what in the hell is going on around here — like you said, I'm on the team, so when we get back to the office, I'm going to call Slocum and ask him myself. And as far as handling him with kid gloves because he's the client, fuck him. Eddie Bennison isn't the only one with a reputation that can be ruined by this case."

CHAPTER 47

After the session in the judge's chambers, Charlie did not feel as upbeat as one would have guessed. He felt good about the way he presented his arguments, *but I couldn't get a final ruling from the judge, and, until I do, that Peters bitch is still hanging over our heads like the blade on a guillotine.*

Trials are wars that are won battle by battle, piece by piece. Charlie Mayfield knew that he came out ahead in today's skirmish, but the damned war was still on! And until it was over and he was the winner, he would have no victory celebrations over any of the little clashes.

CHAPTER 48

R oz Berman and Hugo Shoemaker were in a small conference room down the hall from her office.

"Are you sure you want to do this?" Berman asked, looking to the phone in Shoemaker's hand.

"Damn right," Shoemaker replied as he dialed Todd Slocum's direct number at *Tee Time*. It was about 6:00 p.m. in New York, but Shoemaker knew that Slocum would still be in his office waiting for the daily call that came from him or Berman to report what happened that day at the trial.

And Todd Slocum was indeed in his office, thinking about little else than the trial back in Chicago. As with every lawyer who was employed by any magazine during the past half century, Slocum had the recurring nightmare that someday his magazine would suffer the same fate as that suffered by *The Saturday Evening Post* in the 1960s. The *Post*, then one of the most widely read magazines in the country, published a story in March 1963, strongly implying that Paul "Bear" Bryant, the popular football coach for the University of Alabama, and Wally Butts, the athletic director of the University of Georgia, had fixed the Alabama-Georgia football game. Bryant and Butts each filed lawsuits against the magazine and its parent company, Curtis Publishing, for libel. A jury awarded Butts $3,060,000, at the time the largest defamation award in United States history and an enormous sum in those times. Bryant settled his case, receiving a great deal of money under terms that rendered the settlement tax-free. Totally apart from the monetary loss, *The Saturday Evening Post*, whose reputation for integrity and fair reporting was now destroyed, soon went out of business. The lawsuit unquestionably played a role in the demise of the magazine.

Berman remained in the room while Shoemaker placed his call to Slocum. After a few seconds, she heard him make the connection with New York.

"Good afternoon, Todd. It's Hugo. I'm here with Roz in her conference room. Sorry to call so late, but we spent the entire afternoon in the judge's chambers and didn't get back to the office until just now."

Roz Berman walked over to the phone on the conference room table and pressed the speaker button. Instantly, Todd Slocum's voice boomed throughout the conference room, and was caught in mid-sentence saying, " — so I'm still here in my office anyway. You said you were in chambers all afternoon, Hugo. Sounds heavy. Anything special?"

"Very special," Shoemaker relied. "As you know, a couple of days ago Roz told Mayfield about Elizabeth Peters and suggested that they withdraw their case or we would put Peters on the witness stand to tell her story. We were banking on the hope that they would do either that or ask for a small settlement that we could live with. If they did either, Roz told him, she would not put Ms. Peters on the stand, and Eddie Bennison could live with his wife happily ever after.

"So today, as we showed up for the afternoon court session, we were told to go into chambers where Mayfield had a motion to present. It turned out to be a motion *in limine* — do you know what that is, Todd?"

"Yeah. Isn't that where someone wants to block the evidence even before it's offered?"

"Correct. Obviously, Mayfield doesn't want the jury or anyone else to know anything about Liz Peters or what happened at that hotel. So he asked the judge to prevent the entry of any such evidence. He doesn't even want her to take the stand, and he doesn't want her name or her story mentioned by anyone. And he did it in chambers because the press was sitting out there in the courtroom, and Mayfield didn't want her name mentioned where they could hear it."

"And," Todd Slocum asked, "does this have anything to do with me?"

"Yes, Todd, it does," Shoemaker replied soberly. "The judge is very excited about all of this — especially because Mayfield came up with some convincing evidence that the Peters lady was lying about the Marriott episode. So the judge gave us until tomorrow afternoon to tell him definitely, and on the record, what, if anything, Peters got or is getting for her story. And if she's getting nothing, he wants us to assure him of that on the record. When I say 'on the record,' Todd, I'm saying that the judge wants us to be sworn and give these answers under oath. And he clearly told us that he doesn't want us to duck the issue by saying that we don't know or couldn't find out."

"Wow!" Slocum responded. "He's putting you and Roz on the spot."

"There's more. The judge said that if we can't give him all these answers, then he wants you to provide the answers — in his chambers tomorrow afternoon at four."

The silence on the other end of the phone was deafening. Berman and Shoemaker exchanged glances, each knowing that Todd Slocum was watching his life pass before him.

After what seemed an eternity, Slocum asked, "And how does the judge know about me? How did my name get into it?"

Shoemaker didn't duck the question, and answered forthrightly — almost. "The judge asked us how we learned about Liz Peters and her remarkable story. I replied that we had never met Peters, and that we learned about her from someone at the magazine. The judge pressed for a name, and I mentioned yours. I didn't have a choice."

Silence from the other end of the line.

Shoemaker continued. "Before we talk about tomorrow, Todd, I'd like you to tell us that you didn't make any deals with Liz Peters. And if you did, I want you to tell us exactly what deal or deals were made." After letting that sink in, Shoemaker went on to say, "If you can give us that information now, and in a way that we can relay it to Judge Krause, then maybe you won't have to be there. But just to be safe, we want you in Chicago anyway, in case the judge isn't satisfied with what Roz and I tell him. We want to be able to bring you in to speak for yourself if that's what he wants."

Slocum sounded frantic when he replied. "I already told Roz what they wanted when — "

Shoemaker cut him off. "They? Who is 'they'?"

"There's this guy, Dan Curry. He's a friend of Liz Peters. His wife and Peters work together. Curry lives in Detroit, but he flew to Chicago to meet with Reed and tell him about the Marriott escapade. After they met, Reed called me to tell me about Peters, and he told me that with the information they had we could destroy Bennison and his case against us."

"What's Curry's role in all his, other than being the husband of her friend?

"He told me that he represents Liz."

Shoemaker, who was making notes of the conversation, stopped and looked over to Berman to see if she noticed anything strange in what Slocum had just said. Seeing no action from her, Shoemaker said into the phone, "Todd, you just said a few things that I have to ask you about. First, you said that Curry represented the Peters lady. Is he a lawyer?"

"No. I asked him that. He said he wasn't a lawyer, but that he and Liz had a business arrangement."

Shoemaker closed his eyes. A business arrangement means money, and money means trouble if it's tied to buying evidence. He didn't want to pursue this further for fear of what he might learn, but he knew he had to.

"Okay," he continued, "we'll come back to that. You also said a minute ago that Curry told you that he represented Peters. How did he tell you? Did you meet with him? Or was it over the phone?"

"We met. After he met with Reed in Chicago, Reed called me and asked me to fly out there so he could tell me all about Liz and her story. I did that. Then I called Curry from Chicago and told him I would fly to Detroit to meet with him and Liz. I did that, and we met in Detroit that night — the three of us: Curry, Liz, and me."

"And why did you want to meet with them?"

"Well, I knew that this story she was telling could be important, and I knew that I'd have to tell you and Roz about it, but I was getting it third-hand. Liz told it to Curry, Curry told it to Reed, and Reed told it to me. I wanted to get it straight from the horse's mouth before bringing it to you. And the best way to do that, I figured, was to meet face-to-face with Curry and this woman. Reed gave me Curry's number — he didn't have *her* number. So I called Curry to set up the meeting. I thought I was doing the right thing."

Shoemaker sighed audibly. "Meeting with them is fine, Todd. But what takes place at the meeting could be a problem. So let's get back to where we started. What did Curry say they wanted for all this?"

After a few seconds, a quiet answer came over the line from New York. "Two million dollars."

Roz Berman's face didn't register any surprise at hearing this. Hugo Shoemaker, on the other hand, grimaced.

"But," Slocum was quick to add, "I never gave him a red cent, and I never said or even implied that we'd give him anything. I swear to God, that's the truth."

Roz Berman leaned toward the phone. "Todd, if Judge Krause were to ask you, under oath, could you truthfully and confidently say that you didn't in any way agree or imply that you or anyone else at the magazine would pay anything for Elizabeth Peters to testify or give her story to the press? Could you yourself say that, Todd, under oath?"

"Yes, of course!"

"Okay. We're scheduled to meet with the judge tomorrow at four, after court adjourns. Get here as soon as you can so we'll have some time before then to go over this again. Try to be at the courtroom by noon, and the three of us can have lunch together. Will that work for you?"

"Sure, I'll try to get a flight tonight. Otherwise I'll take an early morning flight and, with the time change, I'd be in Chicago in plenty of time. I'll call if I run into any problems — otherwise I'll see you just before noon." Then Slocum asked the question that Berman and Shoemaker both knew had to be tormenting him: "Will I be in trouble with the judge?"

Roz Berman answered. "Not at all — as long as you can assure the judge that Curry and Peters came to you out of the blue, and that you didn't agree to pay her off."

"By the way, Todd," Shoemaker interjected, "There was something else I wanted to ask you."

"What's that?"

"In this conversation we're having, you keep referring to Elizabeth Peters as 'Liz.' Sounds like you've become close friends. We don't want anyone to get the impression that you and she are pals. So, if and when you talk to the judge tomorrow, make it 'Elizabeth' or, better yet, 'Ms. Peters.'"

TUESDAY

CHAPTER 49

Television shows, movies, and books about trials give the impression that they are action-packed dramas, not unlike the gladiator battles of ancient Rome. In them, every minute is filled with exciting surprises, devastating disclosures, and humiliating admissions. Every word is critical to the ultimate outcome, and nothing is irrelevant.

In truth, however, onlookers would be bored to tears observing what mostly transpires in the courtroom during a trial. Lawyers debate petty objections, court reporters are constantly reading back testimony, judges are having hushed conversations with lawyers at the side of the bench, and 95 percent of the testimony consists of routine background information. Lawyers will ask a witness six questions when one would do, and witnesses' answers are six times longer than necessary. In those movies and TV shows, jurors are shown in rapt attention to every detail; in real trials, they do their best not to nod off.

The next day's proceedings in Judge Harry Krause's courtroom followed that general pattern. Representatives of the Professional Golfers Association and the United States Golf Association spent the morning reading and explaining to the jury some of the incoherently ambiguous rules of golf dealing with the grooves of the club face and the marking of the golf ball on the putting green. They attempted to define everyday words such as "close," "foreign substance," "intentionally," and "so as to give an advantage." There was even some discussion as to the object used to mark a ball on the putting green. The official rules of golf require that the marker must be a "small coin or other similar object," which sounds unambiguous, but there is always someone who will question whether a quarter is a "small coin," or whether a square plastic marker is a "similar object" to a coin.

At approximately 3:30 in the afternoon, just after a witness and lawyer were arguing over the meaning of "addressing" the ball, Judge Krause adjourned the trial until 9:00 the next morning. Then, speaking to the two sets of lawyers seated at the counsel tables before him, he said, "Will counsel please join me in my chambers in ten minutes. Thank you."

In less than ten minutes, all of the lawyers were seated in the judge's chambers in the same seats they had occupied the preceding afternoon. But there was one additional person — a thin, fair-haired man who appeared to be fiftyish, and nervous, was sitting next to Roz Berman. He was Todd Slocum.

"Sally," Judge Krause said as he looked to his court reporter, "we'll go on the record now, but, as I ruled yesterday, the record will be sealed, subject to my further order." Sally Ringer straightened in her chair as she pulled her stenotype machine closer to her.

"Ms. Berman," the judge intoned, "are you prepared to give us the information we were discussing before we adjourned yesterday?"

"We are, Your Honor. I have here next to me Mr. Todd Slocum, Senior Vice President and General Counsel of Tee Time, Incorporated. He can provide that information. Would you like for me to put the necessary questions to him, or would you like to question him yourself?"

"Please go ahead, but first I'll swear the witness." Judge Krause then said to Todd Slocum, "Please stand and raise your right hand." When he did so, the judge continued. "Do you swear, or affirm, that the testimony you are about to give shall be the truth, the whole truth, and nothing but the truth?"

"I do, yes."

Roz Berman shifted slightly in her seat so that she was half-facing Todd Slocum, who sat to her left. She began by asking the routine background questions to establish, for the record, Slocum's name, address, and job title and description. Then she got to the business at hand.

"Mr. Slocum. Did you have occasion to meet with Elizabeth Peters since this trial began?"

"Yes."

"Please explain how that meeting came about."

"Max Reed, a reporter of ours who was a witness in this case, called me the day after he finished testifying to tell me that he had information that might be important, but he was hesitant about discussing it on the phone. Since I was flying back to Chicago that evening, we arranged to meet that night at the hotel where we were both staying.

"When we met, he told me that someone named Dan Curry had approached him and told him all about that night at the Marriott. He claimed that he was representing Liz — Elizabeth — Peters. The next day I telephoned Mr. Curry and asked if I could meet with him and Ms. Peters. I was in Chicago, but I said I could fly to Detroit, where they lived, on my way back to New York. They agreed, and we met later that night in Detroit."

"And where exactly was that meeting?" Roz Berman asked.

"At the coffee shop in the Hilton Hotel out at the airport, where I was going to spend the night."

"And I assume you discussed a subject having something to do with this case."

"Yes."

"Did Elizabeth Peters or Mr. Curry indicate that Ms. Peters could offer testimony that could have a bearing on this case?"

"Yes."

"Now, Mr. Slocum, without you telling us what that testimony might be, did they tell you what it was?"

"Yes, they did."

"And did they describe it in detail?"

"Yes."

"How about substantiation? Did they give or show you anything to substantiate the testimony she could give?"

"Yes, they showed me photographs and also a sworn written statement signed by Ms. Peters."

"Did they give you copies of those photographs and the sworn statement?"

"Well, yes, eventually."

"Could you explain that?"

"At first they didn't want to part with the pictures and statement, but I told them that I needed them to show to you and to Mr. Shoemaker. I explained to them that the two of you were running the case and that I, as house counsel, didn't have any decision-making authority about the trial."

"Mr. Slocum, was there any agreement, express or implied, to give money or anything else of value to Dan Curry or Elizabeth Peters in return for the statement and those photographs?"

"No, absolutely not. There was no such agreement."

"Then why did they contact Max Reed? And why did they meet with you?"

"Well, Mr. Curry said he was representing Ms. Peters, not as a lawyer but as a businessman, and that he was hoping that we would be willing to pay for the testimony that she could give."

"Did he tell you what kind of payment they wanted?"

"Yes. He said they wanted two million dollars."

Judge Krause's eyes widened when he heard this. Even the clicking of Sally Ringer's stenotype machine momentarily stopped when Slocum mentioned two million dollars.

Slocum continued. "He also told me that, if we preferred, they would give the story to the press instead of having Ms. Peters testify."

"Now, Mr. Slocum, I want you to listen very carefully to my next question, and I want you to think very carefully before you answer it. Do you understand that?"

"Yes."

"Did you, at that meeting or at any other time, give any reason for Mr. Curry or for Ms. Peters to believe that you, Mr. Shoemaker, I, or anyone else connected with *Tee Time* would give anything to them — money or anything else — in return for her testimony, or in return for her telling her story to the press?"

"Certainly not!" Slocum answered quickly and without the slightest doubt in his voice, just as he and Roz Berman had rehearsed a half hour earlier. "And I said nothing — nothing at all — from which any such inference could be made."

"Then why did you say, a couple of minutes ago, that you needed the statement and photographs to show to Mr. Shoemaker and me?"

"Because I thought that it was important for you and Mr. Shoemaker to see those pictures and read her statement. I knew we'd never pay for her story, but it seemed logical to me that you should know about it before you heard about it elsewhere — or read it in the papers." Slocum paused for a moment, and then added, "Perhaps I was wrong about that, but I thought you should see the pictures and statement; and, at the time, I thought that the best way to get my hands on them was to imply to Curry that you and Mr. Shoemaker might find a way to make some legitimate accommodation for them. I did that as bait to get the pictures and the statement. And it worked, because they gave them to me without getting anything in return. But I repeat — I never gave them reason to think that you would give them anything."

"And as you sit here today, Mr. Slocum, can you tell us under oath that, as far as you are aware, no payment of any kind has been made — or promised — to Ms. Peters or Mr. Curry in return for her story?"

"Certainly."

"And did you, or anyone else to your knowledge, promise or offer them anything of value — anything whatsoever — if they would take that story to the press?"

"Of course not."

"Thank you, Mr. Slocum."

CHAPTER 50

As soon as Roz Berman was done questioning Slocum, Charlie Mayfield asked, "May I ask Mr. Slocum a few questions, Your Honor?"

"Of course," Judge Krause replied.

"Mr. Slocum. My name is Charlie Mayfield, and I'm Eddie Bennison's lawyer in this case."

"I know who you are, Mr. Mayfield. Your name has become a household word at *Tee Time*."

"Well," Charlie responded, "I'm flattered."

"You might not be if you knew the context in which it's been mentioned."

Charlie Mayfield led the laughter following that comment. Then he composed himself and resumed. "You said a while ago that you told Ms. Peters and Mr. Curry that you needed the pictures and statement to show to your lawyers, Roz Berman and Hugo Shoemaker, and that you purposely implied that they might, in return, make some accommodation. Weren't those the words you used?"

"Yes, those were the words I used."

"And isn't that pretty close to a promise to pay, even if you had no intention of keeping that promise?"

"With all respect, Mr. Mayfield, you're slicing my words very thin. An implication that something might happen is a long way short of a promise that something will happen. The fact is, *they* came to us with an offer to sell testimony; *we* did not go to them with an offer to buy testimony. I did nothing but listen. And if I went a little too far in my eagerness to get my hands on the pictures and the statement, then I'm sorry for that, but I was in an unfamiliar situation that they don't teach us about in law schools, and I was sitting there talking to a guy who was trying to shake me down. As I admitted a minute ago, I might have used the wrong words when I said something about an accommodation, but, nevertheless, I was able to get my hands on the pictures and statement without paying anything — and without promising anything. So, whatever I said to them worked."

"I have one more question," Mayfield said, looking straight into Todd Slocum's eyes. "Since the meeting that night in Detroit at the Hilton Hotel, have you had any further meetings or conversations with either Dan Curry or Elizabeth Peters?"

"I had one conversation with Dan Curry. He called me at my office. It was a few days ago — I think last Thursday or Friday."

"Could you give us the gist of that conversation?"

"There wasn't much. He asked if we were going to pay any money, and I told him no. It got a little heated. He pressed me, and then I lost my temper and told him to get out of my life. I called him a few names and then I hung up on him."

CHAPTER 51

After Charlie was done examining Todd Slocum, and none of the other lawyers had questions for him, Judge Krause excused him from the room. He then asked if anyone else had anything to say regarding Charlie's motion *in limine*.

Roz Berman said she'd like to be heard.

"Please go ahead, Ms. Berman," the judge said, sticking with the last names since they were still on the record, which, at least for time being, would be sealed.

"Your Honor, it's clear from Mr. Slocum's testimony that no payments or other inappropriate conduct has encouraged Elizabeth Peters to come forth with her offer to give testimony in this case. There were no inducements whatsoever. In fact, Mr. Slocum made it obvious in his last conversation with Mr. Curry that under no circumstances would any payments be made.

"So, Your Honor, there is not a scintilla of evidence to suggest that Ms. Peters' testimony is tainted by any misconduct on our part, Therefore, I ask that Mr. Mayfield's motion *in limine* be denied and that we be given leave to call Elizabeth Peters to the stand."

"Your Honor," Charlie interjected, "I also had other grounds for my motion which I could — "

Judge Krause interrupted him in mid-sentence. "That won't be necessary, Mr. Mayfield. I followed your argument very closely, and I'm familiar with all the points you made to support your motion *in limine*." With that, the judge announced, "In fact, I'm now prepared to make my ruling."

———————

After looking to see that Sally Ringer, his court reporter, was ready at her keys, he began. "First, Ms. Berman, I'm in complete agreement with your views on the manner in which the potential testimony of Elizabeth Peters has come forth. On the basis of what I've heard thus far, I find no illegal or unethical conduct on the part of *Tee Time*, or any other defendant, or any lawyer for the defense. Considering the sensitive nature of this testimony, and its surprise arrival on the scene, I can see why Mr. Mayfield's special detector set off alarms. But, after hearing Mr. Slocum's testimony, and hearing nothing to the contrary, I believe they were false alarms. Ms. Peters' motives in seeking payment are definitely impure, but I don't see anything impure on the part of the defendants. Therefore, I will not bar the testimony for the reason that it was ill begotten."

Roz Berman gave an audible sigh of relief. Hugo Shoemaker looked her way and smiled. His reputation had just dodged a bullet.

The Judge was still speaking. "Mr. Mayfield raised other grounds for barring the testimony of Elizabeth Peters, and I'll consider them separately.

"One of Mr. Mayfield's grounds was that the would-be testimony was false. To make his point, he introduced several video tapes and photos to refute Ms. Peters' statement that she went with Mr. Bennison to his room at the Marriott Hotel. To be sure, those tapes and photos showed that Ms. Peters was quite on her own in going to — and entering — Mr. Bennison's room. However, it is not my job to verify the truthfulness of a witness's testimony before it is heard. Veracity is for the jury to decide after hearing the witness examined and cross-examined. Accordingly, I will not bar the testimony on the grounds that it may be false — that would be for the jury to determine.

"Of course," and here the judge looked directly at Roz Berman and Hugo Shoemaker, "you could be taking a big gamble by putting Ms. Peters on the stand to testify. If she were to testify, and if Mr. Mayfield showed the tapes and photos to the jury and read them her sworn statement, they may well conclude that she's lying about the entire Marriott episode. She definitely went to Mr. Bennison's room on her own, in contradiction to her sworn statement. And if the jury believes that she lied, they could pin it on you or your clients."

Charlie Mayfield was biting his lip. If the judge was going to let Elizabeth Peters testify *before* Charlie could bring in the tapes and pictures to show she was lying, it would be too late. By then the jurors — and the press sitting there in the courtroom with their notebooks and cell phones — will already have heard that lying harlot tell about Eddie's penchant for wild sex and violence against women. The possibility that the tapes would prove — an hour after she testified — that she was lying would be of little comfort to Eddie Bennison. By then the story would be all over the airwaves, and the whole world would know about it.

He'd have more to say to the judge on this, but for now he'd bide his time and bring it up after the judge finished with the entire ruling.

Judge Krause continued with his ruling. "Mr. Mayfield raised two other reasons why he believes the testimony of Elizabeth Peters should be barred. In short, these reasons are, first, that the testimony would be irrelevant to the issues in this case, and second, that the testimony would be so inflammatory that the prejudice to the plaintiff, Mr. Bennison, would be disproportionately high compared to any light it might cast on the central issues in this case — so high, in fact, that it would preclude the jury from judging him fairly on the main issues."

Here Judge Krause paused to take a sip of water and to give his court reporter — and her nimble fingers — a deserved respite. After checking to see that she was ready to resume clacking away at the keys on her stenotype machine, he continued. "The question of 'disproportionate prejudice' is a sticky one. All evidence offered by one side is prejudicial to the other side — otherwise there would be no reason to offer it." He looked up and showed a rare smile. "It isn't often that a lawyer offers evidence that is complimentary to the other side." Then he went on. "So the question really is: how prejudicial is too prejudicial?

"This is one of those eternal questions that have vexed judges for centuries. Fortunately for me, I don't have to answer it for our case today." Hearing this, Roz Berman and Hugo Shoemaker looked at each other with puzzled looks on their faces. But Charlie caught the judge's drift immediately, and breathed a sigh of relief.

"I don't have to decide," the judge was saying, "whether the testimony should be barred as overly prejudicial because," and here he glanced at Charlie, "I have decided that the testimony should be barred on grounds of irrelevancy and immateriality. And once I decide that it should be barred for one reason, I don't have to decide whether it should be barred for other reasons. If it's barred, it's barred."

Now Judge Krause leaned back in his chair to explain why he decided that "irrelevancy" carried the day. "The issues in this case are simply these: Did the publications contain lies? Were the lies published with malice, as that term is defined for these cases, or with a reckless indifference to the truth? Did those lies damage Mr. Bennison's reputation? And, if all these questions are answered in the affirmative, then what amount of money will fairly compensate Mr. Bennison for that damage? The first three questions will decide if Mr. Bennison wins. The last would decide how much he should recover.

"Those four questions are the four cornerstones that form the boundary lines of this entire case. No part of the case extends beyond those four corners. In the opinion of this court, Mr. Bennison's alleged proclivity for hotel room sex or female abuse are nowhere within those four corners, and therefore they have no place in this trial. For purposes of this case, those issues have no more relevancy than whether Mr. Bennison goes to church, helps elderly ladies across the street, or remembers his mother on Mother's Day. Accordingly, it is my ruling that the testimony of Elizabeth Peters, to the extent that it is reflected in her statement that has been given to me, should be barred. The plaintiff's motion *in limine* is hereby granted. I ask that Mr. Mayfield prepare a written order for me to sign to effectuate that ruling."

Roz Berman, to no one's surprise, was on her feet. "Your Honor?"

"Yes, Ms. Berman?"

"Even if the testimony of Elizabeth Peters is inadmissible for irrelevancy, as you have ruled, we respectfully submit that we can offer that testimony to impeach the credibility of Mr. Bennison as a witness. The veracity of any witness can be challenged — or impeached — in a number of ways. The most common way to impeach a witness is to point out that he or she has made statements contradictory to his or her testimony. Another way to impeach a witness is to show that he or she has been guilty of moral turpitude — moral turpitude of a nature that would put his credibility as a witness under suspicion. For example, a jury may believe that a person who had been proven to be a liar in the past might likewise be prone to lie while testifying. Similarly, a jury may choose to reject the testimony of a person shown to be morally corrupt."

Judge Krause had enough of this lecture on courtroom basics. "I understand all of that, Ms. Berman. What is your point?"

"My point, Your Honor, is that once the jury hears about Mr. Bennison's behavior with Elizabeth Peters, they may feel that he is a man without morals and therefore prone to lie when it suits his purposes. Therefore, they may believe that he lied when he testified that he didn't cheat or use performance-enhancing drugs. In other words, if the jurors hear what he did with — and to — Elizabeth Peters, they may well conclude that his morals are so poor that his testimony should not be believed. They might conclude that a man who cheats on his wife may indeed cheat on the golf course, and that he was untruthful when he denied it. So, for that limited purpose — to show that Mr. Bennison's behavior with Ms. Peters provides a reason for the jury to believe that he might have lied on the witness stand — we should be permitted to put Ms. Peters on the stand."

Judge Krause was shaking his head even before Berman finished. "Please, Ms. Berman, you insult my intelligence. Do you seriously think that I am so naive that I would believe that you would be introducing this incendiary testimony for the limited purpose of challenging Mr. Bennison's credibility as a witness? *Please!* We all know that you want this testimony for *other* reasons — you want the jurors to despise Mr. Bennison for reasons that have absolutely nothing to do with this case. And you want to hold him up to public ridicule to a far greater extent than your client did with its articles in *Tee Time*.

"My ruling stands, Ms. Berman. And I remind you, and everyone else, that I will not tolerate any leaks about any of this to the press or to anyone else, and that applies to your clients as well as to the lawyers. What has transpired in this room over the past two days will stay in this room, and, as I said yesterday, the transcript is sealed for my eyes only until I rule otherwise. That's enough for today. We're adjourned."

On the way out of the judge's chambers, Charlie Mayfield took the arm of his associate, Pete Stevens. "Call Eddie," he whispered. "Tell him he owes me a drink — the biggest and driest martini they make at the Metropolitan Club."

CHAPTER 52

Eddie Bennison had persuaded his wife, Carol, that they should spend the afternoon going for a walk and doing a little shopping while the lawyers were spending most of the day in the judge's chambers. He knew that they were discussing the Liz Peters problem, and he didn't want Carol anywhere near the courthouse. He knew he'd have to tell her about it and was waiting for the right time. In the meantime, some peace and quiet would be welcome.

The maddening publicity surrounding the trial brought out countless gawkers as well as an endless stream of autograph hounds and well-meaning fans. Even the obsequious attention of the hotel staff was wearing on their nerves. To get some relief from all of this, they decided that when they returned to the hotel they would order dinner from room service and watch a movie on TV.

After dinner, Eddie took a small bottle of overpriced wine from the little refrigerator built into the credenza in their spacious suite and handed it to Carol. At the same time, he pulled out a soda for himself. Then, taking a deep breath, he decided it was now time to bite the bullet. Ever since Charlie told him a few days ago about the threat from Liz Peters, he had been agonizing about whether — and how — to tell Carol about it. Ever since their wedding, they had followed a pattern of not keeping things from one another. *Secrets are verboten*, they often reminded each other, and each was proud to have unfailingly honored that commitment. So, Eddie, realized, he'd have to come out with it, and now was as good a time as ever. *Now was the time.*

He settled onto the settee next to Carol. "There's something we ought to talk about, honey," he said in a voice he didn't recognize.

"Okay, I'll bite. Max Reed was telling the truth about you in those magazine articles, right?"

"Wrong," he replied, trying to manage a smile at her humor. "It's something else."

Carol Bennison couldn't miss the sober tone of her husband's voice and knew this would be not be a joking matter. She looked him in the eye and said, "Go ahead, tell me."

"Well," he replied in obvious discomfort, "remember my telling you about all those groupies who hang around the Tour players?"

"Oh, Lord!" She grimaced, covering her eyes with her hands. "Don't tell me you're running off with one of them! Is she taking my crystal and silver, too?"

"No," Eddie chuckled, "it's nothing like that." He put down his glass still half-filled with soda. "Let me explain. A couple of years ago, when I was playing at Oakland Hills outside of Detroit, some gal tried to pick me up right after I finished dinner at the hotel. It was at the Marriott."

Carol, listening to his every word, didn't know what to expect. But she took some solace in knowing that her husband was an honorable man — as far as she knew. "Okay," she said, "tell me about it, but start at the beginning."

Eddie sat back and, staring out the window, spoke in a quiet voice. "I had dinner in the hotel restaurant, alone, a little earlier, and after dinner I went into the cocktail lounge for a Coke before calling it a night. I had my charts with me and was looking at them to prepare for the next day's round. While I was sitting there, minding my own business, this woman came over to my table from where she was sitting with some other women and started asking me a lot of questions. Then she sat down, but by then I may have invited her to have a seat since she was standing and I was sitting.

"As it turned out, she was a thief — I'll explain that in a minute — and she must have figured that I was a good target. I don't think she knew who

I was, or even if she knew anything about golf, but she kept commenting on my Rolex — she even asked how much it cost, and what kind of car I drove. I decided to get the hell out of there, so I called for my tab, paid it, and headed up to my room — alone.

"I thought that was the end of it, but a little while later there was a knock on my door. I cracked it open to see who was there, and in she walks like she owned the place. The next thing I — "

"Wait a minute, Ed, how did she know what room you were in?"

"I thought about that. I think she must have seen my room number when I signed the tab, or maybe I just told the waiter or waitress out loud what it was."

"So she was smitten by your good looks and Rolex watch. And what happened when this lovely thing came charging into your room?"

"I was just getting out of the shower when I heard a knock on the door. I figured it was the hotel staff wanting to turn down the bed. I wrapped a towel around my waist and cracked the door open to see who was there, and as soon as I did that she shoved the door open and marched right in. I was caught completely off guard. I quickly ducked into the bathroom to collect my thoughts. Then I put on one of those robes the hotel provides and came out a minute or two later to tell her to get the hell out of there or I would call hotel security. But when I came back into the room — there she was, standing at the dresser and going through my wallet. And she had my Rolex in her hand. I exploded — grabbed her by the arm and told her to put that stuff down and leave. Next thing I knew, she starts to spray me in the face — I think it was mace. Some of it got in my eyes. It burned. Scared the hell out of me. Without even thinking, I started swinging and gave her a couple of good shots — right in her face. She grabbed her purse and ran out of the room — I think she was afraid I'd kill her."

Eddie took another sip of his soda and looked directly at Carol. "That's it. Honey. That's the whole story. When she left the room, and didn't take my wallet or Rolex, I thought that was the end of it. I even joked about it the next day with some of the guys at the course."

"So it was a few years ago and it's all over. Why are you telling me about it now?"

"Well, the papers and the TV are covering the trial, and she saw my picture, put two and two together, and decided that maybe she could get some money out of this. So she told some shake-down artist in Detroit about what happened, but, of course, she put her own twist on the story. According to her, I invited her to come to my room, and then I beat the hell out of her without any provocation whatsoever. She even has a picture of her bruised face."

"And did she say that the two of you had sex?"

"Yeah, but we didn't. In fact, she said I was wild, highly passionate, and 'over the top' erotic."

Carol hugged him and said, "Well, that's a relief. Now I know she's a liar."

After a few minutes of silent thought, Carol got to the heart of the matter. "Is all this going to come out at the trial? If so, it'll make headlines all over the world."

"Yeah, right. It's been driving me crazy. The folks at *Tee Time* are threatening to put her on the stand, but Charlie said he had some plan to keep it from coming out, and a while ago his assistant, Pete, called to tell me that everything's cool.

"The judge ruled that none of this can come out at the trial, and the judge warned the other side not to leak any of this to the press. He doesn't want the jury or anyone else to know about it." He smiled and added, "Charlie said we're home free as far as this is concerned. In fact," Eddie added, "you would never have known about it if I hadn't just told you."

"How did Charlie pull that off?"

"I don't know the details yet, but I do know that he came up with some fantastic evidence to prove that this lady is an out and out liar."

"How long have you known that she was trying to come back to haunt us?"

"Three or four days."

She hugged him again. "I'm sorry you had to deal with this alone. It must have been a tough few days."

"It was, and if you ever took the time to do my laundry, you'd know just how tough it was."

She grabbed a toss pillow from the settee and threw it at him.

In spite of the attempted humor, Carol Bennison, usually tough as nails, was fighting tears. She went into the bathroom of their suite to wipe her eyes and tidy her makeup. When she came back, she sat next to her husband and put her arms around his neck. "I love you, Eddie, and I trust you. I even believe you."

WEDNESDAY MORNING

CHAPTER 53

At eight the next morning, Eddie and Carol Bennison were sitting in Charlie Mayfield's office on LaSalle Street in downtown Chicago — an area commonly known as "The Loop" because it is surrounded, or "looped," by the elevated tracks for the metropolitan transit trains known as the "El."

Charlie started the meeting by saying, "I thought this might be a good time for us to review where we stand on the trial, and to outline what we still have to do.

"As things now stand, I'd say we're in pretty good shape. The jury seems to like Eddie, and my instincts tell me that they couldn't stand that jackass, Max Reed.

"That's also the opinion of my 'shadow jurors.'"

"'Shadow jurors?'" Carol Bennison asked. "Who are they?"

"I guess I never mentioned this to you. I have three people sitting out in the courtroom throughout the trial. They hear and see the same things that the jury sees and hears. They tell me when I need to clarify something, or when the other side makes a strong point that I have to refute. And more important, they are trained to study the jurors' body language and facial expressions, and that gives them some idea when the jurors are interested, confused, or bored. They report their impressions back to me, and it helps me keep the jury tuned in to our points."

"Do they discuss their impressions with each other?" Carl asked.

"No, not at all. In fact, none of them knows who the others are. I don't want them talking to each other — I want their individual impressions, and I don't want those impressions influenced by the others. I talk to them separately throughout the trial to get their feedback."

Charlie could see that the Bennisons were intrigued by this aspect of the trial, so he told them more. "It's uncanny," he added, "how accurate they are when it comes to predicting what's going through the jurors' minds. Whenever I finish a trial, I make it a point to talk to the jurors to find out why they decided what they did. Often, they'll tell me that a certain witness, or a certain piece of evidence, was very persuasive to their final verdict, or maybe that something was too confusing. And it amazes me how often they tell me the same things that my shadow jurors were telling me during the trial. So, when my shadow jurors make suggestions on what I should do in the courtroom, I damned well listen to them; to me, it's the same as the real jurors telling me what they're thinking." Charlie looked up to add, "They're well worth the modest cost; and some, mostly retirees, don't charge because they enjoy doing it."

Eddie asked, "Did you say that they believed the jury liked me?"

"They did. My shadow jurors told me that the jury looked very receptive while you were testifying. Many were nodding their heads and even wore slight smiles. On the other hand, when Max Reed was on the stand, some of the jurors were scowling, and they had their arms crossed, which is a classic sign that they aren't buying what they're hearing. And, the best part for me: my shadow jurors themselves liked you a lot — and they believed you. And they know I don't want to hear phony optimism. I don't want 'em puffing me up and building up my expectations if it's not warranted."

Charlie wanted to make another point. "Of course, I myself could watch the jurors and try to read their thoughts. As a matter of fact, I do! I'm trying to read their minds from the very first minute until the case is over, but I'm not as good at it as my shadow jurors are. For one thing, I'm biased, so I might be prone to read them in the way I want to read them; for another, I know too many things about the case that the jurors don't know, so it's hard for me to see the case through the narrower lens through which they see the case. But my shadow jurors see and hear exactly what the real jurors see and hear, nothing more and nothing less, so it's easier for them see things just as the jurors see them."

Eddie and Carol were shaking their heads in awe, continually impressed with the way that Charlie covered all the bases.

Then Eddie looked at his wife and raised his eyebrows to ask if this was a time to tell Charlie about their conversation from the night before. Carol answered with a slight nod of her head.

"Charlie," Eddie said, "we can talk about the Elizabeth Peters thing if you'd like. I told Carol all about it last night."

"Well," Charlie smiled, "that must have been a pleasant conversation."

"It was fine," Carol assured the lawyer. "Eddie doesn't lie, and I fully believe what he told me about that night."

"I do too," Charlie was quick to say. "In fact, I got my hands on some video tapes that support Eddie's version of what happened that night. And those tapes show that the lady lied."

"You're kidding!" Carol exclaimed.

"No, I'm dead serious! I mentioned some of this to Eddie last Saturday morning in my office. Eddie told me, and apparently you as well, that the Peters lady came up to his room after he was already there. But she signed a statement, under oath, saying that they both went to his room together. This is a significant difference. If we could show that she went up there alone, and after he was already there, it would show that her sworn statement was false. It would also support Eddie's version that he went up alone to prepare for his tournament the next day, and to get a good night's sleep.

"And we got lucky," Charlie said. "I was able to get hold of the manager and the head of security at the Marriott hotel in Pontiac, Michigan, where this all look place. As I hoped, they had video tapes covering the elevators and corridors for that night, and they still had them."

Charlie paused to let this all sink in, but Carol could not stand the suspense. "So tell us, Charlie, what did the tapes show?"

"Well, first, the individual frames for the tapes are marked with the date and time, and those dates and times correspond with the date and times we're looking for. The date was August 17, 2007, which was on the Friday night during the tournament at Oakland Hills, and the cameras got her just minutes after Eddie signed a tab at the cocktail lounge. The tab showed the time it was printed.

"Twelve minutes after the tab was printed, which would have been about nine or ten minutes after Eddie signed it, we have a tape showing this woman going up the elevator alone — the tape shows the entire interior of the elevator, and she is unquestionably alone.

"We have other tapes showing her walking down the corridor to Eddie's room, alone. Another shows her standing in front of the door to his room getting all dolled up — putting on lipstick and tidying up her hair.

"And the clincher, if we need one, shows her knocking on the door and when it opened slightly — presumably by Eddie to see who it was who was knocking — she pushed the door wide open and kind of barged right in—just like Eddie said before we saw the tapes."

Carol blurted, "So doesn't that prove that she made this whole thing up?"

"Pretty much," Charlie replied. "She clearly lied about going to the room together with Eddie — the tapes prove that — and lying about that casts doubt on the rest of her story."

Carol now asked the same question she had asked Eddie earlier. "How do you think she knew what room Eddie was in, if he didn't tell her?"

"Easy," the lawyer answered. "When Eddie asked for the tab, he probably told the waiter or waitress what room he was in so the drinks could be charged to his room. Ms. Peters likely heard him say the room number. Or, when he signed the tab, he would have had to write down his room number. She was sitting next to him and it would have been easy for her to see it. Or, after he left, she could have used a pretext to ask the server to show her the signed tab — like saying she wanted to be sure that they weren't overcharged or undercharged — and that would have given her another opportunity to learn the room number."

"Okay," Carol said, "that makes sense. But let me ask another question. Wouldn't it be a good to have more pictures — pictures showing *Eddie* going up in the elevator alone? Surely the hotel has those as well."

"I thought of that, Carol, but decided not to ask for it. I didn't want to tip off the Marriott manager or security guy that Eddie was involved in my inquiry. All they know is that there was a room and bar tab in the name of 'Ben Edwards,' the alias Eddie uses. But if I had them look for his face on a tape, they may have recognized him — remember, his face is well known — and that could lead to unwanted publicity for us. I didn't want anyone being able to make a connection between Eddie Bennison and some woman in a hotel who later had a black eye and split lip. If we ever needed such a tape, I knew I could get it later."

Charlie Mayfield leaned back in his chair, smiled, and proudly announced, "But we won't need such a tape! Yesterday, after showing the tapes we had to Judge Krause, and after I made some other legal points, the judge ruled that Elizabeth Peters cannot testify in the case. He also made it clear that no one on the other side — the lawyers, *Tee Time*, or anyone connected with any of them — should leak, directly or indirectly, any of this sordid story to the press or they would be held in contempt of court. He even granted my request that the transcript of the session be sealed and not available for anyone to see except him."

Charlie leaned back and said, "All in all, it was a very good day."

"And," Eddie said with a big grin on his face, "we had a bet and I owe you a drink."

"Yep. The biggest and driest martini they can make at the Metropolitan Club."

Then Lillian, Charlie's secretary, came in to remind them that it was time to head over to the courthouse for the morning session.

CHAPTER 54

"I would like to call Ward Newton to the stand as an adverse witness," Charlie Mayfield announced at the beginning of the Wednesday morning session of the trial.

A short man with black, curly hair walked hurriedly to the witness stand, as if wanting to get this over with as quickly — and painlessly — as possible. He looked to be in his fifties.

Ward Newton, *Tee Time*'s Vice President of Circulation, was already familiar with Charlie Mayfield's trial skills — not only had it been an ongoing topic of conversation among the magazine's staff, but, a few months earlier, Charlie had taken Newton's pretrial deposition in New York. Although Charlie had been very polite to Newton at that time, it was clear to everyone in attendance that Charlie had done his homework and had a relentless way of getting the facts out of a witness — especially facts that the witness would have preferred not to reveal. It wasn't until the deposition was over and Newton read the transcript that he realized how much information he had given. He then saw that the "polite" Charlie Mayfield could draw as much blood with a hairpin as Lizzie Borden could with an ax.

Now at the trial, and as soon as he finished taking his oath to tell the truth, Newton looked at Charlie from the witness stand with a *please, be gentle* look in his eyes.

"Mr. Newton," Charlie began, "please tell us your name and occupation."

"Ward Raymond Newton. I'm Vice President of Circulation at Tee Time, Incorporated."

"And that's the same *Tee Time* that is a defendant in this lawsuit?"

"Yes."

"Mr. Newton, do you recall sitting in a pretrial deposition for this case, when I asked you questions and you gave me answers under oath?"

"Yes, I do."

"And you had a chance to read over the transcript of that deposition, correct?"

"Yes, I read it."

"And do you stand by the answers you gave me at that time?"

Newton sensed that this was a trick question. If he said that he did stand by those answers, and if one of them hurt the case, he'd be stuck with it. But if he said that he didn't stand by any answers, it could imply that he had lied under oath. He finally answered in what seemed to be the safest way. "Yes, as far as I can recall, I would stand by the answers I gave you several months ago. If I misspoke at that time as to any particular detail, I didn't catch it when I read the transcript, and it certainly wasn't intentional."

"Thank you. Now, would you kindly tell the jury, Mr. Newton, the nature of your job? What exactly does a Vice President of Circulation do?"

"Essentially, my job is to maximize the circulation of our magazine — the number of copies of each issue that we sell. The main way for us to do that is to sell as many annual subscriptions as possible. But we also focus on what we call 'over the counter' sales — that is, sales of individual copies at newsstands and other retail outlets like drug stores and grocery stores."

"May we assume, Mr. Newton, that the majority of *Tee Time*'s readers are golfers or golf fans?"

"That's basically true, but we do have many readers who don't play golf, or play very little. Many become fans from watching golf on television, and develop a keen interest in the sport, even though they don't play it."

"I understand. It's like me being a Chicago Bears football fan and reading about football in the newspapers and in *Sports Illustrated*, but I don't play football."

Judge Harry Krause interrupted the examination to say, "How disappointing, Mr. Mayfield. We all thought that you were a star running back for the Bears."

Everyone in the courtroom laughed at the comic relief. The vision of an overweight, seventy-year old, gray-haired lawyer, wearing a helmet and running down the field dodging tacklers, was too weird to pass up.

"Trying cases is dangerous enough for me, Your Honor — especially in your courtroom!"

More laughs.

Charlie resumed his questioning. "Mr. Newton, before I was so rudely interrupted," and here Charlie winked at the jurors, each of whom laughed again, "we were talking about how you try to pump sales of your magazine. Do you remember that?"

"I do, yes."

"So, if an upcoming issue is to contain a story of particular interest to golf fans, would it be customary for you to put some extra effort into advertising or promoting that issue to the public?"

If the witness seat had a seat belt, this would have been a good time for Newton to buckle up. "Yes, advertising and promoting the magazine is really the main part of my job. That's what the circulation people do at all magazines. And when an upcoming issue contains an article that we expect to be a popular one, we'll put a little extra money into promoting that issue."

"Okay. Now, we all know that the May, June, and July 2006 issues of *Tee Time* contained the articles written by Max Reed about Eddie Bennison, the plaintiff in this case. Are you familiar with those articles?"

"I am."

"And did you, as part of your responsibilities at *Tee Time*, direct that more than the usual amount of money be spent to advertise or promote those particular issues?" Charlie already knew the answer to that question from his pretrial discovery procedures which included an inspection of *Tee Time*'s records in addition to taking Newton's pretrial deposition.

"Yes, I did."

"And isn't it a fact, Mr. Newton, that *Tee Time*, at your direction, spent more than triple the amount to promote those issues — I'll call them the

'Eddie Bennison issues' — than you typically spend, on the average, to promote other issues?

"Well, that's essentially true," Newton answered in a more defensive tone than he intended. He seemed to be almost apologetic about directing the extra expenditures. "For the May issue, we did spend about three times more than we usually spend. However, we didn't spend more than the normal amount for the June and July issues."

"And," Charlie asked quickly, "isn't that because the May issue was so widely read and talked about, and the subject of so many stories in the media — newspapers, radio, and television, including the Golf Channel — that you didn't need to spend money for additional publicity?

"Yes, I think that would be fair to say."

"In fact, wasn't there a postscript to the May story, telling the readers that there would be further revelations about Eddie Bennison in the two following issues?"

"Yes, I recall that,"

"So it was the May issue that really drove sales of the June and July issues, and therefore it wasn't necessary to spend more money promoting the latter two issues. Isn't that right?"

"Yes, I would agree with that."

"Okay, let's find out how it worked out. What was the average monthly circulation of *Tee Time* magazine prior to the 'Eddie Bennison issues?'"

"Just under one and a half million copies per month — about 1.4 million, maybe a little more."

"And what was the circulation of the first Eddie Bennison issue, the May issue?"

"Almost four million."

Charlie feigned surprise. "So you sold nearly three times as many copies of that issue as you were selling of prior issues. Is that right?"

"Yes."

"Then your extra expenditures to promote that May issue paid off, right?"

"I suppose. There was also a great deal of 'word of mouth' publicity from people who read the story. They would tell their friends, who, in turn, bought copies. There were also newscasters and sportscasters who reported on the May story, and that also drove sales of that issue."

"And please tell us — what was the circulation for the June and July issues?"

"More. Each was over five million." Ward Newton shifted uncomfortably and added, "Closer to six million." Ironically, the head of circulation seemed embarrassed by the large circulation of those three issues.

"And did annual subscriptions increase after that issue?"

"Yes."

"And wasn't there also a spike — or increase — in 'over the counter' or retail sales of subsequent issues over the following months?"

"Yes."

"I take it, then, Mr. Newton, that the articles about Eddie Bennison turned out to be a big deal for *Tee Time*. It tripled sales for the magazine for that month, increased sales even more for the following months, and even increased future retail sales and annual subscriptions. Would you rate it that way?"

Ward Newton was getting more and more uncomfortable. "Well, I don't know if I'd call it a 'big deal,' but . . . "

"You're not sure if it was a 'big deal?'" Charlie Mayfield asked incredulously. "Perhaps I'm blowing all of this out of proportion. Tell me, what is the price of a single copy of *Tee Time?*"

"$4.99."

"So sales of the May issue alone generated about 20 million dollars in revenues for *Tee Time*, right?"

"Yes, that's about right."

"And that was many million dollars more than average at that at time?"

"Yes."

"And sales of the June and July issues, combined, generated 60 million dollars?"

"Yes."

"And what is the annual subscription price for your magazine?"

"That depends. We offer many different promotions to sell annual subscriptions. They range from about $25 to as much as $50 for one year."

"And how many subscriptions would you say that you sold as a result of the 'Eddie Bennison' issue?"

"I wouldn't know that offhand."

"Well, let's try to refresh your memory." Charlie went over to the counsel table where his associate, Pete Stevens, handed him a manila folder. He removed a sheet and walked back to face Ward Newton. "Mr. Newton, I have here a memo that you wrote to Mr. Clive Curtis, your magazine's Editor-in-Chief. Mr. Curtis is your boss, isn't he?"

"Yes, he is." The witness remembered his memo — and shuddered.

"Okay. The memo is dated September 24, 2006, which is just a couple of months after the last of the three 'Eddie Bennison' issues. Charlie handed the memo to Newton. "Is that your signature on the bottom of that memo?"

"It is."

Charlie then moved to have the document introduced into evidence, and, hearing no objection, the judge granted the motion and the memo became a part of the official record of the case. Charlie turned to the witness.

"Mr. Newton, please read aloud to the jury the second paragraph of that memo. I highlighted it for your convenience. And, I'll remind the jury that this is a memo from you to Mr. Clive Curtis, the magazine's Editor-in-Chief."

The witness cleared his throat and began:

Max Reed's articles in the May, June, and July issues about Eddie Bennison were a huge success — probably the most successful articles we've ever published. They increased newsstand sales and subscriptions enormously. But even more important, the added circulation increased our advertising revenues to levels we've never seen before. It's hard to estimate, in dollars, what all this means, but I would guess that those three articles, between sales and future advertising revenue, will generate at least 50 to 75 million dollars for us just for this year alone. And our increased subscriptions will certainly pay us great dividends in future years. No matter how we slice it, it was a grand slam home run.

When Newton finished reading, Charlie Mayfield glanced at the jury with an expression that said, *Now we all know why they ruined Eddie Bennison's life.*

Then he approached the witness. "Is it alright with you, Mr. Newton, if we change the subject?"

"Gladly," Ward Newton sighed in obvious relief. Titters were heard throughout the courtroom.

"You were not in the room when Max Reed testified. Isn't that correct?"

"That's correct, I was not in the courtroom."

"After he was done testifying, did Mr. Reed, or any of the lawyers, discuss his testimony with you?"

"Only that he was glad to be done." More titters.

"Mr. Reed told the jury that he had sources for the things he wrote about Eddie Bennison. Do you have any idea who those sources were?"

"No, I have no idea."

"In addition to being a colleague of Mr. Reed, aren't you also a close friend?"

"Yes, I'd say we were close friends."

"And the two of you, with your wives, spend time together socially?"

"Yes, we do."

"And your offices at the magazine are right next to each other, isn't that a fact?"

"That's correct."

"And do you have any idea how long he worked on the Eddie Bennison articles?"

Hoping to help his colleague, Newton answered, "I think he worked on them for quite some time. They were important articles, and I'm sure he wanted to get them right."

"And did he discuss the articles with you while he was working on them?"

"Oh, he might have mentioned it. I really don't recall."

Now Charlie smelled blood. "Let's think about this, Mr. Newton. You and Max Reed are close friends, in business as well as socially, you go out together with your wives, your offices are next to each other, and he's working on the story of his life — a story that will not only make him famous, but will virtually triple the circulation of your magazine. And you are the head of circulation who joyously predicted to your boss, Clive Curtis, that the articles would increase *Tee Time*'s revenues by as much as 75 million dollars in a single year. And with all this, do you seriously think that we would believe that he only 'might have mentioned' the articles to you while he was working on them? Doesn't it seem to you that this would be something that he would be very excited about, and something he would talk about with his friends and colleagues — especially with a friend and colleague who, as head of circulation, would benefit from the obvious increased circulation of the magazine because of those articles?"

"As I already answered, Mr. Mayfield, I don't recall anything specific that he might have said about the articles while he was working on them."

"Well, a few minutes ago you said you had no idea who his so-called sources were. Is that because he never told you, or is it because he told you and you forgot?"

"I doubt if he ever told me. As you must know, reporters don't like to reveal their sources."

"Yes, Mr. Reed made that clear to us." Charlie stole a peek at the jury and gave a very slight shrug of his shoulders, as if to say, *Well I tried to get that information for you. You must be as curious — and as suspicious — as I am about those so-called sources.* Looking back to the witness, he said, "I just thought he might have mentioned their identities in conversations with you or other executives at the magazine."

"If he did, I never heard or knew about it."

Charlie just couldn't bring himself to drop the subject. "But, Mr. Newton, considering that everyone at the magazine knew that this was a tremendous story — 'grand slam home run,' as you described it in your memo to your boss — wouldn't you and the others naturally want to know where Mr. Reed got his amazing information?"

"To my knowledge, no one asked."

Charlie shook his head and chuckled to indicate that the last answer was simply beyond belief. "Mr. Newton, if I were to tell you that you had just won 75 million dollars in the lottery, wouldn't you ask me how I knew that, and who told me?"

"I guess so."

"But when Mr. Reed, in effect, won that much — and maybe more — for *Tee Time* because of his accusations about Eddie Bennison, you're telling us that no one asked how he knew those things, and who told him. Isn't that what you're saying?"

Newton shifted in his seat and softly answered, "Yes."

"Can you see why it's hard for me to believe that, Mr. Newton? Why it's hard for me to believe that neither you nor anyone else at the magazine would think to ask Reed where he got that startling information about Eddie Bennison?"

"I can see why you don't understand that, Mr. Mayfield. Perhaps that's because you're not in the publishing business where certain information — like the sources for stories — is confidential and is not discussed."

"You're absolutely right — I'm not in the publishing business where you turn your heads and don't ask questions. I'm in the law business where we do ask questions — the kind of questions that someone should have asked Max Reed in 2006."

Charlie Mayfield looked to the judge. "I have no further questions, Your Honor."

Judge Krause nodded. "Does the defense have any questions, Ms. Berman or Mr. Shoemaker?"

Hugo Shoemaker deferred to Roz Berman, who replied, "No, Your Honor, but we reserve the right to call Mr. Newton as our own witness later in the case."

CHAPTER 55

As was his habit during trials, Charlie Mayfield spent the noon recess back at his office, where his secretary had sandwiches waiting. This gave him his only opportunity to check his phone messages, dash off a couple of letters, and direct people at the office to take care of a few odds and ends for him that he couldn't handle himself because of being in court nearly the entire day.

It was common for him to invite his client or perhaps one of his witnesses to join him over sandwiches, but today he wanted to spend that brief time with his assistant, Pete Stevens, who had graduated from law school less than three years ago but who already showed enough promise that Charlie sent him to court to argue routine motions, interview witnesses, and prepare court documents for Charlie's review.

"Pete," he began after taking a hefty bite from a hot pastrami sandwich, "that damned First Amendment bullshit is driving me crazy."

Pete didn't catch the drift of what Charlie was getting at, but he knew to be patient and wait for him to make his point between bites.

"Back in 1789, or whenever it was that Thomas Jefferson and those guys got together in Philadelphia to write the Constitution and the First Amendment, all they wanted to do was give people the right to speak without going to jail, and to give newspapers and magazines the right to print things without getting shut down for it. That's all they wanted to do. But over the years, our courts have turned these into some kind of God-given, biblical rights. Now people can burn the American flag, or wipe their fannies with it, and get away with it under the guise of freedom of speech or freedom of expression. And the goddamned press has pressured the courts — including the Supreme Court — to rule that it's okay to lie about public figures as long as it's done without malice. In other words, it's okay to lie and ruin someone's reputation as long as the lie is an innocent one. Or if the press were merely negligent in writing the lie. How can that be, Pete! How can a lie be innocent, and how can writing a lie be a result of mere negligence?

"We learned the first day at law school that people have to pay for harm caused by their negligence. If I'm driving my car without paying attention and run over you, I have to pay you for the harm I caused. That's because I was negligent. You don't have to prove that I intentionally or maliciously ran you down — you only have to show that I wasn't exercising reasonable care. But if a newspaper or magazine negligently or carelessly ruins the reputation of an otherwise highly reputable man, they will get away with it, free and clear. They only have to pay for the damage they cause when it can be proven that they acted maliciously — that is, deliberately or with some evil intent, or with a total disregard for the truth."

Pete Stevens was used to Charlie's colorful attacks on laws that stand in his way. "So where are we going with all this?" he asked.

"As you know, Pete, we have to prove that *Tee Time* was much more than negligent or careless with the Bennison article. We have to get the jury to believe that they treated Eddie maliciously — with evil intent. If we can't show that they intentionally lied about him, we at least have to show that they printed lies about him without giving a damn whether they were lies or not — without even bothering to check. That would constitute a reckless disregard for the truth.

"I think I made some pretty good headway on that today. I think the jury was shocked to learn that the magazine grossed an extra 75 million bucks from those articles, and how excited they were about the success of the articles without caring a whit about what they did to Eddie. And now the jury can see that they did all that for money. Pretty callous, I'd say. And callous rhymes with malice.

"And I take every opportunity I can to remind the jury that Max Reed won't reveal his bullshit sources, and I'm trying to get them to believe that there weren't any sources — and I'll bet there weren't."

Charlie finished his sandwich and took a big swig of soda. "And," he continued, "that's another idiotic thing about our laws in Illinois. They say that a reporter doesn't have to reveal his sources. Dumbest rule I ever heard. Goddamned Reed gets up there on the stand and says, 'Oh, hell yes, I have sources, but I won't tell you who they are.' And we're supposed to believe that crap? He had no sources, and if he did have sources, they were probably something he found in a Chinese fortune cookie."

Pete Stevens asked, "Is there anything I can do on this?"

"Yeah, a couple of things. First, I want some creative thinking on how we can nail down malice on the part of *Tee Time* or Max Reed. Don't assume that I've already done that — we still have a way to go to convince the jury that those guys are bastards, malicious bastards. And I'd like to be able to show that the malice goes all the way up to Globe Publications — they own and control the magazine, they are defendants in the case, and they have tons of money.

"Next, I want you to check with our shadow jurors. Get their impressions as to where we stand on malice. Have we already proved it? If not, what more do we have to bring out?

"Finally, check our research file. It includes a lot of cases and legal articles on this issue. Look for the key words that the courts rely on to find malice. I want to work those words into my questions, and I want to figure out a way to get them into the witnesses' answers. And I want to be sure to slip every one of those words into my closing argument."

Charlie then wadded up his napkin, tossed it into the waste basket, and pointed a finger at his associate. "Here's a job for you, Pete. At the end of the case, when I make our closing statement to the jury before they go out to deliberate, I'll have to hit the malice button hard. I'd like for you to put together a rough draft of what you think I might say on that subject. Mention how badly the articles hurt Eddie, and how much money they made from those articles — and how they were jumping for joy about all that money. Be sure to include the parts of Ward Newton's testimony about all the extra money they spent to advertise the three issues, especially the first one — the May issue. We want the jury to believe that *Tee Time* simply didn't give a damn about the harm they were doing to Eddie, and that they even went out of their way to increase that harm by making all those extra advertising expenditures. In short, Pete, we have to convince them that *Tee Time*'s driving motivation was greed — making obscene profits at any cost, and truth be damned. If that's not malice, what is? And while you're at it, we have to keep harping about Max Reed. We have to make him look like the poster child for lying, malice, greed, and shabby journalism — and, with the testimony we already have, it ought to be easy to do.

"And another thing, Pete. I want to hit them right between the eyes with the last thing that Ward Newton testified to this morning. Remember, I asked him if he or anyone else at the magazine asked Reed about his sources, and he replied — and these were his exact words — 'To my knowledge, no one asked.'"

"This is dynamite, Pete. Here was a sensational story, spread over three separate issues that were the talk of the golf world — a story that would blow the top off *Tee Time*'s sales. It revealed outrageous information about a national hero — an icon. It's unbelievable that the executives at the magazine didn't know where that information came from; it's even more unbelievable that, as Newton confirmed, no one asked. That's because they didn't want to hear the answer: that there were no sources, or that the sources were skimpy or unreliable. They wanted to remain ignorant of that so they could later claim deniability. That's more than malicious, Pete, and it's more than wicked. It's downright evil, bordering on criminal."

WEDNESDAY AFTERNOON

CHAPTER 56

When the afternoon session began, Charlie Mayfield stood and announced, "I will now call Steven Hockett to the stand."

A handsome gray-haired man rose and walked up the center aisle of the courtroom, passed the counsel tables, and stood to take his oath. He was thin, fairly tall, and was wearing a dark blue suit accented with a power tie and a matching handkerchief in his lapel pocket. He could easily be mistaken for a movie star, but his tan and rugged skin revealed a man who had spent a lot of time outdoors.

After the oath was administered, he took his seat in the witness box, obeying Charlie's instruction to smile warmly at the jurors.

"Please state your name and tell us where you live."

"My name is Steven Hockett. I live in Scottsdale, Arizona."

"Your occupation, Mr. Hockett?"

"I'm a professional golfer, Mr. Mayfield. Right now I work as the head pro at the Twin Mountains Golf Club, but I've also competed in professional golf tournaments on the Senior's Tour — it's now called the Champions Tour."

"And for how long have you competed on the Champions Tour?"

"Well, I competed actively from the age of fifty until about five years ago, but then I had to call it quits because of my age. I was sixty-two, and the mental and physical demands of constant competing, practicing, traveling, and being away from my family were wearing me down." He flashed a grin and added, "Most of the guys on the Champions Tour can compete into their mid-sixties, but I couldn't make it that long." This, too, was something Charlie wanted the jury to hear. If they were to decide how long Eddie would be suffering lost winnings, they had to know how long a pro could continue to compete effectively.

"Did you know Eddie Bennison when you were on the Tour?"

"I sure did. We were good friends. We arranged to play many practice rounds together, and, even though we were competitors, we tried to help each other with our games. That's not uncommon on the Tour. And in the early days we often roomed together. He was, and still is, a close friend."

"Mr. Hockett, do you think you knew Eddie Bennison as well as other Tour players knew him?"

"Better. I don't believe any of the players were closer to Eddie than I was. And we've stayed close even after I left the Tour. I'm quite sure that no one played more rounds with Eddie than I did — either practice rounds or competitive rounds."

"Let me ask you this, Mr. Hockett. If Eddie Bennison ever cheated on the golf course, whether in practice or competitive rounds, would you have known it?"

"Oh, sure. Remember, we're in a glass bowl out there. We all watch each other like hawks — not because we don't trust each other, but because we want to see the other guys' shots to learn how the wind is affecting the ball, and where the ball is bouncing. And for the better golfers, like Eddie, we like to see how they are playing certain holes and certain shots, how they are able to hit the ball high or keep it low. What they do will influence how we play our own shots, so we watch them carefully. So we watch Eddie more closely than the others because he plays so well — we all learn from him. And not only are the two or three other players in the group watching him, so are all the fans lining the fairways or watching on television in their homes.

"And there's another reason we watch each other closely. If a player breaks a rule, either intentionally or inadvertently, we have a duty to call him on it. We call that 'protecting the field.' You see, there may be only three or four of us playing together as a group, but there may be another

150 players on the course competing in the same tournament, and it's our duty to protect all of them — the entire field — by calling a penalty when we see a player violating a rule.

"So yes, Mr. Mayfield, if Eddie or anyone else played fast and loose with the rules, we would all know about it — and be talking about it. But it just didn't happen with Eddie. He's totally honorable on and off the golf course, and, like most of us, he treats the rules like they are part of the Ten Commandments."

"Do you think that your opinion on that is shared by other players on the Tour?"

"Absolutely," the witness replied with gusto. "If anyone had something bad to say about Eddie, I would have heard it — and I never heard a word about him that wasn't complimentary. He's not only a great golfer, he's a fine gentleman who is well liked by everyone who knows him. I'm proud to call him a friend.

"And by the way," Hockett added, as if it were spontaneous and not rehearsed, "Eddie wouldn't have to cheat to win; for years he has been the best golfer on the Champion's Tour — by far. And if everyone else cheated, Eddie would still beat them. People have no idea just how good he is."

"Thank you for that, Mr. Hockett. Now, to change the subject, are you familiar with the accusation that Eddie was taking performance-enhancing drugs?"

The witness couldn't resist a broad smile. "Yes, I heard that. It was a big topic of conversation among those of us on the Tour."

"In what way?"

"Well, Mr. Mayfield, we like to think of ourselves as athletes, but not the kind of athletes who depend on brute strength. We make our living with skills that come from sound mechanics, timing, and tempo — brute force and strength have less to do with it than most people realize. Some of the best golfers in history have been short and overweight, and even you could probably beat them in the 100-yard dash."

Considering Charlie Mayfield's age and girth, that last comment brought another smattering of laughter in the courtroom.

"Eddie wasn't the kind of guy who would put that stuff in his body.

He never smoked, and only occasionally would he have a glass of wine or a bottle of beer. He even watched his diet, not to control his weight but to stick with only healthy foods. The idea of him taking steroids or those other drugs that we sometimes find in baseball and cycling is laughable."

"Thank you, Mr. Hockett. Now I'd like to ask you whether it's common for players on the Tour to talk among themselves about other players?"

"Well, sure, I guess I'd have to say that we do that a lot."

"And is it the more successful players who are the topics of these conversations?"

"Sure. You have to understand that there aren't many secrets out there on the Tour. We all talk among ourselves every day during practice rounds, on the practice range, in the restaurants, in our rooms, and even in airports and on planes between events. And it's only natural that the superheroes — guys like Eddie Bennison — are often the topic of our conversations. I'm ashamed to admit that we're like a bunch of old nannies hanging on gossip just to have something to talk about."

"And your point?"

On cue, Hockett replied, "My point is that if Eddie Bennison did anything wrong — like cheating or taking drugs, or like mistreating people or otherwise misbehaving — it would have been a major topic of conversation. I certainly would have heard about it, as would everyone else. And I never heard any such thing — ever."

"Thank you, Mr. Hockett. Now I have one more question. Have you ever heard that Eddie Bennison, or any other professional golfer, leaves dirt or mud in the grooves of his golf club in order to reduce the spin on the ball?"

The witness chuckled. "No, Mr. Mayfield, never. When *Tee Time* magazine wrote that about Eddie, it was a source of laughter on the Tour."

"And why was that?"

"Because it's nonsense. A little dirt couldn't possibly make any difference — anyone who plays golf seriously would know that. And even if it did, how could the golfer know exactly how much dirt to leave in the grooves of the club to get the exact amount of spin he wants? We have enough to think about out there, Mr. Mayfield, without weighing and measuring a few grams of dirt."

"I have no further questions of his witness, Your Honor."

Roz Berman announced that the defendants waived cross-examination of Steven Hockett.

With that, Charlie asked Judge Krause if he would permit them a short recess.

"We'll take a ten-minute recess," the judge announced, rapping his gavel.

CHAPTER 57

harlie signaled his small legal team to meet him in the corridor outside the courtroom, inviting Eddie and Carol to join them.

Once huddled and out of the earshot of others, Charlie quietly said, "I think this is a good place for us to rest," meaning that he was ready to stop offering evidence and turn the case over to the defense to offer whatever evidence they had to show that they did nothing wrong — that everything they wrote about Eddie Bennison was permitted under the heading of "Freedom of the Press."

He added, mostly for the benefit of the Bennisons, "We'll still have the opportunity to introduce more evidence to rebut whatever they offer. That means that we get two bites at the apple, and they get only one — although the judge might let them bring in new evidence to rebut whatever we offer in rebuttal — and so on and so forth. We lawyers have this insatiable need to have the last word, and whenever something new comes up, the other side wants to rebut it and argue about it."

Carol Bennison was shaking her head. "It sounds like this will never end."

Charlie laughed. "We never worry about when it ends, Carol, we only worry about how it ends."

She bowed her head to acknowledge the point, and asked the inevitable question: "And how do you think this one will this one end, Charlie?"

"My gut tells me we're doing okay, Carol, but remember, so far we've been the only ones bringing in witnesses and evidence. We've been the only ones putting points up on the board while the other side is playing defense. But as soon as we rest our case, the situation will reverse itself. Then they'll be scoring the points, and we'll have to sit there and take it. My job will be to keep their scoring to a minimum to make sure that we end up with the most points."

"You make it sound like a game," Carol Bennison said.

"Well, it is kind of like a game, Carol, but not like golf. It's more like Russian Roulette."

━━━━━━━━━

When the trial resumed, Charlie approached the bench. "Your Honor, I'm seriously thinking that this would be a good time to rest our case, but I'd like to defer that decision until I can review the record. Since it's nearly four, may we adjourn until tomorrow?"

Judge Krause, like Roz Berman and Hugo Shoemaker, knew that a plaintiff's decision to rest his case is a big one. If even a single piece of critical evidence was overlooked, it could be fatal to the case. Indeed, whenever a plaintiff rests, it's customary for the defense to make a motion to dismiss the entire case on the grounds that the plaintiff failed to prove an essential element of his case.

Many a case has been lost because a lawyer — usually through an uncharacteristic mental lapse — has forgotten something so obviously important that it was taken for granted. The classic example is the prosecutor who, in the course of trying a murder case, deftly produced the murder weapon — a knife — proved the motive, produced an eyewitness to the stabbing, and offered scientific evidence that the defendant's fingerprints were on the knife, and the victim's blood was on his shoes. But, incredibly, he forgot to offer proof that the victim was actually dead — an essential element in a murder case! The defendant walked out of the courtroom a free man!

Professional courtesy dictated that Berman and Shoemaker give Charlie the opportunity to review the bidding to be sure that he was prepared to rest. And they knew that Charlie, like all other respectable lawyers, would do the same if the situation were reversed.

Roz Berman, without waiting to hear from Hugo Shoemaker, stood. "We have no objection to recessing until tomorrow, Your Honor."

"So ordered," Judge Krause announced. "We'll resume tomorrow morning at nine. The bailiff will excuse the jury until then."

CHAPTER 58

As soon as Charlie Mayfield got back to his office, he summoned Pete Stevens into the conference room. "Pete, I'm leaning in favor of resting our case in the morning. Do you think we have enough in the record on the malice issue? In fact, I want more than malice. We need solid proof that those bastards were outrageously malicious in order to get us a high verdict. Just winning isn't enough; we need to win big. I won't consider it a victory if the jury finds the defendants liable and awards Eddie a lousy 50 or 60 thousand bucks."

Pete Sevens was prepared for the question. "I think we're in good shape, Charlie," he replied with confidence. Looking at notes he had made on a yellow legal pad, he continued. "We have clear evidence that the defendants gloated among themselves about how much money they made from Reed's scurrilous article. That's not only bad taste, but it shows that they had a financial motive to write those lies about Eddie. It has to be easier for the jury to find malice when they see a motive for it.

"But more important, there's plenty of evidence for the jury to infer that Reed had no sources at all, and that he made all this stuff up just to make a name for himself. And if Reed did have sources, there is no evidence that they were reliable or that he took steps to verify what they told him.

"Finally, we have the testimony of Ward Newton that, as far as he knew, no one at *Tee Time* even asked Reed if there were sources for his accusations. And you did a great job of bringing that home to the jury when you had Newton on the stand.

"In fact, that failure to ask about sources syncs with Reed's own testimony when he said that his boss, Howard Wolf, sent him off to the lawyers without even asking if he had the required sources.

"In short, there is ample reason for the jury to believe that there were no sources, and that if there were sources, no one took the trouble to ask who they were or verify their reliability. I did a lot of research on this subject, and I can assure you that we have a hell of a lot more evidence of malice than one usually finds in these cases. Hell, Charlie, we have everything but a signed confession."

Mayfield nodded and smiled. He followed Stevens' analysis and was pleased with the preparation that went into it. But he still had to probe. "That's all fine and dandy, Pete, but what do we do if they bring in a bunch of witnesses who testify that they were Reed's sources, or that they themselves actually saw Eddie cheating or popping drugs? What do we do then?"

Pete Stevens loved these discussions. Charlie, one of the most revered lawyers in Chicago, was his boss, but he was a boss who respected Pete and treated him like a fellow trial lawyer and not like a servant or menial law clerk. And Charlie asked the kind of questions that challenged Pete's analytical powers and sharpened his understanding of the subtle nuances of the law. In law school these were called "rhetorical discussions" and were little more than classroom mental exercises. But this was real-world stuff that mattered.

"If they bring in those so-called sources, Charlie, you'll rip 'em apart. I can just see you cross-examining some jerk who testified that he saw Eddie taking pills. 'What kind of pills? What do they do for Eddie? How often did he take them? Do you know what they are? How do you know they weren't allergy pills? Doesn't your mother take pills?' Hell, Charlie, by the time you're done with him, he'll be reaching for pills himself — probably cyanide!

"And wouldn't it be great if they put some little old lady on the stand to say that she saw Eddie nudge his ball a half inch when he marked it on the green? Or that he didn't clean the dirt out of the grooves of his club before hitting an approach shot? I can hear your cross-examination now: 'How far away from you was he? Are you telling us that you can see—

visually measure—a half inch with your eyes from that far away? Or that there was dirt in the grooves of the club? Really? Well, let's test that.' And then you'll go to the back of the courtroom and put a coin behind a golf ball, pick the ball up, then put it back, and then you'll ask her whether you replaced the coin in precisely the same spot and, if not, how far from the original spot did you place it. Or you'll ask her to tell you if she could see from the witness stand whether there was dirt in the grooves of the club face you're holding in the back of the room. By that time, Charlie, she'll be a total wreck, and she'll say anything you want her to say just to get the hell off the stand."

When Charlie Mayfield looked at Pete Stevens, he saw a young Charlie Mayfield. *I love this kid,* he said to himself.

THURSDAY MORNING

CHAPTER 59

After Judge Krause brought down his gavel to open the Thursday morning session, but before the jury was back in the jury box, he looked to Charlie. "Do you have another witness to call at this time, Mr. Mayfield?"

"No, You Honor. The plaintiff has no further evidence to offer at this time. We rest our case."

"Thank you." The judge then looked to the defense table. "Ms. Berman, Mr. Shoemaker, are you prepared to begin the case for the defense?"

Hugo Shoemaker stood. "We are, Your Honor, but first we'd like to present a motion to dismiss. We didn't know for sure that Mr. Mayfield was going to rest this morning, so we haven't had a chance to put our motion in writing. But, with your permission, I can state our points orally."

A motion to dismiss is a routine motion filed by every defendant at the close of every plaintiff's case. In essence, the motion asserts that the plaintiff's case is so weak that it should be thrown out of court without the defendant having to offer any evidence at all. In other words, the defendant is saying that the court should not waste any further time on such a weak case — that the plaintiff has failed to prove the essential elements of a libel case.

Just as a motion to dismiss is routinely made by a defendant, it is routinely denied by a judge except in the weakest or most frivolous of cases.

After Shoemaker spoke for a few minutes, the judge cut him off. "I will not dismiss the case at this time. In the opinion of the court, the plaintiff has introduced sufficient evidence to justify a reasonable jury to believe that Mr. Bennison has a valid claim against the defendants for libel. This is not to say that I myself would find in the plaintiff's favor, and I'm not saying that the jury would find in favor of the plaintiff, based on the record as it now stands, but only that the jury might find in favor of the plaintiff, and that such a finding would not be unreasonable. And as long as there is that possibility — and I believe that there is — then I cannot take the case away from the jury. The case warrants their review. Therefore, the motion to dismiss is denied."

The judge rapped his gavel. "Court's adjourned for the day. I have a judicial conference this afternoon, so we'll recess until tomorrow morning at 9:00 when the defendants can begin their case."

Judge Krause then turned to his bailiff. "Please bring the jury in, Leon."

A few minutes later, with the jurors in their seats, the judge said, "You good people may have the rest of the day off, but please don't discuss the case among yourselves or with others, and please try not to read about it in the papers or pay any attention to anything about it on radio or television."

CHAPTER 60

Throughout that Thursday afternoon, Max Reed had been holed up in his Chicago hotel room. He was angry, frustrated, and well under the influence of a bottle of Jack Daniels he had been nursing for the past few hours. The Eddie Bennison case was going badly, and he, Max Reed, was certainly destined to be the goat if the jury slammed the magazine for a lot of money.

His last glimmer of hope was when the Liz Peters episode came to light, but then that glimmer faded away when the judge ruled that it had no place in the case. *Damn that Bennison,* Reed thought to himself once again, as he had ever since the lawsuit was filed, *He's a goddamned bum, but he's going to come out of the thing with millions and I'll be the laughingstock of the entire sporting world.*

But it was not in Max Reed's DNA to accept defeat. He had to find a way to get out of this mess, and if he could destroy Eddie Bennison along the way, all the better. Finally, as the afternoon was beginning to fade, Reed decided to execute the plan that had been fermenting in his mind since the judge ruled that Liz Peters was out of the case. Not wanting to use a phone that could be easily identified, he left his room and found a public pay phone a few blocks from the Palmer House Hotel in Chicago where he was staying during the trial, took a deep breath, and then dialed the number he had written down earlier.

A phone rang in McLean, Virginia, on the desk of Lois Sachs, the sports page editor at *USA Today*, the most widely read newspaper in the United States. The sun had already set in McLean, and Sachs was exhausted. It was March, and her long day had been filled with calls and editorial meetings about breaking sports stories. The major collegiate basketball tournaments, the NCAA and the NIT, were in progress, the National Basketball Association finals were looming, and Major League Baseball was in the midst of its spring exhibition season. The necessary coverage of those events had to be blended with the everyday sports news of drug scandals, player drafts and trades, the ever-popular Masters Golf Tournament that was less than two weeks away, and the wide array of other sporting events such as soccer, golf, and horse racing. Lois Sachs' desk was cluttered with drafts of stories needing her approval, telephone messages, and invitations to attend dinners and sporting events. Also on her desk were her two long legs, resting atop the clutter as she leaned back in her swivel chair to relax for a few precious minutes.

"Hello," she sighed, picking up the phone that interrupted the relaxation she so desperately sought. "Lois Sachs here."

Doing his best to disguise his voice, Max Reed whispered hoarsely into the phone, "Is this the Lois Sachs with *USA Today*?"

"Yes, that's me. Who is this, please?"

"Never mind who I am. I'm calling to offer you the scoop of your life."

"Hey, who the hell is this? Is this some kind of joke?"

"Not a joke at all, Lois. I have a story for you that'll make headlines — and not just on the sports pages. You could get the Pulitzer Prize, and Wolf Blitzer will want you on CNN."

Though skeptical, Sachs replied, "I'm listening." Simultaneously, she flipped a switch next to her phone to activate the recorder which she, like many journalists, kept handy for just such an occasion.

"Have you been following the Bennison trial out in Chicago?"

"Of course."

"Bennison's looking pretty good, huh?"

"Go ahead."

"If you check, you'll find that he was staying at the Auburn Hills Marriott Hotel near Pontiac, Michigan, on August 17, 2007. But he may have reserved his room in the name of 'Ben Edwards.'"

"And?"

"And — he was there with a young lady whose last name was not Bennison."

Sachs' reporter instincts were aroused. "And what was her last name, if you know?"

"I know it alright. It's Peters — Elizabeth Peters. And Bennison finished off their little sex party by beating the hell out of her. And she has pictures to prove it, and witnesses to prove that they were together."

"And is there a way for me to contact this Peters lady?"

"Sure, she works at Franklin Advertising in Detroit. In fact, I can give you her address and phone numbers. Got a pen or pencil handy?"

After writing down the information, Sachs asked, "I don't suppose you'd care to give me your name."

"You got that right, honey." And with that the connection was broken.

FRIDAY MORNING

CHAPTER 61

As the Friday morning session was about to begin, Charlie Mayfield felt the vibration of his cell phone in his inside breast pocket. He sneaked a peek at the phone's screen to see who was trying to reach him. It was his office — very unusual since everyone there knew that he didn't want to be interrupted when in court. He scribbled a note and passed it to Pete Stevens: *Call the office — ask Lillian what she wants.* Stevens excused himself and left the courtroom. A minute or two later he returned and handed a note to Charlie: *Lillian said there's a Joe Andrews trying to reach you. He says it might be important.* Pete added Andrews' phone number at the end of his note. Charlie immediately recognized the caller as the Joe Andrews who headed up security at the Marriott Hotel in Michigan where Eddie Bennison had his encounter with Elizabeth Peters. *What the hell is this all about?*

At the first recess, Charlie sped out to the corridor, pulled out his cell phone, and punched in Joe Andrews' number.

"This is Joe Andrews."

"Joe, this is Charlie Mayfield. I understand you're trying to reach me."

"Yeah, Charlie. Remember me? I'm Head of Security at the Marriott out here in Pontiac, Michigan."

"I'll never forget you, Joe. You did me a big favor with those video tapes."

"Well, that's why I'm calling. You wanted the tapes for a certain night a couple of years ago. It was the night of August 17, 2007. Is that right?"

"Yes, that's the date."

"Well, early this morning we got a call from some lady asking about that same night. She asked if we had an Edward or Ed or Eddie Bennison registered in the hotel that night, or someone by the name of Ben Edwards, and if we had anything to indicate that a woman by the name of Elizabeth Peters was with him or was elsewhere in the hotel. As you know from our earlier conversations, we had no registration that night for anyone named Bennison, but we did have a room in the name of Ben Edwards, and that was the room where we had a video of some woman entering. We never knew her name. Are you with me so far?"

"I sure am, Joe. Keep going."

"Okay, and I want to be very candid with you, Charlie. I'm a sports fan, and I read the sport pages every day. I've been reading about this lawsuit out in Chicago, and I'm struck by some interesting coincidences."

"Coincidences?"

"Well, Charlie. You happen to be in Chicago, you're a lawyer, and you happen to have the same name as the lawyer who's representing this famous golfer. Isn't that a coincidence?

"I guess you could say that."

"And this famous golfer's name is Eddie Bennison, which happens to be the same name that this lady was asking about when she called our hotel this morning. I guess we could call that another coincidence."

"I guess we could, yes."

"And the tapes we sent to you showed a lady entering a room registered to a Ben Edwards. 'Ben Edwards' sounds like a pretty good alias for Ed Bennison. Another coincidence?"

"Okay, Joe, we've played this game long enough. Where are we going with all this?"

"Hey, Charlie, don't kill the messenger. I'm only trying to do you a favor."

"Favor?"

"Sure. It's obvious from all this that you're Eddie Bennison's lawyer, and you're trying to get him a gazillion dollars. But to do this you have to make sure that he wasn't screwing around that night at our hotel — and if he was, that no one knows about it."

"And what's the favor you're trying to do for me?"

"I'm trying to warn you that this lady who called us this morning might just blow the lid off the little secret you're trying to hide."

"And how do you think she can do that?"

"Because she works for *USA Today*. In fact, she's editor of the sports page. And she seems to know that a guy named Ed Bennison, or Ben Edwards, was at the Marriot with an Elizabeth Peters on the same night you were asking about."

For one of the few times in his life, Charlie was at a loss or words. *Oh shit!* he thought. USA Today*! This could be the end of the world.*

"Are you still there, Charlie?"

"Yeah, I'm here, Joe."

"I want to assure you that we didn't give her any information at all — not a word. Marriott doesn't need this kind of publicity. But I spoke with her, and I can tell you that she isn't going away. She smells blood, Charlie, and you're going to have to deal with her. Like I say, she isn't going away, at least not peacefully."

"Do you have a name for me?"

"I sure do. Her name is Lois Sachs. I checked her out and she is indeed the sports page editor at *USA Today*."

Joe Andrews then gave Charlie the phone numbers that Lois Sachs had given him. Charlie scribbled it down on a small note pad he always carried in the pocket of his suit jacket.

"Thanks for all of this, Joe. I appreciate it."

"Glad to be of help, Charlie. But since I did you a favor, maybe you can do one for me."

"Anything."

"How about Eddie Bennison's autograph for my son? He loves golf and is an Eddie Bennison fan. His name is Matt. He's sixteen."

Charlie Mayfield chuckled and made a note of the request. "I think I can swing that, Joe. And along with the autograph, maybe I can get Eddie to send Matt a set of clubs."

"Great. And make sure the autograph isn't from Ben Edwards."

FRIDAY AFTERNOON

CHAPTER 62

oz Berman, with Hugo Shoemaker at her side, exited the elevator across from Judge Krause's courtroom at 1:30 sharp on Friday afternoon after the lunch break. Charlie Mayfield was standing there in the hall waiting for them.

"Here we are, Charlie. What's going on? Your message said it was urgent."

"It is. I'd like us to have a short meeting with the judge. I called his bailiff and he set it up. The judge is already there."

"But what's this all — "

"I'll explain when we're in there. Let's go."

When Leon ushered them into Judge Krause's chambers, the judge was in his shirtsleeves, sitting at his desk and holding a pen poised over a newspaper. "Good afternoon," he mumbled without looking up. "Who's the Greek Queen of the Gods? Four letters."

"Try 'Hera,'" Shoemaker replied.

"Oh, of course," the judge said, "I would have known that if I had gone to Yale."

He put the puzzle aside and took a few puffs from his cigar. "Make yourselves comfortable," the judge said motioning to the empty sofa and chairs. "Okay, Charlie, here we are. What's up? Shall I call in my court reporter?"

"I think we can be off the record for now, Judge. But we may want a transcript when you hear what this is all about. It seems that someone violated one of your court orders."

Judge Krause's eyebrows shot up. "Please explain."

"Okay. A few days ago you ruled that this woman, Elizabeth Peters, was off-limits as far as this case was concerned. She could not be called as a witness, and no mention of her should be made. And you made it very clear in your ruling, Judge, that no one should leak anything to the press about her. Do you remember that?"

"I certainly do."

"And you remember the allegations that she and Eddie Bennison had an encounter at the Marriott hotel in Pontiac, Michigan on August 17, 2007?"

"I do."

"Well, it seems that just this morning someone named Lois Sachs called that same Marriott and asked about one Elizabeth Peters and one Eddie Bennison being together in a room at the hotel on that same night, August 17, 2007. And to make this a little more intriguing, Judge, Lois Sachs is with *USA Today* — in fact, she's the editor of the sports page.

"Now I hate to make accusations, Judge, but it's clear that someone tipped off *USA Today*, and it certainly isn't us. It would be totally against our interests for the press to know about those allegations. But it would be very beneficial to the defendants if a national newspaper like *USA Today* broke a story about Eddie Bennison and this Peters woman. After all — "

Roz Berman interrupted Charlie and pointed a finger at him. She half shouted, "Wait a minute, here. Are you actually accusing us of contacting the press in violation of a court order?"

"Not necessarily you, Roz, but someone, and obviously someone who knew about it and would benefit from it. And that would seem to be someone interested in seeing Eddie Bennison lose this case. If not someone from *Tee Time*, then who? As far as I can tell, no one other than the small group of us sitting here knows of Elizabeth Peters, other than her and her friend Dan Curry."

Judge Krause raised his hand to signal that he had something to say. "I agree that this is very serious and I want to get to the bottom of it. And I also agree that Charlie and his client would have nothing to gain and everything to lose if the Peters story were leaked. In fact, Charlie has done everything in his power to keep that story from seeing the light of day. So, as I see it, we have two ways to proceed. First, we can call in everyone who knows about it and ask them under oath if they had anything to do with the leak. Second, we can contact the person from *USA Today*. I think, Charlie, that you said her name was Lois Sachs. We could ask her who tipped her off."

"I already thought about that, Judge," Charlie interjected, "but it won't work. This is an Illinois lawsuit, and she could hide behind the Illinois law that protects the press from revealing their sources, just like Max Reed's been doing from the very beginning. If we ask her who told her about Peters, she'd just tell us that she refuses to answer, and there's nothing we could do about it."

Judge Krause paused to consider the point, then nodded. "I agree. Who at *Tee Time* knows about the Peters story?"

Roz Berman answered. "As far as we know, Judge, it would be either Todd Slocum — he's the magazine's in-house counsel — or Max Reed, the author of the article that led to this lawsuit. They've both appeared here, Reed as witness in open court, and Slocum who testified here in your chambers during Charlie's motion *in limine*. Both of them know about Elizabeth Peters."

"Yes, I remember," the judge said. "Are they both still in Chicago?"

"Todd Slocum is back in New York, but Max Reed is here in town. We wanted him to be available if we needed to call him as a witness when we put on our case, or if anything came up that we'd need to discuss with him."

"Okay," the judge sighed, "call him and have him in my chambers — within the hour. In the meantime, I'll ask Leon to bring some donuts to the jury and tell them to wait for us."

As an afterthought, Judge Krause said, "By the way, Roz and Hugo, I can't direct what you say or don't say to your client, but I'd prefer if Mr. Reed did not know why I want him here."

Roz Berman replied for both. "Not a problem, Judge. We'll just tell him that you asked for him to be here; when he asks why, and he certainly will, we'll just tell him that we don't know."

CHAPTER 63

After about 45 minutes, Max Reed arrived outside of Judge Krause's courtroom, where Berman and Shoemaker were waiting for him. "Did you find out why he wants me here?" Reed asked nervously before anyone even said hello.

"We're not exactly sure," Roz answered. Then, so he couldn't later accuse her of holding out on him, she added, "I think it has something to do with information that might have been leaked, but I can't imagine that it has anything to do with you." She was being honest with him — she could never imagine that anyone would knowingly violate a court order.

Just before they walked into the judge's chambers, Berman whispered, "Just remember, Max, if he asks you any questions, don't play games with him. And for God's sake, Max, be sure to tell the truth. You have nothing to worry about," she added, soon to realize that it might have been the most erroneous statement she ever made.

CHAPTER 64

As soon as everyone was seated, Judge Krause opened the door to his anteroom and asked for his court reporter, Sally Ringer, to come in. As she did so, with her stenotype machine tucked under her arm, the judge said to no one in particular, "I decided to have this on the record."

Once he took his seat behind his desk, the judge looked at Max Reed. "Thank you, Mr. Reed, for coming over on such short notice. I trust it's not an inconvenience."

"Perfectly alright. I was just at the hotel catching up on my email," Reed replied. He instantly felt a surge of relief. *Whew, he seems very friendly. Looks like this is going to be okay after all.*

Judge Krause looked down on some notes he had made, then looked up. "Mr. Reed, do you know anyone by the name Lois Sachs? She's an editor at *USA Today*?"

Oh, shit!

"Lois Sachs?" Reed, stalling, squinted and looked to the ceiling as if he were trying to place a name from his distant past. But his reaction to the question said it all. He may as well have held up a neon sign that said, *"Yes, I know Lois Sachs, I told her everything, I violated your court order, I'm going to jail, I'm getting fired, and I'm going to kill myself."*

"We're waiting, Mr. Reed."

"There was a Lois Sachs in the Sportswriters Guild."

"And have you spoken with her, or otherwise communicated with her directly or through another person?"

"You mean recently?"

"Yes, Mr. Reed. Recently. Within the past few days."

A good liar might have been able to squeak through this, but Max Reed wasn't even a decent liar.

He wrinkled his brow, scratched his head, and squirmed in his seat. Even if he admitted contacting Lois Sachs, he didn't know how to admit it. What prompted the call? What exactly did he say to her? How much did he reveal? He was inwardly screaming for a lifeline from Berman or Shoemaker. *For God's sake, do something,* he silently begged. *Make an objection! Anything! Get me out of this!*

The judge was losing whatever patience he still had. "Mr. Reed," he said sternly, as if he were about to announce a death penalty, "the question is a simple one, and there should be a simple answer. Yes or no. And if I don't get that answer, and get it now, I will hold you in contempt of court and have the sheriff place you in the county jail until I get it. I hope that's clear." He glanced over to his court reporter who nodded, confirming that she got it all. It was right there on the record — the judge's question, Reed's evasiveness, and the judge's warning.

Finally, Reed offered a feeble defense. "I know I'm not the most popular guy around here, but I'm not the kind of person who makes anonymous phone calls to the press."

Judge Krause sat up straight. "Thank you for that, Mr. Reed. I wasn't sure whether Ms. Sachs got her tip through a phone call or other means, such as by mail or email, but you cleared that up for me. How did you know it was a phone call? And how did you know it was an anonymous phone call?"

By this time, Hugo Shoemaker was involuntarily covering his eyes — much like a person watching the shower scene in *Psycho* and sensing what was coming.

Judge Krause stood and walked over to where Max Reed was sitting. He looked down at him and asked, "Did you call her, Mr. Reed? Yes or no!"

Reed, sweating from the bottom of his feet to the top of his head, could not bring himself to confess leaking the Elizabeth Peters bombshell, especially to the most widely read newspaper in the country.

Then the judge's impatience took over. "Enough of this! Sally," looking over to his court reporter, "please bring Leon in here. And tell him to bring one of the sheriff's deputies. But first I want to say something for the record." As soon as Sally Ringer placed her fingers over her stenotype machine, he continued, "I'm sentencing Mr. Reed to the county jail for contempt of court, to remain there until he purges himself of the contempt by disclosing his entire recent conversation or conversations — and any other communications — he may have had with Lois Sachs of *USA Today*." Looking back to the quivering Reed, he said, "When they come for you, Mr. Reed, you might give the deputy the key to your hotel room so he can pick up your toiletries and bring them to you. They don't provide much at the jailhouse."

If Max Reed had a white flag, he'd have been waving it. If he had a towel, he'd be throwing it in. "That won't be necessary. I wasn't trying to be evasive or equivocal, I was just hesitating to find the right words. But yes, I called her."

"We already figured that out, Mr. Reed. And did you give her any details about Ms. Peters' story — her story about what she claimed to have happened between her and Mr. Bennison at the Marriott Hotel in Michigan?"

Reed knew he was cornered, and that denials would get him in even deeper. However, the judge's question gave him a little space, and he rushed to hide in it. "No, sir. I didn't give her any details."

"But you provided her with enough information so that she could get the details on her own, right?"

"Well . . . "

"Did you mention Ms. Peters' name, and how to reach her?"

"I think so," Reed mumbled.

"And did you mention the Marriott Hotel in Pontiac, Michigan?"

Almost imperceptibly, Reed nodded.

"Let the record show that the witness nodded, indicating a 'yes' answer. And the date when Ms. Peters and Mr. Bennison were in that hotel?"

Again, Reed nodded.

Judge Krause looked to his reporter and said, "Let the record show that Mr. Reed again nodded in the affirmative." Then he said to Reed, "Please speak your answers, Mr. Reed. My court reporter can't write down nods. And, weren't you told by your lawyers, Ms. Berman and Mr. Shoemaker, that I handed down an order at the beginning of this trial that nothing was to be said to the press by anyone involved in this case?"

Reed vividly recalled Roz Berman telling him and Todd Slocum when the trial started, and several times since, that no one was to discuss the case with the press. And with her sitting right here next to him he couldn't deny it. "Yes, they told us."

"And didn't they also tell you that, just a day or two ago, I specifically ordered that nothing was to be said to the press, or anyone else, about Ms. Peters and her story about Mr. Bennison and the Marriott?"

"Yes, they did," Reed answered in a voice so low that the court reporter asked him to repeat his answer.

"And why did you choose to violate that order? Did you not think I was serious?"

Beaten, bloody, and nearly down for the count, Reed didn't take the time to think before he gave an idiotic answer. "Sure, I knew you were serious, but, as a reporter, I felt that this is something that the public has a right to know."

Judge Krause wrinkled his brow and looked at Max Reed with utter disgust. "Please tell me, Mr. Reed, why the public has a right to know about such salacious accusations — accusations that may very well be false, nothing more than smoke. Does the public have a right to know what goes on in *your* bedroom? Who made *you* the protector of the public interest, and the one to decide what that interest is? Was that power bestowed upon you when you graduated from journalism school? Or was it handed out at the Sportswriters Guild, where you rubbed shoulders with Lois Sachs?"

"It's just something that all reporters understand. We're taught that at school; we're told that by our editors. We all know that the First Amendment guarantees a free press and freedom of speech, and that's because the public has a right to be informed." Reed was building up a head of steam, and was actually starting to believe what he was saying. "It's like those Supreme

Court cases that say it's okay to burn the American flag, or wave a swastika. Just because something may be offensive or in bad taste doesn't mean that it can't be said or done. Not in this country."

"Well thank you, Mr. Reed, for that informative lesson on civics and on the United States Constitution. I've been a judge for only twenty years, and a lawyer for nearly thirty years before that, and it's helpful to receive instruction on our Constitution, especially from a sportswriter."

In his own mind, Judge Krause had concluded that Reed was more of a gossip columnist than a sportswriter, but he kept the thought to himself. To say that on the record could be used later to claim that he, the judge, was biased and that, therefore, an eventual ruling against the magazine could be overturned on appeal.

Then the judge looked directly into the eyes of Max Reed. "If you're a praying man, Mr. Reed, you should start praying that Lois Sachs runs into a dead end and writes nothing about this. If she writes a single word — or tells anyone else who writes a single word — about Elizabeth Peters and Mr. Bennison, you will have to deal with me, and with every power vested in me by the law. I will be your worst nightmare, and I can ensure that you will never have another moment of peace or a decent night's sleep."

After Reed was excused, Judge Krause told the lawyers that he wanted to make a final statement for the record. "I want the record to reflect my profound disappointment with the conduct of Mr. Max Reed. It was repugnant in every sense of the word. While I'm not inclined to sanction him or the defendants at this time, I feel the need to warn Mr. Shoemaker and Ms. Berman that further violations of my orders — or other misconduct — by anyone associated with the defendants will not be tolerated."

The judge stood and sighed, "It's nearly three, and I'm very upset. Let's all take the rest of the day off. "

CHAPTER 65

After the session ended, Roz Berman asked Reed to come back to her office with her and Shoemaker. Nothing was said during the short walk back to her building, but Berman unloaded as soon as Reed took a seat in her conference room.

"Max! How could you be so fucking stupid? Our entire case — our entire defense — is based on your integrity. We need the judge to believe that you're a responsible journalist, a careful reporter who relies on sources who are themselves reliable. And that you wouldn't go out of your way to hurt someone.

"In the meantime, Charlie Mayfield wants the judge and jury to believe that you are nothing better than a cheap muckraker who deals with slime; that you have no integrity and no professional standards, and that you wouldn't bat an eye at ruining someone with your stories. We were doing pretty well — until today! You made Mayfield's case for him! Now it's obvious to the judge that you don't care how much you hurt people, as long as there's something in it for you. And worse, you did it after you were specifically told not to do it. So now, the judge sees you as one of those tabloid reporters who write anything, no matter how false, and no matter how much it hurts someone. In his eyes, you have no integrity, and you have no credibility. If he thought you had sources for your Bennison story, he sure doesn't now. You lost him, Max, and now we'll probably lose the case as well." With that, Roz Berman screamed, "*Damn you!*" and flung her pen against the wall.

"Wait a minute, Roz," Reed said. "So I pissed off the judge — so what? He can't decide the case. The decision is up to the jury, and the jury doesn't know anything about any of this. I can't see that any harm was done. In fact, we can win this thing if *USA Today* comes out with — "

"Max, you have no idea — not even the slightest idea — how influential a judge can be in a jury trial. For one thing, he makes all the rulings. Second, at the end of the trial he instructs the jury on what to consider when coming to their verdict. But most important, he can send a million silent signals to the jury during the trial — signals that tell them things that will influence their verdict. And the jury watches him for these signals. He might roll his eyes or shake his head when one of my witnesses says something, and then nod and smile when one of Mayfield's witnesses says something. When the jury senses that the judge believes a witness, then they believe that witness. And if the judge does anything to imply that he doesn't believe a witness, or that some piece of evidence is or is not important, then the jury picks up on that and forms the same beliefs.

"In short, Max, if we lose the judge, we lose the jury. And I'm afraid you lost him with that brainless call to *USA Today*. And by the way," she added, "like the judge said back there, you better hope and pray that this Sachs woman doesn't write anything. The county jail is not exactly the Waldorf Astoria, and your cellmates won't exactly be a bunch of choir boys."

Reed, nodding, fully understood the dressing down he got from Berman. "Would it help," he asked, "for me to call Lois Sachs and ask her to forget the whole thing?"

Roz Berman dropped her eyes and shook her head in disbelief at what she just heard. "Max, you don't get it, do you? You're already in deep shit for calling her in the first place, so you want to call her again? With luck, she won't write anything. But if the judge learned that you contacted her again — for any reason — the county jail would be too good for you. He'd sentence you to a hard labor camp in Siberia."

Hugo Shoemaker, who had not said a word until now, lifted a hand to make a point. "Roz, what if one of us — you or I — called this Sachs woman and told her about the court order forbidding any mention of Elizabeth Peters in the case. Maybe we could tell her that she and the paper would be violating that order by printing anything."

"That won't work, Hugo. Even if she believed that, she would take it to her paper's lawyers and they would laugh. *USA Today* is not a party to the lawsuit and is not bound by any of the judge's orders. They are not even in the court's jurisdiction. Further, if we tried that, we'd be taking the same risk as Max if he were to make the call — she'd write how we tried to squelch the story. And you and I are bound by Judge Krause's orders. We'd be held in contempt for simply making the call. Good idea, Hugo, but no, thanks."

CHAPTER 66

Lois Sachs was not into so-called sensational journalism, and she certainly was not one to get excited over news delivered by anonymous phone calls. Nevertheless, it was hard to resist the scoop at which the caller hinted. She decided to follow up, but carefully. As the editor of a national sports page, she knew the downside of maligning a national sport hero — especially one of Eddie Bennison's status. Athletes tend to stick together. Attack a golf hero today, and a football star may refuse to talk to you tomorrow.

More to the point, this would not be the kind of scoop that *USA Today* would relish. It was not the kind of paper that smeared people or took its readers into bedrooms — or motels. Its readers might very well be offended by such reporting. But it was still a newspaper, and this could be news — big news!

She decided that she could at least stick her toe in the water, and to do that she saw no particular risk in calling the Marriott as a first step. She would simply ask if they had any information that an Elizabeth Peters was at the hotel on August 17, 2007, either as a registered guest or as someone who might have signed a tab for a drink or dinner. And she would ask the same question about Edward Bennison or Ben Edwards. If they were both at the hotel at the same time, it would give some credence to the story that the caller had brought to her. If not, she could always forget the whole thing. Sachs knew that hotels are careful about revealing who had been on their premises; yet, having been a journalist her entire working life, she was pretty good at getting information from people reluctant to give it.

But she had bad luck with the Marriott. A dead end. The hotel operator referred her call to the manager, and the manager in turn referred it to hotel security, where she spoke with someone named Joe Andrews. Although the "Peters" name meant nothing to Andrews, he instantly recognized the names of Edward Bennison and Ben Edwards from his recent conversations with Charlie Mayfield, especially since he, Andrews, had easily been able to put the pieces together and realized that Bennison-Edwards was the national golf icon who was currently the plaintiff in a major defamation case who just happened to be represented by one Charlie Mayfield. Andrews was an avid reader of the sport pages, and the connection was hard to miss.

But Andrews wasn't about to give Lois Sachs any of the information she was seeking. For one thing, he didn't want the Marriott name associated with a nationally publicized sex scandal. For another, he felt a loyalty to Charlie Mayfield and didn't want to betray it.

"I'm sorry, Ms. Sachs, but we wouldn't give out that information even if we had it. I'm sure you understand that our guests have a right of privacy, and we respect it."

"I do, yes."

"Newspaper people believe that everyone has a right to know, but the hotel people believe that not everyone has the right to tell."

Lois Sachs did not push him. She recalled that her anonymous caller had told her that Elizabeth Peters could be reached at Franklin Advertising in Detroit, but that was a call she had to think about, not only as to what to say but whether to make the call at all.

First, there was always the possibility that the whole story was a hoax. Peters might be delusional. Maybe she never met Eddie Bennison, but she wanted to see her name in the paper and her face on TV. And if *USA Today* carried a story that even hinted that Bennison did something wrong and it turned out to be false, his lawsuit against her newspaper would make his case against *Tee Time* look like child's play.

Second, what kind of woman would want to go public with a story that she went to a hotel room with a man? And if she thought she could make money out of this by selling her story, that would be the end of the line — a non-starter. *My paper doesn't pay for stories, and that's a firm policy that I'm in no mood to test.*

She finally decided to tell her boss, the Editor-in-Chief, about the mysterious phone call. *The story is too dangerous for me to chase down on my own,* she thought to herself, *but too important to ignore.*

But, as she expected, she was told to drop the story unless she had further corroboration. To proceed on nothing more than an anonymous phone call would be irresponsible journalism. Having no appetite for a lawsuit like the one that *Tee Time* was defending — and the whole world was watching — Lois Sachs' boss was taking the prudent course.

CHAPTER 67

Max Reed had left Roz Berman's office after his dressing down, and now she and Hugo Shoemaker were there licking their wounds. It had been a rough afternoon, with Max Reed spilling his guts about leaking the Peters story to *USA Today*. If the judge had any respect for Reed or *Tee Time* before today, it vanished into thin air when he heard Reed admit to calling Lois Sachs.

Berman had told Todd Slocum to expect a call from her about now, and she now placed it. Once she had Slocum on the line, she pressed the speaker button so Shoemaker could participate.

"Todd, it's Roz Berman. I have Hugo with me."

"Great. I've been waiting for the call. What's up?"

"Well, we had a little surprise this morning. Your boy, Max Reed, can't help stepping on his pecker."

"Oh, Lord, what now?"

"As you know, Todd, the judge ruled that Elizabeth Peters and her story were out of the case. Moreover, he ruled that no one should disclose anything about her and her story to anyone, and specifically included the press. He made that clear to us, and we made it clear to you and to Reed. Well, it seems that good old Max can't keep his mouth shut, so he leaked the Peters story to — are you ready for this? — to the editor of the sports page at *USA Today*. How do you like that?"

"Oh, my God! I can't believe it!"

"You better believe it. He even admitted it — to the judge! And the judge exploded. When he asked Reed why in the hell he did that, Reed gave him some crap about the public having a right to know. Honestly, Todd, the judge was so pissed that I thought he might actually get up and slug Max right in his face. It was awful."

"Why did Max admit to doing that?"

"Well, he hemmed and hawed for a minute or two, but he was trapped. Charlie Mayfield somehow found out that *USA Today* was tipped off, and he reported it to the judge, and then the judge asked Reed if he was the culprit. Once he heard the question, it was obvious that he was the one who did the leaking. He even said that he never made anonymous phone calls, and that was the giveaway because, until then, no one knew that the leak was from an anonymous phone call. At first he fudged, so the judge started to send him to the county jail for refusing to come clean — he even called for a sheriff's deputy to come and get Max, and that's when Max broke down and did a *mea culpa*. It was pathetic."

"Is there anything I can do?" Slocum asked.

"Not about this," Roz Berman answered. "We just wanted you to know. Winning these cases is hard enough, but it's even harder when our own clients stab us in the back. Some dark cloud must have passed in front of the moon the night that Max Reed was born. He caused the case to be filed, and he might cause it to be lost. It's hard to get the jury on our side if the judge sends signals that he doesn't like us."

"I'll have to tell Clive Curtis about this. He already despises Reed."

Berman had more to say. "Actually, I'm really calling about something else. Mayfield rested and now it's time for us. Frankly, Todd, we don't have a lot of evidence to offer. I was hoping that we could produce some of the people who actually saw Bennison cheat or take drugs, but Reed won't tell us who they are. More of that baloney about protecting sources. But if we did produce some of those people to say they saw Bennison do these things, we could be home free. And to do that, Reed has to give us the names of his sources. Without them, we have nothing except Reed's word that they exist, and he's got about as much credibility as Pinocchio."

"I'll give Max a call and see if I can persuade him to tell us about his sources — who they are and where we can find them. I can try to reach him right now — I have his cell phone number."

"Okay," Roz Berman said, "then call us and let us know what he says."

CHAPTER 68

"Hi, Max. It's Todd."

"I guess you heard what happened today?"

"Yeah, I did."

"And you're calling to fire me."

Slocum offered a small chuckle. "No, not at all. We have to stand behind you on this case, Max, and we can't do that if you're not here. Anyway, your job is secure — just like the engineer who designed the gas tank on the Ford Pinto. Ford couldn't fire him after all those gas tank explosions — they didn't want it to look like they were admitting that he did something wrong."

"Gee, that's a consolation. So you'll fire me after the case is over."

"Max, I have to be honest with you. This case is going south, fast. We're going to lose unless we can pull a rabbit out of a hat. And you're the guy with both the rabbit and the hat. You can save the day, Max, and at the same time you can save the magazine and all the rest of us."

"What would you like me to do, set myself on fire? I'm already a dead man as far as the magazine is concerned."

"That's not true, Max. You're a respected guy around here, and throughout the industry. And you have a chance to prove it over the next couple of days. You can win the case for us and be a hero around here, and you can show the world that you're an honest sportswriter."

"Oh, now I get it."

"Sure you do, Max. All you have to do is give Roz and Hugo the names of some of the people who saw Bennison cheat or take drugs. You don't need to give them all the names. Just giving a few names will show that you didn't make that shit up on your own. Then we can call those people in to testify and tell us what they saw Bennison do."

"You know I can't do that, Todd. It would breach a sacred confidence I have with my sources."

"That's bullshit, Max, and you know it! It would be a breach of confidence only if they gave you the information on the condition that you wouldn't reveal their names. But if some golf fan came to you and voluntarily told you that Bennison cheated, and he saw it with his own eyes, and there was no agreement to keep it confidential, then you're free to reveal him as your source. Same thing if one of the pros came to you and told you, voluntarily, that he saw Bennison shooting drugs in the locker room. You would have no duty not to reveal him as a source. Not if he didn't ask you, before giving you that information, to keep his name out of it.

"So tell me, Max, did people tell you about Bennison with the understanding that you wouldn't reveal their names?"

"Well, not exactly. I got it mostly from idle conversations around the club house and the pressroom, from pros and other sportswriters. It was just a subject that came up every so often. And if I ratted on one of the pros who talked to me about Bennison, even with no understanding about confidentiality, our name would be mud on the Tour. We'd never again get even one of them to sit down for an interview, or give us an instructional article. And I'd certainly never do that to another sportswriter."

"But that's a chance we might have to take. If we don't, and if we lose the case, we can be out of business. Who knows what that jury can do? Remember what a jury did to *The Saturday Evening Post* after that article accusing Bear Bryant of fixing a football game? The jury hammered *The Post*, and *The Post* didn't survive the loss. They ended up going out of business.

"We can't let that happen to *Tee Time*, Max, and you can make sure that it doesn't happen. Just give us the names — the names of your sources. At least some of them."

Silence.

Todd Slocum's sigh was audible over the phone. "Max, there were sources, weren't there?"

More silence. And then, "I don't discuss my sources. You should know that, Todd."

MONDAY MORNING

CHAPTER 69

Roz Berman and Hugo Shoemaker had just taken their seats at the counsel table before the Monday court session when Berman's cell phone buzzed to tell her she had a text message. She pulled the phone from her purse and saw the message on the screen from Todd Slocum: *Talked to Max three times over the weekend. Won't budge. Todd.*

She shook her head in despair, then nudged Shoemaker and showed him the message. He, too, showed his deep disappointment. He, like Roz Berman, knew that the case was lost without those names.

"Hugo," Berman said softly, "I have to call Todd. Go ask Leon, the bailiff, to tell the judge that we'd like a few minutes before court starts."

She quickly ducked out into the corridor and dialed Slocum's cell phone number. As soon as he answered she said, "It's me, Roz. What happened?"

"I tried everything, Roz, but I can't get him to identify his sources. I told him it's the only way we can win the case, and this was his chance to be a hero instead of a bum. I even told him that the survival of the magazine — and all of our jobs — was depending on him. But it was like talking to the moon. He wouldn't move."

"Todd, are you sure that there *are* sources?"

"I asked him that very question, and he didn't reply. Then I pressed him, and he said he won't discuss sources. And that was that."

"Any other suggestions?"

"Well, I might be able to persuade Clive Curtis to talk to him. Clive is our Editor-in-Chief and he runs the whole show at the magazine. He has the power to hire and fire, and if anyone can hold an ax over Reed's head, it's Clive. And Clive doesn't take no for an answer."

"Okay, let's try that. Better do it fast. It's our turn to put on evidence, and without the sources, we don't have much to offer. Might be able to stall for a day or two, but that's about it."

CHAPTER 70

Killing time in his hotel room, Max Reed was relieved to have his boredom broken by the ringing of his cell phone. But his relief was short lived — the caller ID on the phone screen read "Clive Curtis." Reed knew that his boss wasn't calling to ask about the weather in Chicago. He took a deep breath and answered.

"Hi, Clive."

Curtis, never one to waste time on niceties, didn't disappoint. "Max, we're up to our goddamned necks in shit, and you're the only guy who can save us. I'm not asking you; I'm *telling* you — give our lawyers some names. Your ass is on the line, Max, and Berman and Shoemaker are the only ones who can save it. But they can't do it with their hands tied behind their backs. You can win the case for us, Max, and at the same time save your ass. All you have do to is give 'em the fucking names."

"Clive, you know I can't do that. It's a sacred rule of our profession."

"You can shove those rules up your fat ass, Max. I'm trying to save a magazine here, and all the jobs that go with it. If you give up those names, a few people in our business might think you broke a trust, but most of them will know you didn't have a choice. But if you don't give up the names, and we lose the case because of your goddamned articles, you will be the joke of our entire industry. You'll go down in the annals of journalism as the biggest hack that ever wrote a story. The journalism world will look at you for generations to come as the ultimate embarrassment — the ultimate disgrace — of our profession. The name Max Reed will be held up as the patron saint of bullshit reporting.

"You can avoid all of that, Max, and you can go from goat to hero — just give us the fucking names! Hell, some of those people would be glad to have you name them; it would give them some stardom — make 'em famous."

Reed was silent, trying to think of what to say to his boss. Clive Curtis interpreted the silence to imply that perhaps there were no sources after all.

"Max — you *did* have sources for those articles, didn't you?

"Of course, I went through all that with Howard Wolf and that fancy Wall Street lawyer, Bernie Cashman."

"But from what I understand, you just told them that you had sources, not who they were. Right?"

"That's right. And I didn't lie to them. They reminded me that I needed multiple sources, and I told them that I knew that. And I did have multiple sources. They knew that I couldn't be expected to reveal their names, and they didn't ask for names. And that's all I can tell you, Clive — I had multiple sources, but I can't reveal who they are."

"Even to me?"

"Even to you."

Curtis, exasperated, took a deep breath. "I've been in this business for forty years, Max, and I can smell bullshit from a mile away. If you really had sources, you could reveal them to me in confidence. I'm a colleague, Max, and I'm your boss. There is no rule or policy anywhere that forbids a reporter to reveal his sources to his boss. And until you do that, Max, I will be forced to conclude — just as the judge and the jury and the rest of the publishing world will conclude — that there were no sources, and that you deliberately lied about Eddie Bennison just to make a name for yourself." And then Curtis half-whispered, "And that's not the kind of reporters I want at my magazine — assuming I have a magazine after all you're doing to destroy it."

"Can I think about it?"

"Sure, as long as you give me an answer within thirty seconds. We have to start putting on our case within the next hour or so, and without those names we have nothing to put on. Without your help, Max, we'll just have to drop our drawers, bend over, and wait for the verdict."

It only took fifteen seconds for Reed to reply. "Okay, I'll call Roz Berman right now and tell her I'm on my way over to the courthouse."

"And what will you tell her?"

"I'll be damned if I know."

MONDAY AFTERNOON

CHAPTER 71

S till waiting to hear if Max Reed was going to break down and give
up the names of his sources, Roz Berman started the Monday
afternoon session by offering some perfunctory evidence. Her first
witness, Malcolm Whiting, was a rules official from the United
States Golf Association who testified about some of the enigmatic rules
of golf. The point was to show how strict and exacting were those rules,
and that little slack is given to their literal interpretation. Berman's intent,
of course, was to show that a violation is a violation, plain and simple,
regardless of its apparent triviality, so that even mismarking the ball by a
mere half inch on the green, or packing the club face grooves with a tiny
amount of dirt, is as serious as kicking the ball out of a sand trap.

"Mr. Whiting, we have heard in this case about the rules pertaining
to the marking of a ball on the putting green, and pertaining to foreign
substances on the face of a golf club. Are you familiar with these rules?"

"Yes, quite familiar."

"And is there any flexibility in the application of these rules. What
I mean is this: is a golfer permitted some latitude in how he obeys these
rules? For example, can placing a golf ball a mere half inch closer to the
hole be a violation of the rules?"

"Absolutely. The rules of golf are taken very seriously, and they are
applied literally. In fact, the sport has been criticized for applying the rules
too literally. "

"Can you give us any examples?"

"Yes, one comes to mind immediately. For many years, the Masters golf tournament, which is held annually in Augusta, Georgia, has been among the most important tournaments in the world. Winning the Masters is the dream of every professional golfer in the world.

"In 1968, there was a very dramatic finish between Roberto De Vicenzo from Argentina and the American Bob Goalby. They were both playing magnificently all week, and when the final round began on Sunday, Goalby was one shot ahead of De Vicenzo. De Vicenzo shot an incredible 65 on Sunday, and finished several minutes before Goalby, who was still on the course. Goalby finished the round with a 66, one behind De Vicenzo for the day, so it appeared to everyone that they finished in a tie and would have to go into a playoff.

"Now," the witness said, looking toward the jury, "I should point out that a player does not keep his own score in professional tournaments. His score is kept by a playing partner — one of the other professionals playing with him. In this case, De Vicenzo was playing with Tommy Aaron, and Aaron was keeping De Vicenzo's score.

"On the 17th hole of that fourth and final round, De Vicenzo scored three — a birdie, since it was a par four hole. The whole world watching on television, as well as the entire gallery surrounding the 17th green, saw him make a three. However, by a tragic error — an innocent slip — Tommy Aaron marked down a four instead of a three for De Vicenzo. He later wrote down the correct score for the entire round — 65 — even after mismarking the score on the 17th hole, but if one were to add up the individual scores per hole on that card for the entire round, it would add up to 66 because of the error. At the conclusion of the round, De Vicenzo signed his scorecard after confirming that it showed his final score of 65 correctly, but he never took the time to check the hole-by-hole scores. Tommy Aaron, then realizing he made a mistake in mis-scoring the 17th hole, immediately notified the officials. However, since De Vicenzo already signed the card with a four instead of a three on the 17th hole, it was ruled that he had to be charged with the four, giving him a final score of 66 — instead of the 65 which was his actual score and the final score on his scorecard. Accordingly, he finished in second place instead of being in a tie for first, and Bob Goalby was declared the official winner of the tournament.

"The rules clearly say that if a player signs a scorecard that shows a higher number on any hole than he actually scored, he must be charged with the higher score, and the fact that the card shows the correct score for the entire round is irrelevant. And if he signs a card with a lower score than he actually had, he would be disqualified.

"So here we see an example of a rule being strictly enforced to punish a player solely because of a freakish mistake by another player. There was no question that De Vicenzo had a birdie three on seventeen and shot a 65 that Sunday and that he should have been in a tie for first place. The galleries saw it, the officials saw it, the sportswriters saw it, and millions of television viewers saw it. But, in the rush of things after the round, the poor guy signed an erroneous scorecard and was punished. His three became a four, his 65 became a 66, and he lost.

"To this day, whenever De Vicenzo is asked about the incident, he says in his broken English, 'I am a stupid!'"

"Thank you, Mr. Whiting, for explaining to us that, in the world of golf, rules are rules, and that they are not merely general guidelines."

"Yes, there have been many examples of this."

"Can you give us another?"

"Sure. The Andy Williams Open was being played at the Torrey Pines Golf Course in San Diego in 1987. Craig Stadler finished his final round on Sunday thinking, as everyone else thought, that he was in a three-way tie for second place. It was then discovered that on the previous day, Saturday, he violated Rule 13-3.5, which forbids a golfer from 'building a stance.' What happened was this: when Stadler was playing the 14th hole on Saturday, his ball had come to rest under a bush in a place that required him to kneel — get on his knees — to hit the ball. Because it had rained the night before, and the turf was wet, he placed a towel under his knees, obviously to keep his pants from getting muddied. He certainly didn't realize that this act, intended to keep his trousers clean, would be deemed 'building a stance' within the meaning of Rule 13-3.5. Ironically, none of the officials or players near him thought anything of it. But a few television viewers called in on Saturday afternoon to mention it, and when the officials reviewed the film the next day, and then checked the rule book, they agreed that Stadler violated the rule and was assessed a two-stroke penalty. Adding two strokes to his score would still have put him high in the money, but, to make matters worse — much worse — Stadler was disqualified and won nothing because he signed a scorecard on Saturday that showed a score lower than he actually had *because of the penalty assessed against him the next day*. That silly penalty cost him dearly. Instead of winning the purse for a third-place tie, or even for a sixth-place finish, which is where he would have finished after the two-stroke penalty, he won nothing — not a red cent — because he was disqualified.

"A very costly mistake," the witness added. "Using the size of today's purses as a guide, the mistake would have cost Stadler several hundred thousand dollars."[13]

Roz Berman got what she wanted from this witness. If Roberto De Vicenzo could be penalized because of the error of another player in writing down his scores, and if Craig Stadler could be penalized for trying to keep his pants clean, then the slightest mismarking of a golf ball or the smearing of dirt in the grooves of his clubs, as Eddie Bennison was accused of doing, were not to be taken lightly.

"Thank you, Mr. Whiting, for helping us understand how strictly the rules of golf are enforced, and how even seemingly innocuous and unintentional infractions can have overwhelming consequences."

Berman knew it was improper for her to make that last statement which should have been appropriate only during closing arguments. But she knew that Charlie was famous for doing the same thing. Finishing with the witness, she turned and gave Charlie a slight wink. *Take that!* the wink said.

Charlie had no questions for the witness, and court was adjourned for the day.

CHAPTER 72

Roz Berman and Hugo Shoemaker were leaving the courtroom after the trial adjourned for the day. They were met by Max Reed, who asked, "Can I walk back to the office with both of you?"

"Of course you may, Max," Berman replied. "I'll even let you carry my briefcase." As they were approaching the elevator bank, she said, "Let's not talk until we get outside. Elevators have ears." Once the three of them reached the street, Berman asked, "What's up, Max?"

"I'm between the proverbial rock and a hard place. Clive Curtis and Todd both want me to divulge my sources, and I honestly think I'll get fired if I don't. But if I do that, I'll be the Benedict Arnold of the publishing world. The entire media industry has worked hard for years to get a free pass when it comes to publishing dirt on well-known people and not revealing who gave it to them. I'd be seen as a traitor to my industry if I gave out the names."

"So how can I help?"

"I was hoping that there might be some middle ground. Like maybe I could reveal my sources off the record. Maybe in a confidential session in the judge's chambers."

"A good thought, Max, but it won't work. We want the jury to know that you have sources and who they are. Whispering it to Charlie Mayfield or Judge Krause in a private session gets us nowhere. It's the jury whom we need to convince that you didn't make all that stuff up about Bennison. And whatever we present to the jury becomes public record." Roz Berman then added, "There are some circumstances where a witness can offer evidence to a jury in a closed session that is kept private from the public and the press, but those involve evidence such as top-secret military operations, or secret formulas in patent cases. We don't have any of that here."

Berman then turned to Hugo Shoemaker who was walking on her other side. "Do you see any way around this, Hugo?" Uncharacteristically for Roz Berman, she was pleading. *There must be some way we can convince the jury that Max had reliable sources without telling the whole world who they are.*

Shoemaker pondered for a moment. "Perhaps Max can testify that he had sources without telling the world who they were."

"He already testified to that. Anyway, Charlie Mayfield will once again try to drag the names out of him on cross-examination. And Max would once again say he refuses to divulge their names."

"But what if he says that he doesn't know the names?"

"Pardon me?" Berman asked, not believing her ears. "How could he not know their names? No one would believe him if he said he didn't know their names. Reporters don't accept sensitive information without asking who is giving it to them."

"But suppose he got the information from fans who never gave their names to him. For example, fans who phoned him and left messages saying that they saw Bennison cheat, but never left their names; or maybe he got unsigned letters to that effect."

Max Reed, walking on the other side of Berman, was listening to all this, which was precisely what Shoemaker intended. Shoemaker was trying to send messages to Reed — hinting as to how Reed could say he had sources without revealing names.

Shoemaker continued. "Of course, it might not be very persuasive if names aren't provided, but it might get Max off the hook as far as his boss, Clive Curtis, is concerned. And it might work for the jury."

Not much was said during the rest of the walk back to Roz Berman's office, but Reed was mulling over what Shoemaker had said about anonymous sources. When they got into the elevator, Berman turned to Shoemaker. "You may have come up with a good idea back there, Hugo.

Let's meet in my conference room in ten minutes. You too, Max."

Once the three of them were all seated at her conference room table, Berman spoke. "We might be able to pull this off, but we'd have to do it right — exactly right! And Max would have to give a flawless performance on the witness stand."

"What would I have to do?"

"First, let me ask you a few questions, and I want you to be straight with me. We can't make any mistakes with this, and you must tell the truth. Are you with me?"

"Sure, tell me what you're thinking."

Berman looked Reed straight in the eye. "Could you testify that more than just one or two people told you about Bennison cheating or taking drugs, but that you don't have their names? They were fans who called you or wrote you without giving their names. Would that be true?"

"Sure, I could testify to that," taking his cue from what Shoemaker had said during their walk.

"I didn't ask you that, Max, I asked if it would be true."

"Sure, it would be true."

"How could we substantiate it? Do you keep a log of the phone calls? Did you keep copies of the anonymous letters?"

"No, there's nothing like that. But I swear to God I didn't make all that stuff up out of thin air. For a long time there has been talk among the sportswriters and the pros about Bennison shooting up with drugs and stretching the rules when it served his purposes. Can I give the names, dates, and places? Well, in some cases I can, but there is no way that I would rat out another sportswriter or pro — that would be out of the question. In fact, none of them said they saw Bennison cheating or taking drugs — they were only repeating stuff they heard.

"But there were stories going around — we all heard them. So when I got those anonymous phone calls and letters, which I would ordinarily ignore, they struck a chord with me. Putting it all together, it seemed strong enough to support my articles. I may be wrong about that, but, as I said, I didn't make it all up — I was hearing things from a lot of people for a long time."

Hugo Shoemaker was frowning and shaking his head as he listened to

Reed. "This scares me, Roz. Even if Max had been hearing these things, the jury may think, nevertheless, that it's irresponsible to publish these serious accusations based nothing more than anonymous phone calls and letters, and on social gossip among sportswriters at bars and restaurants. And if that's what he relied on to write those damning articles, he should have said so in the articles themselves." Looking to Reed, Shoemaker asked, "Couldn't you have written in the articles that they were based on anonymous tips and unsubstantiated rumors? You would still have the big story of the year, your magazine sales would still be through the roof, and we wouldn't be here defending this godforsaken lawsuit. But you wrote those things about Bennison as if they were absolute facts — when they were actually relating nothing more than uncorroborated gossip. And I say that, Max, based on what you're telling us today.

"The fact is," Shoemaker went on to say, "I believed all along that you had reliable, identifiable sources — real people you could name — for those terrible things you wrote about Bennison. And when you refused to tell us who they were, I assumed you were merely exercising your rights as a journalist to protect them. I thought you could name them, but wouldn't. And now today you tell us that you won't name them because you can't — you don't know even their names."

"I just told you that I could name some of the sportswriters and golf pros who were saying that stuff, but I wouldn't do that to them."

Shoemaker exploded. "But they weren't giving you information, Max, they were passing along information that they heard somewhere. You just told us that a minute ago. You can't write stories as damning as these based on gossip that you didn't verify."

Shoemaker tossed his pen on the table and looked to the floor, shaking his head in silent outrage. He had unavoidable visions of his scholarly reputation being forever tarnished by this one case where he was defending a slime-peddling magazine with a gossip-mongering reporter. He shivered to think what the nine Supreme Court justices would think of him when he next appeared in the high court to argue some subtle but critical constitutional point. And he was silently kicking himself because it would have been so easy to have asked Reed the right questions before getting involved in the case in the first place. Had he been told in advance that the articles were based on information from unknown sources, or barroom gossip, he wouldn't have touched this case with a 10-foot pole.

Roz Berman decided to put this issue to bed, once and for all. "Look," she said to both Shoemaker and Reed, "as the record now stands, the jury heard Max say that he had sources but wouldn't name them. In our closing statement, we can tell the jury that he would have named the sources but he chose not to do so, and that would be true in the case of the pros and sportswriters who talked about Bennison cheating and taking drugs. We would say that the custom is so sacred that it has become the law of Illinois, and many other states, which specifically authorizes a reporter to refuse to reveal his sources. And we could explain to the jury that this is a very good law — without it, people would be afraid to expose wrongdoing for fear of retaliation once their name was revealed as the source of the information. Since the founding of this country, our society relies on a free press to serve as a watchdog by informing the rest of us when someone does bad things. And to serve that vital purpose, the press has to cultivate reliable sources to bring them information, but these sources would not bring them information if they could not to it anonymously.

"So we may be able to persuade the jury to believe that Max is actually doing a public service by protecting his sources — a public service that is permitted by the Illinois law. We want them to believe that he had sources but won't name them.

"But if we put him on the stand to say that he doesn't know the names of his sources, they'll think he's a lousy reporter who disgraced Eddie Bennison with nothing more than gossip and rumors. What kind of reporter would write such an explosive story without even knowing the names of his sources?

"So, we might be okay as the record now stands. Max testified that he wouldn't reveal his sources, but the implication was that he knew who they were. So if the jury believes that Max knows their names, but won't reveal them, we might survive. But if he gets up there and says that he has no idea who they are, we're dead in the water. I think we're better off leaving him off the stand altogether, and then using our closing statements to explain why he didn't reveal the names when Charlie had him on the sand. To sum up, we might be able to live with the jury believing that he has sources but won't name them; but we're dead once they hear that he has sources but has no idea who in the hell they are."

Berman leaned back and asked, "Is everyone okay with that?" Hearing no dissent, she looked at Reed and said, "Alright, Max, good news — you don't have to get back on the stand — unless you can come up with some names and save our asses."

Reed was confused by all that Berman and Shoemaker were saying and responded, "Is that really good news?"

"It is for you. If you got up there and testified that you didn't know the names of the people who told you those things about Bennison, Charlie Mayfield would grind you up and feed you to the fish. I can just hear him now. 'Did you ask for their names, Mr. Reed?' 'Did you even try to learn their names, Mr. Reed?' 'Did you try to verify or corroborate their stories, Mr. Reed?' 'Can you show us copies of the anonymous letters you received from your so-called sources, Mr. Reed? Or the phone logs?' 'Do you always write stories based on information that came to you from invisible, unnamed people, Mr. Reed?'

"By the time he'd be done with you, Max, the jury could come to only one of two conclusions: one, that you made all that shit up about Bennison; or two, that you get your facts from tea leaves. Either way, we'd be dead meat."

MONDAY EVENING

CHAPTER 73

Roz Berman left the meeting in a sour mood. As she saw it, her mission was to find a way to convince the jury that what Reed did was standard procedure in the reporting business and that no negative inferences should be drawn from it.

And that's exactly what she set out to do that very evening. As soon as she arrived at her condominium on Lake Shore Drive, she poured two vodka gimlets and took them into the den where her husband, Lou, was in his easy chair reading the paper. He took a sip of his drink and asked, "How was your day? Fighting with Charlie Mayfield all day couldn't be much fun."

"Charlie's not my problem — not today. Today I had to battle with my own team, and it wasn't fun. That goddamned Shoemaker — he's about useful as a trap door on a lifeboat."

"I love your descriptions of people, Roz. God knows how you describe me when I'm not around."

"Well, you wouldn't be around — at least not around me — if you were anything like that elitist Ivy League snob."

"So, what did he do this time?"

"Okay, you already know the problems I've been having with that sportswriter, Reed — he's the one who wrote those horrid things about Eddie Bennison, the golfer who's suing us."

"He's the one with the phantom sources, right?"

"That's him, alright. And I'm beginning to think that that's what they are — phantoms."

"You're kidding! *Tee Time* is not one of those racy rags that looks for scandal around every corner. I read it myself." Lou Berman took another sip of his gimlet, and asked, "But what does this have to do with Hugo?"

"Reed already testified that he had sources but refused to name them."

"As is his right." Lou Berman was an executive in a national public relations firm, and he worked almost daily with people in the media. "Sources are bread and butter to journalists, and 'outing' a source is an act of treason to those guys. It just isn't done."

"But that's not the point. Reed privately admitted to me today that he doesn't know the names of many of his sources — they're anonymous. He claims they told him those things about Bennison in unsigned letters, or through messages left on his phone — letters and messages that he didn't keep. And that idiot Shoemaker wants us to put Reed on the stand and admit that he doesn't know the names of his sources."

"Are you saying that he wrote those stories using only sources he can't identify?"

"Basically, yes. He says he has other sources he can identify, but won't, because they're golf pros or fellow sportswriters, and he doesn't want to piss them off. And even those people were only passing along gossip they heard — none of them ever saw Bennison cheat or take drugs with their own eyes."

"I see your problem. If he testifies that he can't name his sources because he doesn't know their names, he'll look like a boob. But if he testifies that he can name them, but won't, they might think he's a martyr in the finest tradition of his trade. And they might like him for that."

"I agree, and that's what he's already done. And I'll leave it at that without putting him back on the stand. Now I want to reinforce that 'martyr' point by bringing in evidence that Reed is no different than anyone else who writes for magazines and newspapers — that even the most respected reporters and journalists in the country refuse to reveal their sources. But I need to find a strong witness who can say that. And I was hoping you could help me."

"Me? How could I help?"

"C'mon, Lou, you know every respectable reporter in Chicago. You work with those guys every day."

"And you want me to ask one of them to testify for you?"

"No, all you have to do is give me some names. Then I can call and talk to them and figure out if any of them can testify to what I need — or at least give me some direction on how to handle this."

"Would it be better to have someone who writes about sports?"

"No, not at all."

"Give me a few minutes to think on it."

Roz Berman went back to their bedroom to replace her high heels with slippers. When she returned, her husband asked, "How about Clarence Stouffer?"

"Clarence? Wasn't it he and his wife who took us to that charity ball last winter at the Drake Hotel? I think it was for homeless children, or something like that."

"Yes, that's him. But it was for juvenile diabetes."

"Right. I didn't know he was a reporter."

"He isn't. He's Associate Editor of the *Trib*."

"Wow, an editor with *The Chicago Tribune*. Pretty good credentials. Can I call him?"

"Sure." Lou Berman pulled out his cell phone, pushed his finger against the screen a few times, and said, "Okay, get a pencil and paper, I'll give you his home and office numbers." After his wife wrote down the numbers, he said, "If he doesn't remember you, tell him you're married to the good-looking guy who took him for nearly a hundred bucks in our poker game last week."

Roz Berman went into her home office and called Clarence Stauffer. Being an editor of one of the major newspapers in the country, and *the* major newspaper in Chicago, Stauffer knew without prompting that she was the trial lawyer defending *Bennison v. Tee Time*, a widely reported case that could have profound effects on the entire media world.

"Hi, Roz. Great hearing from you. Did Lou hire you to come after me for the money I owe him from our poker game?"

"No," she laughed, "nothing like that. I'm calling because I need some help, and I was hoping that you could give it to me."

"Of course. Does this have anything to do with the trial we're all reading about?"

"It does, yes. When can we talk? It would have to be soon, since it involves that case and what my next moves should be."

"We can talk now, or whenever and wherever is best for you. Remember, Roz, I'm on your side on this one. We're all pulling for you to win."

"Great. I don't want to push you, but if you have a few minutes now, I can tell you about my problem. You may have a solution for me when you hear it, or you may want to think about it for a day or two. Will that work for you?"

"Sure, we're not having dinner until later. We can talk now if you'd like."

"Great, but can we keep this confidential — I mean, highly confidential? I might have to tell you things that could cost me the case if they ever got out."

"Sure, you have nothing to worry about."

"Thanks, and I'll make this very general. I'm interested in you telling me how you people in the press deal with sources for your stories. I know you don't have to reveal your sources, but I need to know what you require before you rely on a source to print a story. In other words, Clarence, can a source be anyone, or does it have to be someone who has well-known credibility? And how many sources are enough?"

Berman really wanted to ask if Clarence Stauffer would approve a story based on little more than anonymous tips that came in the form of unsigned letters or unidentified phone messages, or barroom gossip, but to ask that would telegraph the weakness in her case. And even though Stauffer promised confidentiality, she couldn't take a chance. So she decided to ask general questions at first. She'd decide later whether to ask specific questions that could signal the soft underbelly of her case.

"We deal with that every day, Roz, and there is no a definite answer to your question. As a practical matter, it really depends on the nature of the information provided by the source, and even the number of sources.

"For example, a particularly credible source wouldn't be necessary for routine information that couldn't hurt anyone. If I had a source tell me that it rained last night, anyone who saw it rain would be good enough. I wouldn't require that the information come from a meteorologist. That's not the kind of information that demands a high degree of reliability. On the other hand, if I were writing a story predicting that we'd be having a major storm next Tuesday, I'd want the word of a meteorologist — or maybe two of them — who have proven experience in predicting the weather. The average person would not be a good enough source for me to report a prediction of that significance.

"So, in essence, the rule is this — the more sensational, or technical, the information, the more credible the source must be. And that's only common sense."

"How about the number of sources?"

"There again, it's all a matter of common sense. Neither of us would accept the word of only one person who told us that a Martian spaceship landed in Grant Park last night. If five people told us that, we might have enough to investigate but, to go ahead and write a story of that magnitude, we'd probably want more sources. Furthermore, with information that momentous, we'd ask a hell of a lot of questions to make sure we weren't being fed a bunch of baloney."

Roz Berman was listening carefully, trying to digest what Stauffer was saying and then apply it to her lawsuit.

"This is all very helpful, Clarence. Let me ask you something else, and please remember our agreement to keep this all confidential. How do you feel about anonymous sources?"

"Whoa! Now you're walking on thin ice. Relying on anonymous sources — especially for a sensitive story — is not only dangerous, it's stupid! We don't do it, and that's that, unless the anonymous source tells us something that we already know, or that we can verify through other known sources. Even if an anonymous source told us something that is so innocuous that it couldn't hurt anyone, we still wouldn't use it as grounds on which to base a story."

"But wait a minute, Clarence, I've read a lot of stories in newspapers which mention anonymous sources. I've even seen them in the *Tribune*.

How can you say you don't use them?"

"That's easy to clarify, Roz. When you see that we mention an anonymous source, it's one of two situations. One, if we do happen to write something that we were told by an anonymous source, we say so in the story — we'll say something like 'according to anonymous sources, blah, blah, blah.' In other words, we tell our readers that we don't have a known source, and they can decide for themselves how much credence to give to the story. So, except for extremely sensitive information, we allow some leeway to use anonymous sources, provided we disclose that to our readers.

"Two — the other time we'll mention an anonymous source — is when a known and credible source gives us information on the condition of keeping his or her name out of that story. This is very common. I'll give you an example that you may recall. Last week we wrote a story saying that the mayor was considering the closing of some schools. We got this information from someone very close to the mayor — someone in his inner circle — but that person didn't want his name to be mentioned for fear that it would anger the mayor. So we went with the story, but specifically said in the story that it was based on a source close to the mayor who spoke to us on the condition of anonymity because he was not authorized to speak on the subject.

"So you can see, Roz, that we never base a story on anonymous sources without saying so. And we sometimes protect the anonymity of a source whom we know and believe to be credible."

Roz Berman, busy scribbling notes of the conversation, was pondering her next question when Clarence Stauffer asked one of his own.

"Roz, I know this trial means a hell of a lot to you, as it does to all of us in the press. I just hope for all of our sakes that this reporter for *Tee Time* — the guy who wrote those articles — had more than anonymous sources for the terrible things he wrote about that golf pro. If he didn't, you sure as hell have your work cut out for you."

"I'll be candid with you, Clarence, but I have to remind you that this is all off the record."

"Right."

"Well, the author of the stories claims to have several sources. Some are known to him, and he regards them as reliable, but most are from golf fans who sent him letters or left messages on his phone, and most of the letters are unsigned and most of the phone messages weren't kept. As for the sources he knows, he wants to protect their anonymity — they are other golf pros or people who he otherwise knows. He never got their permission to mention their names. And it's important to him — and his magazine — that he doesn't alienate them. The magazine needs these pros for stories, interviews, and instructional tips.

"Now here's my dilemma. Reed has already testified that he has sources, but he refuses to reveal their names. And he has that right in Illinois. But I'm worried that the jury doesn't believe him. It's easy for them to believe that he's lying when he says he has sources but refuses to name them. So I have two choices. One, I can leave it as it is and hope the jury does believe that he had reliable sources. Or two, I can put him back on the stand to testify that he has other sources but he can't name them because they never gave him their names. But, to me, that sounds worse than saying that he knows his sources but won't tell anyone who they are."

"I'm no lawyer, Roz, but it seems to me that you have only one choice — and that is to play the hand that you're already holding — that he has sources but won't name them, a position he has every right to take. As I see it, if he gets on the stand now and testifies that he relied on anonymous sources — people who he doesn't even know and can't identify — he'll look like a schmuck — either a dumb schmuck or a dishonest one, but definitely a schmuck."

"Thanks, Clarence, that's the route I was planning to take, but it's reassuring to have some confirmation that I'm heading in the right direction."

TUESDAY

CHAPTER 74

When the trial reconvened on Tuesday morning, Hugo Shoemaker stood. "The defense calls Samuel Roberts to the stand." Although Roz Berman handled most of the witnesses for the defense, she agreed that Shoemaker, because of his expertise in First Amendment law, would be a better choice to elicit the testimony of this witness.

A tall, thin man rose and walked briskly to the front of the courtroom. He wore rimless glasses and a corduroy jacket with patches on the sleeves. After taking his oath, he took his seat on the witness stand.

"Please state your name and occupation."

"My name is Sam Roberts. I am a professor at the Northwestern University's Medill School of Journalism in Evanston, Illinois."

"How long have you been a professor at Northwestern?"

"For twenty-three years as a full, tenured professor. Before that I was an associate professor at the University of Florida."

"And what courses do you teach?"

"Several, but my particular focus is on journalistic ethics."

"Have you written on that subject as well as having taught it?"

"Yes, I've written two books and numerous articles on journalism ethics. In fact, that was the subject of my dissertation when I received my doctorate degree — my PhD."

After a few more questions and answers to establish Professor Roberts' credentials, Shoemaker asked, "Dr. Roberts, are you familiar with the practice of reporters and other writers refusing to reveal the names of their sources — that is, the names of people who had given them information on which their stories or articles are based?"

"Yes, of course. Just last year I delivered a lecture in England on that very subject. It was at Oxford."

"Is that a practice that is widely followed by people in the media?"

"Absolutely, and it's a very good practice. It's vital for the health of our society. As a matter of fact, it's one of the reasons that our country is exceptional — it ensures a society and government that have the highest morals on the planet."

"That's a very strong statement. Can you explain to the jury why this is so?"

"Certainly. We often hear the word 'transparent' in the description of a highly moral and ethical government. That word tells us that everything is visible and out in the open — nothing is hidden. And the reason that everything is out in the open goes back to the founding of our country and the enactment of our Constitution more than 200 years ago. Our Founding Fathers gave us a Constitution that guarantees a free press that can act as a watchdog and report wrongdoing on the part of the leaders of our government and our society.

"But the members of the press cannot report those wrongdoings if they don't know about them, and they won't know about them unless someone tells them. For example, the *Washington Post* could not have exposed the Watergate scandal in 1972 were it not for two of its reporters, Carl Bernstein and Bob Woodward, who had been given the damning information by a source identified only by the pseudonym 'Deep Throat.' But this so-called Deep Throat would not give the information to Bernstein and Woodward without the assurance that his name would never be revealed as their source. In fact, it appears that Bernstein had never met him before his revelations, but Woodward had once met him in the White House waiting room outside President Nixon's office. And it was Woodward to whom he first revealed his secrets in a dark garage.

"In any event, the reporters assured him that, if they ever learned his name, they would never reveal it without his permission. Thus, one of the most significant news stories of the century — a story that nearly toppled a government and led to the resignation of a president — would never have been told if Deep Throat thought that Bernstein and Woodward would or could disclose his real identity. It was only the assurance of anonymity, and the trust that it would be honored, that enabled Deep Throat to reveal the wrongs that had been committed by the government.

"There are countless other examples of people exposing wrongdoing because they knew they could do so without fearing the retaliation that would surely take place if their names were revealed.

"So important is the concept of protecting sources that we now have laws known as 'whistleblower laws.' Whistleblower laws are those laws that guarantee protection for people who 'blow the whistle' on others in business or government who have committed wrongs.

"It's worth noting that the policy of protecting those who expose information is woven throughout our society. In addition to the whistleblower laws and the laws protecting a reporter who refuses to reveal his sources, we see it every day in the prosecution of crimes. A very high percentage of criminal convictions directly result from an informer giving information to the police or the prosecutors that leads to someone's conviction. Those informers usually have that information because they themselves participated in the crime in which they are now implicating others. And why do these informers come forward with this information? Because they are promised immunity or a light sentence in exchange for identifying the others. So this is one more example of our society adopting measures to protect those who come forward with incriminating information about others.

"The reasons for these measures is precisely the same as the reasons why we permit reporters not to reveal the names of their sources. If a source feared his identity would be revealed, he would refuse to be a source. And if we didn't have sources, there would be no one to blow the whistle on the wrongdoers in our government and throughout our society."

Hugo Shoemaker had a follow-up question. "I take it, then, Dr. Roberts, that you believe there is nothing wrong or unethical if a reporter refuses to reveal his sources. Am I right about that?"

"You are absolutely right about that. In fact, I would say that it would be wrong and unethical if a reporter *did* reveal his sources without their consent."

"Thank you." Shoemaker was pleased with the way this testimony came in. It gave the defense plenty of ammunition to tell the jury later, during the closing arguments, that Max Reed did nothing wrong by refusing to reveal his sources. Indeed, they would refer back to Professor Roberts' testimony to remind them that Reed was doing exactly what our Founding Fathers would have wanted him to do, although he knew that was a bit of a stretch.

Turning to the judge, Shoemaker said, "I have no further questions of this witness."

Judge Krause looked over to the plaintiff's counsel table. "Mr. Mayfield, do you have any cross-examination of this witness?"

"Yes, Your Honor, I do. But it's nearly eleven, and this might be a good time for a break."

"That's just what I was thinking. Let's take a fifteen-minute recess."

———

Judge Krause turned to address Professor Samuel Roberts, who had just returned to the witness stand after the mid-morning recess. "Professor, do you understand that you're still under oath?"

"Yes."

"Mr. Mayfield, you may cross-examine the witness."

"Thank you, Your Honor." Charlie stood and walked over to a position that he carefully chose. He stood off to the side so that the Professor Roberts would be looking away from the jury while facing Charlie to answer his questions. This position gave Charlie two advantages: first, he could keep his eye on the jurors to see how they reacted to the testimony and, second, the witness would be talking away from the jury instead of to them. He knew that this would irritate Roz Berman, who most certainly had prepped the witness to look at the jury when he testified.

Since lawyers are required to disclose the names of their witnesses and the gist of their testimony in advance, Charlie had known for several weeks that Sam Roberts would be testifying about the practice of not revealing sources. This gave him the time to do some preliminary research on the witness and the subject matter of his testimony, and thus be better prepared to cross-examine him. And in this modern day and age, Pete Stevens, Charlie's associate, was busy clicking away on his laptop computer and doing some real-time research while Roberts was answering Shoemaker's questions.

"Mr. Roberts," Charlie began, deliberately not referring to the witness as "Professor" or "Doctor," terms that would unnecessarily dignify him, "your testimony about those two reporters for the *Washington Post*, Mr. Bernstein and Mr. Woodward, was interesting. Kind of like a walk down memory lane. Isn't it a fact, Mr. Roberts, that Carl Bernstein and Bob Woodward were awarded the Pulitzer Prize for Public Service in 1973 as a result of their reporting on Watergate?"

"Yes, I believe that's true."

"It's definitely true. I researched it myself. And didn't they receive many other awards, along with high esteem and glowing reviews, for their Watergate reporting?"

"Yes, sir."

"And according to my research, which was actually done during the last break by my associate sitting over there with his computer, *The Weekly Standard* called Bob Woodward 'The best pure reporter of his generation — perhaps ever.' And Bob Schieffer of CBS News said that Mr. Woodward — and I'm quoting here — 'has established himself as the best reporter of our time.' Tell me, Mr. Roberts, do you have any reason to deny that Bob Woodward is a world-class reporter who stands at the very top of his profession?"

"No, of course not. The entire world of journalism holds him in the highest esteem."

"And would you say that Carl Bernstein is also a highly regarded reporter whose achievements are noteworthy?"

"Yes, Bernstein and Woodward are both iconic reporters who set a standard that few others can match."

"Based on your career as journalism professor, you could probably name many of the most highly regarded reporters of contemporary times, couldn't you?"

"Yes, I'd say so."

"So tell us, Mr. Roberts, had you ever heard of Max Reed before this lawsuit was filed?"

"No, I don't recall ever hearing his name."

"So you didn't come here today to tell the fine ladies and gentlemen of the jury that Max Reed is in the same class as Bob Woodward and Carl Bernstein, did you?"

"No," the witness smiled, "certainly not."

"In their reporting on Watergate, did Carl Bernstein or Bob Woodward write any lies as far as you are aware?"

"No."

"And do you know if either of them has ever been accused of writing lies that damaged someone's reputation?"

"Well, I would suppose that President Nixon would say they lied, or at least stretched the truth, in their stories that ruined his career and led to his resignation from the presidency."

Charlie Mayfield, along with nearly everyone else in the courtroom, laughed at that answer. "Good point, Mr. Roberts. But do you know if anyone other than ex-President Nixon accused them of lying?"

"Not to my knowledge."

"Didn't it later come out that Deep Throat was in fact a man by the name of Mark Felt, and that Mr. Felt had a very high rank within the Federal Bureau of Investigation — the FBI?"

"Yes, Mr. Felt actually admitted some time later that he was Deep Throat."

"And isn't it true that Bernstein and Woodward took independent steps to verify the information that Mr. Felt gave them?"

"Yes. As I recall, Mr. Felt gave them certain facts which they could double-check to verify the accuracy of his information."

"Let's expand on your last answer, Mr. Roberts. You said that Mr. Felt gave them facts they could double-check to verify his information. I know this is a gruesome example, but would that be like the situation where a person confessing to murder tells the police where the body is buried? If the police double-check and learn that the body was in fact buried in that very same place, it would tend to verify that the confession was true. Is that a good example of what you meant when you said they double-checked things Mr. Felt said in order to verify his story?"

"Yes, that's a very good example. However, there is no evidence that Mark Felt committed any crime."

"Right, and I wasn't trying to imply that he had. I was only trying to establish that Bernstein and Woodward, as good reporters, didn't rely solely on the information he gave them. They went further and verified that information by double-checking certain facts he gave them. Isn't that right?"

"Yes, that's right. They did everything they could to verify that the information given to them by their source, Mr. Felt, was genuine."

"Thank you very much for that, Professor Roberts." Charlie finally called him "Professor," because that last comment scored points for Charlie and Eddie Bennison. Max Reed had already admitted that he took no steps to verify the information he had been given by his unnamed sources. And to milk the last answer for one more drop, Charlie added, "And isn't that precisely why Carl Bernstein and Bob Woodward are regarded as excellent reporters — because they take steps to verify the information given to them by their sources?"

Charlie didn't care a whit how the witness would answer his last question — again, it was the question, and not the answer, that he wanted the jury to hear.

After walking back to the counsel table to confer for a few moments with his associates and Eddie Bennison, Charlie turned and announced that he had no further questions.

"I think this is a good time to break for lunch," Judge Krause announced. And as the lawyers were shutting their briefcases, the bailiff, Leon Poleski, was readying the jurors for their daily lunch in a private room reserved at a restaurant around the corner from the courthouse. The jurors had little choice on the menu, as one might expect of meals served at the county's expense.

CHAPTER 75

Roz Berman had her legal team meet back at her office, where sandwiches and salads were being brought in, and where they could talk without fear of being overheard. Max Reed was not invited to join them.

Once assembled around her conference able, she asked her legal team the same question Charlie asked his team a few days earlier: "Can we rest now, or have we missed anything?"

Hugo Shoemaker stirred in his chair, and Berman picked up the signs of his discomfort.

"What is it, Hugo? Do you think we may have forgotten something?" She knew exactly what was bothering him, but she wanted him to come out with it.

"Shouldn't we explore the pros and cons of putting Max Reed back on the stand?"

"Hugo, we've been through this — over and over again! I'd feel safer putting a keg of dynamite on the stand. Reed is an accident waiting to happen. He doesn't pay attention to the instructions we give him, and he doesn't listen to the questions before he answers them."

"I know all that, but we have to do something to convince the jury that Reed really did have sources. After Mayfield's cross-examination the other day, they may think he made all that stuff up — about the cheating and the drugs — by himself."

"So you think it helps us for him to get up there and say, once again, 'Sure I have sources, but I won't tell you who they are'? If they didn't believe him the first time, why would they believe him the second time? And that would give Charlie Mayfield the opportunity, once again, to make mincemeat out of him on cross-examination. Why give Mayfield another bite at the apple to show that Reed is a deplorable person? The truth means nothing to that man, and he proves it whenever he opens his mouth. So, to sum up, I'll put Reed back on the stand if he's willing to reveal his sources, with names. Anything less than that, he can stay put in his hotel room.

"As the record now stands, we can argue later that there has been no proof of malice or a disregard for the truth. But we'll lose that chance if Reed gets up there and makes an ass of himself, like he did when he testified earlier. His face has 'malice' written all over it! We already had a witness, Professor Roberts, explain to the jury that there is absolutely nothing wrong with a responsible reporter protecting his sources. So let's leave it at that, and we'll pretend that Reed is a responsible reporter. With luck, and if we can keep a straight face, maybe the jury will believe it."

Roz Berman had been toying with another idea since before her telephone call with Clarence Stauffer of the *Chicago Tribune*. She was considering calling a witness — perhaps an editor of a well-respected newspaper or magazine — to testify that it was quite permissible in certain circumstances for a reporter to rely on anonymous sources for a story. But she decided against it after recalling Stauffer's final comment to her: "A reporter who relies on sources he doesn't know and can't identify will look like a schmuck — either a dumb schmuck or a dishonest schmuck — but definitely a schmuck." *And either*, Berman thought to herself, *is a perfect description of Max Reed.*

CHAPTER 76

R oz Berman began the Tuesday afternoon session by announcing that she had no further witnesses, and that the defense was resting. As a courtesy to Charlie, she called him during the noon recess to tell him she'd be resting. This would give him the opportunity to prepare to offer any rebuttal evidence if he chose to do so.

This is a common courtesy, even in hard-fought and acrimonious litigation, especially among lawyers practicing in the same community. The best way to earn a favor tomorrow is to give today.

Charlie stood to announce that he, likewise, had no further evidence to offer.

With that, Judge Krause swiveled in his tall leather seat to face the jury.

"Ladies and gentlemen, you are excused for the remainder of the day. Please be back by nine in the morning, at which time I will give you your instructions for deliberation, and you will then meet among yourselves to reach a verdict. In the meantime, my previous orders are still in effect — do not discuss this case with anyone, including yourselves, until you meet to deliberate, and do not read or listen to anything about this case in the newspapers, radio, or television."

After the bailiff escorted the jurors out of the courtroom, the judge addressed both teams of lawyers who were seated at the two counsel tables. "I'd like for us to reconvene in ten minutes back in my chambers to go over the jury instructions." He then turned, rose, and left the courtroom through the door behind his bench.

Non-lawyers assume that a judge prepares and delivers his instructions to the jury entirely on his own, and that the lawyers are nothing more than bystanders during this phase of the trial. That is simply not the case. Each set of lawyers prepares his or her own set of proposed instructions and submits them to the judge in advance.

Cases are often won or lost by the precise wording of the instructions. That explains why each set of lawyers will argue vociferously over the smallest of details. For example, the more narrowly or strictly that Judge Krause defined "malice" in his instructions to the jury, the less likely it will be for the jury to find the existence of malice. Roz Berman and Hugo Shoemaker would argue hard for such a narrow definition. Conversely, Charlie would fight for a very broad or easy-to-meet definition because a finding of malice was an essential element of his case. And as surprising as it may sound to non-lawyers, there is no single or universally-accepted definition of "malice." Therefore, each team of lawyers would fight for the definition that best suited their case

Ten minutes later, both legal teams were meeting with the judge in his chambers, with everyone holding the instructions proposed by each team. Most of the instructions were routine, dealing with standard issues — such as how to elect a foreperson, casting ballots for a verdict, and so forth. As expected, the more heated arguments concerned definitions of such terms as *wanton or reckless disregard for the truth, malice, damage to reputation, future earning*s, and so forth.

For the definition of *wanton* or *reckless*, for example, Charlie urged the judge to define those terms in the context of simple negligence or carelessness, anticipating that it would be easy for him to convince the jury that Max Reed was negligent or less than prudent when writing about Eddie Bennison. Roz Berman and Hugh Shoemaker, on the other hand, were pleading with the judge for a much harder-to-meet definition, so they wanted it defined as synonymous with such terms as *unconscionable, arrogant, perverse, oblivious to consequences,* and even *intentional willingness to injure.* In their minds, no matter how little the jury thought of Max Reed, they might not believe he was *that* bad.

There was even a dispute over the seemingly uncontroversial term *reputation*. Mindful that the Elizabeth Peters–Marriott story might still leak out before the jury made its final decision, Roz Berman argued that reputation is the equivalent of *character*, and that, therefore, a pre-existing character flaw would mean that Eddie Bennison's reputation was not all that great even without the *Tee Time* articles.

Charlie, on the other hand, was making the case that *character* and *reputation* are two entirely different things — that character is what you *are*, while reputation is what others *think you are*. As Charlie put it, "If everyone thought I was a good, honest man, then my reputation would be that of a good and honest man, and that would be the case even if I were a thief, as long as no one knew about it." He went on to explain that a defendant could pay for damaging the reputation of a bad man if everyone had previously thought that the bad man was a good man. Just as a defendant would have to pay for breaking the good leg of a bad man, he'd have to pay for damaging the good reputation of a bad man if everyone thought he was a good man.

After more than two hours bickering over definitions and other nuances that would comprise the final instructions, the session ended in pretty much of a draw. Each side won and lost a fair share of the arguments. As long as both sides were equally upset with his rulings made during the afternoon, the judge figured he did well.

He would be prepared to read the instructions to the jury after the lawyers presented their closing statements — or closing arguments — to the jury the next morning.

WEDNESDAY

CHAPTER 77

At 9:00 sharp on Wednesday morning, the lawyers were seated at their respective counsel tables, and the jurors had taken their assigned seats in the jury box. Seldom had a Chicago courtroom attracted so many people. Onlookers and an anxious press were crowded into the seats—actually pews—reserved for the public, and many people were out in the corridor waiting for others to leave so they could slip into their vacated seats.

Just as Judge Krause came through the door behind the bench, Leon Poleski, his bailiff, stood to make the same announcement he made at the beginning of each court session: "Will everyone please stand." And after giving everyone a few seconds to obey that command, he intoned in a stentorian voice: "Oyez, oyez, oyez, this Honorable Court is now in session, the Honorable Harry Krause presiding. Please be seated."

Judge Krause took his seat behind the elevated bench, looked around to survey the courtroom to assure himself that all was in order, and then turned to look at Charlie Mayfield. "Mr. Mayfield, you may present your closing statement to the ladies and gentlemen of the jury."

"Thank you, Your Honor." Charlie stood, made a show of trying to smooth the ever-present wrinkles out of his suit jacket, and walked over to a spot squarely in front of the jury box. He carried no visible notes, props, or other aids, but, as he did whenever he made an opening or closing statement, he had a single three-by-five card in the side pocket of his suit. It contained about six or seven key words, which would be all he needed if he stumbled or lost his way. Because he prepared and rehearsed his closing statements carefully, he seldom had to refer to the card, but it was comforting to have it handy.

Charlie assumed a very casual position, with his hands in the pockets of his trousers. He looked slowly from juror to juror, giving each the impression that he was talking directly to him or her. He had those sad-looking, hound-dog eyes that other trial lawyers would kill for. "Trust me," those eyes said. It was those eyes, together with his relaxed manner and warm smile, that combined to portray a very believable, reliable, and trustworthy person — much like the wise uncle or beloved grandfather from central casting.

"First," he began, "I want to thank each of you for taking time from your families and busy lives to come down here and help us out. And I especially want to compliment you for paying such close attention to the proceedings. This is not an easy case for you. The facts are in dispute, and the laws we have to apply are not the kind of laws that we run into every day. The laws of libel and slander — defamation — are often complex, not so much in their reading as in their application. We all know what a lie is, but we can't tell if a statement is a lie just by reading or hearing it. For that, we have to weigh the statement against the facts. We all agree on what a reputation is, but we might not agree on what a specific person's reputation is. And even if we can all agree that a reputation has been damaged by an untruthful statement, we might not able to agree on the extent to which it has been damaged, or what that damage is in terms of dollars and cents.

"I've been talking to juries before some of you were born, and it has never come easy to me. I always worry that I might say something — or forget to say something — that will hurt my client. And I often worry that the cards are stacked against me for one of three reasons. One, because I might have a client that the jury may find unappealing — or just doesn't like; two, the law might not be on my side; or three, the facts might not be on my side.

"But today, these things don't concern me a bit. My client, Eddie Bennison, is a prince of a man, by anyone's standards. He started out with nothing but loving parents and a good work ethic and worked hard to become a household name in the world of sports. He has reached the pinnacle of his profession through hard work and discipline and is an idol of golf fans throughout the world. And with all of that, he's a devoted family man with two children and a loving wife who has sat by his side throughout this trial. And his global popularity is demonstrated by the fact that sponsors have stood in line asking for him to endorse their products — at least they did, until *Tee Time* published those horrific stories about him.

"And you heard from Steve Hockett how Eddie's fellow professional golfers had admired and respected him until the publication of those stories.

"So, I have no concern whatsoever that you won't like Eddie Bennison. His popularity and reputation are beyond reproach, and I have every confidence that you see that.

"My second concern in some cases is that the law may be against my client, but that certainly isn't the case here. The law is crystal clear! All we have to prove to you is that the *Tee Time* articles contained lies, that the lies were told out of malice or out of an indifference or disregard for the truth, and that Eddie Bennison's reputation was damaged as a result of these lies. If you believe that we have proven these three things — and all we have to prove to you are these three things — then you will have to decide how much money will compensate Eddie for the damage caused by these lies.

"So, I think you will agree that our legal hurdles are not all that high. We have to prove only those three things, and I don't think there is any doubt in your minds that we proved all three. Of course we also have to give you evidence as to the extent of the damage to Eddie's reputation and, as I will show you in the next few minutes, we have done that.

"And that takes us to the facts. Let's review the facts as they bear on three elements we have to prove — lies, malice or a disregard for the truth, and a damaged reputation.

"We'll start with lies. Did we prove to your satisfaction that *Tee Time* printed lies about Eddie Bennison? Of course we did. Those articles said, without any doubt at all, that Eddie cheated on the golf course and that he took performance-enhancing drugs. But all of the evidence in this case — every single bit of it — proves that these are outright lies.

"We all know that it's very hard to prove a negative. What I mean is that it's hard to prove that something did not happen. Nevertheless, the evidence in this case shows beyond dispute that Eddie Bennison did not cheat or take improper drugs to enhance his performance on the golf course. All of the evidence in this case — every word of it — tells us beyond doubt that Eddie Bennison did none of the things mentioned in those shameful articles. A review of the evidence will show that I'm telling you the absolute truth — he didn't cheat or take improper drugs.

"Eddie himself testified that he never cheated or took any of those drugs. His caddie, Artie Escalara, also testified that Eddie never did these things. His lifelong friend, and now his business manager, A.J. Silver, likewise testified that Eddie never did these things. Indeed, Mr. Silver actually told you that Eddie Bennison was kind of a square — he actually used the word 'square' — when it came to drinking or drugs; that he wouldn't even touch a cigarette and limited his drinking to an occasional beer or glass of wine. And finally, you heard Steve Hockett, a fellow golfer on the Tour who has been a friend of Eddie's for many years. He testified that Eddie was very careful about what he put in his body. He said that he never saw — and never heard gossip — that Eddie took any improper drugs or medications. And as for obeying the rules of golf, Mr. Hockett actually testified that Eddie was scrupulous about complying with the rules. In fact, Mr. Hockett testified — right here in this courtroom — that Eddie Bennison obeyed the rules of golf as if they were biblical commandments. Those were his very words — that he obeyed the rules of golf as if they were part of the Ten Commandments.

"So there we have three witnesses, besides Eddie, who testified that he never cheated and never took performance-enhancing drugs, and that if he had done those things they would have known it. Each of those witnesses was very close to Eddie. If anyone knew his habits, they did! Now, a skeptic might say that we produced only three witnesses on this issue, four if we count Eddie, but the fact is that the defendants produced *no* witnesses who testified that Eddie did cheat or take improper drugs. Therefore, *all* of the evidence on this issue is that the *Tee Time* articles contained lies about Eddie Bennison, and there is not one shred of evidence that the articles were truthful."

At this point, Charlie, while still looking at the jury, pointed over his shoulder to the defense counsel's table where Roz Berman, Hugo Shoemaker, and their several assistants were sitting, and in a loud voice asked, "So where is their evidence? How do these people justify making those horrible accusations about Eddie Bennison? What is their justification for writing these lies?"

Charlie took two steps forward and put his two hands on the railing in front of the jury box. In a near whisper, leaning forward and looking from juror to juror, he answered his own questions. "I'll tell you how they justify telling those lies. They told them because Max Reed, the reporter who wrote those scurrilous articles, said he had heard that Eddie Bennison cheated and took drugs. And who did he hear that from? I asked him that question a thousand times, and each time he gave me — and you — the same answer. He said, 'I refuse to give you and the jury the names of the people who told me those things.' Let me repeat that so there's no misunderstanding. Max Reed sat up there on the stand and said to us, 'I heard that Eddie did these things, but I won't tell you who told me or where I heard it.'"

Charlie smiled broadly and his eyes twinkled. "Let's just think about that for a minute. He said he wrote it because he heard it, but he won't tell us where he heard it or who told him." He spread his arms and said, "This is amazing! He assassinates the reputation of a decent man with lies, and then refuses to back them up or even tell us where he heard them." And then louder: "What kind of people do this?"

Now — living up to his reputation — Charlie Mayfield pulled the kind of stunt that made him a legend in Chicago legal lore. Again he motioned back to the defense counsel table. "Ladies and gentlemen, sitting over at that table is Hugo Shoemaker, one of the lawyers representing the defendants in this case. Mr. Shoemaker is a famous lawyer. He writes books and articles, and he even teaches law at Yale Law School — an Ivy League school out there in Connecticut. He even appears on radio and television shows."

Shoemaker, sitting there helpless, knew that something bad was about to hit the fan, but he had no idea what it would be. He took a deep breath and gripped the arms of his chair. Roz Berman likewise knew something was coming at them like a raging bull, but she could only sit transfixed, wondering what the hell Charlie was up to.

Charlie's next words came out fast — very fast. He wanted the jury to hear them before Shoemaker or Roz Berman could make an objection. "Would it surprise you if I were to tell you that Mr. Shoemaker, a professor of law at one of the finest institutions in America, cheats on his income tax returns and, on top of that, he is a heroin addict?" And then he hurriedly added, "I know that this is true because someone told me, but I refuse to say who told me, and I won't tell you where I heard it."

Gasps were heard throughout the courtroom, and the members of the press, as one, began scribbling in their notebooks and clicking away on their smart phones. At the defense table, Hugo Shoemaker looked as if he were in a catatonic trance — the proverbial deer in the headlights.

Roz Berman was already on her feet, shouting, "Objection, Your Honor. Objection! This is outrageous! Mr. Mayfield has no right to make these horrific accusations without proof. Mr. Shoemaker is a man of great repute, and Mr. Mayfield cannot be allowed to make these outrageous statements without evidence to back them up. He is attacking an innocent man with outright lies, and we cannot permit this."

Perfect! Charlie thought to himself. *I couldn't have said it better myself!* He turned to the judge, but his words were intended for the ears of the jury. "Your Honor," he began, in a soft conciliatory voice, "Ms. Berman is absolutely right. I agree that I had no right to make those accusations against Mr. Shoemaker without proof. It was a terrible thing for me to do. Indeed, it was inexcusable. In fact," he added, turning to look at the jury and spreading his arms, "I made it all up. Not a word of what I said about Mr. Shoemaker was true. He is an honorable and good man."

And then Charlie put his large hands on the railing in front of the jury box and again slowly looked from juror to juror with those big, sad, "trust me" eyes. "What you just saw, ladies and gentlemen, was a little skit, and we all played a role in it. I played the role of Max Reed, the *Tee Time* reporter who made terrible accusations about Eddie Bennison being a cheater and using improper drugs. Mr. Shoemaker unwittingly played the role of Eddie Bennison who, like Mr. Shoemaker, was the target of *identical* false accusations — *cheating and using drugs*. And you, ladies and gentlemen, played the roles of the millions of people who read and heard of these terrible accusations."

Charlie took a step back, smiled, and continued. "Did Mr. Shoemaker really cheat on his taxes and take heroin? Of course not," and then, looking over his shoulder at Shoemaker, who still seemed to be in a trance, Charlie smiled, and added, "at least not as far as I know."

Then, assuming a very serious pose, he went on to say, "I confess that my false accusations against Mr. Shoemaker were terrible, but that wasn't the worst thing I did. The worst thing I did was to tell you that I based these accusations on what other people told me, but I refused to tell you who they were or where I heard it.

"I said to you exactly what Max Reed said to you and to those millions of readers: 'It must be true because someone told me it was true, but I won't tell you who it was who told me.' But what I told you about Mr. Shoemaker wasn't true — it was a lie, plain and simple. I made it up, but tried to give it a hint of truth by saying that I heard it somewhere.

"I did to Mr. Shoemaker exactly what Max Reed did to Eddie Bennison. We both said terrible things about someone, we both claimed to have sources, and we both refused to name those sources. And I did to you exactly what Max Reed did to his readers — we both lied and then tried to dress it up like the truth with the shallow explanation that we heard it somewhere, but we refused to say where or from whom. But I, at least, later admitted that I was lying. Mr. Reed never did!

"Ask yourselves, ladies and gentlemen, is this right? *Can people be permitted to say these things about others without any proof at all?*"

Charlie smiled broadly, and said. "Actually, you don't really have to answer that question, because Ms. Berman already answered it for you!" With that, Charlie turned to the court reporter and asked, "Sally, would you please read back Ms. Berman's last two or three sentences?"

The court reporter looked to the judge, who nodded, and then she proceeded to unroll the paper coiled within the tray in the back of her stenotype machine. She began to read. "Objection, Your Honor. Objection. This is outrageous. Mr. Mayfield has no right to make these horrific accusations without proof. Mr. Shoemaker is a man of great repute, and

Mr. Mayfield cannot be allowed to make these outrageous statements without evidence to back them up. He is attacking an innocent man with outright lies, and we cannot permit this."

When she finished, Charlie spread his arms wide and looked at the jurors. "You heard it, ladies and gentlemen, with your own ears. Ms. Berman said, correctly, I might add, that I had no right to make those accusations about Mr. Shoemaker. She actually said, and these were her exact words, that I 'cannot be allowed to make those outrageous statements without evidence to back them up,' and that I 'cannot be permitted to attack an innocent man with outright lies.'

"And she was absolutely right! But if she was right to condemn what I said about Mr. Shoemaker, then it would be equally right for you to condemn what Max Reed wrote about Eddie Bennison. As she herself said," and here Charlie whispered his words for dramatic effect, "we cannot permit innocent men to be attacked with lies coming from secret, unnamed sources."

He began to walk back to his counsel table, but then turned back to make another point to the jury. "You know, folks, when I made those statements about Mr. Shoemaker, you may or may not have believed me. But if, instead of hearing them from my lips, you had read them in a highly respected national magazine, I'm sure they would have had a stronger ring of truth. And that, ladies and gentlemen, is a vital factor for you to consider. Max Reed didn't tell just a few people that Eddie Bennison cheated and took drugs, as I did with respect to Mr. Shoemaker. He wrote those false accusations in a magazine that would be read by millions of people all over the world.

"And that's precisely why the law treats written lies, which we call libel, as more serious than verbal lies, which we call slander. The spoken lie — slander — vanishes into thin air once it's uttered. The written lie — libel — has added authenticity, and it has a permanency in that it sits there in libraries, bookcases, and on coffee tables, just waiting for others to read. The written lie stays with us forever, just sitting there, reeking and festering and oozing, always waiting for someone else to read it."

Roz Berman had heard enough. "Your Honor," she said loudly, "may we approach the bench?"

Judge Krause beckoned the lawyers to come to the side of his bench opposite the jury but near the court reporter. They were about to have a side bar conference, that is, a sort of hushed discussion out of the hearing of the jury. The court reporter, Sally Ringer, was preparing to transcribe every word for the record if that's what the judge wanted.

When Berman, Shoemaker and Charlie were huddled to the side of the bench, the judge said to Roz Berman, "I know why you're here, Roz. Do you want this on the record?"

"I sure do."

The judge nodded to Sally Ringer, who, with her fingers now poised at her stenotype machine, leaned forward in order to catch every word of the side bar conference.

"Your Honor," Roz Berman began, "I should have spoken up to object sooner, but Mr. Mayfield's comments about Mr. Shoemaker were so shocking that I was speechless. I'm sure you were as appalled as I was at that outrageous stunt. It's highly improper — in fact, unspeakably improper — to make those terrible statements about Mr. Shoemaker in a court of law. I understand that it was done as part of a distasteful game, but it is nevertheless improper. This ruse of his can have more effect than mountains of legitimate evidence, but this is not evidence. On the contrary, it is the opposite of evidence. Evidence is a compilation of facts, but this demonstration contains nothing factual. Indeed, Mr. Mayfield admitted that it was all false, and that he made it up out of thin air. We cannot allow juries to be influenced by make-believe stories. If the rule were otherwise, we'd have lawyers abandon closing statements and instead read *Cinderella* to their juries."

Judge Krause pursed his lips and shook his head. "I've tried cases for many decades, both as a lawyer and as judge, and I thought I had seen and heard everything, but that little exhibition of Mr. Mayfield's is a new one on me. And I'm not sure what to do about it."

Roz Berman said, "I think you should declare a mistrial, Your Honor, and order a new trial. I'll file a motion to that effect."

The judge shook his head. "Nice try, Ms. Berman, but that is not going to happen. We've been hard at work in this trial now for a couple of weeks, and I'm not about to throw it all down the drain and start all over. What Mr. Mayfield did *may* have been improper, but I'm not sure if it *was* improper. Unusual? Yes, certainly. But unusual doesn't mean improper.

"As I see it, Mr. Mayfield simply used Mr. Shoemaker to make a point. He recalled and demonstrated for the jury two facts that are undisputed — the fact that the defendants accused Mr. Bennison of cheating and taking drugs, and the fact that Mr. Reed refused to reveal his sources. Clearly he has the right to talk to the jury about those undisputed facts. Now, does that right disappear simply because he used Mr. Shoemaker as an example to demonstrate the effect of those facts? I honestly don't think so. As I said a moment ago, it's an unusual tactic, but that isn't enough to make it wrong."

The judge paused to weigh his next words, and then continued. "I'm going to overrule your objection, Ms. Berman, and I'm instructing Mr. Mayfield not to pursue this game playing any further. It was a creative demonstration, Mr. Mayfield, but it's over. Is that understood?"

"Yes, Judge."

"Alright, then. Have you finished with your closing statement?"

"No, Your Honor, I have just a little more."

"Fine, go ahead and finish, but please go to a new subject."

"Thank you, Your Honor."

CHAPTER 78

Charlie was ecstatic that he was able to get away with his little hoax. He knew it made a weighty impression on the jury — he could see it on their faces. He walked back to his table, took a sip of water, and then turned to resume.

"Ladies and gentlemen, you already know the difference between libel and slander, and that libel has a permanence — it doesn't go away once it is written. And when the person who commits the libel is a magazine like *Tee Time*, there are printing presses that belch out millions of copies of the lie, and there are processes to ensure that those millions of copies of the lie are distributed throughout the country and even beyond. And while a slanderous statement vanishes, the printed lie will, as I said before, remain in libraries and on bookshelves, nightstands, and coffee tables indefinitely. And as I already said, it just lies there forever, festering and emitting rancid odors. Twenty-five years from now, someone — perhaps Eddie Bennison's children or grandchildren — could pick up an old copy of *Tee Time* and read that he cheated and used improper drugs.

"So, to sum up the first element in a defamation case — whether the defendants wrote lies about Eddie Bennison, I think we can put that one to bed once and for all. It's beyond dispute that the three *Tee Time* articles about Eddie contained lies. Eddie himself told you, under oath, that he never cheated or took improper drugs. And three other witnesses testified, under oath, that they knew Eddie Bennison well and that he never did the things of which he was accused in the articles. If he had actually done the things of which he was accused, those witnesses testified that they would have known it. But they didn't know it because it never happened.

"And not one single person testified that those lies were in fact true statements. The only people who supposedly saw Eddie Bennison cheat and take drugs are unnamed, unidentified, undisclosed, and, for all we know, are nonexistent figments of Max Reed's imagination — just like my sources for what I said about Mr. Shoemaker.

"So have we proved to you that Mr. Reed's stories contained lies? We sure have. Four witnesses testified, under oath, that they were lies; not one witness testified that they were true. That makes it unanimous as far as the witnesses are concerned — lies!"

Charlie Mayfield again put his hands in his pockets and approached the jury box. "This brings us to the second element we are required to prove — that Max Reed, writing for *Tee Time*, wrote those lies out of malice, or out of a reckless disregard for the facts.

"After we are done with our closing statements, Judge Krause will give you instructions, and in these instructions he will tell you what we mean when we use words like 'malice' or 'disregard for the truth.' He will tell you that malice implies that the defendants did more — much more — than accidentally make an untruthful statement. Malice exists when a defendant deliberately makes a false statement. Or, when a defendant makes a false statement without taking appropriate measures to determine whether it is or isn't true, that is a reckless or wanton disregard for the truth. When a reporter writes something that could be verified, but he doesn't bother to verify it, we likewise have a reckless and wanton disregard for the truth. Similarly," and here Charlie spoke in a semi-whispered tone to emphasize the importance of what he was about to say, "when a reporter writes something based on nothing more than gossip, or unsubstantiated rumor, but portrays it as factual or reliable without bothering to say that it was based on gossip or rumor, and it turns out to be false, it is malicious, and it is a reckless disregard of the truth — it's libel!" And in a louder voice Charlie added, "And it's wrong! It's obnoxious!

"With all of that in mind, let's take a few minutes to review the evidence to see where, in our opinion, Max Reed and *Tee Time* acted out of malice or a reckless disregard for the truth. We don't have to prove both malice and a disregard for the truth — we only have to prove to you that there was either malice or a disregard for the truth. Nevertheless, I think that you will agree that in this case *Tee Time* is guilty of both.

"Allow me to remind you of some of the evidence that proves both of these elements.

"First, you will recall Mr. Reed testifying that he had sources for his accusations but refused to name them. If you believe that he did not have those sources, and that he wrote his stories without sources, that is a reckless disregard for the truth. And, in my opinion, it is more than that. I believe that when a reporter has no sources for the lies he writes, it is such a blatant violation of his responsibilities that it amounts to an act of malice. But, as I said a moment ago, there is no need to find malice if you find that there has been a reckless disregard for the truth.

"And if you believe that he had sources, but that he had no good reason to believe that they were sufficiently reliable for making such horrendous accusations about Eddie Bennison, then that, too, is a reckless disregard for the truth.

"If you believe that he wrote those accusations without taking appropriate steps to verify that they were true, that is a reckless disregard for the truth.

"And if you believe that he wrote those accusations without knowing for sure that they were true, that is a reckless disregard for the truth.

"And, of course, if he wrote those accusations knowing that they were false, that would be the worst kind of malice we could imagine."

Now Charlie made a fist with his right hand and pounded it on the railing in front of the jury box. "And did Max Reed do anything — anything at all — to corroborate these sources, or to verify if their information was true? No, he admitted that he didn't." Charlie then pulled a "reversal" by using the testimony of the others side's witness to make a point of his own. "The defendants *themselves* produced a witness, Professor Roberts, who testified that good reporters make efforts to verify, or double-check, what their sources tell them. But Max Reed didn't bother to do any of that!

Not only did he have no regard for the truth, he actually *avoided* the truth!"

Charlie again dropped his voice to a whisper. "Max Reed didn't even tell his readers that his stories were based on undisclosed sources, and not on his own observations. Instead, he deviously portrayed the fictional cheating and drug use as being undeniably true and beyond question. In other words, he portrayed fiction as truth while concealing the weakness of the basis of that portrayal.

"Now, why would a reporter like Max Reed do that? Why would he write articles knowing they contained false information, or without bothering to verify the truth of what he wrote, or in reliance on sources who he had no good reason to believe were reliable? Well, there are many reasons why a reporter might do that, or why a magazine would allow it to happen. Every reporter likes a scoop — that is, being the first to break a big story. And Max Reed knew that it would be a scoop — a major scoop — to write a story that an iconic, world-famous golfer like Eddie Bennison cheated and took improper drugs. It would not only make him look like a big shot in the publishing world, it could earn him a promotion or a bonus.

"And why would *Tee Time* allow it to happen? Well, you heard their own witnesses say that they picked up nearly 100 million dollars in extra revenue because of Max Reed's stories about Eddie Bennison. Their newsstand sales increased, their annual subscriptions increased, and their advertising revenues increased. And all of these increases were large — they went through the roof. *The magazine made a fortune off Max Reed's lies.* Is it any wonder why they permitted the articles to be published? Is it any wonder why they didn't press Mr. Reed about his so-called sources?" When Charlie uttered the words "so-called sources," he hissed them as if he were a snake.

"When Ward Newton was on the witness stand — he was the head of circulation at *Tee Time* — I asked him point blank if he or anyone else at the magazine asked Reed about his sources, and how did he answer? He sat there and said that he never asked, and, as far as he knew, no one else did either. How can that be, ladies and gentlemen?

"Why didn't the magazine's executives and lawyers ask the same obvious questions that are running through your minds right now? 'Who are your sources, Max? Are they reliable? Did you check them out? What did you do to verify their accusations?' Ladies and gentlemen, these are obvious questions. Why didn't anyone ask them?" Then he asked in a whisper, "Or did they?"

As he started to step back from the jury box, Charlie threw in a comment: "Trusting Max Reed with a computer keyboard was as dangerous as trusting a six-year-old with a machine gun."

Holding his arms out to his sides with palms facing the jury, Charlie asked, "If what Max Reed and *Tee Time* did was not an act of malice, or was not an act made with a reckless disregard for the truth, then what is? What could be worse — what could be more malicious — than what these people did to Eddie Bennison? If they had sources, did they check to see if they were reliable? Did they ask where the sources got their information? Did they take steps to verify the sources' information? Did they do any of these things? These are routine things that are easy to do — assuming Mr. Reed and the magazine wanted to do them. The answer to these obvious questions lies in the testimony of Ward Newton, who admitted, under oath, that 'nobody asked.' And not taking the time to do these routine things seems to qualify as a reckless indifference for reporting the truth, if not being deceitful — intentionally deceitful!"

To change both the pace and the mood of his remarks, Charlie paused for several seconds, and then chuckled and said to the jury, "I hate to quote from an unnamed source, considering what I've been saying about unnamed sources, but there is an age-old adage that says, 'The pen is mightier than the sword.' There are references to that idea throughout history and literature. They are found in the Bible, in letters from Thomas Jefferson, in Shakespearian plays, and even in illustrations in Mark Twain's book, *Tom Sawyer.* This adage was meant to convey the idea that the stroke of the pen could have a greater social impact than the stroke of a sword. Unfortunately for Eddie Bennison, the adage is very accurate.

"With a stroke of his pen, Max Reed cut the legs off of Eddie Bennison's miraculous career; he cut Eddie's earnings to a fraction of what they had been; and he cut the heart out of Eddie Bennison himself. He could not have done more damage with ten swords."

Charlie went over to his counsel table to have a hushed word with his associate, Pete Stevens. He wanted to be sure that he hadn't forgotten anything on the malice issue. Getting Pete's confirmation that he had touched all the bases, Charlie walked back to the jury box.

"We are required to prove to you that those three magazine articles — that is, the lies in those articles — damaged Eddie Bennison's reputation, and that this damage resulted in a monetary loss to Eddie. I don't think there is any question that this is indeed what happened. You all heard A.J. Silver, Eddie's business manager, testify that many of Eddie's sponsors canceled the endorsement contracts they had with Eddie. They did this on the basis of a standard morals clause that gives them the right to cancel if Eddie committed an immoral act, or even if he were merely accused of committing an immoral act in a manner that might diminish his value as an endorser of a sponsor's product. And many of Eddie's other sponsors who did not cancel their contracts just let them expire, and then refused to renew them. Mr. Silver told us that only one sponsor had not abandoned Eddie, but for that Eddie had to sign an exclusive deal — so that to keep that only remaining sponsor Eddie was forced to agree not to sign with other sponsors.

"And you heard other evidence proving that Eddie Bennison's reputation was tarnished by the *Tee Time* articles. You heard evidence that his friends began to shun him, and even his wife was being ignored by former friends. Artie Escalara, Eddie's caddie, told us how the other golfers and their caddies were scornful of Eddie after the articles, and you heard about the heckling from the golf fans who, until those articles, adored Eddie.

"A.J. Silver and Eddie himself testified how Eddie's playing performance deteriorated after the articles. He lost his focus, not being able to concentrate on his game. On top of that, he had to deal with the heckling, the snide comments, the sneers, and the cold shoulders from those he had to confront every day. This all combined to affect his play in a dramatic way. Mr. Silver gave us documentary proof of Eddie's earnings up until and after publication of the blistering articles in *Tee Time*. These records were put into evidence.

"The year before the articles came out, Eddie Bennison earned approximately 15 million dollars from golf alone. That would have come from his winnings on the Tour, his sponsorship contracts, and the corporate outings where he would earn $75,000 to $100,000 to play golf with business executives and their customers and give them golf demonstrations. But, according to Mr. Silver and the records he produced for us, Eddie's earnings began to drop immediately after the articles to about 10 percent of their former level. That would be a loss of about 13 or 14 million dollars per year.

"And for how many years may we expect this tremendous loss to continue? That's a hard question to answer, but it's a question you must try to answer when you go back to reach a verdict later today or tomorrow. Please remember the testimony of Mr. Hockett, another golf professional, who told us that golfers on the Senior Tour can expect to be competitive into their mid-sixties. That would mean that Eddie Bennison, who is now still in his mid-fifties, would have been earning those large amounts for another eight to ten years from now. Those articles were written several years ago, and the evidence shows that Eddie's earnings still have not rebounded. He is still earning about 10 percent of his former earnings after all these years. From all of this, I think you can conclude that the earnings loss from these articles will extend for at least twelve to fourteen years — from 2006 when the articles were published until about 2018 or 2020, when Eddie would be expected to retire — all years when Eddie Bennison could have been winning tournaments, earning endorsement money, and collecting fees for outings, designing golf courses and golf equipment, and writing instructional books and articles.

"So you can do the arithmetic. He will have lost 13 or 14 million dollars per year for a total of about twelve to fourteen years.

"Can we expect that the damage done by these articles will just go away, and the stories about Eddie cheating and taking drugs will vanish? I don't think so! People have long memories, especially when it comes to stories about fallen heroes.

"Let me give you an example. There isn't a baseball fan in the world who hasn't heard about Shoeless Joe Jackson, who played his last baseball game in 1919 — *nearly ninety years ago.* And what do they remember about him? Was it his batting average? No! Was it his reputation as an excellent defensive player? No! Was it the number of home runs he hit, or the number of bases he stole? No! Or that he played for the Chicago White Sox, who won the National League pennant that year? No! The one thing that everyone remembers about Joe Jackson is that he was accused of fixing World Series games in 1919 — almost 100 years ago.

"And what about Barry Bonds? Bonds played for the Pittsburgh Pirates and the San Francisco Giants from 1986 until 2007. Do we remember that he won the National League Most Valuable Player award seven times? No! Or that he holds the record for the most career home runs? No! Or for the most home runs in a single season? No! But what we do remember about Barry Bonds is that he was accused of taking performance-enhancing drugs.

"And as much as I hate to say it, the one thing that everyone will remember about Eddie Bennison is that he was accused of cheating on the golf course and wrongfully taking performance-enhancing drugs. And when Eddie dies — which I hope is a long, long time from now — you can bet that his obituary will mention the *Tee Time* accusations against him. And in the meantime, whenever his name is mentioned, an asterisk will flash though people's minds to remind them of the terrible things — the terrible lies — written about him." Charlie shook his head. "People never forget the bad things they hear."

"There's another old adage that says, 'The bigger they are, the harder they fall.' This case is a perfect example of that. If Eddie Bennison had been an average, run-of-the-mill golfer who barely made a living, he wouldn't be suffering nearly as much from these lies written about him. He wouldn't have had the high earnings to lose. And he wouldn't have the great reputation to lose. If he were just a so-so golfer, the accusations would not have caught fire and been discussed by sportswriters and newscasters across the country. The Golf Channel would have ignored it. In fact, if Eddie had been just an average golfer trying to make a living, Max Reed would never have written those three stories about him. If he really had heard anything bad about Eddie, he would have ignored it. And if he did write about it, the rest of the world wouldn't have paid any attention to him. But Eddie Bennison was by no means an average run-of-the-mill golfer. He was a legend — a national hero — and that made him a target for Max Reed's lethal pen — the same pen that is mightier than the sword."

CHAPTER 79

Charlie paused long enough to take a few swallows of water from the pitcher on his counsel table. Then he returned to face the jurors.

"There is one question that you will have to answer when you go back to deliberate. I talked to you about it a minute or two ago, but I'd like to address it again right now because it's vital, and this will be my last chance to bring it up. When you go back to the jury room, you will have to decide how much money would compensate Eddie Bennison for the lies written about him. I'd like to offer you some thoughts on that. A golfer must be at least fifty years old to compete on the Champions Tour, also called the Seniors Tour. Eddie started competing on that Tour in 2003, shortly after his fiftieth birthday. He was setting scoring, winning, and earnings records right from the start, and continued to do so until the spring of 2006 when the *Tee Time* stories were published. His earnings from golf dropped by 13 or 14 million dollars a year, and they still have not recovered. If Eddie could have been expected to play at his former level until now, five years later, he would likely have continued his earnings until now — but, as we all know, he didn't. Using those former levels as a guide, those articles cost him approximately 70 million dollars from the time they were written until now. And we can only speculate how much longer his earning power will be plagued by these lies.

"Now, as you can see, Eddie looks to be in good physical shape — he doesn't bear any of the signs we often associate with old age. You heard

Steve Hockett testify that many of the golfers on the Senior Tour compete at their former high levels until they reach their mid-sixties. Eddie is now fifty-seven, and I think it's reasonable to assume that he could have continued to compete at his high level for another seven or eight years. Therefore, the loss of his tournament winnings, combined with the loss of his endorsement contracts, plus the loss of invitations to corporate outings, will be continuing for another seven or eight years. It would follow, then, that his total losses from the lying articles would be closer to 200 million dollars. And I'm not even counting the investment income he is losing. Thus, if he had that extra 70 million dollars that he already lost, and invested it conservatively at, say, a 5 percent return, that would be an additional three and a half million dollars per year that he has already lost, and this loss will continue indefinitely into the future, long past the time when he is no longer able to play tournament golf. This is money that he will be losing for the rest of his life!"

"Adding all this together, it is very reasonable to assume that *Tee Time*'s lies have cost — and will cost — Eddie Bennison approximately 250 million dollars as of now and into the foreseeable future.

"So, ladies and gentlemen, when you go back to deliberate your verdict, I am respectfully asking you to do the following: I am asking that you find the defendants guilty of wrongfully and maliciously defaming Eddie Bennison, and I'm asking that you return a verdict in Eddie's favor of at least 250 million dollars to compensate him for his monetary losses.

"If you do that, you will be doing a very good thing. You will be returning to Eddie Bennison that which is rightfully his, and which was wrongfully taken from him by the outrageous lies written about him — and even if you do that, his reputation will still be tarnished for the rest of his life. His legacy will always have that asterisk, that footnote, that will haunt him — that he won because he was a cheat and a pothead."

CHAPTER 80

Charlie then looked into the eyes of each juror, one by one. After what seemed like an eternity, he spoke. "And now, ladies and gentlemen, I have something else I need to ask you — something very important. A few minutes ago I told you that Eddie Bennison suffered a loss of at least 250 million dollars — in lost income alone — because of these disgusting lies printed about him. And if you award him 250 million dollars, you will be going a long way to compensate him for those losses. That would be giving him what the law calls compensatory damages, because that would compensate him for his loss of earnings.

"But he suffered far more than a loss of earnings! He and his family also suffered dreadful humiliation as a result of those lies, and the mental anguish has been indescribable. It is also within your power to compensate him for his mental suffering as well as for his loss of earnings. There is no formula for that. It will be up to you to decide how much money would offset that horrible mental anguish and suffering. And when you decide how to compensate him for his lost earnings and mental suffering, you may — and should — also compensate him for the loss of his glorious reputation. You've heard evidence of how this extremely popular and respected man became a pariah. His sponsors refused to do further business with him, his friends shunned him and his family, people began to speak ill of him, golf galleries heckled and berated him, and sportswriters and newscasters kept reminding the public of his alleged cheating and drug use.

"And how much will it take to compensate Eddie for all of these losses and for all of this damage? That, my friends, is up to the twelve of you. That's why you're here.

"As I said a few minutes ago, I believe that 250 million dollars is fair compensation for Eddie Bennison's lost earnings. How much more would be fair compensation for his loss of reputation, and for the mental anguish and humiliation he and his family had — and will continue — to suffer? That, ladies and gentlemen, is for you to decide. Eddie and I are both confident that you will give this your most serious consideration, and that you will do the right thing. We trust you to do that. Only you can decide how much money, *in addition* to the 250 million dollars of lost earnings, will compensate Eddie and his family for the damage to his reputation, and for the humiliation and mental anguish the Bennison family has endured and will endure far into the future."

It was now time for Charlie to make the final lunge with his saber, and this time with a twist. Again he paused and moved closer to the jurors so that each could see deep into his "trust me" eyes.

"Now, ladies and gentlemen, I am going to ask you to do even more than compensate Eddie Bennison for his lost earnings, his damaged reputation, and his mental suffering. In certain cases, our laws allow you, as a jury, to award punitive damages in addition to compensatory damages. Let me explain. When defendants wrongfully damage a person, we ask that they compensate that person for the loss or damages they have caused. But when the conduct of the defendants is intentional, or so terrible — so egregious — that it shocks our conscience — so terrible that we must take steps to see that they don't do it again, and that others don't repeat the same terrible acts, then we have to make an example of them — we have to spank them and teach them a lesson. And when we have such a case — and in my opinion, we have such a case right here — the jury may — and should — award an extra amount. That extra amount goes beyond compensating the injured plaintiff — it is to punish the defendants for their egregious conduct to ensure that it isn't repeated, and to send a message to others that they should not do the same thing by publishing lies that ruin innocent people. That's why we call it punitive damages —

because it punishes people for conduct that is not only wrongful, but is deliberate, or malevolent, or reckless, or downright nasty — conduct that shocks the conscience.

"We are asking you, ladies and gentlemen, to assess punitive damages against the defendants in this case *in addition* to the 250 million dollars we're asking as compensatory damages.

"And how does a jury determine the amount of punitive damages to assess? How much is appropriate to punish a defendant or defendants for doing such a terrible thing? What amount will deter them from doing it again? What amount will teach them — and others — a lesson? What amount will send a message telling the world that we, as civilized people, will not tolerate this kind of conduct?

"Well, that will be up to you. There is no specific formula for calculating punitive damages. However, there are some common-sense considerations to guide you in deciding the right amount to assess. What are some of these considerations? Well, let's assume that a young, ten-year-old boy deliberately tells a lie. If he had to forfeit one dollar from his weekly allowance, that might be enough to teach him a lesson so he'd think twice before doing it again.

"But if the person who deliberately told the lie was an adult, and not a ten-year-old boy, it's obvious that a one- or two-dollar punishment would not be a punishment at all. To him it would be trivial — a joke. He'd probably laugh at it. But if he had to pay a thousand dollars, or 5,000 dollars, for that lie, he might be discouraged from lying again. And if he had to pay, say, 25,000 dollars for that lie, he'd be even more unlikely to lie again.

"So, ladies and gentlemen, as you can see, an amount of punitive damages appropriate to punish one person might be inappropriate for another person. It might be too punitive, and therefore unfair to him; or it might be too low, and therefore unfair to the person he damaged — or to the person he might damage next time. So the reasonable amount of punitive damages depends on the means of the defendant. The law recognizes this, and provides that a defendant with a great deal of money can be required to pay more for his malicious conduct than we'd require from a defendant of limited means.

"Alright then, let's consider the defendants in this case. What amount would be enough to discourage them — to prevent them — from writing and publishing more lies that ruin the lives of innocent people?

"You will recall that we introduced evidence in this case to show you what the defendants were worth. We introduced financial statements that showed their assets, liabilities, and earnings. And you also heard the testimony of auditors who told you that they examined the financial records.

"It's undisputed that Tee Time, Incorporated, alone has a net worth of three billion dollars, and over the past five years the magazine had an average net profit of 150 million dollars per year." To emphasize his point, Charlie paused to look from juror to juror, and then whispered as if he were disclosing a secret, "That's 150 million dollars of pure profits every year — year in and year out. And even if they were required to pay an entire year's profits, 150 million dollars, as punitive damages, so what? Big deal! It wouldn't mean a thing. Their stockholders might feel a little pinch, but the magazine would continue to operate, and might even continue to print lies. And why not? Who would feel the punishment? Certainly not Max Reed, the writer of these stories — he would continue to get his salary. Nor would Ward Newton, the vice president who brags about the money that the magazine earned from these lies. These people are paid before profits are calculated. Therefore, taking away the magazine's profits for one year would do nothing to deter the people who write and circulate those lies.

"And what about the other defendant, Globe Publications? *Tee Time* is owned by Globe Publications, a large conglomerate that owns newspapers and radio and television stations all over the world. Globe Publications has profited from the lies written, published, and circulated in *Tee Time*. And while they own that magazine, and they profit from those lies, they did nothing — absolutely nothing — to stop their magazine from printing and spreading those lies. Globe Publications owns and controls *Tee Time* — they decided who should run the magazine and how it should be run. They appoint the officers of *Tee Time*, and they indirectly approve the writers and reporters and, by extension, their stories. Shouldn't they also share in the responsibility to compensate Eddie Bennison for the damage those lies caused him? And shouldn't they be punished for their inaction, and shouldn't they be taught a lesson so they won't let it happen again?

"As you review the evidence in this case, you will see that Globe Publications has a net worth in excess of over 60 billion dollars, and annual profits of more than four billion dollars — that's four billion dollars of pure profit — pure gravy — each year! What amount of punitive damages would get their attention? What amount would they take seriously, and not shrug off as a nuisance?

"That, ladies and gentlemen, is for you to decide. As I said before, the first thing you will be doing with your verdict is compensating Eddie Bennison for the damage he suffered because of those lies. That damage would be his lost earnings, his mental suffering, and his loss of an enviable reputation. We believe that 250 million dollars is fair compensation for his lost earnings alone. You will have to decide how much, in addition to that, will compensate him for his mental suffering and lost reputation.

"And the next thing we ask you to do with your verdict is this: assess punitive damages to send a message, loud and clear, to every reporter, every sportswriter, every magazine, every newspaper, and every radio and television station that they must report the truth. No longer can we permit lies — or slipshod reporting — to wreck the lives of good and innocent people.

"We all know about the so-called freedom of the press. That is a good thing, and integral to our society. It's guaranteed by the United States Constitution, and it's part of our heritage. But that freedom carries with it certain responsibilities, and among them is the duty to be fair, honest, and truthful. Nowhere in our Constitution is there a freedom to tell malicious lies — a freedom to destroy lives."

Charlie paused to look slowly from juror to juror. Then he said, looking deep into their eyes, "You are here to perform a solemn and honorable duty. I have every confidence that you will perform that duty well.

"One of my duties when I try a case is to keep my eyes on the jurors. By watching your expressions and even your body language, I can get an idea of how you react to certain witnesses, or to things that we lawyers say. This trial has been going on for many days, and I have been watching each of you. It's obvious that you have all been paying close attention to all that is going on. For that, I thank you, and Eddie Bennison thanks you. We are relieved to know that, with you, our case is in good hands.

"When you go back to deliberate, you should review all the evidence you heard with a questioning mind. And you should likewise question everything I tell you, and everything that Ms. Berman or Mr. Shoemaker might tell you after I finish my closing statement. We are all going to tell you different things because each side is hoping for a different result. But it's your job to base your verdict on the evidence as you see it — and not on how we see it.

"And that's why our jury system is magnificent — the best system in the world for reaching the right decision. You come to this case with open minds and no biases to either side. The everyday experiences you've had for years will provide you with a screen — a screen of common sense. Without realizing it, you have been sifting the evidence in this case through that screen. When we give you different interpretations of the same testimony or the same piece of evidence, that screen will tell you which of us is right.

"And when you go back there to deliberate with your fellow jurors, it will be your duty to stand firm and fight for what you believe. If each of you does that whenever there's a difference of opinion, it will guarantee that you will collectively make the right decision. That's why we have twelve jurors and not only one." Here Charlie cast a glance toward the bench and said, "And with all respect to Judge Krause, that's why we often want juries — and not judges — to decide our cases."

Flashing a broad smile, Charlie moved to the conclusion of his statement. "Lucky for you," he said, "I'm all done. The rules permit me to say a few more things after the defense finishes their closing statement, and I may or may not take advantage of that. It depends on what they say to you. If I have nothing to say when they're done, it won't mean that I agree with whatever they told you. It only means that I didn't think that they said anything important.

"Thank you very much for listening, and for paying close attention since this case began. And thanks also in advance for the conscientious deliberations in which you are about to engage. I am confident that you will come to a just and fair decision."

CHAPTER 81

Judge Krause looked to the defendants' counsel table. "Does the defense have a closing statement?"

"We do, Your Honor," Roz Berman said, quickly rising to address the jury. She and Hugo Shoemaker had had a heated discussion as to which of them would give the closing statement. Shoemaker thought he would do the better job, but he was no match for Roz Berman's persistence. "No way, Hugo, not a chance. You've never talked to a jury in your life. These jurors are my jurors. Like me, they're Chicagoans, and they'd distrust anyone coming out here from the East Coast to tell them what to do. This is going to be a closing statement to average everyday people, not a lecture to a bunch of law students."

Just as Charlie had spoken to the jury as if he were their uncle or grandfather, Roz Berman talked to them as if she were their grandmother — the grandmother who always spoke the truth, gave sound advice, and wanted to be sure that her charges never made a mistake. She wasn't there to tell them — she was there to help them.

"Ladies and gentlemen," she began, in a soothing voice. "Like Mr. Mayfield, I also want to thank you for your attentiveness during this trial. Sitting through these cases can be a strain. You're forced to concentrate on every word you hear, and you constantly worry that you might forget something important. And there is the tedium of having to sit and look interested while we lawyers are arguing about some obscure point that seems trivial. And, of course, there are the hours you spend in the jury room while we are out here or in the judge's chambers making motions and arguing about things. But rest assured that Mr. Mayfield and I have known each other for years, and we have strong respect for one another. The bickering you see between us is strictly professional and never personal.

"I sat here for the past hour or so listening to Mr. Mayfield's closing statement to you. I have to give him a lot of credit — credit for describing to you a defamation case that doesn't exist!

"When I was a little girl — and that was many years ago, long before Eddie Bennison was stealing golf balls at that golf course when he was twelve years old — we used to play a little game with cards; but it wasn't a card game like poker or rummy. We would try to build little houses with those cards, and see who could build the tallest house before it all collapsed. The trick was to make sure that the base was firm and solid so that it could support the cards above it. If the base was not firm, nothing above it was stable.

"What Mr. Mayfield did, ladies and gentlemen, was build a house of cards. Standing there and talking to you, he constructed a house of cards that he wanted you to believe was solid and indestructible. But his house of cards was built with only one card at its base, and this one card was weak, infirm, and unable to support the cards above it.

"And what was that one weak card? It was not a piece of evidence. It was not even a fact. It was nothing more than an inference — an erroneous inference that could support nothing, not even a house of cards.

"Let me explain. Mr. Mayfield's entire house of cards rests on the single card that Max Reed did not reveal the sources who told him that Mr. Bennison cheated and took performance-enhancing drugs. That's it, ladies and gentlemen. Mr. Mayfield wants you to infer from that one single card that Max Reed had no sources, or that his sources were untrustworthy. In other words, Mr. Mayfield is asking you to believe that the refusal to reveal sources must mean that they don't exist or that they are unreliable.

But Max Reed was acting entirely within his rights in protecting his sources. As Judge Krause will tell you when he gives you your instructions, the laws of the State of Illinois specifically provide that a reporter cannot be forced to reveal his sources. It is every reporter's right — and duty — to protect the identity of his sources. The only inference that can be drawn from that refusal is that the reporter is doing what he is entitled to do. It does not imply that the sources are weak or nonexistent; it implies only that the reporter is obeying the law and the standards of his profession.

"Therefore, it is both wrong and unfair for Mr. Mayfield to tell you that you should infer that Max Reed is doing something wrong — or hiding something — by not revealing his sources. Max Reed was simply doing what all good reporters do. And as you heard from the testimony of Professor Samuel Roberts, a professor of ethics in journalism, Mr. Reed was obeying a time-honored practice which promotes a free and watchful press that protects the rest of us from the abuses of government officials and others who violate the standards of our society. If a source feared disclosure, he would remain silent; but, once assured that his identity will not be disclosed, he will step forward and give the information that the public has a right to know. Our society demands this practice. None of us wants to live in a totalitarian country that punishes those who come forward with information of wrongdoing. We see that in other parts of the world, but we don't want to see it in America."

Roz Berman paused to let her plea for patriotism sink in, and then said in a louder voice, "We should not condemn Max Reed for protecting his sources; we should thank him for upholding a vital element of our free society."

Roz Berman took a few steps forward so that her diminutive body was only two or three feet from the jury box. "Mr. Bennison's entire case rests on that one card — that one inference that Mr. Mayfield is asking you to make — the inference that Max Reed must be hiding something by refusing to reveal his sources. But that would be both a weak and an unfair inference, and it cannot support the rest of their case. Like a house of cards, their case must collapse because there is nothing to support it."

Roz Berman walked back to her counsel table to have a few hushed words with Hugo Shoemaker. Then she returned to face the jurors.

"I nearly fell off my chair," she told them, "when Mr. Mayfield asked you to award 250 million dollars to Mr. Bennison. Two hundred and fifty million dollars! I still can't get over it.

"Let's think about that for a moment. Each of you lives in Chicago — either in the city or in one of the nearby suburbs. And each of you must have some idea of what houses cost. If so, you'll probably agree with me that a million dollars would buy a very nice home — a home that many people would consider a mansion. Mr. Mayfield has asked you to award Mr. Bennison enough money to buy 250 of those mansions! And for what? For a single house of cards that will topple over with the first gust of wind!"

Roz Berman then took a deep breath. She had to defuse the most devastating bomb that Charlie had planted during his closing statement. "Mr. Mayfield talked to you about punitive damages. He lectured to you about your power to punish and teach lessons. He even told you to spank the defendants. He actually used that word — spank!

"Ladies and gentlemen, with all respect to Mr. Mayfield, you are not here to spank, teach lessons, or punish. You are here to make a decision — a fair and just decision — based on facts, not emotions. You are not hangmen or executioners — and you are not gods who send people to heaven or hell. You are deciders. It's a very important job, and it's the job you're here to do.

"Please understand, ladies and gentlemen, that I am not conceding that Mr. Bennison is entitled to any amount of money. I don't think he is entitled to anything, because his case is built on a house of cards. The fact is, he has no case at all, and is entitled to nothing at all. Even if Mr. Mayfield, with all of his bravado, asked you for a billion dollars, the fact remains that his client is entitled to nothing, for the simple reason that he has no case. His case — his house of cards — toppled over because it rested on the faulty inference that Mr. Reed had a moral duty to reveal his sources — a moral duty that can be found only in Mr. Mayfield's fertile imagination; it is denied by the law of this state and by our country's constitutional guarantee of a free press."

Berman went on to say a few things about Eddie Bennison's earnings and reputation, but she stayed clear of the issues involving malice or a reckless disregard for the truth. She and Shoemaker agreed that these were weak cards for them to play, and that their best chance to win was to defend

Reed's right not to reveal his sources, a right that Charlie was asking the jury to ignore. If the jury believed that Reed had decent sources and was within his rights not to reveal their identities, they would hold in favor of her clients. She then proceeded to finish her closing statement.

"In closing, ladies and gentlemen, I ask that you come to the right decision. Not the decision that will make you feel good, and not the decision that your neighbor — who hasn't heard the evidence — would like you to make, but the *right* decision based on the law and on the evidence that has been produced in this courtroom, and that you saw and heard with your own eyes and ears. Nothing else matters — only the law and the evidence.

"And when you go back in the jury room and review the evidence, you will see that you won't need a wrecking ball to knock over the Mr. Mayfield's house of cards. All you will have to do is blow on it."

With that, she returned to her seat at the counsel table.

CHAPTER 82

The rules permitted Charlie to speak to the jury one more time, but only to refute or comment on points brought up in the Roz Berman's closing statement. He was not allowed to bring up new issues.

Judge Krause, asked, "Any rebuttal, Mr. Mayfield?"

"Just a few words, Your Honor."

Charlie walked over to the jury with a sardonic smile, shaking his head from side to side. "Hello again," he began. "From where I was sitting, I couldn't see Ms. Berman's face while she was talking to you. So perhaps you could tell me, did she have a straight face when she told you that we should not condemn Max Reed, but that we should *thank him* for fulfilling some kind of civic duty? I mean, I heard her say it, but I can't believe that she was serious."

Charlie turned, as if to walk to a spot further from the jury, but then spun around. *"Thank Max Reed?"* he shouted in disbelief, his eyes blazing and his lips curled, "Thank him for what? For ruining a life? For destroying a career? For crippling a family? For *what?* Max Reed is a despicable excuse for a journalist. He is unworthy of the profession. A peddler of slime whose scandalous stories belong in a supermarket tabloid, if anywhere. And we have Ms. Berman asking us to pin medals on his lapel?

"I'll say this for Ms. Berman — she is loyal to her clients. It takes great fortitude to sit here for all this time defending a man like Max Reed — a man who writes lies for millions of people to read. A man who destroys lives and reputations with ease, and who shows no remorse for doing so. To him, it's just an everyday part of his job. He's a man who wields his pen with no restraint whatsoever — a man who probably puts a notch in his pen for each life he ruins." Charlie turned to look at Roz Berman. "Thank him? I'd as soon thank the devil himself."

Wanting the jury to have a little time to digest what he had to say about Max Reed, Charlie retreated to his counsel table to shuffle through some notes. He then returned to the jury box.

"Max Reed is a repulsive person, but that seems to be a common characteristic among the people at *Tee Time*. For example, let me remind you of what Ward Newton said on the witness stand. You will recall Mr. Newton — he is in charge of circulation at the magazine, and he read to us from a memo he wrote right after Mr. Reed's three articles appeared in the magazine. And do you remember how joyful he was — actually giddy — about how much money the magazine made from those horrible articles? He was cheering about the increased circulation, and the increased advertising revenues, being generated by those lies. And those are the people whom you are being asked to judge. Considering the way they revel in ruining lives to make money, that shouldn't be very hard to do."

Charlie turned to look at the table where the defense team was seated. "And Ms. Berman over there doesn't think that Eddie Bennison should be awarded 250 million dollars. I agree that it's a lot of money, more than most of us will see in a lifetime. But Eddie Bennison has accomplished more than most of us could ever accomplish in a lifetime. And Max Reed and that magazine of his have cost Eddie Bennison more money than most of will ever see in a lifetime."

Looking back to the defense table once again, he continued, "So I'll say this to Ms. Berman: if you think that 250 million dollars is too much compensation for the terrible lies that Max Reed wrote and *Tee Time* printed, you should have told them not to write and print those terrible lies in the first place. I'm here only to seek justice for the wrongs done by your clients — to seek enough money to repay Eddie Bennison and his family for the horrific loss and suffering that your clients caused and now refuse to acknowledge. Don't blame me for what I'm doing; blame them for what they did."

Charlie had intended to say more in his rebuttal, but his instincts told him that this was a good place to end. He wanted the jury to remember his last comment —it seemed to hit the right chord — and he didn't want to obscure it with further comments that would be less impactful. So he thanked them for listening and returned to take his seat at the counsel table.

CHAPTER 83

With the closing statements now completed, Judge Krause swiveled his seat to face the jury. "All of the evidence in this case has been presented to you, and the attorneys for each side have delivered their closing statements for your consideration.

"It's now nearly noon, and we'll stop now for our noon recess. We'll reconvene here in the courtroom at 2:00 p.m., at which time I will give you your instructions for deliberation and for reaching a verdict. That should take about an hour. Then you will begin your deliberations.

"The bailiff has already explained to you that once deliberations begin, they will continue until a verdict is reached. And as he also explained, this may entail you having to spend the night, or maybe two nights. Anticipating this, we have made arrangements for your accommodations at a local hotel that I'm sure you will find very satisfactory. Of course, the county will bear the expenses of your rooms and meals until a verdict is reached, or until it becomes clear that you will be unable to reach a verdict.

"I realize that this is a great inconvenience to you, but we did warn you when you were interviewed as potential jurors that this might happen, and you all agreed to serve in spite of that. Once you begin deliberations, we don't want you hounded or interrupted by the media or by anyone else, and we don't want to put you in the position of having to answer questions from your family, friends, or neighbors.

"As I will instruct you this afternoon, you are not to discuss this case, or any part of it, with anyone — and I mean anyone — except your fellow jurors until after you reach a final verdict and it is announced in open court. And please don't read or listen to anything about the case in the newspapers or on radio or television.

"So I'd like to make the following suggestions to all of you. When we break for lunch, please call your families to let them know that you may not be coming home this evening. After you have your lunch, you will each be driven to your home by one of the sheriff's deputies so you can pick up whatever toiletries and personal incidentals you will need at the hotel. To be on the safe side, I'd take enough for two or three nights — better safe than sorry.

"If you have any questions, please ask the bailiff about them when he escorts you to lunch. If he can't answer them, he'll tell us and we'll get you the answers early this afternoon.

"We truly appreciate the sacrifices you are making to help us resolve this case in a fair and just way. Enjoy your lunch."

WEDNESDAY AFTERNOON

CHAPTER 84

A t 2:00 that afternoon, the judge began charging the jury — that is, reading them their instructions for reaching a verdict. One of those instructions was that the verdict had to be unanimous — agreed to by all twelve jurors. In some cases, the lawyers will stipulate — agree — that their verdict need not be unanimous, and that a consensus by ten or eleven jurors will suffice, but there was no such stipulation in this case. Charlie had asked for it, but, as expected, Berman and Shoemaker rejected the idea. A deadlocked jury is better for defendants than plaintiffs, because the defendants pay nothing unless they lose on a later retrial of the case.

The charge to the jury was completed by 3:30, and the trial went into recess. The jurors were driven to their homes to gather whatever they might need until they could get back to their families. And the lawyers went back to their offices to kick off shoes, loosen neckties, have drinks, and remind themselves of things they'd like to have done or said differently. No matter how well a lawyer performs in a trial, he or she will invariably spend countless hours reliving the trial and commiserating over perceived mistakes.

The plaintiff's team came back to Charlie Mayfield's spacious office. Thanks to his secretary, Lillian Durant, they were greeted by a table laden with snacks, glasses, ice cubes, and an assortment of wines, beers, hard liquors, and soft drinks.

Pete Stevens, Charlie's associate, stood to the side of Charlie's desk and held a drink high. "I'd like to propose a toast to my mentor and boss, Charlie Mayfield, who taught me all I know about the law, and who I'm sure will teach me a lot more in the future. But in all of his teaching and lecturing to me, not once did he ever tell me how to stand up in open court and accuse — *falsely* — one of the most distinguished lawyers in the country of tax fraud and shooting heroin. That is exactly what Charlie did to the esteemed Hugo Shoemaker. I have attended numerous seminars — and read almost everything ever written — on trial technique, and never has such a cornball demonstration been discussed."

Stevens turned to his mentor and said, "Charlie, that was the goddamndest thing I ever saw — or ever heard of! It was downright crazy! But y'know, I think it worked. I really do! Once you pulled that nutty stunt, you had the jury in your pocket. I was watching them. When you began your closing statement, they all had stern looks on their faces, and they wore expressions that said, you have to convince me, and I'm not that easy to convince. But as soon as you pulled that bullshit with Shoemaker you had them eating out of your hand. Whenever you made a point, they were nodding so hard that I thought their heads would fall off. They looked like those little bobblehead dolls that you see on the dashboards of cars.

"And they were doing it again during your rebuttal. When you made that comment to poke fun at Roz — you know, asking if she had a straight face when she said we should all thank Max Reed for performing a civic duty — I thought they were going to stand up and cheer. And when you finally finished, I expected them to yell 'Encore! Encore!' I wouldn't have been surprised if they jumped out of the jury box and carried you around the courtroom on their shoulders, all the while singing Handel's 'Hallelujah Chorus.'"

This performance by Pete Stevens brought laughs from everyone in the room, and no one laughed heartier than Charlie Mayfield, who held his glass up to salute Pete. "Thank you, Pete. But what I did back there with Shoemaker was not nearly as risky as what you just did. Right here, in front of my valued clients, Eddie and Carol Bennison, you accused me of using cornball tactics and doing a nutty stunt. I consider that defamatory!"

Carol Bennison couldn't let that pass. "Sue him, Charlie! Sue the bastard! We don't tolerate defamation around here!"

Eddie Bennison stood, holding a Styrofoam coffee cup high. "Since the evidence in this case proves that I am a square, non-drinking, non-smoking, non-drug-taking wimp, I'd like to propose a toast with a cup of coffee."

He looked down at Charlie, smiled, and spoke. "Charlie, I never told you this, but when those articles came out in *Tee Time*, I got calls from lawyers all over the country wanting to take my case. Even the people at National Container back in Tulsa said they'd find a lawyer for me. But A.J. Silver, as my business manager and agent, insisted that I call you, and it was the best advice I ever got. From the first time we met — right here in this office — I knew you were the right choice, and you never gave me reason to doubt it.

"You not only took my *case*, Charlie, you took me. And you took Carol. We have been emotional wrecks since all this happened to us, and you were far more than our lawyer — you were our psychiatrist, our pastor, and our savior. You gave us hope when were we down.

"And just when I thought we had seen the worst, along came that terrible lady from Detroit — Elizabeth Peters. I thought that was the end of my life — and certainly the end of my marriage." Eddie made a slight bow. "But you handled her, Charlie, just like you handled everything. It's like you are always out ahead of everyone else, looking for bumps and potholes in the road, and then smoothing them out before we get there. And you seem to be able to see around corners. We don't know how this case will come out, but no matter what the jury does, Carol and I want to thank you, Charlie Mayfield, from the bottoms of our hearts.

"And I'd like to give special thanks to Pete, here, who has been a real star. I watched the way the two of you worked during the trial. You're a great team. It was just like in the movies where a surgeon sticks out his hand and someone always hands him the right scalpel or sponge. Every time Charlie needed a piece of information, or a document, Pete had it right there for him. It was great to watch the two of you work together — wonderful teamwork.

"And I can't sit down without saying one more thing. Charlie, would you please ask Lillian to come in for a moment?"

Charlie buzzed his secretary from the phone on his desk, and in a few seconds, Lillian Durant came in.

"Lillian," Eddie Bennison said, "I want to thank you for all you did on this case. I must've called Charlie here at the office a thousand times during the past few years, and if he wasn't here, you tracked him down for me, or relayed my questions to him, and then you tracked me down to give me his answers.

"I couldn't begin to count the times I've been in this office since I hired Charlie, and that includes many nights and weekends. And I've never been here when you weren't here, Lillian. I've seen you pounding away on your computer, making calls and retrieving documents for Charlie, ordering in lunch, keeping our coffee cups full, and always with a smile on your face. Charlie might have been the star of the show, but I know you were backstage giving him his props and making sure that his other clients knew he wasn't abandoning them."

Eddie went over to Lillian and gave her a hug. "You told me once, Lillian, that your husband was a golfer and that he was a fan of mine. What's his name?"

"Harold."

"Is Harold right- or left-handed?"

Bewildered by the question, she answered, "He's right-handed."

"Good. You go home tonight and tell Harold that I've arranged with my golf equipment sponsor to have a complete set of new clubs, along with a golf bag and twelve dozen balls, delivered to your home. Charlie already gave me your address. And also, Lillian, I know that you know how to reach me. Please let me know if you, Harold, or any of your friends would like to attend any of our Tour events. I'll be sure you get complimentary passes — not just for the course but also for the clubhouse. And that offer goes for as long as I'm playing on the Tour."

Lillian Durant was fighting back tears. "That is so generous, Eddie."

"Nonsense. It's the least I can do. You've been a big help, and no matter how much Charlie pays you, it's not enough."

Carol Bennison couldn't resist the temptation to add a comment of her own. She stood, held up her glass of wine, and said, "I'd like to echo everything that Eddie said. Living with him after those stories came out about him has not been easy, but Charlie, you, Pete, and Lillian have helped him more than you'll ever know. You were the lights at the end of his dark tunnel. No matter how low he was, or how deep his despair, he always seemed buoyed up after talking to you or returning from a visit to this office. You all pitched in to give him the hope and the confidence he needed to get through all this."

Carol walked over to Charlie, bent, and kissed him on the cheek. "Charlie, you worked hard to prove that Eddie never cheated or took those awful drugs. And he didn't. Now, if he ever needed drugs, it would have been to get him through this trial — but he had you and your team, and you were the best medicine in the world for him." Then she walked over to Pete Stevens to give him a hug.

Again succumbing to his compulsion to have the last word, Charlie Mayfield took the floor. "For myself, and for Lillian and Pete, I want to thank Eddie and Carol for their kind words and thoughts. And, if we score a touchdown with the jury, we'll all have a lot more than our mutual thanks to spread around. As President Lyndon Johnson once said, there are some awards we can wear, and there are some we can eat. We hope the jury's verdict will feed us all for a long time."

"Any predictions, Charlie?" This from Carol Bennison.

The lawyer laughed. "Juries are less predictable than the stock market. We've won cases I thought we had lost, and we lost some that I thought we had won. So don't ask me, Carol. You'd have as much luck asking a gypsy fortune teller."

"But you must have some feeling, Charlie," Carol replied, "some premonition."

Charlie looked down toward the floor and nodded slowly. "Well, my gut feelings are pretty good. And earlier today I talked with our shadow jurors — do you remember my telling you about them?"

Eddie and Carol both said they remembered.

"They think everything looks good for us, and they are notorious for not being overly optimistic."

Then he added, "And I had another source who thinks we're okay."

"Who would that be?" Eddie asked.

"Leon Poleski, Judge Krause's bailiff. He gave me a wink and a slight nod when we left the courtroom today, which I took to mean that we're in good shape with the jury."

Carol Bennison raised a hand. "I don't understand."

"Well, you wouldn't, Carol, because this is all new to you. But Leon has been sitting in that courtroom for years, and he has seen more trials than I will ever see in a lifetime. He has developed an uncanny ability to predict what juries do. And remember, Leon is the person who escorts the jurors back and forth between the jury room and the courtroom, and he's the one who sits with them during lunch. Even though the judge tells them every day not to discuss the case with anyone, including among themselves, it's only natural that a few words pass among them to indicate their feelings about a particular witness, or about the lawyers. Leon picks up on these things. So, when he gave me a wink and a nod today, I took it as a signal that he was picking up good vibes from the jury."

With that, Charlie rose and walked over to refill his drink glass. When he returned, he said, "But please, don't mention to anyone what I said about this. Leon is not infallible. More important, I don't want him to get in trouble, and I don't want anyone to get the impression that we're getting unauthorized information from courthouse personnel. In fact, I may be reading too much into all of this."

"Not a problem," Eddie was quick to say. "Neither of us will say a word about that — ever!"

Carol nodded. "Not a word, Charlie."

"Okay," Charlie said. "Now I'd like to say a few things about our wait for the verdict." With that, the Bennisons snapped to attention. "Eddie, you and Carol are about to experience the most agonizing hours of your life, and you will be helpless to do anything about it. Your fate will depend on something over which you have absolutely no control. This could take us hours, perhaps well into tomorrow — or even the next day or beyond. The judge and Leon have our phone numbers, and they know how to get hold of us at any time during the day or night. And it's possible that the jury may have a question before they reach a verdict, in which event we'll be notified."

"What kind of questions might they have?" Eddie asked.

"It could run the gamut. They might ask about a procedure, like whether they can call home. Or maybe one of them will get sick and they'll ask what to do. I once had a case where a juror sent word to complain that she was being bullied by other jurors.

"Those are the easy questions. Sometimes they'll send a message that they want some clarification on a point of law. For example, in this case they might want to ask something about malice, or whether a lie has to be intentional before it can be called libel. Whenever they ask a question, the judge will call us and we all haggle about how to answer it. Then the judge will send back his answer, or call them back into the courtroom if he thinks it makes more sense to explain the answer in person.

"But there's one question I dread more than any other."

"What's that?" Carol asked.

"It's when they ask what to do because they're deadlocked and can't reach a verdict."

"Then what happens?"

"Depends on a lot of things. If that happens after only an hour or two, the judge will tell them to go back and keep trying. But if it happens after several hours, or after a day or so, he'll ask if they think it's possible to reach an agreement if they spend more time. If it appears that they have little hope of that, he may declare a deadlock, release the jury, and order a whole new trial."

"Oh, Lord!" Eddie exclaimed.

"Right," Charlie said. "None of us wants that, including the judge. Well, on second thought, the defendants might like it because it would mean they don't have to pay anything — not yet, anyway. And if there's a second trial, it's usually good for the defense because they'd know what to expect from us, and they can be better prepared than they were the first time."

There was a lull in the conversation as everyone was digesting the unappetizing thought of having to go through another trial.

Charlie broke the silence. "I suggest that we finish up here, and then go grab a bite to eat. If we don't hear anything by then, Eddie and Carol should go back to their hotel or, better yet, go out to a movie or go for a long walk.

But, before we break, let's all be sure to share our phone numbers — cell phones, hotel phones, and home phones. I'll call if we hear from the judge or from Leon, and you call me if you have any questions. And please, be patient. This can take some time. And don't try to read anything into it if there is a long wait. It shouldn't be taken as a good sign or a bad sign."

"What if it's an early verdict?" Eddie asked. "Like in the first hour or two?"

"Well, like I said, we shouldn't read too much into it. Some lawyers say that a quick verdict is good for the defense, because it tells us that the jury didn't have to take the time to get to the question of damages. In other words, if they like the defense side, all they have to do is vote 'not guilty.' But if they like our side, they have to vote 'guilty' and then get into the question of how much to award Eddie. That can take some time. So longer deliberations are often good signs for plaintiffs, unless it means that they're deadlocked and we have to start all over.

"But it's still a guessing game. Once I got a big verdict — about three times more than I asked for — and the jury was out for only a couple of hours. Hardly enough time to elect a foreman. And that was a complicated case with more issues than we have in this one. So who knows?" he asked rhetorically, shaking his head.

Within minutes, everyone went his or her own way to start the vigil, and Lillian Durant came in to gather up the glasses, plates, and uneaten food.

CHAPTER 85

As one might expect, the mood over at Roz Berman's office was much different than the one at Charlie's. This had nothing to do with the prospect of winning or losing, but rather with the personalities.

At Charlie's office were Eddie and Carol Bennison, whose personal lives would be drastically and permanently affected by the jury's verdict. But no one at Berman's office faced the prospect of personally having to dig into his or her pocket. If they lost, the payment would come from corporate coffers out in New York with the financial loss, if any, ultimately spread over hundreds of thousands of shareholders.

Further, Roz Berman and Hugo Shoemaker, as defense lawyers, were paid basically by the hour, and their fees were not materially affected by whether they won or lost. Of course, they wanted to win as badly as Charlie did, but more for pride and reputation than for immediate financial gain. Charlie, on the other hand, had real skin in the game. He had taken Eddie's case on a one-third contingency fee, meaning that he would receive one-third of whatever the jury awarded Eddie. If Eddie lost and got nothing, Charlie would likewise get nothing. But if Eddie hit it big, then Charlie, too, would have a big payday. So, while Roz Berman, Hugo Shoemaker, and Charlie Mayfield all wanted to win, and perhaps equally so, Charlie stood to win or lose far more, in terms of dollars, than Berman or Shoemaker.

Legal scholars and commentators have debated forever the pros and cons of contingent fees. Those in favor argue that such an arrangement offers the chance for a non-wealthy plaintiff to hire a good lawyer to prosecute his or her case. Thus, the minimum-wage worker who loses a leg in an auto accident can hire the best of lawyers to sue the negligent driver who caused the accident. But if there were no contingent fee arrangements, he would be out of luck because he could not afford to hire a lawyer who would charge several hundred dollars per hour. Still, in many countries, contingent fees are not permitted on the reasoning that legal ethics dictate that a lawyer should be an advocate for his client and not his financial partner.

There was another reason why the atmosphere was different at the two lawyers' offices. At Charlie's, the senior lawyer was reaping the kudos of his grateful clients. At Berman's office, on the other hand, there were no grateful clients to praise and thank their lawyer — the clients were impersonal corporations half a continent away. Eddie's life would be dramatically and personally affected by the verdict, whichever way it went, but life would go on without much change for the people at *Tee Time* or Globe Publications — except for Max Reed, who feared that his job, and his entire future as a sportswriter, hinged on the awaited verdict.

And while Charlie Mayfield regarded the case as *his* case, neither Roz Berman nor Hugo Shoemaker could claim the case to be *his* or *hers*. It was *their* case, and victory or defeat would have to be shared between them. In the meantime, each was internally blaming the other for the way it was handled. Shoemaker thought that Berman alienated the jury with her brassiness. To a man of his gentility, a woman should be "sugar and spice and everything nice," and that was definitely not Roz Berman. In the meantime, Roz Berman believed that Shoemaker, with his disdain for rough play, hampered the style she adopted so often to rack up her impressive record of victories. Had it not been for Shoemaker's reticence, Roz Berman would have put Elizabeth Peters on the stand without first giving Charlie advance notice, and it was that notice that enabled Charlie to block the testimony with his motion *in limine*. Ever since that ruling, Berman could not look at Shoemaker without thinking, *Damn you, Hugo Shoemaker, for making me tip our hand to Charlie! If I had my way, I would have had Elizabeth Peters on the stand before Charlie knew what hit him.*

Further, if the case were lost, each knew that the other would blame him or her. And with all the interviews, seminars, public appearances, and lectures that were sure to ensue, regardless of the verdict, there would indeed be plenty of opportunity to revisit the way the case was handled. That was one of the disadvantages of a highly publicized and well-covered case: if it's lost, everyone sees the defeat, and everyone is a Monday-morning quarterback who is quick to second-guess the strategy and skills of the losing side. To this day, Marcia Clark and Chris Darden have not lived down the humiliation of losing the O.J. Simpson case, perhaps the most closely followed trial of all time, every minute of which was carried on national and international television. And instead of receiving empathy or understanding for their loss, they were — and still are — vilified, rightly or wrongly, for the way they handled the trial.

There were two other people that afternoon in Roz Berman's conference room: Max Reed and Todd Slocum.

Slocum asked, "What do you think, Roz? What's your best guess as to what the jury's going to do?"

When the same question was put to Charlie a few blocks away, he answered that it was anyone's guess, but then he went on to give the reasons for his optimism — the feedback from his shadow jurors, Charlie's own take from observing the jurors, and the almost imperceptible signals from the bailiff. He had given an honest and complete answer, as best he could.

Roz Berman, however, answered in the manner of many lawyers who, rather than risk predicting the outcome of the case, build alibis they may need if they lose. And Roz Berman was a master at building alibis.

"Frankly, Todd," she began, "from the very beginning I foresaw some problems we'd have to deal with, but they've turned out to be worse than I thought."

"What kind of problems?"

"Well, first, we knew all along that the jury could be very impressed with Eddie Bennison, but he turned out to be even more impressive than I anticipated. He was an excellent witness. Smiled at all the right places, gave all the cute answers that Charlie told him to give, and did everything right. I half expected him to jump into the jury box and start giving golf lessons."

She then turned toward Max Reed. "I hate to say this, Max, but the impression you made on the jury was just the opposite. They saw you as the guy who attacked a national hero. And it looked to the jury like you were devious — hiding behind sources who you refused to name."

"But I — "

"I know, Max, you were just doing your job, but doing some jobs well can be very offensive to some people." She paused and added, "I suppose executioners run into the problem all the time.

"The fact is, I'm worried that they see you more as a gossip columnist than as a legitimate sportswriter."

Sighing and shaking her head, she added, "But don't feel too bad, Max, you weren't the only one to get under the jury's skin. When Ward Newton was on the stand, Mayfield had him read that memo he wrote telling his boss that those three articles about Bennison were the most successful articles ever published in *Tee Time*, and that they were worth at least 50 to 75 million dollars in revenues. He said they were 'grand slam home runs.'

"So, as the jury sees it, Eddie Bennison was a national hero whose career was ruined by a bunch of guys at your magazine — the same guys who were cheering and bragging about how much money they made by ruining that career." She looked around the room and added the final punctuation mark: "That memo of Newton's could cost the magazine a ton of money."

Roz Berman was doing more than building alibis to be used if things went badly. Like many lawyers, she had a tendency to paint an overly bleak picture to her clients. This served two purposes. One, it was a warning to be prepared for a bad result and to lay the groundwork to deny later that any guarantees of success were given. And second, if they ended up winning the case, the lawyer could claim to be a hero for winning a case that was expected to be lost. The lawyer who predicted a good result made the client feel great, but, by doing so, he risked looking that much worse if the case is lost.

After putting her alibis in motion and presenting the possibility of a loss, Roz Berman knew that something more was expected of her; she still had not answered Todd Slocum's question. "So, Todd, to be perfectly candid, I think this thing can go either way. There's a lot of sympathy for Bennison, but we have something going for us. The American public loves to read dirt about people. Let's face it, that's why the supermarket tabloids sell so well. That's why everyone reads the gossip columns. That's why some of those cable TV shows are so popular. Everyone says terrible things about other people, and the public eats it up. The jury can support that thirst by voting for us — by saying that it's okay for the Max Reeds of the world to write these kinds of stories. It's the American way! We want them to believe that a verdict against us is a suppression of the free speech and free press that America has come to honor. That's what I'm hoping for." She paused and added, "But it's a long shot when those stories are written about a national icon like Eddie Bennison."

CHAPTER 86

It was just after six in the evening in New York, but Doug Timbers, *Tee Time*'s Vice President of Public Relations, showed no signs of getting ready to call it a day. He was at his desk, his suit jacket thrown over a chair, necktie pulled down, and shirt sleeves rolled up past his elbows, asking rapid-fire questions to the others sitting in his office.

"Gail, what's the latest news from Slocum?"

His secretary responded, "I spoke with Todd ten minutes ago. He's huddled with our lawyers right now, and they seem to think that we won't know anything until tomorrow morning at the earliest. The jury didn't get the case until about an hour ago, and the judge told them to expect to spend the night, maybe two nights — he even sent them home to pick up whatever they'll need at a hotel."

"Did Todd make any predictions?"

"Well, he sounded pretty glum. He said our lawyers were preparing him for the worst."

"Wonderful," Timbers replied sarcastically. "Just wonderful."

He then turned to a young man sitting off to the side. "Jerry, how are we doing on the releases?"

"We're all set," Jerry Bank said as he pulled a few sheets of paper from a folder. "I have two press releases ready to go, one if we win and one if we lose, just like you wanted. If we win, the release will say that the verdict reinforces our respect for the jury system, which once again has seen the wisdom of the constitutional mandate of an American free press.'"

"That's fine. And if we lose?"

"I'll read that one. It says, 'We are disappointed by the outcome of the trial, though we understand that Eddie Bennison is an extremely popular figure who was obviously very attractive to the jury. But that attraction is no justification to disregard the constitutional mandate of an American free press. We intend to file an appeal to a higher court, and we have every confidence that we — and the Constitution — will prevail.'"

"Okay, Jerry, I like the message, but I don't want to glorify Bennison by saying he's 'an extremely popular figure.' See if you can change that part, and then show it to me."

Timbers had something else to say. "There's a good chance that the verdict won't come in until tomorrow — maybe even later than that. In the meantime, we're sure to be getting calls. And if we do, you all know what to say, right?" He pointed to a woman seated and facing him from the other side of his desk. "Tell us, Marie. Tell us what we say when we get a call before the verdict is in."

"We give the standard line — that we're confident, but beyond that it's our policy not to comment on pending litigation."

"Correct. And if anyone makes a statement that goes further than that, they'll answer to me."

CHAPTER 87

Back in Chicago, the rest of the night was quiet. However, the wheels inside the lawyers' heads were spinning nonstop. Each team was in its respective office, quenching thirsts, nibbling on snacks, and waiting.

Charlie had downed his third martini of the evening. Roz Berman was sipping from a cup of coffee while staring with disgust at Hugo Shoemaker, who was nursing his fifth cup of tea. With each, he went through a meticulous and unvaried routine — dropping in precisely one-half of a sugar cube (from a supply he carried with him), making precisely eight dips of a teabag (from a supply he carried with him), and giving three stirs of the spoon. Although totally innocent, this performance with his tea was one more thing about Shoemaker that had been getting under Berman's skin.

As she had told one of her law partners, "I wish to hell that this guy would scream or throw things once in a while, but all he does is wince whenever I reach into my bag of tricks. He makes a bigger deal out of his cup of tea than I do preparing a seven-course dinner, and you should see what he goes through when he orders in a restaurant — he grills the poor waiter with a thousand questions: Is it spicy? Is it salty? Is it lean? Is it cooked in vegetable oil? Could the chef add a little oregano? The bastard won't let me cross-examine a witness as thoroughly as he cross-examines these poor people who bring him his food."

Berman realized that her reactions to Shoemaker were a bit harsh, but waiting for a verdict always made her tense. Still, the law professor had been testing her patience ever since they were both hired to defend the Bennison case. Whenever she wanted to use a meat ax, he wanted her to use tweezers. Whenever she wanted to kick a door in, he wanted her to knock gently. To Roz Berman, the stuff of classrooms was not the stuff of courtrooms. She wanted to win this case more than any she had ever tried, but the professor was cramping her style and making victory next to impossible. And for this she resented him. If the case were lost, the world would view her as the loser. It was her case. No one would remember that the professor had his thumb on the scale.

THURSDAY MORNING

CHAPTER 89

It was 7:30 a.m., and Charlie Mayfield, in bare feet and pajamas, was plugging in the coffee pot when the phone rang. The shrill sound gave him a jolt. He took a deep breath and answered.

"Hello?"

"Charlie, it's Leon. We have a verdict. The judge would like everyone in the courtroom at 11:00."

Another deep breath. "That's nearly four hours from now, Leon. Why so long?"

"Well, the jury's been at it most of the night, and they just told us they had a verdict about fifteen minutes ago. We want to give them time to shower and change, and we're giving them a big breakfast at the hotel. They earned it, Charlie — this has been a big ordeal for them."

"Of course, Leon, that's fine. We'll be there at 11:00."

"Great. See you then."

"Wait, Leon. Is there anything else you'd like to tell me?"

"Like what?"

"Like whether they gave you any indication of what the verdict will be."

"Hey, Charlie — you know better than to ask me that. Even if I knew, I couldn't say a word."

Yeah, right.

"And there's another reason the judge wants to wait until 11:00."

"What's that, Leon?"

"He wants me to call the press and give them time to get people over here for the reading of the verdict."

"I should have guessed."

"Yeah, they gave me a number to call — I think it's for the press pool. Whoever answers will know how to reach all of them."

"Okay, Leon. Thanks. Have you called Roz yet?"

"Gonna do it now. And Charlie?"

"Yes."

"Good luck. If I was on that jury, you'd be kissing me on the lips at 11:30."

Charlie laughed out loud. "I'll keep that pleasant thought in mind, Leon. See you in a few hours."

CHAPTER 90

Charlie did nothing for the next ten minutes, taking that time to get his thoughts in order. He had no idea what the verdict would be, so he had to be prepared for any eventuality. Preparing statements to the press, answering the questions he could expect from Eddie Bennison, deciding how to soften the blow if he had to deliver bad news and anticipating everything else he'd have to do during the day, depending on the verdict. But his first task was clear.

He dialed the Hyatt Hotel and asked to be connected to the Bennisons' room. Carol answered.

"Carol, it's Charlie. I hope I didn't wake you."

"You didn't. I couldn't sleep a wink last night. Too nervous."

"Is Eddie there?"

"No, he went down to the workout room a half hour ago. Should I go down and get him?"

"No, don't do that. Let him get his workout in. But when he gets back, tell him we have a verdict and — "

"A verdict? Really?" Her anxiety was unmistakable. "Did we win?"

"Don't know, Carol. It's going to be read in open court at 11:00 this morning. But I'd like you and Eddie to meet me in my office by 9:00 or 9:30 at the latest. We have to be prepared to deal with whatever happens."

"We'll be there."

"Okay. And listen, Carol — within the next few minutes, the press will know that a verdict is coming down this morning, and they may corner you at the hotel or on the way over to my office. They can be relentless, so please, Carol, be nice to them but don't — under any circumstances — answer any questions. They might make it tough for you, but just blame me. Tell 'em that your lawyer told you not to speak to them until everything is over. And Carol?"

"Yes, Charlie."

"See if you can get A.J. Silver to join us when you come to my office this morning."

"A.J.? Why A.J.?"

"He can help us decide on what to say to the press. In fact, since he's Eddie's business manager, the reporters will be sure to pepper him with questions, just like they will with us. I want us all singing from the same hymnal."

———

The Bennisons, along with A.J. Silver, were ushered into Charlie's office a few minutes after 9:00 by Lillian Durant. Because it was early and knowing that they all came on short notice, Lillian had coffee and sweet rolls laid out.

"Okay," Charlie began, "everything we've been working on for the past few years comes down to today. We don't know whether it's going to be good or bad, so we have to be prepared to go either way.

"From the legal side, there isn't much we have to think about right now. If we win, we celebrate; if we lose, then we'll have time to decide on our next steps."

Although A.J. Silver had a law degree, his practice never brought him near a courtroom, and litigation procedures were a mystery to him. "Charlie," he asked, "I don't know what you mean by 'next steps.' Wouldn't we just appeal if we lost?"

"Sure, we'd have to consider an appeal, but there are steps to take before we get to that. I hate to talk about losing, but it's a possibility we can't ignore. If the verdict comes in against us, the first thing we do is ask the judge to poll the jury. He will then ask each juror if he or she voted for that verdict, so we can be sure that the vote was unanimous. The law requires a unanimous vote, not only on liability but also on damages.

"Then we'll have thirty days to file a motion for a new trial. If we do that, we have to give reasons why the first trial was tainted. The standard reasons are to point to errors the judge made in certain of his rulings — reversible errors that were so serious that they could have changed the outcome of the case."

Carol Bennison asked, "Were there any of those errors?"

"Nothing glaring, but I'd have to go through the record, word for word, to be sure. Most of the rulings on evidence went our way, so there isn't much for us to complain about on that score. In fact, the most controversial ruling in the case — and it was the most important ruling — went our way. If we win, the other side may use that as a reason to ask for a new trial."

"What ruling was that?" Eddie asked.

Charlie wrinkled his brow into a frown. "I'd rather not get into that right now."

Charlie realized that his deflection of the question was awkward, but he had no choice. The controversial and important ruling he had in mind was the ruling keeping the Elizabeth Peters episode out of the case. Charlie didn't want to bring that up with A.J. Silver in the room; there was no reason for him to know that Eddie had been accused of shacking up at a Marriott Hotel in Detroit and slugging the woman in question. Fortunately, that entire issue was handled privately in Judge Krause's chambers, and Charlie wanted to keep it that way.

He decided it was best to get to the immediate issues. "We're going to have our hands full with the press this morning, and we have to be ready for it." He looked around to be sure he had everyone's attention.

"They already know that the verdict will be announced in the courtroom at 11:00 this morning. The judge asked his bailiff to call them right after he called me."

"Why would the judge want them there?" A.J. Silver asked.

"It's not that he wants them there, A.J. But trials are open the public and the press, and they have every right to be there. If he hadn't agreed to call them, they would have been camped out at the courthouse since yesterday afternoon.

"Also, knowing Judge Krause, I suspect that he wants them there so he could give them a few warnings."

"What kind of warnings?" Silver inquired.

"He'll probably warn them not to hound the jurors with questions about why they did what they did. Also, he may ask them to respect Eddie's privacy — especially if the verdict goes against us.

"Now, let me tell you a little about those press people. You won't get their questions from nice little flowered notes they send you. No way! What you'll get are microphones and cameras shoved in your face when you least expect it, and not only today but in the weeks to come. They'll corner you walking out of your front door or walking into the grocery store. They'll phone you and everyone you know.

"And the questions they ask won't be pretty ones. If we win, they'll be asking you, Eddie, what you plan to do with the money. And they'll ask you about that, too, A.J. And Eddie, be prepared for them to ask if you cheated on the golf course or took drugs.

"We'll go over some of these likely questions this morning and decide how to answer them. The important thing is this — be nice to them, and don't act like the questions are out of line or that they're imposing on you. If you cooperate, they're more likely to write nice things about you. But if you give them a hard time, they can make you look really bad in print. Remember, this is their job, and they think it's the most important job in the world."

"What about a prepared written statement?" Silver asked.

"For today, we'll have two written statements prepared, one if we win and one if we lose. I'd like for you to work on them, A.J. They should be fairly vanilla — how we respect the jury system, that the judge was fair, that the jury worked hard, that freedom of the press is not a freedom to ruin people's lives with lies — that kind of thing. And I'd like them worded as if they were coming from Eddie or, better yet, from Eddie and Carol."

Charlie took a large bite from a sweet roll, and followed it with a few gulps from his coffee cup. "There's another thing I want to mention. Once the case is over, the jurors are free to discuss it with anyone. So, whether we win or lose, I'll interview some of them — or have someone else interview them — to find out how they feel about certain witnesses, or certain pieces of evidence. I'll want to know if there was anything that was confusing to them, or that they didn't understand. That's critical information for us to know in the event we ever have to re-try the case."

"Re-try it?" Carol Bennison asked in dismay. "You said that might happen if the jury was deadlocked. But they're not deadlocked."

"Well, as I tried to explain earlier, Carol, whichever side loses can ask the judge for a new trial because some errors were made. And if that happens, I want to be sure to do a better job the second time — not use the witnesses they didn't like or didn't believe and do a better job of explaining things that may have been unclear to them."

"But," A.J. Silver asked, "you said a while ago that the judge might warn the press not to contact the jurors. Then why is it okay for you to contact them?"

"Good question, A.J. The judge knows that lawyers need to do this for their clients and for their own self-improvement. And they know that we'll be respectful of the jurors and only ask questions that can help us evaluate the job we did. On the other hand, the judge knows that reporters can be relentless in badgering people for information that leads to big headlines and sensational stories, naming the jurors and exposing them to the public. He doesn't want the jurors to be subjected to that. Of course, he might allow them to contact the jurors, but only on the condition that they behave."

The discussions and speculations went on until the door to Charlie's office opened and Lillian Durant leaned in. "It's 10:30," she whispered apologetically.

Charlie smiled. "Thanks, Lil, for reminding me — we sure don't want us to be late for this."

CHAPTER 91

Judging from the number of people crowded into and just outside of Judge Krause's courtroom a few minutes before 11:00, a bystander might have thought that the county was giving away free parking passes. One could only wonder how word of the upcoming verdict could spread so fast.

Just as Judge Krause, with robes flowing, entered from the door behind his bench, Leon Poleski announced, "Everyone please rise!" And as the judge took his seat in the tall leather chair that faced the courtroom, the bailiff declared, "Oyez, oyez, oyez. This Honorable Court is now in session, the Honorable Harry Krause presiding. Please be seated."

After several seconds, everyone was seated and the room was perfectly quiet but for the muted sound of the ventilation system.

The judge looked toward his bailiff seated off to his side. "Please bring the jury in."

Leon Poleski walked out of the side door and in less than 30 seconds returned, followed by the twelve jurors. During the trial there had been fourteen of them in the jury box, including two alternate jurors who were empaneled against the possibility that one or two of the twelve regular jurors would become ill or otherwise be unable to continue. The two alternates were excused when all twelve of the regular jurors began their deliberations.

The twelve took their previously assigned seats in the jury box, with the exception of Ralph Jensen, a high school principal who had been elected to be the jury's foreman. He took the first seat in the first row, and the juror who had previously sat in that seat took Jensen's regular seat.

When they were comfortably seated, the judge said, "We understand that the jury has reached a verdict. Is that correct?"

Ralph Jensen stood. "We have, Your Honor."

"And has it been signed by each and every one of the jurors?"

"Yes, sir, it has."

"Please read your verdict aloud."

Jensen cleared his throat. He took a quick look around the courtroom but avoided making eye contact with anyone seated at either of the two counsel tables. Then he looked down to read from the verdict form held in his trembling fingers and read.

"We, the jury, find the defendant, Tee Time, Incorporated, guilty of wrongfully defaming the character and reputation of the plaintiff, Edward Joseph Bennison . . . "

These words were met with an immediate applause from the courtroom, and within seconds there were the sounds of pens scratching on notebooks and the slight clicking of text messages being typed out.

Judge Krause rapped his gavel to hush the noise. At the plaintiff's counsel table, Charlie Mayfield nudged Eddie's arm. Both Eddie and Carol, who had been inconspicuously holding hands, tightened their grasps and let out the breath each had been holding without realizing it.

"We do not find Globe Publications, Incorporated, guilty of wrongful defamation."

Showing no emotion, Judge Krause asked, "And has the jury agreed on an award of damages?"

"Yes, Your Honor." Looking again at his paper to be sure he made no mistake, the foreman continued. "We award compensatory damages in favor of the plaintiff, Edward Joseph Bennison, and against the defendant Tee Time, Incorporated, in the amount of 247 million dollars."

Charlie, concealing his excitement, leaned over to whisper in Eddie's ear. "An odd number. That tells me that some were higher and some were lower, so they ended up with a compromise. Happens all the time."

Ralph Jenson, the foreman, was not done. "We further award punitive damages in favor of the plaintiff, Edward Joseph Bennison, and against the defendant Tee Time, Incorporated, in the amount of one billion dollars."

Charlie jolted, and then leaned to whisper to Eddie, "So much for odd numbers."

With this last announcement, the courtroom burst into pandemonium. Everyone, it seemed, had something to say or someone to call. There was even the clapping of hands from onlookers having no official business, some of whom were the courthouse regulars — usually retirees who enjoy watching trials and making friendly wagers on the outcome.

Within seconds, newscasts throughout the nation were being instantly interrupted to report the verdict.

The judge asked if any of the lawyers wanted the jury to be polled. Roz Berman stood and said that she would. With that, Judge Krause looked at his list of the jurors and then asked each, by name, if he or she voted in favor of the entire verdict — in terms of both liability and damages — as read by the foreman. Each replied for the record in the affirmative.

Judge Krause then said for all to hear, "The court accepts the jury's verdict and will sign an order consistent with that verdict. Mr. Mayfield, please prepare such an order for me to sign, and try to have it for me by 3:00 this afternoon. But run it by Ms. Berman and Mr. Shoemaker as to form. If there is any disagreement as to the form, then you should all meet with me at 3:00. I'd like to wrap this up today."

The judge then turned toward the jury. "Ladies and gentlemen, please accept my sincere gratitude for the time and effort you put into this case. It required a great deal of patience and concentration because of the complexity of the issues, and I know that there was added pressure on you because of the public's interest in the case. You will doubtless receive both compliments and criticism for your verdict, but we know, as you know, that your verdict was the result of thoughtful consideration after a careful review of all of the evidence. If you should have detractors, it's only because they weren't here to see and listen to the evidence that you saw and heard with your own eyes and ears.

"Before I excuse you and send you home to your families, I'd like to alert you to something. Some of you — if not all of you — may be contacted by the press who will want you to tell them what went on back there in the jury room. You have no obligation to talk to them or answer their questions, but you are free to do so if you wish."

The judge then looked out to the courtroom. "And I'm admonishing the people in the press to respect the privacy of the jurors. I can't order you not to contact them, but if I learn that you are harassing or bothering them, I will consider it an act of contempt for the judicial process and will deal with it accordingly."

Then he returned his eyes to the jury. "It's also possible that you will be contacted by one or more of the lawyers in this case, or by their representatives, to ask you some questions. They do this in order to get an evaluation of what kind of job they did, and thereby improve their skills for future cases. This is normal and customary. You have no obligation to talk to them, but you are free to do so. Again, thank you. You are excused."

With that, Leon beckoned the jurors to follow him out of the side door of the courtroom.

The judge rapped his gavel. "Court is adjourned." He stood and exited out of the rear door.

CHAPTER 92

The instant that Judge Krause left the courtroom, Carol Bennison let out a scream and threw her arms around Charlie's neck. And she whispered in his ear, "It isn't the money, Charlie. We have enough money. But you gave Eddie his life back. You proved to the whole world that he's an honorable man. We knew it, and now the whole world knows it — because of you." She kissed him and said, "I love you, Charlie Mayfield."

The atmosphere was gloomy at the defense table. Todd Slocum had his head buried in his hands. Not only could this verdict very well put the magazine out of business, but it was also a personal kick in his stomach. He could have prevented publication of the defamatory articles, but he didn't. And he could have hired lawyers who would have been a better match for Charlie Mayfield, but he didn't. In short, he was the company lawyer, and it was therefore his head that was on the line when a verdict like this decimated the company.

On the other side of the defense table, Roz Berman and Hugo Shoemaker were huddled, each trying hard to appear calm and unshaken.

"Did he say a billion dollars, Roz? With a 'b'?"

"That's how I heard it."

The professor was shaking his head in disbelief. "I think that would make it the highest defamation verdict in American history."

"Congratulations, Hugo, on setting a new record. Now you'll be even more famous than you were before." She paused and added, "And the billion is only the punitives. There's another quarter of a billion in compensatories."

CHAPTER 93

I f any verdict ever called for a celebration, this was the one.

Back in his office, and after all the hugs and high-fives, Charlie suggested that the team have dinner together. In addition to Eddie and Carol, Charlie invited his associate, Pete Stevens.

Carol replied, "Only if you and Pete bring your wives. I've been holed up with all you guys for weeks, and I'd like to be with pretty people for a change."

"Done," Charlie responded. "I'll have Marge there. And Pete, can you be sure to bring Debbie?"

"Sure."

Charlie looked over to A.J. Silver. "I was hoping you could join us, A.J."

"Love to, and I'm sure that Sara can be there too. Any suggestions on where to go?"

"I was thinking about Gibsons on Rush Street. Best steaks in Chicago. In fact, I called there this morning and made a reservation, and they can put us in a private room. We'll need that privacy because, by tonight, the whole world will know about the verdict, and the last thing we need is a bunch of people running over and asking for Eddie's autograph — or a handout! Seven o'clock. It's all set."

Carol was laughing. "You mean you made the reservation before the verdict came in?"

"Sure. Why not? I could always cancel it if we lost."

"Okay," Eddie said, "Gibsons on Rush Street it is. Seven o'clock."

"Perfect!" Carol said. "That gives us the whole afternoon to shop at all those great places on Michigan Avenue."

Seeing Eddie wince, Charlie put his hand on Carol's shoulder. "Just remember, Carol. It may be a long time before we see any money out of this thing. Let me explain. Ordinarily, a winning plaintiff can collect on a judgment as soon as it's entered. However, we have to wait until the judge rules on any motions for a new trial. And if *Tee Time* appeals and posts a bond—usually twice the amount of the judgment—then we have to wait until all the appeals are done, and the judgment is affirmed, before we can start to collect. And you can bet that *Tee Time* will be posting an appeal bond to keep everything on hold."

Then, getting back to the case at hand, Charlie said, "Knowing Roz Berman, she'll file a thousand motions to set aside the verdict, to get a new trial, to lower the amount of the verdict, and God knows what else. And after she loses all of them, she'll file an appeal — and post an appeal bond — that could keep this thing in limbo for a couple of years or even longer. She'll do this stalling in the hope that we settle for a lower amount just to get it over with."

"That doesn't seem fair," A.J. Silver said.

"Well, it's not. But the good news is that interest runs on the judgment until it's paid, and in Illinois, the interest on judgments is 9 percent."

"Nine percent?" Silver exclaimed in bewilderment. "Hell, I couldn't do that well with the money if they paid it tomorrow. I might be able to get Eddie 4 or 5 percent, but never 9 percent, unless we made risky investments that I'd never make. I hope for Eddie's sake that they stall for a long time, as long as we can get 9 percent."

"It's not quite that easy," Charlie said. "These New York companies with their fancy New York lawyers are famous for shenanigans to avoid paying judgments. There are games they can play to put the magazine under the protection of the bankruptcy courts. Probably a Chapter 11 proceeding, which would bar us from going after the assets until they go through a reorganization. If they do that, and if it works, then we could be left out in the cold for a long time, and then be forced to take pennies on the dollar."

"That's terrible!" Eddie said. "How could they get away with that?"

"Maybe they can't," Charlie replied. "It wouldn't be as easy as I'm making it sound. The good news is that Tee Time, Inc., as a company, has a net worth of over three billion dollars, which is nearly three times more than the judgments we got against them today. So, at least mathematically, there is enough there to pay us no matter what they do — or what they try.

"For now, my biggest job is to make sure that the verdict stands up: no new trials and no reversal if they appeal."

"If they do appeal," A.J. Silver asked, "what court would it go to?"

"Good question," Charlie replied. "Ordinarily, appeals from the Illinois trial courts go to the Illinois Appellate Court, and from there to the Illinois Supreme Court, provided that they choose to take the case. Considering the importance of the issues, I'd bet that our state Supreme Court would agree to hear the appeal. And since our case involves issues with the United States Constitution — specifically the First Amendment — the defendants might ultimately be able to appeal to the federal courts."

"Is that good or bad?" Silver asked.

"I don't see it as good or bad. Our case on the First Amendment is strong, and the jury's verdict shows that there is strong proof of malice — and that's the main thing a federal court would be looking for in a case like this. In fact, we tried the case as if it were being tried in the federal courts, using the same evidence and arguments we'd use there. We did that because it's the federal courts that set the rules for applying and interpreting the First Amendment.

"So, folks, as far as I'm concerned, we have a very strong verdict. The big question isn't *if* we collect — it's when we collect."

Eddie asked, "If there were any weakness in our verdict, Charlie, where would it be?"

Charlie chuckled. "My answer might surprise you. Our biggest problem as I see it is that we won too much! Sometimes a verdict is so high that a judge refuses to uphold it. Do any of you remember that crazy case where a jury decided that McDonald's had to pay a lady nearly three million dollars after she spilled hot coffee on her lap? And she spilled it herself!"

They all nodded to show that they did indeed remember that case.

"Well, the judge who heard that case later reduced the amount of the verdict from nearly three million to a much lower amount — a few hundred thousand. A judge is permitted to do that when he believes that a verdict is outrageously high and bears no relation to reality or to the evidence. So it's possible — but I don't think probable — that Judge Krause or some appellate judge might decide that our verdict is just too high. Let's face it, the two awards today come to a total of about one and a quarter billion dollars. And that might be enough to put *Tee Time* out of business. Some judge might decide that that's too severe a penalty for three lousy articles about a golfer."

Not wanting to dampen the mood more than necessary, Charlie explained himself. "Now don't get me wrong. I'm just talking theory here in order to give you the complete picture. But in my opinion, our judgment is rock solid and it won't get overturned. And that's what we're going to celebrate tonight. Seven o'clock at Gibsons on Rush Street."

THURSDAY NIGHT

CHAPTER 94

Charlie was right to reserve a private room at Gibsons. The party was recognized as soon as they walked in through the door, and within minutes, people approached with smart phones for taking pictures, and with menus and napkins and anything else on which Eddie Bennison could sign an autograph. It took several minutes before they were ushered to the private room where they could finally settle down and relax.

"Whew," Eddie said, "they must have known we were coming."

"I don't think so," Charlie replied. "Actually, I took a page out of your book, Eddie, and made the reservation in the name of 'Ben Edwards.'"

"Then what the hell happened when we walked in?" Pete Stevens asked.

"Well," Charlie offered, "of all those people who were eating and waiting on tables when we came in, many of them obviously read the newspapers and watch the local news on TV. Today's verdict was all over the news, along with Eddie's picture, and it only takes one or two people to spot him before the whole place knows."

After the waiter brought drinks to their private room and took the dinner orders, Eddie tapped his ballpoint pen against a stein of beer to get everyone's attention. "May I please have the floor for a minute?" he asked.

Everyone stopped what they were doing and gave him their attention.

Eddie lifted the beer and spoke slowly and seriously. "I don't know if beer is a suitable beverage on which to make a toast, but it will have to do. I have about one of these a month, and this is the perfect night for me to indulge."

He looked from person to person, and continued. "I have both a toast and an announcement to make. The toast is an obvious one." Holding his stein higher, he said, "To Charlie Mayfield, I declare my everlasting gratitude. And Charlie, this is not only for me, but also for every person who might ever feel, as I did, the sting of a vicious reporter, newscaster, magazine, or newspaper. What you accomplished with this trial, Charlie, will make all those people think twice before doing to others what they did to me."

Then Eddie turned to face Pete Stevens. "And Pete, I also raise my glass to you. We all know how helpful you were to Charlie, and how valuable you were to the successful outcome. I get a lot of credit for winning golf tournaments, Pete, but I know darn well that I'd never win any of them if it weren't for Artie, my caddie. He gives me what I need to win — sometimes the right club, sometimes the right advice, and sometimes just being there next to me. The reassurance I get from him is vital. You do for Charlie what Artie does for me. Charlie and I couldn't get along without you guys. That verdict is a tribute to all you did."

Before he sat down, Eddie said, "And I also want to toast Marge Mayfield and Debbie Stevens. You are both married to wonderful and talented men, but I have no doubt that their accomplishments can be traced to the love and support they get at home. As beneficiaries of their talents and accomplishments, Carol and I thank you both."

Everyone in the room applauded Eddie's thoughtful expressions of gratitude.

"Now," he said, "I'd like to make an announcement." Certain that he again had everyone's attention, Eddie looked over to A.J. Silver. "I suppose I should have discussed this first with A.J., my wonderful friend, agent, and business manager. I promised A.J. many years ago, and regularly ever since, that I'd never make an important financial decision without first asking him. He begged me to make that promise, and I'm glad I did. He saved me from making a lot of mistakes. Heck, it's gotten to the point that I hesitate to buy a pair of shoes without running it by A.J. He'll probably explode when he hears what I have to say next."

A.J. Silver playfully held his hands over his ears. "I have no idea what you're about to say, Eddie, but you're scaring the hell out of me."

"As you all know, Charlie is entitled to one-third of whatever I get out of this case. The entire award comes to about one and a quarter billion dollars — Lord, I can hardly say that without fainting. Now, I know we may end up getting something less; maybe we'll end up agreeing to less in return for a quick payment without appeals, or maybe the judge will reduce the verdict like the judge did in that McDonald's case over the hot coffee. Or maybe we'll lose altogether on appeal. On the other hand, we may end up with more, considering that we're entitled to collect 9 percent interest on the judgment until it's paid.

"What Carol and I would like to do is this." He looked at A.J. Silver, shrugged his shoulders as if to say, *Sorry, pal,* and continued. "We'd like to donate our share of the verdict to charity. We haven't yet decided on — "

"Eddie!" A.J. half shouted. "You're talking about giving away over 800 million dollars!"

"I know that, A.J. Carol and I have discussed it, and this is what we want to do."

"You discussed it? When? We didn't know about the verdict until this morning. This is too big a decision to make in a few hours."

"We've been talking about it for months. We didn't think it would be this much, but we don't see where the amount matters."

"So," A.J. asked, his head shaking in bewilderment, "who are the lucky charities who will be getting all this money?"

"We thought we'd create a foundation to hold and invest the money and make annual donations to deserving charities, particularly where golf is involved. Places like First Tee, which supports junior golf, and perhaps some that help minority and disadvantaged kids. I'd even like to fund a college golf scholarship program and name it for Walt Clerke — remember, he's the one who got me started in golf when I was a kid.

"We'd like you to help us run the foundation, A.J. If you could invest the money with a 5 percent return — and that shouldn't be a problem for a guy like you — that would produce about 40 million of income every year, and after paying operating expenses, we'd still have a tremendous amount to give to the charities."

Silver still wasn't convinced. "For years I've been helping you and my other clients accumulate and protect your money, and now you want me to help you give it away."

"Look," Eddie explained, "you've done a great job for us, A.J., and, thanks to you, Carol and I have plenty of money to enjoy a good life. And with what Charlie has done for us with the trial, I have my reputation back — plus a clear mind that will help me go out and start winning golf tournaments again. So life is good, and now we can help make life better for other people, too. This foundation would be very important us; golf has been good to us, and now we can do something for golf.

"Let's not forget," Eddie added, "that when we hired Charlie to file this suit, all we wanted was for me to get back my good name and to prove that I wasn't a cheater or druggie. And that's what we got. Even if I didn't get any money out of this, it would have been a wonderful victory. The money is gravy, and I'd be honored to share it with others who need it more than we do."

"Well," A.J. sighed, tossing his napkin on the table, "at least the deduction will come in handy."

"Deduction?" Eddie asked.

"Sure. I need to double-check this, but I'm pretty sure that you will have to pay income taxes on the money you'll be getting. You can claim a deduction for money given to a charity. Without that, you could be paying hundreds of millions of dollars in taxes. Even after the deduction, you'll be paying so much in taxes that the government might even name a battleship for you."

Charlie Mayfield raised a hand. "May I make a point, Eddie?"

"Of course."

"If you really do this, we have to decide whether to announce now that you're planning to give the money to charity, or whether to do it after all the appeals are over and you actually have the money in hand."

"Does it make any difference, Charlie, when we announce it?" Carol Bennison asked.

"Well, it might. If Eddie announced it now, and then later changed his mind, he'd look terrible. It's okay for people not to give money away, but if they say they will, and then they don't, they get accused of all sorts of things — lying, breaking promises, and even conniving."

"Conniving?" Carol repeated.

"Sure," Charlie replied. "People might suspect that Eddie said he was going to give the money away just to make himself look good in the eyes of the public and the judges who will be hearing the appeals. But, once he wins the appeals and the verdict is upheld, if he doesn't follow through and give it away, it will look like he said it just to hoodwink everyone. If you think that Max Reed's articles about him were bad, can you imagine what they'd write after Eddie breaks a promise to give nearly a billion dollars to charity?

"So my advice, Eddie, is to say nothing about this unless you are absolutely, 100 percent sure that you're going to follow through with it."

Then Charlie stood up, tapped his glass with a spoon, and said, "Marge and I would also like to make an announcement."

The others all snapped to attention.

"Marge and I share your desire to be charitable, Eddie. So we're thinking that we might slip an extra twenty dollars onto the collection plate at church next Sunday morning."

FRIDAY MORNING

CHAPTER 95

AJ. Silver's office issued a press release the next morning.

PRESS RELEASE

Professional golfer Eddie Bennison today expressed his gratitude over the verdict handed down yesterday by a Cook County, Illinois, jury in a suit Bennison filed against Tee Time *magazine and other defendants. In 2006, the magazine published stories implying that Bennison had cheated on the golf course and, in addition, had taken performance-enhancing drugs to explain his phenomenal success over the previous few years on the Champions Tour.*

The jury awarded Bennison $247 million in compensatory damages and an additional $1 billion in punitive damages. The entire amount was assessed against Tee Time.

"I never lost faith in the American judicial system," Bennison said, "and I want to compliment the jurors on their patience and on their understanding of the all of the issues presented in this case. And I especially want to thank my lawyer, Charlie Mayfield, who never let me lose confidence in the case or in myself. Today is the first time since the summer of 2006, when those horrible stories were written about me, that I awoke in the morning without a heavy heart. My honor has been restored, and I hope that I will be able to say the same for my golf game.

"My wife, Carol, and I are already making plans to share our good fortune

with several charities in and out of the world of golf. We will do this through a foundation to be funded with the money from the jury's award."

CHAPTER 96

As expected, *Tee Time* used every means possible to get out from under the massive verdict.

On the judicial front, the magazine filed a motion for a new trial based on several grounds. Their lawyers asserted that Judge Krause committed many errors, focusing primarily on his ruling that Elizabeth Peters would not be permitted to testify to her alleged sexual tryst with Eddie Bennison, and the ensuing physical assault, at the Marriott Hotel near Detroit. In keeping with Judge Krause's earlier ruling, this part of the motion was filed under seal and not made a part of the public record. Only Judge Krause and the judges on the reviewing courts would be able to see it. The defense further argued that Judge Krause committed an error in not granting a mistrial when Charlie, to make a hypothetical point during his closing statement, falsely accused Hugo Shoemaker of cheating on his tax returns and using heroin. The reasoning of the defense was that this stunt made a mockery of the trial and was so egregious — so outlandish — that it unduly influenced the eventual verdict.

Finally, the defense argued that the cumulative effect of Charlie's gratuitous comments to the jury, for which he was reprimanded by the judge on several occasions, unduly prejudiced the jury.

To be sure, trials are inevitably punctuated with errors. There are so many procedural and evidentiary rules that total compliance is virtually impossible. However, a mere violation of one of those rules is not necessarily grounds for a new trial or for a reversal of the final judgment. For that, the error (or cumulative errors) must be so significant — so material — that they would likely have affected the outcome of the case.

Thus, an insignificant error, such as when a lawyer asks a question calling for irrelevant evidence, is not grounds for a mistrial or reversal. Indeed, most of these trivial errors are ignored or are corrected with the sustaining of an objection or by the judge giving an instruction to the jury to disregard the evidence that came in because of a harmless error.

When Judge Krause denied the motion for a new trial, the magazine next filed a motion for a *remittitur,* that is, a motion asking the judge to reduce the size of the verdict, asserting that it was grossly excessive. While not common, *remittiturs* are granted when a runaway jury gets so carried away that it returns a verdict that is higher than any test of reason could justify. An example of this was the infamous McDonald's "hot coffee" case which Charlie had mentioned to his clients. In that case, an elderly woman sustained burns when she placed a coffee cup between her knees while riding in a car, and some of the coffee spilled over the lip of the cup onto her lap, causing burns. The jury returned a verdict assessing $2.7 million against McDonald's, but the judge, on his own motion, ordered a *remittitur* reducing the verdict to only a fraction of the amount set by the jury.

When the motions for a new trial and for a *remittitur* were denied, the magazine began the lengthy appeals process. The first appeal was to the Illinois Appellate Court, where the verdict was upheld. Since the loser in the trial court is entitled to only one appeal as a matter of right, the magazine next filed a petition for leave to appeal to the Illinois Supreme Court. Only a very small percentage of these petitions are granted, and granting the petition only assures that the higher court will hear the case; it doesn't mean that the trial court judgment will be overthrown. In Eddie Bennison's case, the Illinois high court granted the petition, heard the appeal, and then affirmed the appellate court decision upholding the verdict.

Because the case involved issues relating to the First Amendment of the United States Constitution, *Tee Time* then sought redress in the federal courts, which led to an eventual hearing before the United States Supreme Court. The nation's highest court agreed to hear the case because of its importance and because the Supreme Court felt that it was time to review and, if necessary, clarify the defamation laws with respect to public figures where malice and a wanton or reckless disregard for the truth were often misunderstood requirements for liability.

As expected, the four conservative justices, sympathetic to the large corporations that control the media, voted for a reversal of the verdict against *Tee Time*. However, the four more liberal justices were in favor of upholding the verdict. The ninth justice, who was often the "swing vote," sided with the liberal wing to uphold the verdict. Thus, Judge Krause's original judgment, based on the jury verdict, was allowed to stand, and the judgment was therefore officially — and finally — upheld by a five–four vote in the Supreme Court.

All of these motions, petitions, and appeals took over three years to conclude, during which time the interest on the judgment against *Tee Time* amounted to over 300 million dollars and resulted in a total award of over 1.5 billion dollars.

CHAPTER 97

t was no surprise that, when it was finally time to pay the judgment, *Tee Time* did not have the cash to pay it. Globe Publications, its parent company, tried desperately to sell the magazine to generate the funds, but the value of the magazine had diminished considerably because the judgment in the Bennison case virtually destroyed its credibility and any good will that it previously had. As popular as *Tee Time Magazine* had been with golf fans before the Max Reed articles, those same fans abandoned the magazine in droves after the jury found that the articles were false and, worse, were written with questionable —or perhaps nonexistent — sources.

So, while the evidence at the trial showed the net worth of Tee Time, Incorporated, to have been in the neighborhood of three billion dollars, the verdict diminished the value of the magazine to the point where Globe Publications was lucky to net just under two billion for the sale. Fortunately for Eddie and Charlie, that was enough to satisfy the jury's verdict — with a little left over for Globe Publications.

EPILOGUE

Until Globe Publications was able to sell the magazine, Max Reed was kept on the payroll. Firing him, they reasoned, would imply that he was wrong to have written the Bennison articles, and they couldn't take that risk while the appeals were pending. The company that bought the magazine from Globe, however, had no such concerns, and, once the sale was completed, they wasted no time in giving Reed his walking papers. It was his last job as a sportswriter.

Todd Slocum, the Chief Legal Officer of Tee Time, Incorporated, knew his future with the magazine was tenuous. He wisely resigned and returned to his home town in Missouri, where he joined the small law firm that represented his father's lumber business. Writing wills and handling divorces was a far cry from his prior life in the fast lanes of the New York media world, but he blended nicely into his new community, slept well, took up golf, and never looked back.

Elizabeth Peters had the good fortune of marrying a young man she met on an online dating site. And she had the good sense never to tell him, or anyone else, of her professed one-night stand with "Ben Edwards" at a Marriott Hotel in Pontiac, Michigan.

Dan Curry, of course, regretted the fact that he was never able to cash in on the Liz Peters story, especially after seeing what the case was actually worth. But Elizabeth Peters, now that she was remarried, told him that she would not cooperate with him in trying to squeeze any money out of a story that she now wanted to be kept in secret. It was only when she threatened to deny the story and ever having met Eddie Bennison that Curry reluctantly agreed to walk away from what he thought would be the biggest payday of his life. *I was so close*, he lamented. True to form, he couldn't totally let go; he told the story from time to time in bars, but no one took him seriously — just another delusional drunk.

No one at *Tee Time* took the loss harder than Clive Curtis, the Editor-in-Chief. *I shouldn't have allowed those goddamned articles to be published*, he said to himself over and over, and to anyone else who would listen. *They were ticking like time bombs, but instead of listening to the ticking I made the mistake of listening to those friggin' lawyers who kept telling me that we were protected by the First Amendment. I should have trusted my instincts and told them to go to hell. How many times have I told my staff, "trust your instincts," and "If it looks too good to be true, then it probably isn't true — it's bullshit!" But there I was, asleep at the switch while the worst articles in the history of journalism slipped past me.*

Within a week after the magazine was sold by Globe Publications, Curtis was summoned to the office of the new owner's president. Of course, Curtis was expecting the worst. "Clive," the president began, "I don't know what the hell to do with you. You're a great editor and highly respected in the industry. We need your talent around here, plus you know the people at *Tee Time*, and we need that knowledge. On the other hand, the biggest publishing disaster in my lifetime occurred on your watch — you could have stopped it, but didn't.

"So here's the deal, Clive. I don't want to lose you — not completely. But I have to put you in the penalty box for a while. So I'm going to send you to St. Louis, where you'll hold the title of Editor-in-Chief of one of our recent acquisitions, a small start-up called *Collegiate Sports*. You may have heard about it — it's a monthly magazine — well, not exactly a magazine, but more of a newsletter, covering college sports, mostly football and basketball. Averages about 24 pages an issue. It doesn't have much in the way of circulation, and the advertising revenues are lousy, but the readership is growing steadily and the reader loyalty is high. The male millennials seem to love it, and we think it will be a good asset down the line.

"I think it'll be good for you to get out of New York and get your batteries recharged — and get that damned Bennison case behind you.

"And by the way, we'll have to cut your salary and benefits a little, but that'll seem like a big raise since you'll be in St. Louis and not New York where you can't eat lunch for less than fifty bucks.

"Do a good job out there, Clive, and we'll get you back on the ladder heading upstairs. But promise me, don't trust the damned lawyers to decide whether to put a hot story in *Collegiate Sports*. You're a seasoned newspaper man with a good head. Trust that head — and nobody else's."

Clive Curtis could have jumped over the desk and kissed the guy! Here he was, thinking he was about to get canned, and instead he was being handed an opportunity for a fresh start without any of the old baggage. And to get out of New York, where he sensed that everyone he knew was ridiculing him, was a big plus. Under these circumstances, a salary cut was the least of his concerns.

———

While the appeals were running their course, Globe Publications made numerous overtures to Charlie Mayfield in an effort to reach a compromise on the final judgment. Essentially, Globe offered to withdraw its appeals and immediately satisfy the judgment if Eddie Bennison, in return, would accept a smaller payment. The proposal had merit, but Globe was demanding too much of a concession for a quick and final payment — its first proposal was for a 50 percent concession, and they never increased it significantly. While the decision to settle was Eddie's, he insisted on not making any decision without Charlie's full endorsement. After all, Charlie had "skin in the game," since his fee was to be one-third of the final payment. Charlie preferred to play hard ball and either hold out for a much better offer or take the chance that the judgment would be upheld and collect the entire amount, plus interest. But all he would say to Eddie was, "Discuss it with A.J., Eddie. He's your business manager. But don't get seduced by their offer to make a quick payment. Remember, you're earning interest on the judgment until it's paid, and that's something like $2 or $3 million every week. So what's the rush?"

Eddie, with Carol's assent, decided not to accept the settlement for the lower amount. He'd gone this far, and it didn't seem right not to see it through to the end. Anyway, he already had what he wanted the most from the litigation — his reputation — so it was worth rolling the dice for the full amount.

———

When Globe Publications finally paid the entire judgment, plus interest, after selling *Tee Time*, Eddie, true to his word, created the Edward Bennison Golf Foundation. The charter of the foundation specified that it was intended to "foster an interest in golf, enhance the popularity of golf, and encourage participation in the sport." He named a board of trustees with A.J. Silver as its chairman. Other trustees, who were paid expenses plus a small stipend, included Pete Stevens, Charlie's associate, and Arturo Escalara, Eddie's caddie. Included as one of the trustees was Mickey Laster, Eddie's college roommate whose father had hired Eddie to work at National Container. To round out the board, Eddie appointed his friend from the Tour, Steve Hockett.

One of the first grants made to the foundation was to fund four college scholarships each year for graduates of Kewanee High School. Those eligible for the scholarships either played on the golf team or had a letter of recommendation from the golf professional at either Midland Country Club or Baker Park, the public municipal course. The provision for a recommendation from a local professional was intended to make the scholarships available to females and others who hadn't actually had an opportunity to learn the game while still in school, but were nonetheless endorsed by one or both of the local golf professionals who knew them and saw promise in their futures. There was no mandatory requirement that the recipient play high school golf, or intend to play college golf, because Eddie's primary intent was to provide college educations for promising students. As a way to acknowledge his first mentor in the game, who was no longer alive, Eddie named this the Walter Clerke Memorial Scholarship.

Once the details were worked out, this scholarship program was extended to other high schools near Kewanee.

Further, the foundation would make substantial grants to the Evans Scholars Program, which provided college scholarships to caddies who could not otherwise afford to go to college.

Eddie also wanted his foundation to pay the expenses of two deserving first-year touring professional golfers, one on the Champions Golf Tour and the other on the regular PGA Tour. However, this would have to wait for A.J. Silver to figure out how — and whether — such a program could be qualified as a charitable endeavor and thereby protect the entire foundation as a charity for tax purposes.

———

The jury's verdict had been handed down a few weeks before Eddie's and Carol's two children, Betsy and Wally, began their summer break from school. As soon as their school terms ended, the entire family flew to Orlando, Florida, where Carol and the kids explored every corner of Disneyland and Epcot Center while Eddie devoted eight to ten hours each day to his golf game. He had played virtually no golf at all since a couple of months before the trial started, and he was intent on getting back on the Champions Tour as soon as humanly possible.

To his great relief, his game seemed to have held up fairly well during the long layoff. The daily exercising and stretching he had been doing was paying off. After only a few days, he was striking the ball solidly, nearly as well as he ever had, and he was soon able to control the shape, distance, and trajectory of his shots better than he had expected. His plan was to defer any decision on when to get back into competitive golf, but the encouraging results of those first days of practice motivated him to get back on the Tour and play in a few tournaments as soon as the fall season got underway.

It was easy for him to decide on the perfect venue for his reentry back into tournament golf. A major Champions Tour event — the Senior PGA

Championship — was scheduled to be played in September at the Southern Hills Country Club in Tulsa, Oklahoma. Having lived and worked in Tulsa since before starting on the Tour, Eddie knew he'd have many friends and well-wishers in the gallery, and he'd be able to sleep in his own bed. Because he had won the Senior PGA Championship once before, he was exempt from qualifying, but he knew that in any event he would be granted one of the rare sponsor's exemptions because of his national popularity and as an attraction for the hometown fans. Best of all, he knew the Southern Hills course like the back of his hand. It was one of the more challenging courses in the country, but Eddie knew its subtle nuances, and he knew that his course knowledge would give him a slight edge over the rest of the field.

Satisfied with his decision as to when and where to get back on the Tour, he knew the first step he had to take to implement that decision — and that required an immediate phone call.

"Hey, Artie. It's me, Eddie."

The excitement in Artie Escalara's voice was unmistakable. "Eddie! How's it going down there in Florida?"

"Great, Artie. Good, solid contact, and I'm back to shaping the shots as well as ever."

"Yeah — just like riding a bicycle. Comes back to you in no time. Tell me, Eddie, how's the distance control?" Artie knew that Eddie's one weakness — and a minor one at that — was his ability to add or take away 3 or 4 yards on a critical iron shot. It's that one talent that changes 30-foot putts to 10-foot putts, and that in turn will convert a couple of pars each round into birdies. It's common knowledge among professional golfers that it takes birdies to win — pars will put food on the table, but they won't put trophies on the mantle.

"Really good, considering the layoff. I've been spending a lot of time on that, and it's paying off."

"That's great, Eddie. Wish I were there to help."

"Well, Artie, that's why I'm calling. I'd love it if you could come down here for a couple of weeks and watch me. I want you to see what I can and can't do so you can be there to help when we get back on the Tour."

"When are you planning to get back out there?"

"September. I'm entering the Senior PGA Championship at Southern Hills."

"That's a major event, Eddie. And on a tough track like Southern Hills? Are you sure you're ready for that?"

"I'm ready. Remember, Artie, my home's in Tulsa and I've played the course a thousand times. And I'll be surrounded by friends. If I have to face all those guys on the Tour again, that's where I'd like it to be."

Then Eddie asked the question that Artie was dying to hear: "Are you ready to get back on my bag, Artie?"

"You kiddin' me, boss? I've been going crazy, waiting for this phone call."

Eddie laughed. "Great, Artie. Book a flight and let me know when you'll get here. You'll stay with us — we rented a large condo, 'cause I have the whole family with me, but there's an extra room with your name on it."

"You know, Eddie, we've only talked a few times since that verdict came down. Everyone down here — especially my relatives — must think that I had a piece of your action. I've never seen so many people with their hands out. Seems everyone has a sick mother or a sick car."

"Just get me winning again, Artie, and you'll be able to take care of them."

"Well, I've been able to help the relatives out a little with the money you've been paying me since we left the Tour." After a moment's pause, Artie went on to say, "I can't tell you what it meant to me, Eddie, for you to keep me on the payroll throughout this whole mess. And of course, that check you sent to me . . . "

Artie didn't have to finish the sentence. Eddie knew he was referring to the $250,000 Eddie sent him the day after the verdict was handed down.

"Don't mention it, Artie. It'll be our little secret. And there'll be some more for you when the judgement is finally paid. You helped me in the courtroom with your testimony as much as you ever helped me on the golf course." Then Eddie added, "By the way, Artie, that was not part of your salary — it was a gift, so don't pay any income taxes on it. It was just a token of my appreciation."

"You call that a token?" the caddie exclaimed. "I haven't even told my family about it — they'd be all over me like flies on a fresh turd."

Eddie laughed out loud, as he always did when Artie came up with one of his picturesque metaphors. "By the way, Artie, make sure you book a first-class ticket for your trip down here. We can afford it now, and I'll take care of it."

"Fantastic! I'll try to find some clean gringo clothes to wear so they don't throw me out of first class and into the back of the plane."

———

With Artie by his side, Eddie's practice time in Florida became even more productive. By the time they boarded their flight to Tulsa, Eddie felt as ready as he ever had. Even the delicate little chip shots and pitches — the shots that suffer the most from a long layoff from golf — were "hunting" the hole as well as ever.

Walking into the Southern Hills locker room to get ready for his first practice round on the course, Eddie was greeted by his fellow competitors with warm handshakes, hugs, and high-fives. They all took vicarious pleasure in his victory. Everyone in public life, whether it's an athlete, actor, or politician, fears the power of the press, and, right or wrong, none of them believes that the press is completely fair. So, in effect, Eddie's battle was all of theirs, and his victory belonged to all of them.

After a half-hour warmup on the practice range, Eddie went over to the putting green and rolled a few putts to get the feel of the greens. Then, when he was comfortable with his putting stroke, he and Artie walked over to the first tee to start his practice round with his long-time friend and fellow competitor, Steve Hockett, who had testified at the trial. Fans surrounding the tee applauded Eddie, and their applause was much more enthusiastic than the polite clapping of the hands that normally greets a player arriving at the tee for a practice round — there were actual roars!

He removed and waved his hat rather than slightly tapping it as was the custom, and smiled broadly in appreciation of the warm greeting. He then circled the tee and took the time to slap the hand of everyone there, constantly uttering his thanks.

Finally, after Hockett hit a very respectable drive, Eddie walked to the center of the tee box, teed up his ball, and then stood behind it to look down the long, narrow, downward-sloping fairway at the end of which, 464 yards away, was the small, distant green. Few courses have hosted as many major championships as Southern Hills, and few started with as intimidating a first hole as this one.

After visualizing the drive he wanted to hit, he addressed the ball, took a last look down the fairway, did his familiar waggle, and took the long, smooth swing that reflected the "tempo, tempo, tempo" that Walt Clerke drilled into his head nearly fifty years earlier on a small, nine-hole course back in Illinois.

Crack! The perfect sound of club against ball was music to the ear. The long, high, towering flight of the ball, starting out slightly to the right and then curving ever so gracefully back to dead center, evoked the *oohs* and *aahs* of everyone witnessing that magnificent first drive. Eddie turned, smiled broadly, and again doffed his hat to acknowledge the gallery's reaction to the shot. Then he began his walk down the fairway with his arm around Artie Escalara's shoulder.

Artie, with teary eyes, looked up at him and, with just three words, made the world glow again. "We're back, boss."

NOTES AND REFLECTIONS OF
TONY JACKLIN

1. There is a staggering difference in the distances that today's pros hit the ball compared to a few decades ago. While today's professional golfer will routinely strike a ball with a 7-iron that flies 180 to 190 yards in the air, that was certainly not the case when I was competing. The standard rule of thumb for all of us, including for Jack Nicklaus and Arnold Palmer, with whom I had played often, was a simple one: our normal shot with a 7-iron would carry 150 yards; we would use the 8-iron for a 140-yard carry, and a 6-iron for a 160-yard carry. That was the standard for nearly all of us.

    I assure the reader that this huge difference has nothing to do with the comparative strength and power between today's pros and the pros from our time. Instead, the increased length of the flight of the ball is attributable to the ball itself. Today's golf balls simply go farther! The variance is nearly 40 yards with the middle irons such as the 7-iron. And the difference with the driver is laughable. True, today we see better clubs and customized club fitting, and the golfers might take better care of themselves, but it's the ball that makes the big difference.

2. A word about amateur and professional golf. Until more recent times, society held the successful professional golfer in much lower esteem than his amateur counterpart. In 1966, while competing in a tournament at Royal County Down, a renowned course in Ireland, I was not permitted in the clubhouse because I was a professional! Only the amateurs were allowed entry. This had been a long-standing tradition, not only in the United Kingdom but even in the United States, to an extent. A professional who objected to this nonsense — and in a most flamboyant way — was the inimitable American professional Walter Hagen.

Hagen played the British Open in 1922 at Royal Cinque Ports Golf Club, and he was clearly miffed at his reception by the British establishment. He and his fellow pros were not given lockers or even permitted in the clubhouse, which was reserved for private members. As a protest, Hagen parked his chauffeur-driven Austin-Daimler automobile in front of the clubhouse and used it as his private locker room. The club members were stunned to see him sitting inside putting on his shirt, or sitting on the running board changing his shoes. Carrying his protest one step farther, he had his chauffeur meet him later on the 18th green with a chilled martini and a tailored jacket.

Unfortunately for him, he finished in 53rd place and was savaged by the British press, but Hagen, not to be daunted, got his revenge the following year, 1923, by finishing second at Royal St. George's Club. When the tournament ended, he was asked to present the claret jug to Arthur Havers, the Englishman who won. In true form, and still irate over not being permitted in the clubhouse, Hagen stood, pointed to a local pub across the road which had welcomed him all week, and announced to the assembled crowd, "We'll present the trophy to the new champion over there."

3. Maladies other than routine aches and pains have always plagued golfers. Orville Moody, who was known as "Sarge" because he had risen to the rank of sergeant in the United States Army, had won the US Open in 1969. When later competing in the British Open, his severe allergies forced him to place a handkerchief over his face to filter the pollen. It looked to all as if the American marching down the fairway was Jesse James or The Lone Ranger.

4. As you might expect, the touring pros have only in recent years had the benefit of fitness trailers and other lovely accommodations. Today's Tour pro is fed and treated much better at the events than we were. Before the player tees off, he will be treated to a nice breakfast buffet, and a tasty lunch will await him after the round. And while he's eating or working out in the fitness trailer, there are people there to re-grip or re-shaft his clubs and check the lofts and lies and sharpen the grooves of each club. Indeed, the golf equipment representatives are all over with clubs, balls, gloves, and shoes, begging the pros to try, use, and keep them (without charge, of course).

5. Compared to the fans at other sporting events such as baseball and soccer, golf fans are relatively well-mannered and treat the players with respect. When they do heckle, it can have a bad effect not only on the target of the heckling but on his playing companions as well. This collateral damage was often seen when Gary Player was actively competing. Gary, who was a South African, was often heckled because of his country's practice of apartheid during those years. Fortunately for him, he had become accustomed to the ugly comments and was able to put them out of his head. But some of his playing partners were not so stoic and were distracted and thrown off their games by the remarks that were aimed at Gary.

6. As the reader can see, the role of the Tour player's business manager is both broad and important. For the marquee player, his business

manager's office will surely do more than invest his money and secure endorsement contracts. The duties may extend to making plane and hotel reservations, finding the right doctors, therapists, trainers, and coaches, and even arranging for drivers and perhaps babysitters.

And then there are the regrettable stories of business managers who, through negligence or otherwise, have made horrible investments that cost their athlete-clients untold millions of dollars. Worse, there have been sad instances of business managers who have deliberately fleeced their clients out of fortunes.

7.   I'm sad to report that the disparity of purse sizes today, versus a few decades ago, can be measured in terms of light-years. In 1969, I won The British Open, and my first-place prize money was 4,250 pounds, or $5,525 in terms of US dollars at the 1969 conversion rate. By contrast, the winner of the 2017 British Open, Jordan Spieth, received $1.845 million in US dollars.

And in 1970, I won the US Open, for which first place paid $30,000. In 2017, Brooks Koepka's check for winning the US Open was more than $2.2 million!

Looking at it another way, I received less for winning the 1969 British Open than Adam Scott was paid for finishing in twenty-seventh place in 2016, and Satoshi Kodaira, a player who finished in a tie for forty-sixth place in the 2017 US Open, took home nearly $6,000 more than I did for winning the same tournament in 1970.

8.   Before plane travel was commonplace, and certainly before the advent of the private jet, the touring golf professional in the United States would drive from event to event by car, often with his wife. To reduce expenses and the burden of driving, two such couples might drive together or, more likely, two or three fellow professionals

would drive together. On the longer drives, as when the tour moved from the West Coast to Florida, that drive could take a week. In the meantime, three or four caddies would drive nonstop, changing drivers all the way, and make the trip in half the time.

My ever-creative caddy Scotty Gilmore, mentioned below in Note No. 10, replaced the engine of his car (which he named "Poppy") with a truck engine to facilitate these cross-country drives. To accommodate the larger truck engine, Scotty had to cut a hole in the car's hood — making Poppy easily identifiable at the Tour stops.

9. The duties of the caddie have changed considerably over the years since I've been playing professional golf, mostly in ways that the fan in the gallery would not notice. For example, an important part of the player's preparation in a tournament is to hit balls on the practice range before (and sometimes after) each round. Today we are provided with baskets of new, clean balls to hit onto the range, and they are left there for someone to pick up later. But, not that long ago, we had our own practice balls. We would hit those balls toward our caddies who stood out on the range to retrieve them. This could be a suicide mission! There they were, standing side by side and trying to distinguish which pro was hitting which ball. Even with our presumed accuracy, we had the hapless chaps running back and forth and from side to side, dodging each other and the flying golf balls, all the while looking into the blinding sun, or through an early morning mist.

Another example of the caddie's changing duties has to do with measuring distances from various points on the course to the hole. Electronic or laser range finders are not permitted during play, nor are there yardage markings on sprinkler heads or concrete discs on the Tour fairways. During my earlier years as a tournament golfer, our caddies would have paced the course from various spots to the front and center of the putting green, and would then make the appropriate daily adjustments for the precise pin placements for that day. In more recent years, outside resources have been providing (for a fee) "yardage books" for each course that include not only yardages from specific points to the front, center, and back of each green, but also diagrams of the greens showing general slopes and distances from side to side and from front to back. This replaces much of the guesswork on which the earlier touring pros had to rely.

10. The fictional Artie Escalara is, in some ways, modeled after my wonderful friend and caddie in the 1970s and 1980s, the inimitable Scotty Gilmour. Scotty was not merely an excellent man to have on my bag; he could be as entertaining as he was helpful. In commenting on how the role of the caddie had changed over the years, from a virtual laborer to a valuable strategist, Scotty succinctly observed, "Today, the caddies carry briefcases." And that says it all.

    The reader should know that the Tour competitors and their caddies were like one big family that was together for most of the year. And the caddies were colorful family members indeed. Many had unforgettable — and often descriptive — names such as Tobacco Lou, Black Rabbit, White Rabbit, and Deputy Dog. My dear caddy and friend, John Gilmore, was known as Scotty for his Scottish heritage. And my caddy in 1968 when I won the first of my two Greater Jacksonville Opens was "Creamy Caroline," who had previously caddied for Arnold Palmer. Creamy was well known for using a baseball mitt to catch balls on the fly when on the practice range. (See note 9 above.)

11. Thankfully, the situations described here are quite rare. The players on Tour are gentlemen. To be sure, there is the occasional player who might break a competitor's concentration with an offhand comment, or by standing a bit too close when the other is about to strike the ball, but, as I say, it's extremely rare and usually non-intentional.

It's worth noting here that irritating a fellow competitor can invite danger. Every player has the responsibility to watch and see that the others do not, accidentally or intentionally, violate a rule. Further, we may want a competitor's opinion as to where our ball crossed a hazard line. In such situations, it would be comforting to know that the eyes watching us belong to a friend. (This point is not as valid today as it was a few decades ago when there were precious few "officials" available to make rulings. In those days, players were more often asked to help with rulings; but today, with the abundance of officials on the course, it's a rarity where a competitor is called upon to interpret a rule.)

12. I can personally verify that Lee did indeed say this. I know because I was the player to whom he said it!! I'll never forget the day — not for the remark, but for the golf. It was in 1972, on the first tee at the World Match Play competition in Wentworth, England. It was a 36-hole match, and we had just finished the first 18 holes and Lee was four-up on me. After his "You just have to listen" remark, we both played fantastic golf, and it seemed like an aviary with all the birdies and eagles! After the next nine holes, I was actually one-up after shooting 29, but, alas, I ended up losing one-down after I parred and Lee birdied the 36th hole.

13. This story of a rules infraction being reported by a television viewer is not an isolated event. In the spring of 2017, Lexi Thompson, a popular competitor on the Ladies Professional Golf Tour, was a victim of such a call. Lexi, who was leading a tournament with only one day left to play, had a very short putt of only about one foot, which she had marked with a coin. The television camera showed a close-up view of her inadvertently replacing the ball ever so slightly to the side of where it had been (and not any closer to the hole), perhaps by one-quarter of an inch. One or more viewers called in to report this, and it was later verified by the rules officials who reviewed the film and then assessed Lexi with a two-stroke penalty

for replacing the ball incorrectly, and another two-stroke penalty for later signing an incorrect scorecard. Without the penalties, she would have won the tournament by four strokes! The total penalty of four strokes meant that, instead of winning the tournament, she finished in a tie for first place and then lost in a sudden-death playoff, costing her over $200,000 in prize money. However, under the rules of the LPGA Tour, unlike those of the PGA Tour, she was not disqualified for signing a card with a lower score than she actually had after the penalties.

In 1957, during a professional tournament on the Old Course at St. Andrews, the South African golfer Bobby Locke had marked his ball and then moved his coin one putter-head's distance to the side so that his coin would not be in the line of Bruce Crampton, who was next to putt. Locke forgot to move his coin back to the original spot before he putted, and his mental error was reported by one or more television viewers. Since the penalty would have been two strokes, but he won the event by three strokes, he was permitted to retain his first-place finish. Under the then-rules in the United Kingdom, he was not disqualified for signing an incorrect scorecard that showed too low a score. For those interested in trivia, this was the first instance of "trial by television": that is, the first time a television viewer called in to report a rules infraction that led to a penalty.